YURI RYTKHEU

A Dream in Polar Fog

Translated from the Russian by Ilona Yazhbin Chavasse

archipelago books

RAINMAKER TRANSLATIONS

Archipelago Books
25 Jay Street #203
Brooklyn, NY 11201
www.archipelagobooks.org

Library of Congress Cataloging-in-Publication Data
Rytkheu, Yuri Sergeevich, 1930–
[Son v nachale tumana. English]
A dream in polar fog / by Yuri Rytkheu ;
translated from the Russian by Ilona Yazhbin Chavasse.—1st ed.
p. cm.
ISBN 0-9749680-7-2
1. Chukchi—Fiction. 2. Chukotskii avtonomnyi okrug (Russia)—Fiction.
I. Chavasse, Ilona Yazhbin. II. Title.
PG3476.R965S613 2005
891.73'44 — dc22
2004027875

Distributed by Consortium Book Sales and Distribution
1045 Westgate Drive
St. Paul, MN 55114
www.cbsd.com

Jacket photograph: *Glacier Bay, with Iceberg,* Asahel Curtis.

This publication is made possible with public funds
from the New York State Council on the Arts, a state agency.

NYSCA

A Dream in Polar Fog

I

On the morning of September 4, 1910, the inhabitants of Enmyn, a settlement spread out on the shore of the Arctic Ocean, heard an unusual clamor. This was not the cracking of shattered ice, nor the rumble of an avalanche, nor the crashing of stones down the rocky precipices of the Enmyn cape.

Just then, Toko was standing in his chottagin,* pulling on a white kamleika.† He thrust his arms carefully into the wide sleeves, touching his face to the material, inhaling its smell – had a good airing out in the freezing wind. Otherwise all he touched – traps, Winchester, snowshoes – everything would be permeated with that smell.

A crashing noise roared in his ears. Toko quickly stuck his head through the neck-hole, and sprang out of the chottagin in a single bound.

Where, only yesterday, there had been the white people's ship, a cloud was spreading. There were ice splinters under his feet.

People rushed out from all twelve of the yarangas. They stood in silence, looking out toward the ship, and making guesses about the explosion.

Now Armol' came up to him.

"Likely, they were trying to crack the ice . . ."

* *Chottagin* – the cold, outer part of the yaranga.
† *Kamleika* – a cloth overall, worn over fur-lined clothing.

"I think so, too," Toko agreed. "Let's go." And the two hunters set off for the ice-bound ship.

The cloud over the ship was dissipated, and in the dawn twilight you could make out a hole in the ice under the bowsprit. There were more and more chunks of ice underfoot, strewn all about the ship.

The deck rang with agitated voices, long shadows flickering across the portholes.

Toko and Armol' slowed their step. The others caught up with them.

"Blood!" Toko exclaimed, bending down to the tracks that led from the hole to the ship.

"Blood!" the people echoed, looking down at the stains on the ice and on deck.

From the frozen-through wooden belly of the ship came a long, drawn-out moan, just like the howl of a wounded wolf.

"Trouble in the ship!" cried Toko, and leapt up on deck.

Gingerly opening the door, he saw white sailors, crowding in the small cabin. The steam from their breath floated under the low ceiling. Tin lanterns, fueled with seal blubber, gave off barely any light.

A blast of icy wind had rushed into the cabin alongside Toko; a tall, lanky sailor with his neck wrapped in a colorful scarf shouted something, sharp and angry. Toko didn't know the white men's language, but understood that he was being thrown out. He beat a hasty retreat, sensing an upraised fist with the back of his eyes.

The people of the Enmyn settlement were standing by the side of the ship. Silently, with their eyes, they asked Toko about what had happened, but he only shook his head and joined the waiting crowd.

The ship had come to Enmyn ten days ago. It must have strayed far north, into the gulf that separated the Invisible Land* from the continent, and had to run at top speed to evade the approaching ice fields. Still, the ice had caught it, and held it tight to the rocky shores of Enmyn.

* Invisible Land – Wrangel Island

The whites came ashore. Their faces were marked by despair and fatigue. They went from one yaranga to another, but unlike their predecessors, they had no interest in pelts, whalebone, and walrus tusk; what they asked for was warm clothing and deer meat. There was no deer meat to be had, and the whites were not scornful of taking walrus livers instead. They gave a meager trade for the clothing, but still the goods were indispensable and made to last – needles, axes, saws, cauldrons.

The captain – tufts of hair on his cheeks, and dry, rough skin stretched tight over a long hard bony face – conversed with Orvo, who had once sailed on a whaling ship, and even lived in America, asking him all about the way to the gulf of Irvytgyr, and gazing mournfully at the ice-bound horizon.

Orvo felt sorry for him, and tried to make him understand that a strong southerly wind might still push the ice floes offshore. This had happened not just in the beginning of winter, but even at its peak, in those dark days when the sun wandered beyond the horizon, not daring to poke its face out into the frost.

The captain only sucked his pipe in silence, and sighed.

Two days ago, a wind started to rise from the south. It drove the snow from the peaks down to the fast ice,* and a wide crack that led to the open water appeared by the side of the whites' ship.

The sailors revived and stayed aboard, watchful for an opportunity to break free.

In this kind of wind, the ice floes behind Enmyn's promontory would shift a little, and you could hunt nerpa, to supplement the summer's reserves.

The hunters would leave at dawn, to make the most of the short daylight out on the ice, and return dragging a heavy kill behind them. Chot-

---

* Fast ice – sea ice that forms and fastens to the coastline: its edge is dynamic – sea-ice cracks form and enlarge while ice floes may break off. It can extend for only a few meters or for several hundred kilometers from its point of attachment. Fast ice usually ends where the water reaches a depth of 25 m.

tagins were ablaze with light, the well-fed people singing songs, and the muffled drumming of the yarars* floated down to the ice-bound ship.

The winter promised to be a good one: The meat larder pits were filled to the neck, laden with a mix of walrus kymgyts,† wrapped in walrus hides, and whole seal carcasses, minus skins and flippers. That summer, the people of Enmyn had hunted well, had traded well, and the stores of tobacco and tea were so plentiful that even Orvo, who knew the true value of the white people's goods, was generous enough, from time to time, to treat the destitute ship's captain to a pinch of tobacco.

Orvo walked up to Toko and Armol.

"They should have waited a bit," he said thickly, nodding toward the ship. "A south wind coming."

"The man is moaning. I went over, but they yelled at me, threw me out."

"Maybe they didn't mean it like that," Orvo conjectured. "Sometimes the white man says a tender word just so, and then it sounds like curses."

"Should I go up again, maybe?"

"No, wait." Orvo held him back. "When they need our help, that's when they'll call us. No need to stick our noses in it. The whites have a kind of gathering – it's called a trial. People, dressed all in black, kiss an open book; and then they decide who will be strangled with a rope, and who will be shut up in the house of twilight."

"These are their punishments?" Armol' was horrified.

"Well, the crime can be great, too," said Orvo with a sigh.

A loud groan sent a shudder through the gathering. A rectangle of light appeared as the door swung open, and the captain stepped out on deck. Squinting his eyes into the crowd, he shouted:

"Orvo!"

"Yes! It's me!" Orvo readily replied in English, and limped toward the wide plank that served as a gangway.

* *Yarar* – a drum made from a stretched walrus stomach.
† *Kymgyt* – a roll-up of walrus meat.

He peered into the cabin's gloom as he entered and made out a figure laid out on the low bunk. On top of the blood-stained covers lay a pair of hands, swathed in white canvas. It was the young man whom everyone called John, and the people of Enmyn, *Sson*.*

John lay on the bunk with his eyes closed, quietly moaning. His damp, sandy hair was plastered to his forehead, his nostrils quivering as though catching some intriguing aroma. A shadow lay under his lowered eyelashes, just like under a snowcap.

The captain pointed to the wounded man, to his hands.

"John boom!"

Orvo was looking at the prostrate young man, and beginning to guess what had happened without the captain's explanation. The sailors, in their impatience, had decided to blow up the ice field that separated their ship from open water. Orvo had seen it done before. They would bore a hollow in the ice, stuff it with large paper-wrapped cartridges, set fire to a thin rope, over which the fire would quickly run. The ice would shatter, sending shards high into the sky. Sometimes this helped. But today's thunder was to no avail. The explosion failed to make a single crack.

"Should have waited," Orvo concluded. "Maybe, a wind will come and push the ice offshore."

The captain nodded in agreement, signaling to the people crowding by the bedside to disperse. Orvo came closer. It seemed that the young man had gotten it in both hands – in both wrists, to be precise.

"Orvo!" the captain called.

The old man turned and saw a smallish metal flask on the table.

"There are still seventy dollars left. Here they are." The captain laid down a crumpled wad of paper notes, the kind that Orvo had not much faith in, despite knowing well that the whites liked them no less than the metal ones. "John has to be taken to a hospital. Or else he'll die."

On hearing those words, the wounded man gave out a loud moan and

* This is not merely a question of mispronunciation. In Russian, the word *sson* means "sleep" or "dream." (TN)

raised his eyelids. Orvo was standing close to him, and could see his blue eyes, dimmed with pain.

"It's a long way off, the hospital," Orvo sighed. "In Anadyr'. Sson might not make it."

"There is no other way," the captain shrugged. "We've got to help the lad."

"Got to help," Orvo concurred. "I will talk to my comrades."

The crowd was still milling about the side of the ship. In the east, beyond the sharp peaks of faraway icebergs, it was dawning, but the starlight hadn't weakened, and the constellations flickered as brightly as though it were night.

Orvo was slowly making his way down the ice-covered plank.

"What's happened?" Toko was the first to ask.

"Sson had his hands blown up," Orvo informed him. "He's in a bad way. Has to be taken to Anadyr'."

"To where?" asked Armol'.

"Anadyr'," Toko repeated. "There's a Russian doctor there, attached to the regional governor."

"Who's going to drive him all that way?" Toko said doubtfully. "What if he dies on the journey?"

"He can die here, too," Orvo observed, and after a pause, added, "They've got nothing to pay. All that's left is a bottle of the bad fire-water, and a small heap of paper money."

The men lowered their eyes, and took a long time peering at the toes of their torbasses. In the silence, the wounded man's moans escaped through the thin cabin planks.

"Who is he to us?" Armol' broke the silence. "A stranger, a white man. Let them do as they please. We didn't wound him, so it's not our concern."

"Armol' speaks rightly," Toko agreed. "What good have they done for us? They don't even have any tobacco. Racing the dogs all the way to Anadyr' and back – that'll take just about the entire moon! So much feed wasted! No time to go hunting, so who's going to feed the ones left behind in the yarangas?"

"And you, Toko, are also right," Orvo agreed.

He stood there, feet planted wide, furiously thinking. The people speak rightly: Why should they help the white man, who has his own shamans, his own customs, his own lands?

When he lived in Alaska, and the cough bent him in two, who helped him then? What help was there for the one who wandered by the garbage pits and fought the dogs over scraps? It wasn't any better aboard ship, either. They didn't seat him at the table, along with everybody else. After lunch, the cook would bring a bucket out for him, where everything was heaped together – bones, meat, the sweet, the bitter, the salty. He ate, and the whites watched him, laughing. When they spotted a white she-bear on a drifting iceberg and killed her, taking her cub on board, the sailors treated it with more care than they did Orvo, a human being, a hunter of walrus and whale and those same polar bears.

The moans grew louder. Little by little, it was becoming brighter, and the imprisoned ship was emerging from twilight; a snow-covered deck, icicles on its rigging, and yellow lights moving behind the frosted port-holes.

"Everyone, go back to Enmyn," Orvo said, and started first for the yarangas, turning his back on the ship.

The others drifted after him. The creaking of snow under their lakhtak* soles drowned out the wounded man's moaning.

But before they could reach the shore, they heard the captain calling after them.

"Orvo! Orvo!" The captain was shouting as he ran to catch up. "Wait! I have something to talk to you about."

He clutched at the old man's sleeve, dragging him back.

* *Lakhtak* – bearded seal, sometimes known as sea hare *(Erignathus Barbatus).* (TN)

Orvo shook off the captain's hand, and said, with dignity:

"The three of us will come: Toko, Armol', and I."

"All right, all right," the captain nodded vigorously, and loped back to the ship.

The wounded man had been moved to some other room. He was not in the wardroom. Where he had lain, Orvo now saw three Winchesters, a zinc box of cartridges, and a large steel two-handed saw.

"If you take him to Anadyr', and bring back a paper saying you delivered him safe and sound, these Winchesters will be yours," the captain said.

Toko, who had never owned a proper gun, only a small shotgun, rushed over to the Winchesters. This kind of generosity was unheard of! Three Winchesters, with cartridges, in exchange for a month-long journey!

"And he'll hand over the guns right now?" Toko asked Orvo.

"I'll find out." Orvo started to talk to the captain in English.

They talked and argued for a long time. Then the captain grabbed one of the Winchesters and held it out to Orvo.

"He says that he's willing to give us only one Winchester now, and the others when we come back."

"He won't cheat us?" Toko was unconvinced.

"Sure, we'll trust him, just like that." Armol' spat to the side. The captain looked at him with displeasure, then moved his eyes to the floor, to where the yellow slug of spittle had landed.

Toko elbowed his friend, and whispered:

"It's not done to spit inside the wooden yaranga."

The captain walked over to the Winchesters, picked one up and, almost forcibly, made Orvo take it. He then took the magazines out of the remaining guns, and handed them to Armol' and Toko. He said something, with an important look, and Orvo quickly translated:

"The captain swears that these Winchesters will be waiting for us onboard the ship until we come back. As a security, he is giving us the nests for the bullets."

Armol' and Toko looked at one another, and Toko said:

"We agree."

All three of them left the cabin and walked down the plank onto the ice. The crowd had returned to the side of the ship, waiting in the cold for further news.

Orvo, Armol', and Toko walked side by side, heading for the yarangas. A silent crowd followed them, farther and farther away from the ice-covered ship.

"We should have also asked them for a small wooden boat," Armol' said with regret.

"They gave a good price. No reason to be put out," said Orvo sensibly. "Now taking one of their cloth yarangas, that's another thing. The wounded man isn't used to spending the night in the tundra, and anyway, one of those cloth tents is a good thing. Who knows, we might end up keeping it. Cut it up for kamleikas."

Toko entered his chottagin. His wife already knew everything. She took out clothing for a long journey, from a large sack – a wide kukhlianka with the fur facing out, an under-kukhlianka made of baby deer hide, double-thick trousers, three pairs of torbasses, mittens, a chamois ochre-dyed kamleika, a loose overall trimmed with thick wolverine fur, and a piece of bear skin – for sitting or sleeping on.

Toko took his winter dogsled with birch runners off the roof, found a long lakhtak harness, and went off to find the sled dogs.

2

John had not lost consciousness for an instant, but the pain in his wrists was so strong that he felt nothing outside of it, and it seemed to him that an opaque curtain of agony rippled between him and the rest of the world.

Each sudden move brought on the memory of the blinding fireworks that had reared up in a blaze before his eyes a few hours ago . . .

Having swallowed a large mug of coffee with condensed milk, John experienced an incredible surge of strength, and was even somewhat surprised to realize that at no point in the last few days had he been quite so sure of the favorable outcome of this, his first arctic voyage.

Stepping out of the cramped, smoky wardroom, John filled his lungs with frosty air and threw an almost tender look at the deserted rocky shore, where dark spots marked the dwellings of the local people. A sharp joy pierced him at the thought that he, John MacLennan, had been born far away from this wretched place. A feeling akin to pity for the dispossessed stirred in his breast when he glanced over at the cluster of dwellings, the little pillars of smoke, barely visible in the twilight.

. . . John MacLennan had been born in Port Hope, to the family of a librarian, who lived on the shore of Lake Ontario. Their house stood on a street that led to the shore, and in the distance, there was the gently bobbing yacht, *Good Journey*. Still, it was not the yacht but books that called the junior MacLennan to faraway seas. The poems of Kipling, the vague insinuations of seasoned mariners, hinting of distant lands, of night squalls and morning shores, undiscovered by civilized man.

After spending two years at the University of Toronto, John, despite the admonitions of his father and mother, and the pleading eyes of his fiancée Jeannie, darling Jeannie, the little schoolteacher, set off on his long journey. He crossed the continent by railroad. From Vancouver, he made his way to Nome, and there . . . there were plenty of ships to choose from. Whalers, merchant ships of the "Hudson Bay Company," some incredible slop-buckets, haphazardly equipped for sailing the Arctic seas, snow-white yachts from the United States, filled the spacious harbor.

John MacLennan soon found his future boss Hugh Grover, almost a fellow countryman, and the owner of a merchant schooner, in a port saloon. The ship's owner, who was also its captain, hailed from Winnipeg and, like John, had become irresistibly entranced by the sea in his youth, drawn by the the stories of his uncle, who had once sailed the Hudson Bay. Hugh Grover turned out to be this uncle's sole heir when the latter died, collapsing on the green lawn in front of his house, having trimmed it himself moments before.

Aboard the ship, filled with a motley crew, most of whom had trouble remembering their homeland, John took up a privileged position, and although it was not customary for the captain to have an assistant, John became one, and moreover, became a close friend of Hugh Grover's.

Everything was going smoothly. Steadily climbing north, along the edge of the Arctic Ocean, and making short stops to trade with the aborigines, Hugh and John dreamed of setting a record and reaching the mouth of the distant Siberian river Kolyma. This would have been a huge event in the history of sailing the Russian Arctic, and the names of Hugh Grover and John MacLennan could have been preserved for posterity on the maps, like those of Franklin, Frobisher, Hudson, and other great men who had conquered the snowy silence.

On fire for explorers' glory, Hugh and John didn't hear the muttering of the crew and had forgotten about the calendar, relentless in counting down the days of the short northern summer.

Beyond Long's Bay, when the mouth of the great Siberian river was very near, so near that the waters carried the mangled trunks of taiga forests, swept off her banks and out to sea, there appeared on the horizon a harmless-looking white stripe – the most terrifying sight in the whole of the Arctic Ocean.

Only then did Captain Grover come back to his senses; he wrenched the wheel sharply, and turned the *Belinda* back.

By evening, the white stripe became a clearly recognizable ice field. The captain ordered raised sails and shouted down to John, in the machinery chamber, to squeeze every drop of energy from the old motor.

For three days they ran, and the ice field relentlessly followed, always gaining. In the evenings, when darkness descended over the water, and the ice was lost from view, the sailors' hearts filled with hope that they had outrun the white death at their heels.

But by morning, as soon as pale dawn rose over them, the ice shone more brightly than morning light, and the sailors, standing around in despairing silence, could hear the grind and crackle of ice floes.

Soon the ice had caught *Belinda* in its grasp, and tightly embraced her. Now the ship moved along with the ice field, unable to change course or find refuge on a beach.

There was no need now for motor and sails, *Belinda*'s speed depended on the speed of the north-easterly wind that was driving the churning ice floes toward the Bering Strait. The ship's hull creaked, but it still held.

The last hope they had was that the ice would carry the vessel through the straits and into the open waters of the Bering Sea. This hope grew stronger with each passing day, but when their goal was almost within reach, the ice came to a stop by the cape of Enmyn, and the ship was pushed to a rocky outcrop and immured there.

"We'll have to spend the winter here," Captain Grover said gloomily.

"We're not the first, and we won't be the last. At least there are natives ashore."

However, a working relationship with the natives proved difficult to manage. The locals could not believe that there was nothing to trade aboard the ship, that everything had been traded long ago, that the hold was crammed full of polar fox pelts and walrus tusks.

Among the natives, they discovered a man who spoke a little English. He was something like an elder or leader of the group, though strangely, the inhabitants did not accord him any visible honors; it seemed that the respect toward this man was rooted in something else entirely. He was called Orvo. Unlike the other, difficult to pronounce local names, Orvo's had a reasonable sound, and there was no need to twist your tongue – as, for example, when John attempted to pronounce the name of Orvo's daughter, Tynarakhtyna.

Orvo gave the sailors some hope, hypothesizing that a south wind may yet push the ice offshore, opening the way to the Bering Strait.

A hint of the change in weather had come two days before. The ice had begun to shift slightly, and a wide crack of water opened up almost directly in front of *Belinda,* pointing straight on course.

After a short conference, they agreed to try blasting with dynamite the ice ridge that still separated the ship from the water.

The sailors bored hollows in the ice.

Early in the morning, just after breakfast, John MacLennan descended to the ice. He paused briefly by the side of the ship, taking in the beauty of the rising dawn, and then slowly moved toward the drilled holes, carrying the blast charges and fuse. He placed large paper-wrapped cartridges into the ice holes, buried them in snow, and tamped it down with his feet. He adjusted the fuses and set fire to the main one. A spitting blue flame raced toward the charges.

John walked back to the ship and sat down on an ice-crusted boulder. Silently, he counted down the seconds. There was an explosion. Against expectation, it was muffled and weak. But the ground trembled and John could feel the ice that had seemed forever glued to the rocky shore move slightly under his feet. Came three more, louder blasts. After each, John was covered in ice dust and small splinters.

He waited for the fifth. What had the explosives done to the fissure? Did it widen, as he and Captain Grover had plotted? But there was no reason to look, not until the fifth blast had sounded.

The allotted seconds came and went, then again as many.

John peeked out from his shelter. No smoke, no flame. He waited a little longer and, deciding that the previous blasts had buried and extinguished the fuse, he went back to the fissure. It had become no wider; the explosives were useless. The four charges had merely enlarged the hollows, and did not even reach down to the water. The fissure looked exactly the same as before.

The fifth cartridge was smothered in crushed ice and snow. A little smoking tail protruded from the clump. Not thinking, John kneeled and started to clear away the snow, trying to reach the cartridge.

And then it exploded. That first instant, John saw a blazing light, as though it were the Northern Lights rearing up in front of his eyes. Then the sound wave hit his ears, compressing his eardrums. John fell forward and lay there, until he could feel an acute, bone-piercing pain flood his face and hands. It was then that he started screaming. He screamed and could not hear himself, holding out the bloody tatters of fur mittens, the rags of his own fingers, and some kind of bluish-red strings that dripped bright crimson blood onto the snow.

Sailors were coming down from deck. Captain Grover ran to him.

"What have you done, boy!" he shouted, carefully lifting John. "Help me! Hold him up!"

The sailors approached John gingerly, throwing suspicious glances at the remains of the fuse and cartridge.

"Don't worry," John rasped, "all the cartridges have blown."

While they were carrying him to the ship, he keenly felt that it was life itself, along with his blood, that was running out of his body. It was an astonishing sensation that grew into horror. And when they lowered him to the bed in the tiny wardroom, he moaned and begged:

"Won't you stop the bleeding!"

One of the sailors was quick-witted enough to bind a rope across his wrists. The blood stopped gushing, and now John felt his entire body suffused with fire, the hot stream pulsating in his wrists, his toes, and his mouth filling with foul, metallic saliva.

"Will I die?" he asked of Hugh, who was standing at the head of the bunk and nervously plucking at a sideburn.

"You won't die, John," Hugh answered, "I'll do everything I can to save you. You will go to a hospital. To Anadyr'. There's a doctor there."

"You'll wait for me here?" pleaded John.

"How can you ask a friend that question?" Hugh was offended. "We're clamped so tightly to this shoreline that we couldn't move an inch even if we wanted to."

"Thanks, Hugh," John sighed. "I always knew you were a true friend."

"Damn, if we had open water from here to Nome, you'd be in a hospital in three days!" the captain avowed despondently. "I give you the word of an honest man: We will wait for you."

John looked at the captain's steadfast face, whose sympathetic, thoughtful expression somehow lessened the pain and fire raging through John's entire body.

"You'll go on the dogsleds to Anadyr'. I'll fix it so they treat you well," the captain promised.

"And they won't do anything to me?" asked John.

"Who?" Hugh didn't quite understand.

"You know, these savages, the Chukchi. Their faces don't inspire my trust. These people are just too unsavory-looking. Unwashed and unschooled."

"They're an honest enough people," Hugh reassured his friend. "Especially if you pay them well."

"So be generous with them Hugh, won't you?" John's voice held a note of pleading. "Give them anything they want . . . I'll make it up to you later, in Port Hope."

"What are you talking about!" Hugh was indignant. "There's no reckoning between friends!"

When Toko appeared on the doorstep, and the captain shouted coarsely at him to leave, John said:

"Don't be like that with them, Hugh. Treat them more gently."

"I'm sorry, John. You're probably right," the captain mumbled, flustered, and asked for Orvo to be fetched.

John was barely following the captain's conversation with Orvo. The Chukcha's English was so atrocious that you had to strain to understand him.

John closed his eyes and felt the revolting wave of nausea rise up in his throat. He could barely manage to hold on until Orvo's departure, strangely unwilling to show his weakness in front of the man.

The captain ordered for John to be moved into another cabin, and the wardroom cleaned up.

The sailors moved the wounded man. They carefully removed his clothes, and dressed him in fresh, clean underthings. Over that, a woollen shirt, thick canvas trousers and double-thick knitted socks, and then they dressed MacLennan in some just-bought Chukcha fur-lined winter garments. Hugh dragged over John's trunk and an enormous sack of provisions.

"There's coffee, biscuits, sugar, tins, condensed milk, and a flagon of vodka," Hugh enumerated, businesslike. "And in the trunk, I've put another change of underclothes, your papers, letters, and photographs of your family."

"Thanks, Hugh," John was struggling to smile, "but there was no need to bring the trunk. I imagine I won't be in Anadyr' for that long."

"The papers and money will come in handy. You'll have to pay for the treatment."

"You're right, Hugh," John replied. "It's so good to have you near at a time like this. I will never forget your kindness. This morning has made you closer to me than a brother, closer than father or mother. Thank you, Hugh . . ."

Captain Grover, not usually a sensitive man, took his handkerchief out of his pocket and dabbed at his eyes; he was sincerely touched. He was genuinely fond of the boy. He had noticed him back there, in Nome, in the port saloon, and thought that John would make a good companion for him and help him while away the time, surrounded as he was by the rough and delinquent gang of which his crew was comprised.

Grover had wasted much breath to prove to John how naïve the younger man's outlook was, in this cruel world where everyone seeks a warm place to lie and a bigger, fatter piece of the meat. He'd conducted long, inspirational talks with the boy, at times when the rest of the crew was engaged in luring women onboard. He stroked John's shoulder, which quivered in outrage, and spoke to him, eliciting compassion for the wretches who have only one joy in life – to get drunk when the voyage ends and their share is doled out, or to eke out a moment of carnal pleasure during a lengthy, exhausting trip.

John, equipped for the journey, lay on his back, thinking about the wealth of kindness and sincere compassion in the man who, at first, had seemed to him only a cynic and a materialist . . . Undoubtedly, Hugh was right in some things. In many things, really. But he was just too cynical and forthright. He'd spoken so disdainfully of the Chukchi, and now he was forced to ask for their help. Of course, they would be well-paid, but if there had been even a grain of trust between the indigenous people and the crew of the *Belinda,* John would feel much easier now, setting off on a long journey to the unknown Russian town of Anadyr'.

3

Three dogsleds drove up to the *Belinda* and the drivers, having first hammered their ostols* into the ice, ascended to the deck.

Three Chukchi entered the scrubbed wardroom, and the captain, politely and amiably, ushered them toward the table, which held three impressive silver goblets full of rum.

John was propped up on the couch. Clad in a fur-lined kukhlianka, fur-lined trousers and kamuss† torbasses, in an overall trimmed with wolverine fur, he was almost indistinguishable from the drivers.

Grover passed a goblet to each, and, signaling for them to wait a moment before drinking, he made a little speech:

"You are entrusted with the life of a white man. You must deliver John MacLennan to the Russian town of Anadyr' safely, wait there until he is recovered, and then bring him back here. You know how much we value the life of our friend," here, he nodded in John's direction, "and on your heads be it, if anything should happen to him." After a pause the captain continued in a completely different tone, "But if everything goes well, a rich reward will await you. Orvo, you understand what I'm saying and can translate for your fellows."

While Orvo translated, Toko was looking over the wounded man. He

---

* *Ostol* – a metal-capped stick used for braking the dogsled.
† *Kamuss* – The skin from a deer's thigh.

didn't like his icy, cold eyes. They had the strange quality of looking right through a person, as though that person were an empty place.

Toko could feel John's stare pierce him through, giving rise to such a strange chill in the pit of his stomach that not even the fiery rum could chase it away.

Orvo finished translating Captain Grover's speech:

"Curse the hour I agreed to this! He's got me, the wily one! I was swayed by the Winchesters. And now what can we do? We'll have to take him. And he's like a hungry louse. If anything should happen to him, it'll be our heads . . . What do you think? We will go, eh?"

Orvo addressed Armol', but the latter, only half-listening to the translation of the captain's speech, caught nothing except the last words and nodded silently.

And Toko, after a moment's hesitation, quietly said:

"I've never, ever had a real Winchester."

The wounded man was carefully carried from the wardroom and lowered onto Orvo's dogsled, where a little deer-hide canopy had been prepared for him. The remaining two sleds were loaded with provisions, dog feed, John's trunk, and extra clothing. Besides that, a small cloth yaranga was lashed to Toko's sled in case they had to spend a night in the tundra.

They might have set off long ago, if every sailor had not considered it his duty to touch his face to John's. Captain Grover took the longest time doing this, until tears ran down John's cheeks. It was strange to see a grown man weeping.

Toko stared at the ice-floe eyes that were melting now with large hazy tears, and a feeling akin to pity, mixed with triumph, moved within him. John caught his glance, hid his own eyes and swiped at his tear-filled eyelashes with the enormous deer mittens covering his mangled hands. The pain of it made him grimace.

Orvo shouted at the dogs, and the sled moved off slowly. The sailors ran after them, seeing off their shipmate and making John even more upset, hanging his head lower and lower, until his face was completely hidden inside the fur-trimmed hood of his warm overall.

The dogsleds came ashore, leaving the ice and the ship behind them. When they rode past the yarangas, Toko braked his sled a little and stole a glance at his wife, who stood outside watching the departing sleds. Their eyes met, and this was to be their only farewell. Toko, remembering the sailors' leave-taking, had the sad thought that, after all, it would not be so bad to press his face to his wife's, to breathe in her scent and hold it in his memory during this long journey to far-off Anadyr', where he had never been before.

The sled dogs ran across the frozen lagoon floor. There was little snow yet, and large expanses of clear icy surface stretched from one shore to the other. The pack tried to run down the powdery strips laid out by the snowstorm, where their paws found a less slippery purchase, but the drivers kept turning them toward the ice, over which the sleds' runners could fly forward most easily, almost catching up with the dogs in their harness.

Toko was looking back at the yarangas that little by little disappeared into the snowy expanses, dissolving in the looming darkness, at the familiar crags that framed the horizon. With his eyes, he held on tight to his own yaranga, the one that he'd built with his own hands, collecting driftwood under the craggy cliff-faces and waiting his turn at the division of a hunt's spoils to get some walrus hides for the roof. He had saved up the nerpa blubber, pouring it into sealskin bags; he had cut out lakhtak belt-strips to offer to his deer-herder friends, in return for deer hides to make his polog*... The yaranga turned out as well as anyone else's and seemed, to Toko and Pyl'mau, even better and cosier, because it was their own home. They'd only been married for three years, but it was as though they had lived a long life side by side; they could guess the other's desires without words and long explanations.

* *Polog* – the sleeping chamber inside a yaranga.

The outline shape of his home faded from view. The horizon grew flat and empty, with nary a sign of life. Now it didn't matter where you looked – forward, backward, to the side: It was the same everywhere.

Toko's sled was running last. At the head of the column, Armol' was opening the way. And Orvo, who was driving the wounded man, rode in the middle.

The little tent atop Orvo's sled was fashioned in such a way that John was looking backwards rather than ahead, so that the snow flurry from under the dogs' paws didn't hit him in the face, and so that the wind couldn't blow into the hood of his overall.

The white man was sitting up straight, watching the running dogs. His blue eyes were darkened with pain, or perhaps fatigue. Or maybe it really was the sadness of leaving his comrades and embarking on such a long journey. Who knows what kind of thoughts may be springing to life in a head like that, covered with hair so light it seems to have gone prematurely gray.

John could feel the intent stare of the brute whose sled followed his own. What strange and narrow eyes he has! What can you make out behind slits like that, like the narrow chink in grandmother's piggy-bank. And yet, if you look carefully, you'll fall into them, as into a bottomless crevasse. An utter mystery that no man shall penetrate. What could he possibly be thinking about, this young Chukcha?

The sled stopped rattling as they came over the calm smooth surface of the lagoon, and the pain in his hands died down. For a long time, John's eyes clung to the *Belinda*'s masts, those two black smudges in the fading light that tied him to his own world. But over there, where the dogs were heading, the unknowable awaited him; that and the chance of life.

And the masts disappeared. A gaping void in his head, as though all his brains had been dashed while the sleds bumped up and down the ice dunes. Only somewhere deep within his conscience, a terror; terror before this monstrous expanse without end, before the cold that was already creeping under his kukhlianka, terror of the people who bore him across the snow, of their bottomless black eyes that watched and watched him – as though he were walking a closed circle with an abyss at every side.

What was left of his palms and fingers? Sometimes John tried to wiggle them, as it seemed to him that they were whole, only the pain resonated strangely in his elbow and shoulder, where there was hardly a scratch. Afraid of the pain, John was trying to think. To think of anything at all, only to drive away this feeling of his own self-disappearing. Is this how vastness impresses itself on a man: as though drawing him into itself and dissolving him, leaving no flesh, no blood, no thoughts . . .

Realizing that it was better to sit with eyes closed – at least he didn't see this endless white space – John leaned back on the deer hides folded behind him and tried to sleep, to get away from this melancholy landscape, from his gloomy thoughts and the ache gnawing at his hands.

Armol', riding in front, began braking and then came to a halt. This meant that it was Toko's turn to take the lead position and open a trail for the others.

Toko shouted to his pack and overtook the two sleds. It was soft snow, not the mid-winter kind that is tamped down firmly by windstorms and then smoothed by an icy blizzard's rough palm. This snow was easy on the runners, but hard on the dogs. At times they sank to the belly into the fluffy snowdrifts, the snow clinging to their coats and paws.

Over the rises and at the tallest snowdrifts, Toko would jump off his sled and jog alongside it, holding on to the baran.* It was warm, and Toko would throw back his hood, running bareheaded until his hair was covered with frost.

Then he would topple onto the sled at a run, so that the lakhtak strips

* *Baran* – a handlebar in the shape of an arch over the sled.

lashing its wooden frame together groaned, and the pack leader turned back his head to give the driver a look of reproach.

Orvo was submerged so deeply in his own meditations and winter clothes that it was impossible to read the expression on his face, much less his thoughts. Orvo was mentally going over his actions in the last few hours, growing sure that he had made a mistake in submitting to the worst of temptations – greed. Yes, it went without saying that those goods were excellent. And yet they had lived without such things, lived as Orvo's ancestors had done, without tobacco, tea, the bad joy-making water, woven cloth, metal needles, and had managed to hunt with bows and arrows. These new things, brought by the white men to Chukchi shores, had only complicated life. The sweetness of sugar also held a bitter tang. How does one know what's best? Yes, he had lived in the white men's enormous settlements, but what could he say, having seen only the tawdry port saloons and municipal dumps?

That world had not sat well with him, but who can vouch that the white men like the Chukchi way of life? All people live their own way, and there's no use making another person do as you do, changing his customs and habits. If you don't stick your nose into another's life but only try to work to mutual advantage, then there will be no quarrels. It's no good when the white man enters the life of an arctic shore . . . The thoughts buzzed in his head, allowing him no peace. Oh, why had he agreed to take on this cripple? He's got an unkind stare, and his face looks like the face of a man drained of his last drops of blood . . .

The eastern horizon had paled and only the brightest of the stars remained in the sky. The backbone of a far-off mountain range sheltering the valley of the Big River that led to Anadyr' rose jagged and sharp against the blue of the sky, its uncapped peaks glinting ominously under the rays of a sun that was creeping unseen beyond the horizon.

Orvo rose up out of his overall and shouted to Toko:

"We'll make a stop, go over the runners!"

As soon as Toko made to brake his sled, the pack leader stopped and the rest of the dogs followed suit.

On hearing Orvo speak, John opened his eyes. The sled's steady rocking over a smooth snowy path had come to a stop.

Again his eyes met those of the Chukcha riding behind him, and marveled how much the other's appearance had changed, right down to the cut of his garments. Even his eyes different, and his expression were . . . What could it be? And only at Toko's approach did John realize that the drivers had switched places. He thought of how alike they all were, and that he'd have to learn to know them from one another.

Toko came closer, discussed something with his companions, and looked over at John. The latter could make out something akin to a smile on that face, dark like the cover of an old leather armchair. He returned the smile, drawing back his cold-numbed lips with difficulty.

"Look, he's laughing," Toko remarked with surprise, pointing with his finger.

"Why shouldn't he smile?" Orvo replied. "He's a person, too. And if he can smile, it must mean that he's not doing so badly as all that. Maybe we'll deliver him safely to Anadyr' after all, and get the Winchesters in exchange . . ."

"Yes, we've got to look after him," said the practical Armol'. "Maybe it's time to feed him? Go on and ask him, Orvo."

Orvo pointed to his mouth, then to John's mouth, and worked his lips.

John had not felt hungry, but it was certainly lunchtime and he nodded his head to indicate agreement. While Orvo headed for the dogsled with John's own provisions, the other drivers upended their sleds and went about cleaning the runners, chafing them with wet hides. They sprayed the runners from their own mouths, drawing in warm water from flat Scotch whiskey bottles, kept next to their bare stomachs under the fur clothing. Having used all the water, they stuffed the bottles with snow and slipped them back into their kukhliankas. John couldn't suppress a shudder, just thinking about that freezing glass touching bare skin.

In the meantime, Orvo had brought over the sack that Captain Grover had so carefully packed, opened it up, and began gesturing to find out what John would like to eat. John chose a salt pork sandwich and a lump of sugar.

Having finished their work, Armol' and Toko came closer and watched the feeding of the white man with undisguised interest.

"Just look at those teeth!" exclaimed Armol', awed. "White, sharp, like an ermine's."

"Yes," Toko agreed. "If he bit you, you couldn't shake him off."

"He could chew through metal, much less bone," added Armol'.

John stopped chewing. The humiliation of it, his helplessness and sense of injury, drove away his appetite.

Orvo had understood him and quietly said to his fellows:

"You could stand back a little. Haven't you ever seen a person eat? He's shy of us!"

"All right," Toko concurred, and called to Armol':

"Let's go, let the white man eat."

John gave Orvo a grateful look and, swallowing the last bit, said hoarsely:

"Thank you."

"Yes! Yes!" Orvo nodded vigorously and continued in the Chukchi tongue:

"Now we can keep going. We have to make the mountain spine by nightfall. There we'll stay with Il'motch, and we'll sleep in a warm tent, and have plenty of deer meat, too."

John suddenly felt unbearably thirsty. The dry, cold food hadn't left him a drop of saliva, and his tongue was thick and parched in his mouth.

"Drink?" he asked, and mimed drinking some liquid, throwing back his head.

Orvo grasped his meaning immediately, and reached inside his clothes. He brought out the same kind of bottle as his comrades', used his teeth to pull out the dirty rag that did for a cork, and held it out readily.

John couldn't conceal a grimace of disgust and had to screw his eyes shut before he could touch his lips to the bottle's neck. He drank the warm water with greedy gulps, hurrying, choking, making an impossible effort of will to chase away the thought that the warmth of it came from the old driver's body. When he took his lips off the bottle, he saw Orvo's flat smiling face, incredibly similar to the stylized picture of an Eskimo in the National University Museum in Toronto.

John managed a smile. He had wanted to show his gratitude with it, but something sparked inside him, and the resulting smile was sincere, not forced.

The drivers took up their places and the dogs pulled the sleds toward the mountain range, which rose up relentlessly against the travelers, taking up more and more of the horizon and shattering the line where earth and sky met.

The air became more and more blue, as though someone enormous and invisible were thickening the color. The snow that stretched ahead was blueing, the bumps, the hillocks and snowdrifts were blueing, and the sky too, lighting up the stars; the blue seeped into the sleds' tracks, into the dogs, the harnesses, and Toko's face, framed by wolverine fur.

Night was descending over the tundra.

4

Like a lullaby, the congealing darkness damped the sound of sled-runners over snow. Within the even rocking of the sled and the cozy creaking of its leather fastenings, John drifted in and out of sleep, remembering his last autumn at home, the blazing fires of maple-leaf fall. Forgotten details were taking on symbolic meaning, and resurrecting them in memory was sweet and surprisingly pleasant.

A narrow path, almost invisible in the grass, led to a shady corner that was proudly called the city park. You could have counted all its trees on your fingers. There was a set of brightly colored swings in the middle of a grassy stretch, and John and Jeannie liked to climb aboard and push one another, to the disapproving comments of strolling mothers. And when they finally had to give up the swings to children, they would lie on the grass for hours, watching squirrels cavort in the branches overhead.

A horn trill would bring them back to reality; John's father blowing into a seashell, gathering the family to a late lunch . . .

The way was definitely becoming steeper. It was hard on the dogs, and the drivers went on foot to spare them. Now it was Toko's turn to bring up the caravan's rear. He walked alongside the sled, holding on to the baran. The slope was covered in deep snow, his feet kept sinking, and he kept thinking how good it would be to sit down on the sled, or at least place your foot on one of the runners and ride a little, cooling your straining heart with a deep breath.

Toko looked at the somnolent white man, tucked in cosily atop the dogsled, and felt a muffled irritation take hold of him. He didn't fight against the feeling now, didn't try to convince himself that the sled was occupied by an unfortunate and sick person whose very life was in their hands. Toko's tired, hungry, and frustrated mind saw only the cause of all this hardship. He remembered the strong white teeth that noisily crunched hard biscuit, the white throat greedily gulping water, the icy blue eyes and that semblance of a smile . . . Yet beyond all this beckoned the image of the new Winchester – a weapon that would make his life worthy of a real man. No animal could evade him then, and he would never again feel ashamed of himself when one escaped from right under his nose. With a good Winchester you could hunt white fox in the tundra. Even in the bright whiteness of snow, a sharp eye can discern a different shade – a sable creeping, following mouse tracks across the snow. You could get three-dozen by spring with a Winchester. Cure them nicely and hang them outside for the dry cold wind to bleach the pelts even more and fluff up the downy fur.

And when the ice broke and you could see a ship's sail, then you could come down to the shore without hurry, sensitive to the white tails streaming behind you. The trader's eyes will spark to a greedy glow, he'll clutch the fox pelts. Then you can ask for plenty of tobacco, a good pipe, buy a knife and a string of big glass beads for your wife.

You didn't even have to wait for a ship. You could get on your sled and set off on a long journey to Irvytgyr, to the ancient settlement of Uelen where the trader Carpenter lives, the one who is almost like one of the natives, as he's taken a native from the other side of the bay – an Eskimo – for his wife, and has made children with her. He trades fairly and never tries to burden a tundra-dweller with a useless item.

A Winchester is certainly a good thing, and it's worth driving the white man to a far-off place, all the way to Anadyr', for such a weapon.

John could barely see Toko's exhausted, overheated face. The thickening gloom filled his field of vision, already shadowed by his overcoat's thick wolverine fur hood. Armol', walking in front, was shouting at the dogs and cracking his whip. Old Orvo, though invisible to John, was breathing loudly and heavily, often joining in Armol's exhortations.

The dogs suddenly took off with a burst, although the sleds were still crawling up the gently sloping incline. John felt the leather fastenings moan as Toko jumped back on, but they continued to gain speed. Armol' rushed by, through a whirlwind of snow. He was braking with all his might, but the dogs flew on ahead – as though there had been no long day's crossing in the deep tundra snows.

There came the sound of human voices, and then a stranger clad in a long chamois robe rushed to Orvo's aid. He grabbed hold of the baran, and the dogsled began to slow down, finally coming to a halt in front of a yaranga that had seemingly appeared from nowhere.

Ignoring the pain, John peeked out of the tent and looked around curiously. The yaranga was markedly different from those on the shore. It was smaller and did not have wooden walls. The roof, stitched together from a multitude of shorn deer hides, turned into walls as it came down, anchored to the ground with large stones, and packed down with snow for extra hold. A palisade of wooden stakes projected over the roof and exhaled a homey curlicue of warm smoke.

This was the camp of the reindeer-herding Chukchi. John had heard of them before, and had even seen one such reindeer-herder back in Enmyn. The latter hadn't dared ascend to the ship's deck. Instead he stared at the white people from afar, hiding neither his curiosity nor his amazement. He seemed to have been a little afraid.

But here, the reindeer-herding folk, exchanging a few words with the new arrivals, immediately surrounded Orvo's dogsled to stare at John. They traded loud comments with one another and unceremoniously pointed their fingers at the white man, propped up helplessly on the sled.

"Sitting like a frozen crow!"

"Look how furry his cheeks are!"

"But the mustache is all white . . ."

"That's just hoarfrost . . ."

"Wrapped himself up, like an old woman."

"Move off, move off!" Orvo shouted at the mouthiest ones.

John hadn't understood a single world, but could feel that he was being laughed at.

A murky rage was kindling in his heart. He shifted a little, stretching muscles that had grown numb with sitting still, lifted himself from the sled and stood on his feet. He could barely believe that he was able to move unassisted. It was such a boon that he almost shouted his joy out loud. Holding himself in check, and with only a triumphant glance around, he took a few steps on weak, trembling legs.

"Look at that," said Toko with surprise, "he's walking!"

He looked John in the eye and could suddenly discern a warm yellow light glowing in the icy blue depths. That's how a hunter, clambering over hummock-churned fast ice is guided home by a blubber-filled stone lantern that calls to him from the shore. It was the look of a worn-out man who has suddenly found his sought-after shore, a place where he can breathe freely and feel the earth firm beneath his feet. It was the look of a man who rejoiced.

And Toko smiled back at him.

Orvo called to John and led him into the yaranga.

John followed meekly, carefully holding up his bandaged hands. They had to bend low at the yaranga's entrance. Even from afar, John had felt the comfortable warmth of smoke, and on entering the yaranga he was engulfed in steamy air. The smoke wound its way up from the fire, pooled by the deer-hide cupola and left through the smokehole, through which peeped the darkened evening sky.

Orvo led John through to the center of the dwelling and got him down onto a low seat that turned out to be a lengthy log, covered over with deerskins. To sit on, it was fairly uncomfortable, and John took a long time settling until he found the right position.

The chamber was quite roomy. Not far from the entrance, a fire blazed, giving off enough light for John to be able to thoroughly look over the yaranga. A large sooty cauldron, clearly of foreign make, was over the fire. Some sort of stew was bubbling away inside it, and John, who'd gotten hungry, could smell the aroma of boiled meat through the bitterish smoke.

The dancing flames flickered over two bustling women, both naked to the waist. They resembled mermaids, with their glossy sloping shoulders, bare breasts, and long matted black locks of hair that fell over their faces. The lower halves of their bodies were imprisoned in ungainly fur cocoons, with ballooning trouser-legs and fur-lined footwear, ornamented with embroidery.

The women gave John frightened glances and switched to whispering. It was not hard to guess that they were talking about the strange guest.

Next to the wall, down the entire perimeter of the yaranga, there were leather sacks, evidently the food stores, wooden vessels, bales of deer hides. One corner was piled with freshly skinned deer legs, the tendons hanging down. A scalped deer head, likely readied for cooking, stared ahead with cloudy, lifeless eyes.

John made an effort to pull his eyes away. Above him, deer carcasses hung from the wooden rafters and were awash in the thin smoke from the fire.

Behind him was the fur polog, its rectangular walls sewn from reindeer hides. The front wall was raised and the polog's inside clearly visible, but it was empty, save for a dead grease lamp.

The curious were peeking through the low door. First to appear were the children. Swathed in furs, hoods trimmed with dense pelt, they looked like little balls, and only the button noses and shiny olive-black eyes suggested they were human beings. Pushing aside the children and sticking their hands inside the dwelling, the women percolated with questions while their eyes took in John.

There was the sound of male voices. Orvo, Toko, and Armol' entered the yaranga. Strangers followed behind them, evidently the camp's inhabitants. Toko was dragging John's food pouch on his back, and Orvo carried his little trunk.

"We'll sleep here," Orvo told John. "Wind coming down from the mountains, it's to no good."

"I'd like to go outside for a minute," John muttered shyly.

At first Orvo didn't understand him. John had to repeat his request a few times. Toko was watching him carefully, and suddenly, though he hadn't understood a word, said to Orvo:

"No need to translate here! It's clear enough."

And he motioned for John to follow him.

They stood within the silence of the invisible and boundless dome of the sky, thickly scattered with large stars. John had never imagined before that stars could be so bright. They flickered on high, marking the lines of constellations he'd known from childhood. He was looking at the sky and trying not to think of the cold touch of Toko's fingers. He was thinking that he'd have to steel himself in order to survive this, to steel himself and learn to mentally leave this place for far reaches, inaccessible to this simpleton who can't even deal with something as simple as an ordinary button.

Toko was saying something quietly, probably uttering his Chukchi curses, but what difference did any of it make if you couldn't grasp the words!

Still, how majestic was the silence! The taut wind, blowing steadily, without gusts, resembled a cold stream born of a glacier. The moon was rising over faraway ridges, and the mountain peaks glittered mysteriously and strangely . . . What a pity that man, when he is young, looks to God so rarely, sure as he is of his own strength! Perhaps this was it, that moment when your soul converses with It, the one and only . . .

Toko had finally managed the buttons. Why, why have so many buttons in a place where it's so easy to do with one? Truly the whites are miserly where it is easy to be generous, and yet wasteful in ways beyond understanding. Rearranging the folds of the kukhlianka, Toko looked up into John's face. The other was standing, head thrown back, and the vaulting sky was reflected in his icy eyes. A strange kind of sadness marked his face, as though while Toko was grappling with the buttons, a new person had appeared in John's stead, a person with a strange, shaman-like expression. Alarmed, Toko gave John a little push.

The white man roused, his eyes filled with a live warmth again, and he said something short, tender, probably a word of thanks for Toko.

Inside the hut, Orvo invited John to come inside the polog, whose front curtain was now closed. He had to crawl inside on his belly. The rectangular room was lit by a grease lamp. Its flame was steady and bright. A woman was crouching in front of the brazier, directing its blaze with a little stick like a conductor's baton. Toko helped John find a comfortable position and pulled off his outer clothing. It was warm and light inside the polog. John's shattered wrists barely hurt at all. The pain was somewhere bone-deep, and if you paid no attention to it, it was almost as though it didn't even exist.

He could hear voices behind the fur-lined wall, the footfall of soft torbasses on the earthen floor. The edge of the curtain moved, and a head came through. It was with difficulty that John recognized old Orvo. Next to Orvo, Armol's head emerged, and then appeared the man who had been the first to greet the travelers. Soon, a row of shaggy heads ranged from corner to corner before John and Toko. They chatted to Toko all at once, sometimes addressing John himself through Orvo.

John was curt in answering their questions about his health, and observed the profusion of heads that stared at him, like some sort of a nine-headed monster, with some annoyance.

John's irritation was stoked by a sharply rising feeling of hunger. Finally, unable to bear it a moment longer, he addressed Orvo, asking him to take the food out of his sack.

"Don't hurry so," Orvo answered calmly. "We'll have some real food in a moment."

His head disappeared and was immediately replaced by a long wooden trough, filled to the brim with steaming boiled meat. The smell was so strong and savory that John, unable to help himself, swallowed convulsively.

Orvo, who had popped up again behind the dish, gave a triumphant shout and passed an order to Toko, explaining, it seemed, how the white man should be fed.

Toko grabbed an enormous meaty bone off the dish and pushed it in front of John's face. The warm meat touched his lips, and John drew back, appalled by such rough manners.

But instead of an expression of shame, Toko's face clouded with surprise and questioning. After a moment's thought, an idea transformed his face. He called out:

"Sson!" and, clasping the meat in his teeth, cut off a slice close to his mouth, almost nicking his own nose with the blade.

He purposely exaggerated his chewing and slurping to show how tasty the meat was.

But Orvo, who may have known that the white man takes his food in a different manner, or who may have simply guessed it, cut the meat into small pieces on the wooden platter, speared one piece with his knife and raised it to John's lips. So feeding began.

The meat was delicious, tender and juicy, but completely bland. After two or three slices, John attempted to explain to Orvo that the mistress of the house had evidently forgotten to salt it, but Orvo said decisively:

"Salt no!"

Then Toko unceremoniously opened John's clothes sack and discovered a small linen bag of the precious white granules.

Orvo neatly salted John's share of the meat, and even added some to the meat broth that finished off the plentiful feast.

After the food, everyone began preparing for sleep. The master's wife carried in some rolled-up deer hides. John's allotted sleeping place was by the back wall, next to the grease lamp. Toko settled down close to him. The brazier and the steaming meat had made it warm, almost hot, in the polog. Toko divested himself of his fawn-skin under-kukhlianka with one smooth move, and was left bare to the waist. But after a while even this seemed too much, and he pulled off his undergarments too, completely naked now, except for a piece of deer hide thoughtfully provided by the yaranga's mistress, which he draped between his legs.

When all the other men followed his example, John asked Orvo to help him get rid of at least his warm fur-lined shirt and trousers.

Orvo folded the removed garments under John's head, making something of a pillow. John sank back on it and lowered his eyelids. A blessed peace was stealing over his body. The journey was turning out to be less frightening than he'd thought.

John lay on his back. All around him was the buzz of incomprehensible conversation. It acted as a soporific, like a quiet ocean tide or a gurgling stream. Before he fell into a deep sleep, the kind face of Captain Hugh flickered across John's consciousness. Only, for some reason, his hair and close shave were that of a Chukcha deer herder. But John had no time to be surprised at this – he was asleep.

5

Orvo slowly packed the tiny pipe bowl with tobacco and, drawing deeply, passed it on to Il'motch, the yaranga's owner.

Il'motch took the pipe and carefully tucked the stem into a narrow gap between his sparse teeth, making sure not to open his mouth too wide, lest he lose even a small part of the precious tobacco.

Armol' was following the elders' movements, but didn't dare ask for even one drag for himself.

"Three days, you'll be climbing toward the pass," Il'motch was saying, almost without moving his lips. "Three days and three nights out in the freezing wind, without shelters, without firewood, without deep snow. You won't be able to take much provisions, so you'll have to starve a bit, and the dogs will, too."

Licking tobacco juice off the pipe stem, Il'motch finally passed it to Armol'. The young man gripped it convulsively, and drew in deeply.

When it was Toko's turn, Il'motch was continuing in a normal tone:

"The white man needs to be taken to Anadyr', there's nothing you can do about that. Go back, and you'll anger the captain, but if he dies – who can tell what trouble you'll get for that . . . I'll say, it's a hard yoke you've roped yourselves into."

Orvo glanced over at the sleeping John, and, with a sigh, admitted:

"Got greedy, I did. But you could work five years and still not have enough for three guns. There's little demand for whalebone now, they pay badly, and the whites only want white fox nowadays. And you well know, on our shore it's better to hunt the white fox out on the sea, when he follows the white bear, scavenging for leavings. You can't leave traps on the ice – they just get swept away."

"A gun is a very good thing," Il'motch agreed, and looked longingly at Orvo's cooling pipe.

Catching his glance, Orvo started reaching over for his tobacco pouch.

Toko looked down at John. Eyes closed, the white man did not seem so alien. Just a sleeping person with very light hair and tightly shut eyelids, irises trembling behind them, watching a nameless dream.

"Give you some foodstuffs," said Il'motch, attentively watching Orvo pack tobacco into the pipe bowl. "In the fall, we had a good many deer downed in the first blizzard. There'll be plenty of meat . . . If the road is good, then sure, you'll manage the pass, too. And then it's down and down – into the valleys. The Kereks will be roaming there, and the bow-legged Karamkyt.*

"The ones that ride stags?"asked Armol'.

"The very ones," Il'motch nodded. "They're a hard-up people. Big eaters, though."

"Going through their camps, it's nothing but grief," Il'motch continued. "They're not big on sharing food, and their yarangas are cold."

For some time, there was silence in the room. The wind, having gained strength toward nightfall, beat at the yaranga's deerskin sides.

"Comes from the mountains," said Il'motch, softly. "We'll be snowed in by morning."

They all held their breath, listening to the wind.

The flame in the grease lamp was dying out. The women, done with

* *Karamkyt* – Evven deer herders.

their household duties, were bedding down for the night, stripping off their clothing and climbing under deerskin covers.

Il'motch sucked on the empty pipe, and handed it to Orvo.

"Time to sleep."

In the middle of the night, John awoke with a vague feeling of anxiety. At first he couldn't make sense of where he was. Just now he had dreamt of splitting logs in the cellar of his parents' house in Port Hope, while looking forward to the pleasant hours he'd spend in front of a crackling fire. He kept on chopping, and the pile of wood grew higher around him. The logs fell on top of each other, forming a tall stack about to topple over. His arms ached, his shoulders were shot through with pain. John glanced at the swaying stacks from time to time but, strangely, carried on chopping until a river of logs flooded over him. He made an effort to climb out from underneath it – and woke up.

At first he thought that he must be in his own cabin on board the *Belinda,* but in the very next instant a mounting throbbing in his hands brought him back to reality.

Outside the yaranga's walls, a gale thundered – battering at the deerskins, threatening to tear the fragile-seeming dwelling from its moorings and carry it off into the measureless breadth of the tundra. But the dwelling clung tightly to earth. It shook, it moaned, but stayed put. It must have been one of those terrible blizzards that John had read about in the accounts of polar explorers, and then heard told of in the port saloon at Vancouver, and later in the Alaskan capital, Nome.

There were times when the gusts were so fierce that John could feel the dwelling lift up from the ground, as though ready to fly after the storm.

And yet both the yaranga's inhabitants and guests slept soundly, in spite of the wind's roar, which threatened to overwhelm their mighty snoring.

John squirmed around on his bedding. It was stifling and he felt thirsty.

The moans and groans of the wind outside tolled in his ears. His wrists, which he'd managed to forget for a moment, were making themselves known with a sharp pain that rose higher and higher, moving from elbow to shoulder, and from there, pounding at his head in time with his heartbeat.

The air inside the yaranga was so close that he could almost feel it, liquid, against his cheek. It adhered to the body, making it difficult to breathe.

John remembered that nearby, three steps away from him, was a fur curtain that could be lifted. Navigating in the dark, he started to crawl quietly toward the front partition of the room. He kept bumping into naked bodies before he could feel the loosely hanging curtain with his forehead. Using both elbows and head, he stuck his face into the chilly front section of the yaranga and breathed in the cold air, awash with the reek of damp skins, with pleasure.

The storm's howling was louder here than inside the fur-lined polog. Tiny snowflakes drifted in, falling on his face. Stumbling about in the dark had cost John a great deal of effort, and he felt shattered. A strange fever gripped his body, flooding him with hot blood, and the only thing that dulled the pain and agonizing thirst was the cold air. Half-in and half-out of the inner chamber, John drifted off again, to the sound of the wind. He slept fitfully – not real sleep, but rather a doze punctuated with short periods of wakefulness. He was constantly jarred awake by the dogs, who licked his face with their rough tongues, and the pain racking his limbs.

Toward morning his thirst became unbearable, and John decided to try and reach a thin layer of snow that had drifted in to cover the floor of the outer yaranga. He inched forward slowly, crawling over a wooden headrest, and felt cold air coming closer in the darkness, even imagining that he could see the white snow – although this was only the distant reflection of the blizzard in the yaranga's smoke hole.

John lost his balance, landing on top of his crushed hands, and gave a loud moan as the pain overwhelmed him.

Toko, awakened by the moan, rushed to John's side and helped him back to his bed.

The sleepers began shifting around. A woman slid out from underneath a deerskin coverlet and, miraculously finding a space among the tangled multitude of bare limbs and bodies, began to make a fire.

Lying still had lessened the pain somewhat, and John stared curiously at this savage daughter of Prometheus, who, in the murk of the inner chamber, was twirling a stick with remarkable dexterity. The end of the little stick was slotted into an indentation in the middle of a wide board. Soon there were sparks flying out from under the stick, and within a few moments a blue tongue of flame appeared; it was immediately carried over to the lamp, to skitter cheerfully over a small mossy knob that floated in the grease.

The dwelling's inhabitants were climbing out of their fur blankets, plastered with adhering deerskin hairs. Rubbing their faces perfunctorily, they made quick work of getting dressed. Old Il'motch disappeared from the room, followed by Orvo, Toko, and a woman.

John was left all alone with the flickering light of the lamp. Unable to stop himself, he called out for Orvo.

The old man stuck his face inside the fur curtains and looked inquiringly at John.

"Bring some water," the other asked.

Instead of Orvo, it was Toko who brought water. Carefully supporting the wooden vessel, formerly an ordinary ladle that had lost its handle, Toko poured water into John's wide-open mouth, and looked at the sick man tenderly, with unabashed regret.

John lay back and thanked Toko. The man gave a wide smile, and nodded his head with a show of sympathy, motioning toward John's bandaged hands.

John put on a martyr's face, to indicate his being in pain. Toko wanted to say something else, but there were no words, and he was far from confident with gestures – so he simply came over to John and gave him an encouraging pat on the shoulder.

All that day John lay inside the inner chamber. After a plentiful breakfast, the fur curtain-wall was raised and he could observe the goings-on of the yaranga's life.

The deer herders would often come in from the cold, covered in sticky snow, bringing with them a bit of the snowstorm and making the constantly stoked fire splutter and waver. John's fellow travelers went off somewhere and came back worried. They took a long time brushing every snowflake off their clothes and threw compassionate glances at the white man.

By evening the storm had reached its peak. Once, the yaranga shifted as though some binding had been torn off. The men ran outside with loud shouts, and their agitated voices could be heard through the crashing wind.

Before the evening meal, the host picked out a few skinned deer legs from a pile and tossed them to his guests. Greeting this bounty with approving exclamations, the guests took out their hunting knives and set speedily to work, stripping the bones of their meat and tendons. All this went straight into their mouths, accompanied by the loud lip-smacking of unconcealed pleasure.

Having scoured the bones, the eaters started tapping on them carefully, so that the bones would crack. The first to accomplish this was Toko. He drew some pinkish marrow out from the splintered bone, and biting off half, offered the rest to John. Or rather, just pushed it into John's mouth, so quickly that its recipient hadn't the chance to refuse the offering. There was nothing for it but to chew and swallow the marrow. It turned out to be not merely edible, but delicious.

After Toko, everyone clamored to treat John, offering him the fattest and pinkest bits of marrow. Orvo moved closer and struck up a conversation about the weather: The wind being so strong had likely broken the ice shelf around the coast of Enmyn.

John was dumbfounded by this news. If Orvo's assessment was right, it meant that the *Belinda* had open waters into the Bering Strait. Now the only thing that could hold Hugh Grover back was John's absence. What a pity! Maybe it was better to turn back? Especially as it seemed that they had barely made a fifth of the journey? If they went back, the *Belinda,* at a good clip, could gain Nome in three days. And there was a hospital there.

"Orvo, we have to go back immediately!" said John, agitated.

He had to repeat the words a few times before Orvo could make sense of them. His face lengthened, and John assumed that the old man was worried about his reward.

"Everything that Hugh promised, you'll receive," John assured him fervently. "Even more. I swear it will be more."

John was so overwrought that he was suddenly aware of a thick fiery wave rising up in his chest, cutting off the air and bringing tears to his eyes.

"We'll think about it," said Orvo evasively. "There's time. We won't go anywhere until the wind dies down."

Orvo had answered John in the Chukchi language. Remembering himself, he switched to English. He explained to John that, of course, they would turn back, as soon as it was certain that the ice rim had broken. Studying the expression in John's eyes, Orvo could see clearly that the young man was in a bad way. And not because of the news of broken ice, but because of what they had all feared most.

It is called the blackening of the blood. This often happens to people with frostbitten limbs. After a few days the skin of the affected area blackens, as though singed by an invisible fire. A mysterious flame devours the person, eating him from the inside. Death comes quickly.

The only way to save him is to amputate the stricken organ. In his day, Orvo had seen many people with severed fingers and toes – a common thing in the North. The majority had performed the operation themselves, and saved their own lives thus. And yet only a real enenyl'yn* would dare attempt cutting off whole hands and feet, one with the vast experience passed down from generation to generation.

Orvo called Il'motch over and showed him John's fevered eyes.

"His blood is beginning to go black," he said quietly, as though the Canadian could have understood Chukchi speech.

Il'motch pressed his wide rough palm to John's forehead and confirmed, "Like a kettle on the boil."

John was growing angry: Did they think him gone mad, just because he wants to return to the ship? Couldn't they understand that he'd be better off sailing to Nome in three days than bouncing around on a dogsled, for God knows how long, in search of some mythical Anadyr', which may not even exist!

He started to explain this to Orvo, quickly and angrily, but it seemed that the old man just let it go over his head, busy with his own thoughts.

The blizzard would last no less than three days. More than enough time for the black blood to rise to the heart and consume the man. A white man, entrusted to Orvo and his comrades. And when John died, it would be better for them not to return to the shore since the whites are capable of destroying a whole settlement to avenge one of their own. So it was a few years back, when the Neshkan people killed a sailor, a rapist who had dishonored a very young girl. The whites brought their ships nearer to shore, and opened gunfire on the yarangas. Those who were not fast enough fleeing into the lagoon perished from the bullets. Then the sailors came ashore, plundered the empty yarangas and set them on fire. And that for a single dead man.

* Enenyl'yn – shamans (literally – those who can fly).

Orvo raised his eyes again and shot John a look almost of hatred. John shuddered; no one had ever looked at him that way before.

"The guns will be yours," he repeated, and felt how dry his mouth was and the fog that was filling his head, bringing unconsciousness. Gathering the last of his strength, he tried to look Orvo in the eyes. "You'll get a big reward," he rasped, slumping onto his side.

"Trouble," said Orvo, returning to the chottagin. "The burning has begun."

"What are we going to do?" Armol' asked, frightened.

"Don't know," said Orvo in a hollow voice. "Wait – until he dies. Then wait for the ship to leave."

Toko rose silently from his place and went up to the patient. John lay on his side. His eyes were half-closed, and he was mumbling something in his own language, over and over repeating: "Mam, Mam" – calling his mother, likely.

Toko settled him more comfortably. The sick man opened his eyes for a moment but failed to recognize him.

John was breathing heavily, the air escaping his gaping mouth with a whistle, and even from a distance the heat of it was palpable.

Toko returned to the men, sitting at a remove. Orvo was stuffing his tiny pipe bowl with trembling fingers.

"We have to save him," Toko said.

"It can be done, if the black flesh is cut off," Orvo answered.

"Even so," Toko said slowly. "He'll live. Better to bring him back without hands, than dead."

Orvo furiously sucked the pipe and then uttered with great irritation: "And what will you tell the whites when they say there was no need to take off the black flesh? How will you be able to convince them that it had to be done? You know nothing of these people; they're born convinced that they are always right, and that the opinion of someone whose skin is a different color can't be of any worth."

"So what are we to do, then?" Armol' spoke up.

"Maybe, do it like this," Il'motch cautiously suggested. "Not think about who he is, but as though it was one of ours in trouble."

"But we have to bring him back!" Orvo was almost shouting. "How will I face the captain when I bring him a stump of a person? He won't even be able to feed himself, much less go hunting!"

"The white man lives by many means, not just hunting," Toko countered.

"We could call for Kelena," mused Il'motch. "She will be able to sever the black flesh. She has done it before. Do you know Mynnor?" He was addressing Orvo.

"I know him," Orvo nodded. "Walks on his knees."

"That was Kelena's work, taking off his feet," declared Il'motch, with a touch of pride. "So she can help here, too."

"She still has the power to speak with those?" Orvo shifted his eyes in the direction of the smoke-hole.

"Even better than before," Il'motch confirmed. "Especially when she tells the future with a deer shoulder blade. As though the naked truth lies before her. She is a powerful person."

Orvo looked around at his fellows, as though searching for support. His eyes were fearful and uncertain. Neither Toko nor Armol' had ever seen the old man like this.

"All will be well," said Toko, reassuring himself. "The main thing is to get him back alive. Alive is better than dead. They can ask him what happened, and then they won't blame us."

"I suppose you're right," Orvo said, still uncertain, and nodded to Il'motch: "Call for Kelena."

6

Kelena threw back the sleeve of her kerker* and bared one stringy, dried-out breast, which drooped like an empty leather bag. She ordered an extra pair of braziers, so that there was enough light. The men obeyed her without question, spreading out a well-scrubbed leather rug, while Orvo sharpened the shaman-woman's knives with great concentration.

Kelena went up to the patient. Her face was long and thin. Tattoo lines disappeared into deep wrinkles like footpaths in the tundra hills. Bristly hairs sprouted from her wide nostrils. But her hands and her eyes were astonishing. Toko couldn't tear his eyes away from her fingers, marveling that a woman could have such powerful hands. Kelena's eyes burned with yellow light, as though each eye housed a blazing grease lamp. It seemed, whenever the shaman-woman cast her eyes into a shadowy corner, that she shone a torch into the darkness.

Despite her unattractive appearance, Kelena aroused neither fear nor revulsion. Perhaps it was due to the huge strength and confidence emanating from her tall, withered frame, that people inevitably felt reassured and trusting toward the big and kindly woman who could not fail to help them.

"To save this man, we must slaughter a dog," said she to Il'motch, quietly, but with authority.

* *Kerker* – a female's one-piece fur suit.

"Get one from Orvo," Il'motch replied.

"But we have still got a long way to go," Orvo objected.

"Armol', go and bring a puppy from my yaranga," said Kelena, taking charge.

While Armol' was off on his errand, the sick man was moved closer to the center, and the braziers were raised high on supports, so that their light could fall from above. Kelena laid out her instruments on a clean bleached piece of sealskin: sharpened knives, needles and bones, tightly wound thread made of deer tendons, pieces of fur and long strips of clean, soft deerskin.

Armol' carried the struggling puppy into the room.

"Il'motch, Orvo, you're to help me," instructed Kelena. "The dog must be killed."

Il'motch took the puppy, and Orvo bent down to help the shaman-woman unbind John's tightly bandaged hands.

"You, young ones, don't go far off," ordered Kelena, "you may be needed. If he starts to scream and struggle, get on top of him and hold him down."

"All right," Toko nodded, feeling his mouth dry up.

Kelena shrugged off her kerker, now clad only in a narrow loincloth. As though out of nowhere, a little bottle appeared in her hands. She took out the plug with her teeth, tested the contents on the tip of her tongue and, forcing John's clenched teeth open, poured the liquid into his mouth. John thrashed and flailed his arms, but Kelena held him down with a knee.

Some time passed, and John lay still. Even his breath seemed to steady.

Then the shaman-woman carefully inspected her blades, spat down on each one, rubbing the spittle into the knife with her palm, and looked satisfied. Raising her face upwards, she was motionless for a while, eyes shut, whispering charms. A strange thing, but it seemed to Toko that she was speaking in the white people's language. Was it because it was a white man she was about to heal?

Finished with her preparations, Kelena cautiously peeled back the bandages from John's broken hands. Where they were stuck to the skin and hard to lift, the shaman-woman wet them with fresh dog's blood. As the blackened skin appeared, a sweetish suppurating smell filled the room, making everyone breathe faster and harder.

The sight that awaited them could not even be called the remains of human hands. Everything was mixed together in a bloody mess – clumps of fur from the mittens, smashed finger bones, shreds of flesh and skin. Unable to stand it, Toko turned away.

"More blood, more blood," called Kelena. "Let the puppy blood wash your wounds and give you a dog's endurance."

With effort, Toko turned back to where Kelena was doing her work. She moved quickly and purposefully, as though she were handling walrus flippers or deer legs, not human hands. The blade slid over joints, separating the bones and leaving large, hanging folds of skin. Tossing aside a severed hand, Kelena picked up a needle threaded with deer tendons. A straight, beautiful seam began to stretch across the stump, and little droplets of blood marked the needle's wake.

The shaman-woman's face was covered in perspiration. Sometimes she would wipe the sweat from her forehead with an elbow and sniff impatiently. Having finished with one hand, she moved on to the other.

And then what everyone was dreading happened: John became conscious. At first he looked up, surprised, at the shaman-woman who was bent over him with her knife. Then, his face twisted in a grimace of horror and revulsion, he let out an awful scream and thrashed under her hand.

"Hold him," Kelena shouted. "Hold him tight!"

Toko and Armol' threw themselves over poor John, tried to weigh him down. But the white man was still strong and quick. More than once he managed to throw off their combined weight. But, ultimately, what can a cripple do? Orvo and Il'motch came to help.

"He mustn't move his hand!" were Kelena's orders. "You, Armol', hold his arm, and the rest of you, don't let him move."

Finally, they were able to bear down so that John couldn't move a muscle. Toko was almost lying on top of him, face to face, feeling John's hot breath on his skin.

John's large blue eyes were frozen with terror. Big tears rolled out from an overflowing blue lake, quickly running down his cheek and somewhere behind an ear into a thicket of light hair, wet with perspiration.

He was muttering something. Quickly, hurriedly. His tone conveyed pleading, horror, promises, pain, rage . . .

Without having understood a single word, Toko answered him.

"Just bear it for a little while longer. All will be well. This woman is saving your life, don't fear her . . . Your pain is hurting me too, but it must be borne. To go on living, it must be borne. You want to see your land, your mother, your loved ones, don't you? Maybe you have a wife? You'll come back to them alive. Without hands, but so what? White people have many jobs that don't require hands. So you'll do that kind of job. Besides, you folk are clever with gadgets and contraptions, you'll manage to fix something in place of hands. You've figured out many things; big fire-breathing boats like mountains roaming the seas, you've forced flame into a little jar, and it burns there with a noisy blue heat. Came up with guns, food in tins . . . All will be well, Sson."

"Grab him tighter," Toko heard the shaman-woman's voice, "I'm going to start sewing."

Toko leaned over John again and continued over his muttering.

"Kelena can sew. She'll make you a seam you'll be proud of – brag to all your friends. Deer-tendon threads are strong, they won't tear . . . Don't twitch, there's only a little left now. The blizzard will end, we'll drive back. It won't take two days to get to Enmyn, and you'll see your friends again. The ice has gone, it's a clear way. You'll sail off . . . Just a little more, now. It's hard for me too, looking into your eyes . . ."

John lost consciousness again, or else decided that resisting was useless, and Toko realized that it was easier to hold the white man down.

Through half-closed eyelashes, heavy with tears, John watched his torturers. When the terrible hag swam into view, sharp knife in hand, he had thought that they were intending to eat him. And right away he recalled tales of cannibals, devourers of human flesh, of savages who roast their prey over dying coals. He could smell his own burned flesh, the singed hairs of his beard.

He writhed and screamed, trying to reach Toko's dark, sweaty face with his teeth, trying to reach the treacherous and bloodthirsty brute that fed him from his own hands, cared for him, only to pin him down later, until each of the others had cut off a tasty morsel.

But it was an unequal battle. Toko lay on top of him like a boulder, and there was an incredible amount of weight in the young man. It was useless to fight. And it was then that John was seized by such self-pity that he couldn't restrain his tears. They rolled down his feverish cheek, calling up an overwhelming feeling of bitterness and irreparable damage. He had never been so helpless. Perhaps only somewhere in the foggy deep of childhood, in a life lost forever. Still, it was not the life he'd already lived that he grieved for, but that he'd never go home, never appear on the doorstep as the conqueror of polar seas. All the joys of the world will be for those who, at that moment, haven't an inkling of death. They will belong to Hugh Grover, his friend, the only one, maybe, who is hoping for his return. Poor, dear Hugh! Freezing in an ice-bound little ship that seemed so strong and secure, waiting for his friend.

It was as though a stone slab were weighing him down, and not a human being. A slab reeking revoltingly of sweat, rancid seal fat, and something else, filthy and unbearable.

Nausea assailed him. The pain had grown numb and, oddly, moved to his heart. But maybe he was dead, and all that was happening didn't matter. And the heavy weight – it was only the weight of the gravestone, laid over his final resting place. John closed his eyes and willed himself not to open them again, to shut out the hateful features, shiny with grease and sweat. He sensed some kind of commotion. They were doing something with his hands! But what?

John opened his eyes again. Strange – he had always been certain that the Chukchi had narrow slits for eyes, yet this one had enormous black irises, with intense sorrow and pity in their depths.

"What are you doing to me?" John shouted. "Let me go! You'll pay for this!"

"Just stick it out a little longer," he heard the voice of Orvo answer back. "Only a little while left."

"What are you doing to me?" John was howling.

"Taking care of your hands!" Orvo shouted back at him. "Taking off black flesh, saving your life!"

"Dear God," John moaned. "My hands! My hands!"

He did not feel the shaman-woman Kelena carefully tying soft deerskin strips over his stumps. But suddenly he understood that these primitives had cut off his fingers, barring the way for gangrene. What barbarism! A good surgeon could surely have rescued at least two, three fingers on each hand . . . And they . . . What if that horrible witch had chopped off both his hands?

John opened his eyes and saw that Toko had let go of him and was now sitting beside him, studying his face.

"He's come back!" Kelena pronounced it with joy. "He's moving his eyes."

"What have you done to me?" John asked quietly, addressing Orvo.

"Saved your life," came the old man's exhausted reply.

"What have you done with my hands?"

"It had to be done," Orvo answered. "Your flesh went black. Death stood close beside you, and you would have shut your eyes forever. There was only one way out – to take away the black flesh and black blood. And that's what she has done." Orvo nodded toward the shaman-woman, who was wearily packing a tobacco pipe with a huge convex mouthpiece.

"Oh, my Lord," John sobbed, and burst into tears, mindless of the others. "Who's going to need me without hands?"

Kelena wiped her bloody fingers with a wet cloth, smoothed her hair and looked at John with a smile.

"What's he wailing about?" she inquired of Orvo.

"Crying over his hands," said the old man.

"Understandable," the shaman-woman nodded.

She walked closer to John and softly stroked his head.

At the touch, John turned sharply and saw the old woman's hideous face. Her skin was like something baked in a roaring fire. Her burning eyes held untold tenderness. It was awful – compassion and ugliness intertwined!

He made a move to push the old woman away, but lost consciousness again, sinking back into the furs.

Kelena tucked him in, saying, "He'll sleep a long while."

Gathering her instruments neatly into a special leather bag, she began collecting what was left of the puppy and what she'd cut off with her knife, wrapping the stuff in a square of deerskin.

She looked around, hummed approvingly and called out to Orvo, "You'll help me."

There were dogs in the chottagin, curled up asleep. A fine powdery snow drifted in through the smoke-hole, and the blizzard shone down with a faint, mysterious light.

Kelena lifted the stone that held down the pelt hanging over the entrance, and instantly, the wind rushed into the yaranga, tousling the dogs' rough coats. The pelt flapped and buckled in her hands.

Orvo rushed to help the old woman.

As soon as they were outside, Orvo and Kelena were caught up in the whirlwind. Orvo followed the old woman, who had steamed forward into the wind at a clip. He was beginning to worry about going too far from the yarangas when, all of a sudden, the shaman-woman stopped dead in her tracks. She stood there like a broken-off fragment of a mountain crag, set in the face of the gale. And the blizzard's gusts passed around her, quickly raising a snow funnel around this living, motionless idol. She stood still for some time, whispering prayers and incantations, then reached down and dug a deep hole in the snow. Into the hole she lowered the puppy's remains and the severed hands of the white man.

"Hands and bones . . ." Kelena was chanting. "Only hands and bones. The white man will go back to his land. Maybe they will make new hands for him there, but these that stay here, let them be no trouble for our people. We are tundra people, and our life is different to his, whose hands remain here. They will lie in peace under the snow, and in the spring, when the sun digs them out again, the crows will come and do with them as is their custom. They are a wise folk, they know what to do . . ."

Kelena turned to Orvo:

"Say it after me! You who do not see, but can hear us! Let the white man's anger blow past us like a springtime storm. We saved his life. Teach him this, and make him understand what we did."

Orvo repeated the words after the old woman, wind bursting into his mouth, cutting off the air, stuffing his throat with snow. He spat, but obediently echoed the shaman-woman's every word.

Strange that most of the charms Orvo had heard before had been assortments of unrecognizable words, resembling those of the Koryaks, or Eskimos, or even of the Evven people . . . A regular person couldn't understand them, even if they were his own and had been handed over to him by a shaman. Yet here, the shaman-woman was speaking in ordinary language, despite the gravity of what they were doing, burying a white man's hands.

Finished with the ritual, the old woman tamped down the little snow mound and started back, into the wind. She walked, slicing through the taut, thick air with her long skinny body, walked straight and stubborn, without slowing. Orvo followed behind, amazed by the old woman's strength.

Brushing snow off her clothes, once inside the chottagin, Kelena asked Orvo:

"What did the white people promise you?"

Orvo listed the agreed-upon items and added:

"I fear, though, that we'll have nothing. We didn't get him to Anadyr'."

"True enough," Kelena drawled sympathetically. "The white man will never understand us."

7

The blizzard died down in the night. On waking, John heard neither the wind's howl nor the rustle of snow on the roof. Behind the hide walls, beyond the deerskin polog where the sleepers snored, stillness had spread like a mantle.

It was with a sense of pleasure that John gave himself to the silence, to his own tranquillity of soul, to the gradual rebuilding of his strength. He could tell that he was better: His postoperative fever had gone, thanks to the ministrations of old Kelena.

The shaman-woman often came to look in on the patient, bringing different kinds of potions and infusions. Convinced now that these people meant him no harm, John entrusted himself to their care and was surprised at himself to have thought so badly of them. True, as for his questions about what the shaman-woman had done with his hands, Orvo answered evasively, pointing to his small knowledge of English. John tried to draw Toko into a conversation, but the latter would turn away as soon as he guessed what the white man was asking.

The polog awoke all at once. A woman approached the brazier, made a few energetic passes with the lighting-stick, and the steady light of the moss floating in deer fat lit up the sleeping chamber.

"We'll have some food – and then, back on the road!" Orvo informed John cheerfully. "Got to hurry back to shore, before the ice locks in again. In such a wind, the sea could be clear all the way to the American shore . . .

Shame about your insulting Kelena yesterday . . . She did all that she could. And even more than that. You've still got two fingers on your left hand, and on the right – half the little finger, and a bit of the middle one. You're not a total cripple . . ."

Getting dressed with Toko's help, John walked out of the polog. His breath caught in the frost, and he had to squint against the blinding whiteness – despite there being no sun, but rather only a milky-white stripe spilling over the jagged horizon, the sign of a polar day in winter.

The herd's owner had already corralled the deer. The horned beasts shied back in terror at a human's approach. The Chukcha deer were not domesticated. Lassoing a well-fed buck, their host pulled him close. Two young lads fell upon the stag, wrestled it down to the snow and plunged their knives in his neck. A woman set a leather vessel to catch the crimson stream.

The stag was quickly skinned. John watched the herders' movements avidly, and although the scene was not a pleasant one, he consoled himself with the thought that this was their way of life, their means of existence.

Some boys brought a quantity of transparent river ice on their sleds, the women hung an enormous cauldron over the blazing fire and started another fire nearby. Orvo, who had been helping to skin the deer, carefully punctured the stomach and poured its contents into the cauldron. A woman diluted the mixture with blood, and began mixing it with her bare hands, up to her elbows in the bloody mash.

Despite the solid frost, all the men were walking around bare-headed, and the women shrugged off the sleeves of their kerkers for greater mobility, leaving almost half of their torsos open to the elements.

A few more deer were slaughtered for the dogs. Having finished their labors, everyone went inside the chottagin and settled close to the fire, waiting for the food to arrive.

As usual, John's small trunk and linen sack of provisions had been placed in front of him. John asked Toko to spread their contents over a low wooden table. The yaranga's inhabitants were clearly intrigued by the mysterious and unfamiliar items: sugar cubes, hard biscuits that looked like white wood chips, and tins of canned food.

John asked for Kelena to be called in.

The old woman arrived, and sat herself down across from John.

"Let her choose what she likes best," John said.

Orvo translated. Kelena looked at the white man intently, and reached out to stroke the fair hair.

"You'll give me what you think fit," said Kelena. "I'm not paid for my efforts, since a human life isn't to be bought or paid for. It's there, or else it's not. There is no other way about it. Each person has got to save the life of another. Though, what kind of person are you! You won't be able to live with us, since you won't be able to get food for yourself or for your progeny. And yet, I'm thinking that you're not last among your own people, because just look at your eyes – proud and intelligent. Yes, you've lost your hands, but you haven't lost your wits. If they help you to survive among your own kind, then I must have done a good thing . . . And that is how we are, us shamans. We are called to do good for people – to heal, to forecast weather, to tame evil spirits. Ours is a hard life. Not much joy in it, except when we see a person getting well, or when Narginen grants us kind weather, warm spring, and quiet winter. Be happy, young white one. You ended up here with us, true people of the tundra, like a brown bear among the polar white."

Orvo managed to render most of the old shaman's speech in English.

John listened to the woman and the old man attentively and then pointed to a packet of tea, needles, sugar – and bending his head ceremoniously, asked the shaman-woman to accept all this.

Kelena accepted the gifts with dignity.

Then Orvo filled some cups from a bottle of vodka.

"Bad joy-making water," he explained, and opening his mouth wide, quickly downed a cup. The others followed his example.

Toko handed John his cup.

Then the boiled meat and fresh deer's blood soup were served.

John, cheered by the vodka, resolved to follow his companions' example in everything. Their host brought in a bone spoon, and fixed it to John's stump with a deer-tendon cord.

The soup tasted a bit burnt, but was quite edible. Each spoonful brought on a feeling of satiation and strength. When came the turn of the meat and fresh bone marrow, John's stomach was over-full. His fellow-travelers, however, not only ate several enormous chunks of deer meat, but also managed to empty a gigantic teapot full of strong tea. Yet as to sugar, everyone was quite frugal. John's jaw dropped when he saw Kelena, after five or six cups of tea, signal the end of her tea-drinking by removing from her mouth the same tiny piece of sugar she had bitten off at the beginning – and neatly pack it away in a bit of rag.

"Would you look at that!" John couldn't help exclaiming, and he gave the shaman-woman two more pieces of sugar from his stores.

The dogs, well-rested over the days of blizzard, pulled well, and soon the sled caravan left the grazing camp and its welcoming valley by the foot of the mountain range far behind. John looked back for a long while, seeing the yarangas' smoke in the blue twilight. A kind of new, unfamiliar feeling trembled in his breast; it might have been gratitude toward the people he was leaving behind, people that had treated him with such warmth and compassion; or perhaps the happy expectation of seeing Hugh Grover, who waited for him at the Enmyn cape; or perhaps it was the understanding that he'd escaped the bony hand of death that had been cast over him . . .

Toko sat sideways on his dogsled, also glad to be going home. Even if the captain doesn't put up the reward, to hell with the Winchester, it could have been worse. What if Sson had died on the road, or after his fingers had been cut off? Then they would have had to forget the way back home and find another place; probably, they'd have to hide out in the tundra. It goes without saying, tundra folk live well, especially if their herd is as big as Il'motch's. The food is right outside the yaranga, and all you have to do is keep an eye on the deer in a blizzard and keep the wolves off. But the wandering! As soon as you're used to a spot, you've got to roll up your yaranga and go find another . . . Toko considered the deer-herding life compared to the life of a sea hunter and concluded decisively that, although the shore dweller hasn't got a four-legged food supply waiting by the yaranga walls, still his life was far better. You can leave the yaranga on an early morning and look out onto the same unbroken line of the horizon.

There's nothing better than running the dogsleds in such weather, right after a long hard snowstorm, when spent nature seems to be resting after the last days' work. Silence hangs over everything, horizon to horizon, and the sound of gliding runners, the dogs' uneven breath or human voices, travels far and wanders the air, bouncing off icy crags and snow-bound hummocks.

There's barely any frost. Spit – and the spittle lands on the snow, without having been frozen to an icy white lump in midflight. You can ride on top of the sled for long stretches, without having to jog alongside it for warmth.

Making nearly half the distance between the mountains and Enmyn, Orvo signaled a rest stop – to give themselves and, more importantly, the dogs a breather.

They made camp on the ice-bound river shore, putting up the tarpaulin tent. It was cramped, and only by bunching together could all four adults fit inside. Really, the tent had been meant for John, but he'd insisted strenuously on all the drivers piling in.

By some miracle, Orvo had managed to find a few dry twigs and make a fire. For a nightcap, each man received a mug of hot tea, strongly laced with vodka.

Dragging in all the deerskins he could find on the three sleds, Toko made a fluffy bed for John.

"I'm as healthy now as any of you," John declared. "I shouldn't have any special treatment."

Everyone bedded down helter-skelter.

Wriggling from side to side, John asked Orvo:

"Do you like this sort of life?"

"What sort?" At first Orvo didn't understand.

"The life that you lead out here, in the snows, in the frost?" John clarified. "There are other lands, you know, where life is more comfortable. It's warmer there, and there aren't such terrible snowstorms, like the one we've just lived through. You can weather one blizzard, at most two or three, but all your life! It's impossible! Take you, Orvo – you've seen other countries and other lands. Didn't you like them? Eh?"

"I liked them," Orvo said, uncertainly.

"You see. That means your homeland must be less comfortable," John concluded.

"Maybe so," Orvo agreed, and turned on his side with the intention of falling asleep, but John was evidently determined to make up for all the days of his silence.

"So what's the matter?" he asked. "Look here, the entire American continent is peopled with men who came over from other places. These men crossed enormous distances in search of a better life, in search of a better land."

"It's no good to us," Orvo answered. "We believe that we live on the best land in the world. That's the beauty, that no one wants it except for us . . . I've seen our neighboring Eskimos forced to leave the coastline, because gold was found there."

John was quiet for a moment, then uttered thoughtfully:

"Well, maybe you're right. Maybe it's only because the Chukchi and the Eskimos settled in the worst lands that they've escaped annihilation."

Such talk chased away Orvo's desire for sleep, and no matter how he twisted and turned, on his side, on his back, still he couldn't fall asleep.

Growing sure that neither John nor Toko nor Armol' was asleep, Orvo decided to broach a worrying and important question whose gravity bore no comparison with any of John's deep and meaningful queries.

"What do you think," Orvo asked, "will the captain give us the promised reward?"

"Why wouldn't he?" John was surprised.

"Because we didn't get you to Anadyr'. And the work that the Russian doctor ought to have done, was done by the shaman-woman Kelena."

"That's no matter," John shrugged. "I only have to say the word, and Hugh will give you not only what he promised, but more besides. Have no doubt – your reward awaits you."

"Do you hear that?" Orvo couldn't hold his tongue. "He says we'll be paid in full!"

"That means I'll have a new Winchester!" exclaimed Toko.

John looked at his excited companions with a patronizing smile. How little these savages needed to be happy! No more than an old Winchester, one that's only good for the garbage heap in another world.

The reassurance that their reward would be paid in full, so agitated John's fellow travelers that for a long while there was nonstop talk inside the small tent, and Orvo himself promised John that they would do everything in their power to get him back to the ship at top speed.

John barely closed his eyes that night.

No sooner had his eyelids begun to inch down, than he could see before him the ship's silhouette against the black crags of Enmyn, Hugh's kind manly face, could hear the voices of his comrades, and good old English speech instead of this barbaric babble, where you can't tell where one word ends and another starts.

Morning came in the shape of a light crimson stripe over the eastern horizon. After a hurried snack, the travelers were under way and heading for the shore.

The drivers ran alongside their sleds, so as not to exhaust the dogs and conserve strength for the long unbroken journey ahead.

By the time the Northern Lights blazed across the sky, the dogsleds had reached the south side of the lagoon. If you listened carefully, you could already hear voices rising from the settlement, dogs' muted barking, a child's cry.

Sensing the nearness of home, the dogs ran without urging. Toko overtook Armol', then Orvo, and together with John broke into the lead position. The pack had been about to make a turn for the yarangas, but Toko shouted at them and steered them toward the seashore, to the craggy shelter where the *Belinda* lay.

Awakened by the barking, people were spilling out of their yarangas. They ran after the sled, shouting something, but it was impossible to make out a single word against the furious gallop of the pack.

The sled flew down the shore. Joyfully, tenderly, John looked out into the open sea that was soon lost from view over a dark horizon. Not a single piece of ice – the storm had cleared the water's expanse: Sail away to your heart's desire.

But the place where the *Belinda* had lain was empty. Toko held back, but John yelled something impatient and motioned ahead into the darkness, closer to the crags. Toko started the sled again, and drove slowly, wary of falling off the high shelf of fast ice and into the water.

John peered into the darkness, trying to discern the lines of a ship, until his eyes ached. He begged Toko, pleaded with him to come closer to the water's edge, but the sea was empty. Under the crags it was empty, too.

Joy was beginning to turn into worry and fear: What had happened to them? A shipwreck? But surely someone, even a single man, must have survived?

Slowly, almost by touch alone, and sensing the open water, the dogs nosed their way forward. The shouts of those who'd run after the sled were growing louder:

"Come back!" the people were screaming after them. "The ship is long gone! Nothing there, come back!"

Toko looked at John. But the other, not understanding the Chukchi language, was scanning the empty black stretch of open water in desperation. When his eyes met Toko's, he shuddered.

"Is it true?" he asked Orvo, who'd made his way forward.

"Yes," said the old man, head bent low. "They sailed on the very first day, as soon as the sea was clear of ice. They were in a great hurry, and didn't even come down to make their farewell."

"It can't be! It can't be!" cried John, and facing the sea, he howled: "Hugh! Hu-u-u-ugh! Why don't you answer me? Have you abandoned me? Oh God, but it's impossible!"

He jumped off the sled and ran for the edge of the fast ice.

"Hold him back, he'll fall into the water!" Orvo shouted fearfully.

Toko caught up with him and grabbed him from behind.

John was struggling, kicking, but Toko held him close.

"Hugh, come back for me! Don't abandon me here, don't leave me with these savages! Oh, Hu-u-u-gh!"

John fell to his knees, and then forward, prostrate. He couldn't speak at all now. His body convulsed with sobs, and his throat produced a drawn-out, animal howl – the cry of a man betrayed by his own tribe.

The Chukchi, observing the white man's grief, stood motionless; not one of them had made a sound until John went quiet, pressed flat against the ice.

All around, silence reigned. And the people imagined that they could hear the rustling draperies of the Northern Lights overhead.

Toko approached John cautiously. The other's eyes were wide open and gazing straight ahead into the distance. It seemed that he was seeing something far away, something that neither Toko nor any of his kin were ever to see. Yellow foam adhered to the corners of his mouth, and his face had taken on a strange aspect. It was as though a countless number of years had flown over his head, and it even seemed to Toko that there was a glint of gray in the hair escaping from underneath John's fur-lined hat.

"Take him back to the yaranga," Toko heard Orvo's quiet voice.

Toko clasped John around the middle and prepared to lift him up. But John, though slowly, rose by his own effort and leaning on Toko, limped toward the yarangas, black against the snow and the spill of the Northern Lights.

And from the north, wordlessly, without wind or wave, with barely a rustle, came fields of ice – to shut up the wide waterway so recently opened by the storm.

8

John MacLennan moved in with Toko.

At first he lived inside the polog together with the rest, but then Toko, seeing the white man's discomfort in living next to them, partitioned off one corner of the chottagin, to create for John a space somewhere between a closet and a dog kennel. Feeling generous, Toko built him something resembling a bed, laying some roughly sanded wooden planks over whale vertebrae and covering the whole with deerskins. Still, this "room" was a cold one, unbearably so on snowy nights – then, John would shyly clamber into the polog and settle close to the grease lamp, reaching his frozen stumps out to the hot flame.

He examined them and was astounded by the skill with which the sutures had been laid. The deer veins fell away after a time, and the even stitch-marks stood out against his white wrists. His left hand still had a whole little finger and a middle finger that was only missing a fingernail. On the right, an orphaned little finger wiggled dejectedly, and a pitiful half-finger stuck out from the middle.

At first John couldn't look at his mangled hands without breaking into tears, but then grew used to them, and even felt surprise at the loss of his former self-pity.

Living in the polog, John discovered a simple but important rule – if you want to survive, don't miss your chance to have an extra meal. It could well be that tomorrow there will be nothing to eat, and those who dwell in the yaranga will have to chew on half-rotted leather cords, clean out the meat pits, pry bits of blubber and flesh from the sides of wooden store bins.

More than once he'd caught his host's contemptuous glance, but paying no attention, continued to hurriedly stuff chunks of half-boiled nerpa into his mouth, and take enormous gulps of blood soup.

Toko's wife Pyl'mau treated the white man better than did the others. In any case, she was not as rudely curious as Enmyn's other inhabitants, who – as if in jest, but really with the most serious intentions – would pull John's covers off his body and try to peep at him undressed.

Pyl'mau was a young woman in the prime of health, with a round, ruddy, grease-glossy face. She was always bustling about – cooking meals, grinding seal blubber in a stone mortar, curing skins by soaking them in a trough full of stale urine, and then stretching them on the snow. Hers was the care of home, dogs, and infant – whom she always carried around on her back, outside of feeding him and changing the strips of moss that served as diapers.

Toko went hunting early in the mornings. In truth, it was still closer to night, since the hunter needed to greet the dawn out on the ice in order to make full use of the short daylight to spot a seal in the dark waterholes and kill it.

John watched Toko's equipping himself for the ice with curiosity. A white hunting overall fashioned from a rough light-gray canvas flour sack was always hanging in the outer chottagin and smelled of freezing wind, salty sea ice, and the crispness of a mounting blizzard.

Next to the coat-kamleika, in a bleached sealskin case, rested the yaranga's greatest treasure – the old 30x30 Winchester, with a neatly trimmed gun-stock and a locked sighting. Next to the Winchester – an akyn, a wooden sphere with sharp hooks attached to long leather ribbons. This was used to drag the kill up from the ice hole. Two walking sticks were propped against the wall – one with a sharp point, for testing ice thickness, the other blunt, ending in a flat round piece for packing down snow. Finally – a pair of snowshoes, which John initially mistook for tennis rackets.

Every morning, Toko would put on all this gear in a particular order. Besides the above items, he also wore accoutrements that were probably of great significance, but John had difficulty guessing their purpose. Among them, tiny figurines of marine animals, leather strips, bone buttons.

These figurines, John hazarded, were in some way connected with similar items nestling in the yaranga's nooks and crannies. Sometimes Toko conducted long and earnest discussions with them. What these discussions concerned – John could only guess. Even later, when he began to understand Chukchi speech, he could not make sense of these allegorical exhortations and pleas. These were conversations with the gods, private and heartfelt talks, where only the direct conversants could understand one another, and the joining in of a third would have been pointless.

While Toko was busy adjusting his hunting gear, Pyl'mau got breakfast going. In good times, when there was some store in the meat pits, the morning meal consisted of frozen ground meat and a few pieces of the previous night's boiled seal. All this was washed down with a few mugfuls of brick tea, which Toko shaved off onto a clean wooden board.

Food was served on a long wooden platter of somewhat dubious cleanliness. At first, John would transfer the food to his own tin plate, but on consideration, decided that it was much more advantageous to eat from the common dish when the deciding factors are speed and strength of tooth.

Finally, Toko would pull the sackcloth overall over his head, festoon himself with various pieces of gear, take up the first walking cane in one hand and the second in the other, and stride off into the blushing horizon, gradually dissolving in the thick predawn blue.

John would usually stand by the yaranga in silence, and follow the bread-winner with his eyes, until the latter disappeared among the ice-hummocks on the shore.

He'd return to the yaranga and sit by the dying brazier, giving himself over to a kind of meditative doze. He tried hard to avoid dwelling on the past, dispersing thoughts of his lost friends, the green gardens of Port Hope and the caressing waters of Lake Ontario. With a malicious pleasure, he told himself that he'd become almost like one of the savages that surrounded him, primarily focused on food, warmth, and sleep. With a kind of nasty inner glee he observed his habits, ingrained since childhood, fall away like a useless old skin. It hadn't taken very long before he felt quite comfortable not brushing his teeth, or indeed washing his face. He had long since exchanged his underwear, rotting from sweat and grime, for a bit of fawn skin.

At first, John had been appalled by Toko's manner of house dress, when the latter, crawling into the polog, would strip naked but for the meager, largely symbolic piece of fur.

As for Pyl'mau, she strolled about the dwelling clad only in a thin loincloth, and her large breasts – so full of milk that there was always a warm white droplet at the end of her dark, almost black nipples – swung to and fro with a stately dignity.

All this became fairly commonplace for John, and he would have followed his host's example long ago, if it hadn't been for his white skin, whose contrast to the surrounding dark bodies excited unhealthy curiosity. The reddish down on his chest had elicited such a scream from Pyl'mau, that John had been seriously frightened. John's body, for all its defects of red hair and unbelievable pallor, was a favorite topic of conversation among Enmyn ladies for a long time.

Despite it being winter, the days were quite long. In order to be of some help to Pyl'mau, John sometimes took the baby, singing him half-forgotten lullabies and even telling him stories.

In good weather, John would harness himself to a sleigh made of two halves of a walrus tusk and criss-crossing wooden slats, prop up the little boy and take him for a ride around the lagoon, stopping by the neighboring yarangas on the way.

The entire settlement numbered twelve yarangas, and John came to the conclusion that their inhabitants were all closely linked by blood. The majority of the women were from other settlements, and even had Eskimos from the Cape Dezhnev counted among them. To tell the truth, though, in appearance they were no different from the Chukchi women, and one had to be well versed in the language to be able to distinguish them by their accent.

He especially liked visiting Orvo. Little Yako was handed over to the care of old lady Cheivuneh, and Orvo would sit John down and pack him a pipeful of the precious mixture of tobacco and wood chips. The men would smoke and converse. Usually the conversation consisted of Orvo's questions and John's long-winded answers about the beliefs and customs of the white folk. In turn, John tried to find out what powers the Chukchi obeyed and what gods they worshipped. Either he didn't understand Orvo very well, or it really was so, but John could find no evidence of authority or rank, nor even of a leader among the Chukchi. Each lived according to his own judgement, and matters of importance to the whole settlement were settled without too much debate – reason and practicality prevailed. People treasured the good will of their neighbors. Thorny issues were usually referred to Orvo, whose authority rested largely on his experience, since the old man possessed neither wealth nor unusual physical strength. In fact, his yaranga might have been shabbier than those of some others.

Around noontime, Pyl'mau would call her lodger in and feed him an extra snack. By midwinter, noon was spelled by the sun's edge peeping out from a faraway mountain range. The snow grew pink, and the frost lessened, the chilling breath of the wind died down and stilled.

At times like this, the polog wasn't as hot as usual, because in the interests of economy only one grease lamp would be lit, and only half-strength at that. The grease was conserved. In the murk, Pyl'mau managed not to slice off her fingers, shaving bits of kopal'khen onto a wooden dish. The lumps of fat in the walrus meat were somewhat rancid and greenish. It took John a while to get used to this sort of food, yet later on he even found a certain piquancy of flavor in the slightly rotting kopal'khen.

Twilight descended, long and quiet. The sound of a man's footsteps carried far, and the creaking under John's feet would wake the dogs, stretched out and slumbering in the forty-degree cold. Lamps were being lit inside the chottagins. Their flickering light flowed out through wide-open doors and lay on the snow.

The moon rose, and shadows began to creep into human tracks, hide behind the ice-hummocks. By the hour of the first hunter's appearance on the invisible line dividing earth and sea, the northern half of the sky would be aglow with the many-hued tapestries of the Northern Lights. In profound silence, under the vaulting sky, the dance of pure colors commenced.

At such moments, John was overcome with a strange trepidation – as though he were listening to an organ from the immeasurable cathedrals of beyond. There was no sound, but the feelings born of the gigantic symphony of colors were akin to music in their majesty and depth.

Tears would burn in his eyes, his soul stilled and his thoughts turned to goodness and brotherhood. John would enter Toko's yaranga with a feeling of enlightenment and turn a tender gaze on Yako and Pyl'mau. At such moments he found the young woman rather attractive; he would make her blush with his unusual stare and incomprehensible words

"There's something about you," John would say, addressing Pyl'mau. "And your name – Polar Fog – promises not just a storm, but also some kind of change of atmosphere. If you had a good bath and put on a dress, and had shoes on, instead of these old torbasses – why, I imagine you could even be called pretty . . ."

The hunters were returning to the settlement. Not always with a kill. John became as adept as the women at recognizing whether a person was laden or empty-handed, from afar. But until the hunter was clearly visible, the watchers were too cautious to voice their guesses.

This winter, there were a few lucky days when each hunter brought in a haul, some dragging whole strings of nerpa, and trailing long bloody prints in the snow.

When she was certain that Toko was indeed towing a seal behind him, Pyl'mau would fill an old and worn little pitcher with water, trying to include a sliver of ice, and with solemn ceremony step out to greet her husband.

Toko would approach the yaranga slowly, firmly planting his feet in the snow, plunging deeply the sharpened end of his walking stick. Half a step from the dwelling's entrance he would halt and unhurriedly unbuckle his hunting harness used to drag the kill. Thus freed, he'd reach for the pitcher – but wouldn't drink right away. First of all he'd wet the seal's muzzle with water, as though giving it a drink after their long and fatiguing journey together.

Only then would Toko hold the mug in both hands and drink, deeply and with great pleasure. Still, no matter how thirsty he may have been, the hunter would leave a few drops of water at the bottom, spilling them out in the direction of the sea as an offering to the gods that had granted him a rich kill.

After this ritual, Toko would cease to be a significant personage who was fully aware of his importance, and turn back into himself – happy to answer questions about the condition of the ice, wind direction and the currents of the Arctic Ocean.

Meanwhile, John helped Pyl'mau drag the seal inside the yaranga. Here the animal would be stretched out on a walrus skin and left to defrost for a few hours.

Toko would pick up a piece of stag antler and start to pummel the snow out of his outer garments. Taking off his canvas overcoat he'd neatly place it back on its peg, clean the Winchester, carefully roll up the rope. Shaking the snow off his torbasses and kukhlianka, Toko would then crawl inside the polog and there divest himself of everything else.

This signaled the beginning of the evening meal. The first to appear was a wooden dish of pickled greens. The greens were immediately disposed of, but all manner of delicacies were already waiting their turn – seal kidneys, liver, mashed and frozen-solid meat. All this, in John's opinion, was consumed in monstrous quantities. Finally the main dish of boiled meat came forth. It was heaped upon the platter in enormous chunks, and a tasty steam rose up to fill the crowded polog, breaking out into the chottagin through a vent and teasing the dogs.

Soon enough, John stopped marveling at the wealth of food consumed at the evening meal, as his appetite was scarcely less than that of Toko, who'd spent all day out on the spiky ice cover of the Arctic Ocean.

Finished with his dinner, Toko would lie down on the deerskins and play with little Yako, smoke, or simply follow his wife's movements.

Pyl'mau would poke the seal with her finger and, if it seemed ready to be butchered, she'd take out her woman's knife, one with a wide sharp blade. Making a few preliminary slicing passes, as though marking out a pattern, she'd begin taking the seal apart, pulling off the skin together with its layer of blubber. To someone unused to it, the seal looked a lot like a person stripped naked, and John used to have to turn away at first. Dividing skin from flesh, Pyl'mau would then slit open the stomach cavity and joint the carcass. She was well versed in the beast's anatomy, and her knife never hit bone.

At times there was no fresh meat for a while, and a fruitful day's hunt would be celebrated with an impromptu feast, featuring much bone-picking. And at the end they'd slurp up thick, delicious broth until they were about to burst.

Often enough, while a carcass was being butchered, the chottagin rang with light footsteps – that was how a visitor indicated his presence to the hosts. Then someone's tousled head would poke into the polog. Usually a woman. Some chatter would follow, sometimes even a simple piece of gossip, something even women of high latitudes can't do without. The visit would end with Pyl'mau placing a sizeable piece of meat and blubber into the visitor's hands. At times, there came so many such visitors to Toko's yaranga that only some trifling bits of a whole nerpa were left, barely enough for two or three meals.

But this was a fair and magnanimous tradition. It did not occur to either Toko or Pyl'mau to let a neighbor depart empty-handed.

John had tried to explain to his hosts that even if there were no choice in the matter, one could at least reduce the quantity given to each visitor.

"Each person wants to eat his fill," Toko would answer. "If you can feed a hungry person, then feed him."

"But a person doesn't live one day at a time. You need to save something for the future, for yourself," John would counter.

"And when I have no luck, and come back empty-handed, I will not be ashamed to go to those I have fed," Toko would return.

Everyone would go to sleep pell-mell on the deerskins, heads toward the polog's entryway. A long, well-sanded log served as a pillow. John's ears constantly ached, until he figured out how to sleep on his back.

Pyl'mau retired last of all. Dampening the brazier's flame, she'd feed little Yako his evening meal and sing to him, rocking gently in rhythm with the simple melody.

The fire would die down, the lullaby would fade away, the thoughts milling in John's head would run together, and he'd sink into a deep sleep.

9

John had arranged his own corner in such a way that it somewhat resembled a ship's cabin. The discovery prompted him to turn to Toko, who understood the white man's wish and cut a round "porthole" in the wall, stretching a walrus stomach, normally used for making yarars, over the window.

Orvo paid John a visit every day. He was crafting leather attachments for John's stumps. At first, Orvo had made some from lakhtak skin, but it turned out to be too soft, and he had to replace it with walrus hide. The walrus attachments had holding loops and hooks for a variety of instruments. Now John could use a knife with relative facility and neatly spear food with a three-pronged fork.

On a little table, fashioned from an old retired sled, John spread out the uncomplicated remains of his former life. These included a few thick woollen socks knitted by his mother. He held them in his stumps and silently buried his face in them. He wasn't aware of the sailor's sweat permeating them; for him, they were his home, the image of his living room, the flicker of coals in the fireplace, the dull shine of a silk-upholstered armchair, the aroma of ancient perfumes, powder, and his mother's bluish-gray hair, her fingers with their carefully polished fingernails . . . A wall barometer – his brother's gift. And here was his watch, with its massive cover. The hands have stopped long ago. Strange, but in the whole time he'd been living in Enmyn, John had had no need for a time-measurement more precise than the change of night to day. Gingerly hooking the watch with his holders, John wound it up and brought it to his ear. The clock ticked loudly and brassily, and the plaintive ring of its coil echoed a distant, departed era. Needless to say, the ones left behind in Port Hope may have been living differently now, but for John, their way of life was forever engraved in his memory.

Among the multitude of things that had become useless, and even out of place in John's new life, there were a few pencils and an almost unused notepad bound in thick leather. Once, John had dreamed of filling it with the tales of his own adventures and then publishing the notes somewhere like the *Daily Toronto Star*, maybe even turning them into a whole book, like the volumes kept behind thick glass in the university library in Hart House.

With a condescending smile, John picked up the notepad with two holding hooks and blew on the pages to open them. The first page was emblazoned with scribble:

> . . . *I'll probably never get used to alcohol. It's something shameful: empty posturing, cockiness, cynicism. You look at someone like that in the morning and can't even believe that you were just like them, and even thought that this is the only way to be . . . And that woman who left my room this morning. Who was she? Had she let me know her real name? She was crying as she told me that in my stupor I'd called her "Jeannie."*

On reading this John turned around, as though someone could have stood reading over his shoulder, then managed to grasp the page with his grips and somehow tear it out with an audible crackle. The sheet fell to the ground. John bent down to get it, but just then Orvo squeezed into the "cabin." He never knocked.

"Tyetyk," he proclaimed loudly.

"Yetti," John replied, recalling with chagrin that by Chukchi custom it was the yaranga's owner or occupant that must be first to offer a greeting.

"Tyetyk," Orvo repeated, and deftly scooping up the sheet of paper, placed it on the table.

"Written-down talk," said the old man with respect.

"It's not needed anymore," John said. "I was going to throw it away."

"Throw it away?" Orvo was astonished. "Throw away written-down words? How's that?"

John, himself surprised, said, by way of explanation:

"I don't need them anymore."

The old man looked at him sideways. He had always imagined that the whites only wrote down the most important, most sacred words. That's why they write them down, because they want to save them. Just like all those chants and prayers a shaman learns by heart, weighty words that are needed in difficult times.

"If you don't need them," Orvo said slowly, "then let me take them."

"What good are they to you?" John smirked. "You'll never be able to read them, anyway."

"Maybe never," Orvo humbly agreed. "But I'm thinking: You can't just take written-down words and throw them away. To my mind, it's a sin . . ."

There was something unusual in the old man's voice. John looked at him, wavered for a moment, then nodded:

"All right, you can take this paper."

Orvo smoothed out the page and began scanning the lines with concentration. And John was struck by his expression. It seemed that the old man was reading the words and understanding what was written.

"You know what," John said, reaching for the sheet of paper, "maybe you're right. It's not good, throwing away what's written. Let me have that bit of paper back, and if you really want to have a written note, I'll write you another one."

"As you like," Orvo immediately agreed, and handed back the sheet.

Placing it back inside the notepad with some difficulty, John suddenly remembered that writing another word was unlikely now that he had no fingers. Orvo caught his glance and said uncertainly:

"We'll try to make holders for a pencil. Yes, we will try."

"You think we'll manage something?" John was doubtful.

"You learned to feed yourself with the little fish-spear, you can wield a knife, dress and undress yourself," Orvo enumerated. "Maybe you will learn to write."

John looked at the notepad and pencil and uttered with some passion:

"If I can do that, I'll write you words that are truly worth keeping!"

Orvo didn't like to leave things undone. The very next day he brought over an assortment of leather holders and tacked them onto one of John's stumps.

"How many do I need?" John teased him with a grateful smile.

"If something doesn't work, we'll take it off," Orvo answered.

Following John's instructions, he sharpened a few pencils and attached one to a leather loop. The notepad lay open on the table. John looked steadily at the sheet of paper and drew a line. It came out crooked, and the pencil tip skidded off the edge of the sheet and broke.

Orvo had been carefully observing the white man's movements. Unhooking the broken pencil from its holder, he looked the whole attachment over and declared:

"Needs to be made a different way. Now it's as though you're trying to shave with a spear. The pencil should be shortened, and the holder attached at the wrist. Then it will be more like a finger."

Upset at the setback, John was listening to Orvo's words without much interest, as the familiar bitter malice welled up inside him, directed at no one in particular. He blamed his own sometimes too-lavish imagination that painted his future in lively colors each time he considered it. He saw himself in a university lecture hall, bent over a desk. Instead of hands – ugly stumps, and aided by the mechanisms that kind old Orvo made for him, he was writing. He was writing, and all those around him were gazing at him, their eyes harboring pity . . . Pity, and maybe even contempt.

His heart trembled, and he turned away.

But all you needed to communicate in the present circumstances could be done with plain human speech. Simpler *and* better. It would be laughable if, for example, he, John, had sent a love letter to Pyl'mau and she answered him on a pink scented sheet. Picturing Pyl'mau with an envelope rather than the woman's knife in her hands, John let out a chuckle and told Orvo:

"No need to do anything about it. It would be better if I learned to shoot."

"Well now, that's true enough: that will be easier than writing words again," Orvo replied. "But maybe we should give it another try."

"But tell me, Orvo, what use would that be to me here?" John responded. "Maybe I don't even intend to go back to the world where they read and write – and here with you, what use is there in being lettered?"

"At this time, probably no use," Orvo slowly uttered. "But I have a feeling that a time will come, and our people will need the paper-talk, and our own language will need signs like yours."

"I doubt you'll ever get there," John persisted. "And anyway, what for? What is the point? Your way of life doesn't require literacy or books, so why not go on living as you've always lived? Maybe that really is the best and most sensible way of living . . . Even though you won't fully understand me, I'll tell you this: The closer man is to nature, the more free and untainted he is in his thoughts and in his actions. When I was studying at the University of Toronto – that's a big school, where a person is pumped full of all kinds of knowledge, mainly useless – I had a friend who would say that the appearance of man was an evolutionary mistake, since man brings discord into nature's biological equilibrium . . ."

John glanced at Orvo, and cut his own speech short:

"I'm sorry, Orvo. I can see you don't know what I'm talking about." And he laughed. "The further your people stay away from the white man and his mores, the better it will be for you."

"Maybe that is true, and maybe not true," said Orvo, with his usual candor, and added: "Yet, the gun you're intending to shoot again, that was thought up by white people."

The day came when Orvo, Toko, and John set off for the fast ice, bringing the Winchester along.

A hundred or so steps, and the yarangas disappeared from view. In the north, as far as the eye roamed, ranged an ice-bound sea. Monstrous conglomerations of ice rose to dozens of meters in height. Here and there were bluish iceberg splinters.

Close to the horizon, the craggy shore stretched up toward the sky, and its steep sides, eaten away by the tides, stood out blackly against the snows. In a few spots, the gloomy crags were vertically laced with frozen waterfalls, and the snowcaps shadowing the crags' bulges promised future avalanches.

The steep shoreline turned into gently sloping hills on the continent. Against the otherwise solid backdrop of snow, one hill was crowned with a set of whale jaws, firmly anchored to the earth.

"What's there?" John asked, motioning toward the dark bones.

"The grave of the White Woman," Orvo answered him.

"White Woman?"

"Not really white," the old man amended. "She's called that because she was born and lived on a shore that was white with ice and snow. It is said that all who live on this shore are her children. That means we are too."

Moving a little further down the sea ice, the men halted and began setting up targets. There were three – in descending size order.

Orvo dragged a knot of ice and trimmed it with his hunting knife, fashioning it into a shield with a window and rest for the Winchester barrel. Toko took up a battle position and tried out the weapon. The smallest of the targets exploded into tiny pieces at his first shot.

"Works," he said with satisfaction, and motioned to John. "Now you."

Yesterday, there had been a new addition to the many implements on John's leather cuff – a small loop, angled so that he could use it to hook the Winchester's trigger. Settling comfortably behind his shield and bracing his feet against the ice, John took aim. Aboard the *Belinda,* he'd been considered a good shot. But now his heart beat so violently, it was as though there were suddenly much more room in his ribcage. The sight line kept wavering. John lowered the barrel and took a few deep breaths. Meeting Orvo's eyes, he caught a sympathetic and encouraging look.

Regaining his breath, John took aim once again. The shot rang out. His eyes swimming with tears from the strain, John couldn't make out a thing.

"Try not to move your shoulder," he heard Orvo's calm voice say.

"The bullet went a little high," Toko clarified. "Your aim was right, it was only that you moved your shoulder."

With his fingers, Toko showed him the margin of error. And although it was rather dubious, exactly how his eye could have caught the bullet in midflight, John believed him, and this time aimed more steadily.

He could tell from the sound that the bullet had hit home.

"Got one nerpa!" Toko enthused.

John's heart filled with a hot wave of pleasure: He can shoot! He will no longer be a freeloader in the eyes of these savages. He can procure food independently, and will be able to look not just Pyl'mau, but Toko, Orvo, and the acid-tongued, mocking Armol', in the eye.

"Try again?" he asked Toko.

"We shouldn't waste the cartridges," Orvo said, collecting the Winchester. "Come summer, the white men's ships will come and you'll get a gun of your own."

On the way back, John's stride was firm and confident. Once again he was a real human being! And maybe his dreams of returning to his own people were in vain. If he stays here, he'll become a provider just like Toko, Orvo and Armol', and all the other Enmyn people. His life will be measured by the filling of his stomach. The time will come, and he'll marry a woman of this tribe, breed a litter of kids needing nourishment and clothes, and when his hunter's luck runs out, they'll quietly die inside the polog, without light, without fire. He'll learn the tribe's traditions and possibly even grow to believe in their spirits and gods . . . And no more will his eye be ravished by a green forest hue, nor warm water caress his body, nor his heart stutter in the presence of a beautiful woman. He will take on a Chukcha's appearance, and his inner world will be no different from the polar animals inhabiting these parts . . .

But who can say what manner of life is right for a man? The life of that left-behind, almost unreachable world where Hugh had sailed, abandoning his countryman, one to whom he'd sworn loyalty and friendship?

Or this life, the one John first touched in his misfortune, and the one he is living right now, sometimes even forgetting that he is not a complete man. Would he be content, returning home far different from the man who is awaited there, and for the rest of his life hearing words of consolation, words of pity . . . A cripple?

Clearly, there's no need to be too enamored. It's more than possible that life in these parts only seems attractive from an outsider's point of view, and only at first glance. Maybe, delving more deeply, John will learn unpleasant things, too. But on the other hand, he's lived here long enough to be sure of the wholesomeness and sincerity of these children of snow and frost . . .

The days were spent in labors. As soon as Orvo or Toko returned from hunting, they would pick up John and set off again for the icebergs off the shore for some shooting practice. One after another, the ice masses shattered, the winter silence was rent by the blasts of the gun's report, and each shot imbued John with a feeling of self-confidence.

In the evenings, he would sit down at the rickety little table and try to write. The letters came out huge and tried to climb one upon the other, but already they were letters rather than senseless scrawl.

And when he managed to trace the name Jeannie on the sheet of paper, he was so transported that he shouted into the chottagin:

"Look, Toko, look at what I did!"

Toko stuck a worried face through the door flap.

John showed him the piece of paper with large childish letters, upon which the beloved name was crookedly inscribed.

"See, I wrote that! With these two hands I wrote it, understand?"

With an effort, Toko began to comprehend what John was talking about. By the standards of that world, Sson has probably accomplished much. But for Toko, the most important thing was that the white man had learned to shoot, which meant that now he wouldn't starve to death.

John felt himself coming back to life and was pleased; and yet more and more often he returned to the fleeting thought of remaining here forever, becoming like Toko, Orvo, forgetting the troubles and complexity of his old world. Sometimes John could picture himself in his new friends' shoes, look at himself and his ilk with their eyes, and it was then that doubt assailed him. Yes, perhaps this is it, a true and meaningful life, a life worthy of man.

One afternoon, Orvo came to mend a broken holder for the gun trigger. They sat in John's little room, and the old man began to sew a leather loop right onto John's leather-encased stump.

"Listen, Orvo," John said quietly, "what would you say if I decided to stay here forever?"

"We'd be glad of such a brother," Orvo answered without hesitation.

From the ease of his reply, John understood that the other had taken his words lightly.

"This is a serious talk, Orvo," John said. "I want to hear what you have to say, what advice you have for me."

Orvo bent down to John's wrist, and bit off the thread.

"What can I tell you?" he uttered thoughtfully. "Seagulls live with other seagulls, crows with crows, walruses with walruses. That is how it's meant to be. Although, man is not a beast . . . But it won't be easy for you. You'd have to become just like us, after all. Not just shoot, fish, dress and speak like us . . . But why are you asking me about this?"

"I admire the way you live," John answered. "It seems to me that your way of life is the kind of existence worthy of a man. And that's why I'd like to remain among you. But what will you say to that, what will your tribesmen say?"

Orvo was silent. But it was plain from his face that he was wrestling with opposing feelings.

"It is good that you praise our people. But I tell you again: It will be hard for you . . . We are glad to welcome you into our family, but you're not alone in the world. You have loved ones. They still wait for you. And another thing I'll say, Sson. Now you see our life as more or less tranquil, because we had good fortune with the autumn hunt, and in the summer we bagged plenty of walrus and even harpooned a whale. For a few years now, illness has not visited us. People are hale, fed, cheerful, and so it seems to you that ours is a good life. Even the weather brightens what you see: I can't remember such a warm and calm winter as this one. But now, think about our life when the autumn hunt is meager, and it's hard to put away a reserve of food. And then the winter will come bitter and snowy, and the sea will be sealed in ice – not a crack or patch of water . . . Then comes famine. And with famine, illness. People die like flies on a cold night. You'll be eating the scrapings off the meat pits, the rotted meat, and boiling lakhtak harnesses to fill your empty belly. I say to you again, Sson, we've grown fond of you, but you could not bear this life of ours . . ."

John thought about these last words for a long while: If even Orvo sees him as only partially a man, then how would it go for him over in Port Hope?

Yet, another time, almost as if in passing, Orvo said to him:

"Well, if you like it here with us – there's no hurry. Stay as long as you want."

10

Events came, whose meaning John could not fathom. There were times in the middle of the night, or early in the morning, when Toko would spring up from his deerskin and go outside, where the snow was creaking under his friends' torbasses. Careful footsteps receded further and further, toward the coast. As the days lengthened, so did Toko's absences. Sometimes he disappeared until evening, returning only when the long sun sank behind the dark crags of the western cape.

"Where does he go off to?" John got up the courage to ask Pyl'mau.

"To talk with the gods," Pyl'mau said simply, as though the gods were their nearest neighbors and could be approached without any formalities.

"So what do they talk about?"

"A woman isn't meant to know such things," said Pyl'mau, and having considered for a moment, added: "But I think they are talking about seals, walruses, and the weather."

"Important talks, then," John remarked.

But he asked no questions of Toko, who was worried and withdrawn.

On those days that Toko had not gone out, they would set off hunting. The sun rose early. The long shadows of ice hummocks and crags quickly grew smaller and smaller. The snow was dazzling. So as not to get sunblind, Toko and John fashioned sunglasses out of thin strips of leather with narrow slits to see through. These eyepieces severely limited one's field of vision, but then again, you didn't have to worry about the sun's sly rays.

Within a few days, all of John's exposed flesh became so tanned that in color it was hardly different from Toko's skin.

"I've become almost like you," John would say, displaying the darkened patches of skin.

"Truly," Toko would agree, with inward satisfaction. Sson, this helpless, pathetic person who had not had the slightest inkling of how a real man ought to live, was gradually becoming an actual human being. He's even changed his walk, and now goes with a slight spring in his step, putting his foot just so, so that it won't slip. And doesn't stuff his mouth with snow, as he used to in those early days. He's learned that it's better to wait until they get home. The snow only intensifies your thirst . . . Not long from now, Sson won't be any different from real people. He'll be able to go along, not just hunting, but to the ceremonial sacrifices, which Toko attended most mornings. Soon, they will perform the most important of the sacrifices. They will take the winter-weathered hide boats off their high supports, carry them to the sea and bury them in snow so that the meltwater wets the boats' walrus-hide shells, dried out over the winter. That morning all the gods will receive gifts, they will be addressed with solemn words, and the men themselves will gain new strength, for the time is nearing when the walruses return to the sea, and hunting walrus requires great strength. Sometimes they will have to drift on the sea for several days on end, only rarely clambering onto an iceberg in order to butcher the kill and cook a repast over a walrus-fat flame . . . Even now they might take John along to the sacrificial gathering, it's only that Orvo has said it wasn't yet time . . .

Toko was teaching him the hunter's art, while Pyl'mau corrected his speech. Each time, before pointing out an error, she would burst into ringing peals of laughter, and the laughter transformed her face. She would turn into an enchanting woman, and it was by force of will that

John pushed away his masculine stirrings. Besides, inside the polog, Pyl'mau habitually wore only a narrow loincloth. Her darkly glowing body seemed as though carved of teak, her full breasts were still firm. He avoided being left alone with Pyl'mau . . . And then, those nightly sighs and deep breathing . . . It was all happening an arm's length away.

He called up a vision of Jeannie in his imagination, tried to remember everything, even the most insignificant details; yet each time, instead of a pale little face surrounded by flaxen curls, it was Pyl'mau's smiling face that appeared, her full lips and white teeth. This despite the fact that John had never seen her brush her teeth in his presence.

The morning of the most sacred ceremony arrived. The day before, John and Toko had been late in returning from the sea. They were dragging three nerpa apiece. Both were exhausted – their way had been long and arduous; they kept having to walk around puddles of meltwater on the ice, their feet sinking into the softened and porous snow, cold water sloshing inside their low sealskin torbasses.

Early in the morning, John opened his eyes and heard Toko tell him:

"Sleep, rest some more. I won't be back for a while."

A bleary-eyed Pyl'mau was bustling around the oil brazier, warming up yesterday's meat. John turned on the other side and fell back asleep. When he awoke, Pyl'mau was kneading a deerskin. Three lamps burned brightly. Pyl'mau sat completely naked, bracing her feet against the softened inner side of the hide. John studied her through half-closed eyes. By the lamplight, her skin, despite its swarthiness, took on a rosy glow. When Jeannie had a suntan her breasts remained white, and even glowed palely in the night when she walked toward him, nude . . . But here, the woman's skin color was even, matte and warm. It was all he could do not to run his palm over it, feeling that warmth. The impulse was so insistent and torturous that John couldn't conceal a moan of physical pain.

Pyl'mau stopped her work and peered at him intently. John pretended to be asleep and screwed his eyes shut tight. Suddenly he felt the touch of Pyl'mau's hand, and opened his eyes.

Pyl'mau was sitting next to him on the deerskin bed.

"Is it bad with you?" she asked compassionately.

Unable to utter a syllable, John only blinked.

"I know that it's bad," Pyl'mau said with feeling. "You rarely sleep well. Talking in your own tongue, calling out for someone. I understand you. When Toko took me for a wife and brought me here, oh, I felt so bad! As though they tore out my heart and left it back home . . ."

"You weren't born here, then?" John asked.

"No, I'm from far off," Pyl'mau answered. "From another coast. One day the Enmyn people drove into our settlement, and among them was Toko. I took a look a him, and he looked at me. We went to the tundra, to the places where the grass is soft. And when the time came for them to leave, I told my parents that I'd be setting off with Toko. And I've lived here ever since. The first year, I was so sorry, I cried so much!"

"So you . . . do you . . ." John stumbled. He had wanted to ask Pyl'mau whether she loved Toko, but didn't know how to say *love* in the Chukchi language, and so phrased it this way: "Is it good, your living with Toko?"

"Very good!" Pyl'mau said without hesitation. "He is such a man! Kind, tender, strong! Even in the black winter nights, when all around is frost and darkness, with him I feel happiness and light. And our son, Yako, he's like a little round moon." Pyl'mau threw a tender glance at the corner, where the little boy was sweetly snoozing.

She still held her warm palm pressed to John's forehead. Her body gave off a faint odor of perspiration. Speaking of Toko, she had closed her eyes and softly nodded her head.

John felt that in a few more seconds something terrible, irredeemable, was bound to happen. Throwing off Pyl'mau's hand, he sat up sharply, pulled on his clothes and bolted out to the chottagin.

Pyl'mau looked quizzically in his wake and even called softly:

"Sson!"

The outer door slammed shut in answer.

It's hard for the fellow to get used to the strangers' life, strangers' speech, strangers' food . . . And that it should happen, he turns out to be a good man, though white. At first, Pyl'mau just couldn't get used to his pale skin and the auburn beard that covered half his face. Amazing – John's beard even grew on his chest, and what's more, was curly!

More than once, in the dawn hours, Pyl'mau watched the men savor those last slumbering moments and grew still, as though entranced, looking deeply at one man and then the other. Sometimes, from some depth of consciousness, a stray thought surfaced: Why not be the wife of two men? Aren't there men with two wives? How many years now has Orvo been living with both Cheivuneh and Ve'emneut? It's hard to even think of his two wives as separate people. They're always together, and after the long years of sharing their lives, their voices and even their looks have grown similar . . . In the village where Pyl'mau herself was born, there were plenty of men with two wives. Her father's friend Teki, one of the deer people, he had three wives!

Pyl'mau let out a heavy sigh and, in a fury, frenziedly set to kneading the uncured deerskin with her rough and calloused heels.

Human voices rang out sharply between the clear sky and the snowy earth of the early-morning calm. A crowd was discernible at the edge of the settlement, where the row of yarangas came to an end, and the Sacred Whale Jaws were set into the ground. John slowly started making his way toward it. The icy crust that came with the nocturnal frost was crunching underfoot. He could feel a soft and pliant layer of snow underneath, already too soft to support a laden dogsled.

The hide boats had been lowered from their high trestles and lay keel up on the snow. These unusual boats – wood, walrus hide and lakhtak bindings – were a revelation to John. Not a single metal part, not a nail or screw in them. Three people could easily pick up and carry a vessel that stayed afloat carrying fifteen men or two to three walruses. Still, with all respect for these astonishing boats, John felt a tremor imagining the fragile wood and leather construction weaving a path among the ice floes, each of which were easily capable of holing a ship's side.

John came closer. Armol' was holding up something resembling a large wooden dish. Then John saw that many other men held the same kind of dish. Except that some men had larger ones, more like trays, and others had tiny wooden bowls. Dogs loped about underfoot. They were amazingly quiet, neither barking nor growling, as though they understood the meaning of the sacred ritual.

Orvo was barely recognizable. The old man wore a long robe of a light brown chamois hung with colored ribbons, with tassels of white deer-skin, with thin leather threads ending in beads, with bells, with silver and copper coins. A snow-white, black-tailed ermine dangled from his back.

Orvo was speaking, his face turned to the sea. The speech was evidently intended for the gods only, since the rest of the people were not listening to the old man, but rather talking amongst themselves. Intoning a few words, Orvo would take the nearest man's tray or bowl, scoop up a handful of sacred food and throw it to Dawn and to Dusk, to North and South. The dogs were carefully picking up the sacrifices and silently following the old man about.

Three hide boats lay on the snow. Orvo slowly walked around each one. By the front end, he would stop and take a long while muttering, touching his hands to the dried-out walrus skin. Sometimes he would raise his voice, but no matter how hard John listened, he couldn't make out a single word. It seemed to him that Orvo was speaking in some other tongue, not Chukchi.

There were also boys among the crowd of men. They were full of dignity, and primly followed the procession around the hide boats. The vaulting sky, the dark distant crags touched with blue, the quietude that seemed almost to be listening to their prayers; all this affected John to a surprising degree, and with a pang he remembered the Sunday service at the church in Port Hope, the dressed-up parishioners and the organ's song, reaching down into the most sacred depths of his soul.

John did not acknowledge a God and did not go to church. His father believed that each man had the right to live as he saw fit and should not prevent others from doing the same. John's parents were regular church-goers, but he suspected that his father did not believe in God, and only went to Sunday services because it was the expected thing.

But here, on the edge of the Arctic Ocean, John suddenly yearned to enter the cool cathedral twilight and, instead of this endless sky, see a tall dome and rainbow dust motes dancing in the multicolored sunbeams that pour through stained-glass windows.

The talk with the gods came to an end. Orvo addressed the people. The boys, holding their shirt-ends like baskets, were making the rounds of those with sacrificial food dishes. Having filled up, the kids raced each other for the yarangas to cheer their mothers and sisters with the remains of the divine feast.

Toko noticed John and, with a nod in his direction, said something to Orvo. The old man motioned John closer.

"Soon we'll put the hide boats to water," Orvo said, joy suffusing his voice. "Look there," he pointed to the sea, covered with ice hummocks and snow. "Look higher, at the sky. See a dark stripe? That's the reflection of clear water. It's still far-off, but soon the south wind will start blowing and the sea will come nearer to Enmyn . . ."

"And a ship will come for you," Toko added.

"Well, before that ship gets here, I'll have plenty of time to go hunting with you, maybe even bag myself a walrus," John said cheerfully.

People had crowded in all around them. Curious, John peered at one of the dishes. To his surprise, the gods' food was no different from that of the people. It consisted of small pieces of cured deer and seal meat, neatly chopped lard cubes, some kind of herby grasses. Orvo scooped up a bit of the sacrificial feast with his calloused palm and held it out to John.

"Now we'll carry the hide boats to the shore and pack them in snow," he explained, chewing loudly and with relish. "Little by little, sun will melt snow, and water dampen leather. The leather will become softened and taut. And by the time the hide boats are ready, the ice will have gone from our shores . . ."

"Got it," John said confidently, unwilling to look like an ignoramus in front of the other Chukchi, despite not having understood a word of the explanation.

Walking back to the yarangas with Toko, he was thinking that these people are far from being as ignorant as he had first taken them to be. They've got their own calendar, their own idea of the movement of heavenly bodies . . . and as for medicine, you can only bow down in admiration. John remembered his own lack of trust in the shaman-woman who'd saved him from certain death, and smiled inwardly; he remembered too, how he once used to confuse Toko and Armol', and how all the Enmyn Chukchi seemed to him to have the same face. Yes, they do have their own culture, one that adapts to the harsh existence that falls to their lot. These people have managed to preserve all the best features of humanity in an environment that would be the death of many a wild beast . . .

John glanced at Toko and tried to imagine him in a different set of clothes, different surroundings. He transported Toko to the middle of the Port Hope Catholic cathedral, dressed in a velveteen jacket, trousers, shoes, and a starched white collar. But the picture turned out so incongruous and alarming that he couldn't repress a smile.

"You in a cheerful mood?" Toko asked.

"Tell me," John turned to him, "could you live in another place?"

"What other place?" Toko didn't quite understand.

"In the lands where I'm from, for example."

Toko was striding forward silently. The question had been put to him in all seriousness and he was bound to give a substantive answer.

"If I had to," Toko slowly uttered. "If there were no other way out. But maybe I couldn't survive it even then."

"But why?" John objected. "I am living in your land, after all."

"Because you have the hope of returning," Toko answered. "It's as if you're a visitor here. The ships will come, take you back to your warm homeland, to your family and friends. Time will pass, and your life here will seem to you a vague dream. You know, there's a sort of dream that you can never remember clearly . . . A dream in polar fog . . ."

"A dream in polar fog?" John mused, and after some thought, made the objection: "No, the things I've lived through here I will never forget . . . Toko, I wanted to ask you: What would you say if I decided to stay here forever, on your shores?"

"Well, you could live among us, too," Toko said thoughtfully, "but you do have a chance of returning, and your loved ones probably haven't lost hope. Maybe afterwards you'll come back to us. We need the white people's friendship, because they have more skill and knowledge than we do. They've thought up things that make a man's life easier."

"I worry that interaction with us will bring your people nothing but trouble," John said harshly.

"Look at how long I've known you, but I never heard anything ill from you," Toko said, smiling.

A fire blazed inside the chottagin. Pyl'mau melted some snow and handed it to John for his face washing. John gripped a clean white rag between the two short wooden holders that stood in for fingers, wet it and made a few passes over his face. Toko washed his face too, something he'd picked up from his white friend.

Faces washed, the men sat down to breakfast.

"We need lakhtak," Pyl'mau remarked to the men with increasing frequency. "There's nothing left for shoe soles. If you don't get some, you'll end up going barefoot."

The hunters would go out to the fast ice. The long-awaited south wind had lost its way in other lands, and the ice-sheets were firmly welded to the craggy shore.

Flocks of wild duck took flight over the far land spit.

Toko shook John awake early in the morning. They breakfasted on cold nerpa meat. Pyl'mau put a few pieces of boiled nerpa into a leather satchel for the road.

"What's this? We're taking food? But when we go out on the sea, we can't take even a little bite along!"

"That's custom," Toko answered. "For duck hunting we can take some food along, but it's sin to take it to sea."

"Don't you think that some of your customs simply make your life more difficult?" John inquired while helping to hitch up the dogs.

"There are some rules in life that make one person's life difficult, but help all people together," came Toko's meditative reply, one that convinced John that it was better to drop the subject altogether.

Their path ran along the shore. John and Toko were by no means the first to go out – the snow was already marked by the passing of a good many dogsled runners. On approaching the Pil'khyn Strait the hunters picked up speed. Armol' had taken his younger brothers along. The boys held eplykytet* in their laps, and were picking through walrus teeth for slinging. They were smilingly contemplating John, decked out with two eplykytet.

"Hey, Toko, how is he going to manage throwing an eplykytet into a flock?" Armol' shouted from his sled.

"He'll manage," Toko assured him. "He's already tried it on the ice, in the lagoon."

For a few days now, John had been mastering the art of eplykytet throwing under Toko's supervision. This turned out to be a great deal harder than learning to shoot a Winchester. The very first attempt almost ended fatally – for Toko. The eplykytets, sliding off John's stumps, whistled past Toko's head at half a finger's breadth. And another time, John even managed to hit himself. Despairing of ever taming the disobedient device, John informed Toko that he would do without duck. But Toko was resolute:

"A true man must be able to tackle everything!"

"Well, it's not as though I would take these bones with me to Port Hope!" John shook the eplykytet up and down. "I've got a decent shotgun at home."

"No great feat to bring down a bird with a gun," Toko rejoined. "You try it with this."

And once again, patiently, he set to demonstrating how to swing the bunch of walrus teeth on their thin sealskin thongs overhead, until he finally taught John to launch the eplykytet in the right direction.

In places, snow had already left the shingled promontory, and from afar the dark bald spots resembled patches on an endless white canvas.

* *Eplykytet* – a device for hunting birds, consisting of a bone or lead weight on a long string.

The patches were where the hunters disposed themselves, looking out for the flock of ducks that flew overhead from the opposite end of the lagoon.

Toko had decided on a little hillock where the shingle was dry, and led the dog pack off to the shore, so they'd not see the ducks and frighten them off by barking. Armol' and his brothers settled down nearby.

"When the flock moves closer, we need to lie down and be still," Toko was admonishing his comrade. "Jump up only when the ducks are right overhead."

John listened and nodded quietly, charged with the kind of excitement familiar to any hunter.

For some time, John and Toko talked quietly, scanning the horizon line. The flocks were flying either to the left or to the right of them.

"Maybe we should try another spot?" John suggested.

"Be patient. The ducks will come to us, too," Toko answered calmly.

And truly, very soon an enormous flock came into view not far from where they lay. The din of beating wings grew with each passing moment. The dense dark stripe resembled a racing hurricane rather than a flock of birds. The roar was like that of Niagara Falls.

Toko and John pressed tight against the damp shingle.

Crossing the shoreline, the ducks rose sharply upwards, yet they were still flying so low that John felt the wind generated by their wings. The eplykytets whirred upwards. They numbered four instead of two. Somehow Armol' and a younger brother of his had turned out to be close by. Three ducks, bound in leather thongs, plummeted to the ground.

John raced toward them, but was beaten by Armol' and Toko.

Armol' handed him back his eplykytet with a caustic little smile.

"Missed," he said.

John was nonplussed. For some strange reason, every time he came across Armol' he felt an odd kind of disquiet and often caught himself talking to the man in an obsequious, even guilty, tone. This time, too, John quietly said:

"I can't do it yet."

"Hard for a white man to learn our way," Armol' pronounced, tying two of the ducks together by their wings.

The second flock was much larger than the first. Once over the shingled sandbank, it blocked the sunlight. This time, John also had some luck. His eplykytet wrapped itself around a large fat lylekeli.*

"Fortune has favored you," was Toko's restrained praise.

"Got lucky," said Armol'.

In truth, there was such a profusion of ducks that you could have thrown an eplykytet blindfolded.

By the time the sun crossed to the western side of the sky, Toko and John had almost three dozen of the ducks.

John, flush with triumph, was promising Toko:

"As soon as I get home to Canada, I'll send you a shotgun, right away. One shot into such a dense crowd and you can go back with a full sled!"

"I'll look forward to that," Toko said, uncertainly.

When their sled was running over the beaten path back, Toko settled himself comfortably and launched into song. John had heard Chukchi singing before, but could glean no great pleasure from the doleful, plaintive melody. It seemed to him that everyone just sang the same song. There were almost no words, and one could only guess at the feelings that overwhelmed the singer.

It was hard for the dogs. During the day the snow had melted in the sun, becoming too loose for the sliding runners. Again and again, John and Toko would jump off the sled and help the dogs.

* *Lylekeli* – a drake.

The Sacred Whale Jaws loomed ahead, the track became more solid, and now they could have a rest.

"Why is your ancestress called the White Woman?" asked John, as he recalled that according to Chukchi legend, the woman who was buried under these bones had given birth to the Chukchi people.

"That was what they called her," Toko answered.

"And why whale bones in particular, over her grave?"

"She gave birth to whales as well as to people, didn't she?" Toko answered in a matter-of-fact tone.

"Whales?" Stunned, John was about to inform Toko it was nonsense, but then the absurdities of the Bible came to mind, and he only asked:

"Can you tell me something about her?"

"Every child remembers this legend," said Toko, "and you should know it also, because you too might be a whale's brother."

"A whale's brother?" John had to ask again.

"Well then, listen," Toko said, leaning back comfortably. "The old men tell us that a time long ago, a beautiful young woman lived on this shore. And such a beauty she was that even the great sun forgot to leave the sky as it gazed on her, and the stars would shine in daylight just to get a glimpse of her. Out of her footprints grew lovely flowers and pure water springs appeared.

"The beauty often came to the seashore. She loved to look at the waves and to hear their murmur. She would fall asleep to the whispering of the wind and the wave, and then the sea creatures would gather onshore to get a look at her. The walruses climbed up onto the pebbled beach, the seals watched her without blinking with their great round eyes.

"One day, a big lygirev* was swimming past. He noticed the crowd of sea beasts on the shore, grew curious and finally swam up close. When he

---

* *Lygirev* – a Greenland whale.

saw the beautiful maiden, he was so taken with her that he forgot where he had been going.

"When the weary sun sat down for a rest on the horizon, the whale returned to shore, touched his head to the pebbly beach and turned into a fine young man. The beauty saw him and lowered her eyes, shy. And the young man took the maiden by the hand, and led her into the tundra, to where the grasses are soft, to the carpet of flowers. And so became the custom – each time the sun set toward the line of the horizon, the whale would come back, turn into a man, and live with the beauty as a man with his wife. The day came, and she knew that she would soon bear a child. Then the whale-man built a spacious yaranga and lived there with her, and returned to the sea no more.

"Little whale calves appeared. Their father housed them in a nearby lagoon. Whenever they got hungry, the babies would swim to shore – and there was their mother, coming out to meet them. The little whales grew quickly, and soon the lagoon was too small for them, they wanted to be let out into the freedom of the wide sea. It pained their mother to see them go, but what can you do – whales are a sea folk. Her children swam off to the sea, and the woman was with child again, except that this time she gave birth not to whales but to human babies. Meanwhile the whale children did not forget their parents, often coming to shore to frolic in front of their mother and father's eyes.

"Time passed. The children grew up, the parents grew older. The father no longer went out hunting, now his sons brought the food. Before their first sea hunt, their father called them to him and gave them a word of parting:

"To one who is strong and brave, the sea is a life giver. But remember: your brothers the whales and your distant relatives the dolphins and porpoises, live there. Do not hunt them, but take care of them . . .

"Soon the father died. And the mother was too old now to see her sons off on the hunt. The whale-people increased in number, the sons all took wives and each had many children. More and more food was needed, as the whale's descendants became the Chukchi and the Eskimo people, hunters of sea life.

"Came one bad year, when there were few beasts to be had by the shore. The walruses forgot their watery way to the settlement, and the nerpa had retreated to distant islands, so the hunters had to go further and further to sea – where some were lost on the ice, and some in the fathomless depths.

"But the whales continued to cavort and play cheerfully close to shore. And then one of the hunters, a son of the White Woman, said:

"'Why don't we hunt the whales? Just look – mountains of blubber and meat. One carcass will feed all of us and the dogs through the winter.'

"'But have you forgotten that they are our brothers?' the people answered him.

"'What kind of brother are they,' the hunter scoffed, 'if they live in the water, and not on land, their bodies are long and huge, and they don't know a word of human speech.'

"'But they say . . .' the people tried to set him straight.

"'Old wives' tales for little children,' snapped the hunter. He fitted out a big hide boat, taking with him the strongest and most skillful oarsmen.

"It turned out to be an easy job. One whale swam to the hide boat himself, as he had always done upon seeing his brothers come out to sea. But this reunion spelled his death.

"They harpooned the whale and dragged him to shore; to haul him onto the beach they had to call up all the villagers, even the women and little children!

"The one who had killed the whale went to his mother's yaranga to tell her what a treasure he'd gotten for his people. But the mother already knew, and was dying of grief.

" 'I killed a whale!' the hunter exclaimed, entering the yaranga. 'Pulled in a whole mountain of meat and blubber!'

" 'It was your brother you killed,' his mother answered. 'And if today you have killed your brother just because he does not look like you, then tomorrow . . .'

"And then she died."

Toko fell silent.

John was silent too.

"And everything went from there," Toko said finally, "so now even when a human kills another human, nobody is much surprised."

There was lively commotion in the settlement. Each yaranga blazed with a fire, and blue pillars of smoke rose steeply into the clear sky. Down and feathers floated around in the air – they were plucking ducks inside the chottagins, cauldrons were on the boil, and delicious clouds of steam roused the appetites of both the people and the dogs.

Pyl'mau had stoked up a great fire inside the chottagin. She took some ducks right off the sled and set to cooking.

John and Toko unhitched the harnesses, stored away the sled on its wooden supports, chopped up some kopal'khen and fed the dogs. On entering the chottagin they both took off their hunting footgear. Looking over John's torbasses, Toko noticed a small rip in the sole, and showed it to Pyl'mau.

"Need lakhtak," Pyl'mau said. "You'll end up barefoot by summer, there's no leather for shoe soles."

"Tomorrow we'll go out to the fast ice," Toko replied.

John had slipped off to his tiny room. Shutting his eyes, he could still see the endless duck swarm flashing by, and his ears still hummed with Toko's voice, recounting the ancient legend.

John rose from his pallet, took out his notepad and wrote:

21 (?) May, 1911. Enmyn settlement. Today I went duck hunting and used a weapon first employed by people of the Stone Age. And I felt like one of those people, and treated my friend Toko accordingly. But what he has told me is very far from primitivism. This legend holds so deep a meaning that I doubt if Toko himself can comprehend the import of what he told me. Bible parables are like a child's mumbling compared to the idea that pervades the deep poetry of this legend . . .

Then John wrote down the ancient tale, trying hard to recall the smallest details.

And yet I suspect that Toko's telling me the tale was not without a purpose. Perhaps thus was his way of introducing to me, through allegory, the idea of universal brotherhood – that unattainable dream of mankind, rooted in the first beginnings of history.

Reading over what he'd written and carefully inspecting the handwriting, John noted with satisfaction that his writing had improved. It was more even, and the letters almost ceased escaping between the lines. After another satisfied glance, John stuck a pencil in the holder-clasp and continued:

If only a year ago, someone had told me I would find that the native women here possessed undeniable charms, I'd have called him a brainless fool and taken it as an insult. It seems that each woman is beautiful in her own place. My imagination can't set Jeannie in this hut, just as Mau would seem out of place in our living room at home. And yet, both of them – Jeannie and Mau – are lovely enough to arouse a man's feelings. Being among these people has obviously done me some good. I've started to look at many things more simply, and that means more precisely and more open-mindedly. I know already that I'll have a hard time leaving them, and even at home, in Port Hope, my ears will go on ringing with Chukchi speech and I'll dream the dreams of this shore . . . Dreams in polar fog. And too, I feel that although I may be covered in grime, it's as if I've shed something, some sort of bark that kept me from feeling another man's joys, pains and emotions . . .

"Sson, time to eat!" he heard Toko's voice call. "Come out here."

John paused for a moment over the open notepad, then shut it and came out into the smoky chottagin, where Pyl'mau was moving around in the firelight.

She placed a large wooden dish filled with duck meat onto a little low table. This time there were no knives – bird flesh being quite susceptible to being torn apart by teeth.

When their hunger pangs were quelled, and their eyes strayed seeking tasty tidbits, Toko spoke:

"We need to get some lakhtak. If a keral'gin* comes, we'll go out on the ice. We'll go lightly, without the dogs. No need to get nerpa. We've got plenty in storage, all the barrels are full of fat, soon the walruses will be in season – what are we going to do with it all? We'll go looking only for lakhtak."

"Surprising, that all through the winter, only we two never came across any lakhtak," John said.

"It happens," Toko replied. "Someone is lucky, someone else is not. It's rare good fortune to down a lakhtak. You can trade a piece of its skin to the deer-people for fawn skins . . ."

Pyl'mau didn't interrupt the men's conversation. From time to time, she would get up, add some more duck to the plate, and stealthily move

* *Keral'gin* – a northeasterly wind.

her eyes from one to the other. And the insistent thought was rattling around in her mind: Why can't a woman do as a man does? Why is what he's allowed not given to her?

The ice that stretched over the sea was riven with cracks, pitted with meltholes from which the sea exhaled. There was almost no snow at all left on top of the ice, and despite a thick layer of dried grass and the fur chizhi they wore, their feet felt every inch of the painfully hard surface.

It was a hot business, the going. John could feel a trickle of sweat run down the furrows alongside his spine. Toko walked ahead of him. Never slowing, he kept a rapid, even pace. Exerting the last of his strength, John drove himself onwards. The Winchester that hung from his back in a white leather case, grew heavier with each step, and even the wooden akyn was starting to feel as though it were made of lead. Only his self-esteem forbade him to ask for a rest. He was breathing heavily and beginning to stumble, when Toko suddenly halted in front of a melting ice hummock.

"Let's have a look at what's ahead," he said, and motioned toward the ice hummock's peak.

"Have a look," John called back, "I'll wait down here."

"All right, then." Toko took out his hunter's knife and fell to carving out some footholds in the ice. Transparent ice chips flew down to John. He caught a few small ones and put them in his mouth to alleviate the dry heat.

Toko clambered on top of the ice hummock and, putting a hand to his eyes, painstakingly scanned the horizon. Coming back down, he announced:

"Open water is very near. Let's go."

And he set off again.

Lagging behind, drenched in sweat, John was thinking irritably that his torbasses would have lasted quite well enough until the first ship arrived.

He wouldn't need new ones at all. Except perhaps as a souvenir of his sojourn in the distant Chukchi lands. He would hang them up in the living room, so that anyone coming for a visit could see them. And then he'd tell the story of how the Chukchi beauty Pyl'mau (he would call her by her full name then, not the name he'd grown used to calling her – Mau), would shape the water-resistant soles with her teeth, and then he would get up, take the torbasses from the wall and show them Pyl'mau's teeth marks, preserved forever in the leather sole. Besides the torbasses, he'd have to take along a kukhlianka, his hunting gear and the snowshoes. Some of the items he could donate to the National Museum in Toronto, and he must remember to have some beaded slippers made for his mother and Jeannie. Just like the kind Pyl'mau had.

The open sea came into view suddenly, without warning. Water blended with sky, and the faraway ice floes were hard to tell apart from clouds. It was as though the still watery surface rose up to meet the edge of the sky, and the vastness that opened out was enough to take your breath away. John's emotions were also shot through with the thought that this was the way home, back to his own world, where he was born, where he'd grown up, where he belonged.

"We're there," Toko drawled with satisfaction, and gave a few deep sighs.

Considering this an adequate resting pause, he now began fashioning a hideout.

"It would be better if you set yourself down a bit farther away," he told John. "That way we'll get the lakhtak faster."

"You're right. But how will I recognize a lakhtak?" John was doubtful.

"But you've seen them."

"Just dead ones, already killed," answered John.

"In the water, lakhtak look about the same as nerpa," Toko started explaining, "except that he's bigger and his whiskers are rough, and almost always black."

"Let's not guess," John suggested. "I'll just shoot at everything, and then we'll sort out which is lakhtak and which is nerpa."

Toko scratched his head, winced, and unwillingly consented:

"All right. But do your best not to get too many nerpa. What's the sense in killing the animal for no use?"

He helped John make a hideout, and then the hunters separated.

Quietly, the ocean breathed. Water splashed by a thick faultline in the blue ice. Toko looked over to the eastern side of the sky, to where a distant cape pointed a long black finger at the vastness of the seascape. The sky above the crags was clear, nothing to indicate a change of weather. But you had to be careful in springtime. The wind could suddenly change, and the crevasse-covered ice could break into ice floes from a light breeze and carry the hunters out into the open sea.

It was a long slow wait for the lakhtak, time marked by the drops of water that fell noisily from the ice to the surface of the sea.

Nerpa kept on popping up over the water's surface. They swam unhurriedly, and were sometimes so close that Toko could have reached them with his little boat hook.

A shot rang out. Toko leapt to his feet and raced to John, who was already unwinding an akyn over his head. A dead lakhtak was floating in a widening pool of blood. John threw his akyn just beyond it, jerked it back and hooked the animal.

Together, they could barely haul the dead lakhtak onto the ice. Toko didn't need to inspect the creature to know that he had exactly the kind of hide required for hunting shoes – sturdy and thick.

"You've bagged a lakhtak!" Toko exclaimed, with a look of admiration and gratitude for his friend.

"I had trouble recognizing him," John admitted with a smile. "More like I felt it really: that this was a new kind of beast. So I decided that this was indeed lakhtak, and I pulled the trigger."

"Well done!" Toko praised him. "Now all you've got left to do is harpoon a walrus, go out whale hunting and spear an umka – a white polar bear."

"Nerpa, ducks, and lakhtak are quite enough for me," John said, and there was sadness in his voice, "too much for me, even . . ."

"How about switching places with me?" Toko offered. "We'll sit together, it won't be so dull, waiting."

"Is one lakhtak not enough for us?" asked John.

"True enough, but we've only just got here," said Toko, looking away.

John could feel a shade of upset in his voice. And really, their return would not have painted a pretty picture: a white man, a cripple, with his kill, and Toko empty-handed.

Toko deftly pierced the bearded seal's whiskery lips, threaded a boat-tugging rope through the hole and dragged the animal over to his hide-out, made from large blocks of ice.

Toko took up his post, and John got down nearby, his Winchester poised.

A nerpa appeared in the distance, slowly making its way toward the hunters. John was looking into her eyes. Noticing him, the ringed seal dove underwater.

"Why has the nerpa got such human eyes?" John asked. "Maybe she, too, is related to some human folk?"

"And why not?" Toko replied. "Every beast has relations among people. And those of us whom the wind carries off and imprisons in the ice, they slowly start to turn into tery'ky, changelings. The person goes wild and can't live like people do. He wanders about the tundra and the mountains, attacking animals and eating their flesh raw."

"Have you ever seen these tery'ky?"

"Once, I saw one."

John turned around to face him, thinking that Toko was joking. But the Chukcha's face was serious.

"I was still very young then, unmarried. Hunting lakhtak in the spring, just like this. I saw an animal on the ice. Started creeping up on him. I was crawling a long time, froze my hands and knees. But just as I was about to aim – I see that it's a tery'ky. He popped his eyes out at me, and he's grinning. I bolted to my feet and ran out of there. Ran all the way back to the settlement, without a rest."

"So what did he look like, then?" asked John.

"Smooth. Completely naked. Only a thin reddish fur on his body . . . Horrifying to look at."

They heard a splash. A whiskered head came up through the water's smooth, still surface.

"Shhh." Toko took aim. "Don't you shoot. I'll do it."

John lowered the muzzle of his Winchester.

A lakhtak was rapidly approaching shore. Evidently, he was intending to climb on the ice and warm himself under the spring sunshine. Two smooth waves radiated from the sides of the whiskered head. John was amazed at his speed. The beast was very close when the shot rang out. The bullet hit his head. Death was instantaneous, but sheer inertia still propelled the bearded seal to the shoreline.

Toko grabbed a light boat hook and threw himself onto the edge of the icy escarpment. He tried to maneuver the lakhtak onto the metal hook, but it turned out to be missing just a bit of reach, the length of an index finger. Toko bent over the edge of the ice barrier, hanging over the water. He had almost managed to reach the seal and was about to lunge forward to hook the carcass, when, all of a sudden, he was sliding down the ice, and a loud crashing crack and a fountain of spray, he fell into the sea. And immediately went under. Surfacing, his face contorted in terror as he made ungainly attempts to stay afloat.

Remembering that the none of Chukchi could swim at all, John rushed to the icy edge, thrusting out to the drowning man the first thing that came to hand – a Winchester.

Toko caught the faceted barrel and grabbed it tight. The sharp foresight cut into his palm, keeping his hand from slipping.

John made a supreme effort and, pulling backwards, dragged Toko halfway up. His water-logged clothes streaming, the not-so-tall and certainly not portly Toko became remarkably heavy. Toko bent over the edge of the ice-shelf. John felt easier. He looked down at his hands, and the hairs on the back of his neck stood up: slowly, the thick hide loop that had been sewn onto his leather-covered stump was sliding down . . . But Toko was almost completely on top of the ice. John shifted the whole of the weight to his left hand, where the leather ring held fast, and tried to move his right hand further up, behind the trigger.

And then a gunshot rang out! John snapped around, jolted, not comprehending that the Winchester had fired in his own hands. When the recognition pierced his brain, and his eyes registered a spreading crimson stain under Toko's limp form, he couldn't hold back a terrified scream.

"Toko! Toko! Was it really my Winchester?"

"You hit me," Toko moaned quietly. He let go of the gun's barrel, and his body began a slow descent toward the sea, leaving a wide blood trail on the ice.

John lunged forward and grabbed Toko's kamleika with his teeth, pulling him away from the edge. Making sure that there was no more danger of falling in, John turned Toko over on his back.

His face was leeched of color and deathly pale. Slowly, painfully, Toko opened his eyes and his dry lips whispered:

"The blood is leaving me . . ."

John moved his eyes to the wound. Ringed with a large bloody stain, a dark hole rent the kamleika. It was not very big, not even a finger's breadth. Blood gushed from it in uneven spurts.

"Close it with snow . . . Snow dipped in water . . ."

John threw himself into gathering the meager remains of gray unmelted snow. He scraped up snow with his stumps and packed it over the wound. Carefully cutting open the kamleika and kukhlianka, he laid Toko's chest bare. The snow, quickly saturated with blood, was melting. Then John pulled off his kamleika, tore it into wide strips with his teeth, and tried to wind them tightly around Toko's chest.

The wounded man was groaning quietly, without opening his eyes. Finished with the bandaging, John leaned close to Toko's face and asked:

"How are you doing?"

"Cold, and I'm thirsty . . ."

John put a handful of snow into the open mouth.

"How am I going to get you home?"

"Leave me here, go get the sled," Toko managed.

"No, I won't leave you."

"Sson, you're not to blame. It could happen to anyone. It's not your fault."

John looked at the lakhtak stretched out nearby with hatred, as though the animal were responsible, and then an idea came to him like a lightning bolt:

"Toko! I can drag you back on the lakhtak skin!"

No time to waste, John took out his knife, stuck it into the holder loop and fell to skinning the carcass. He left a layer of blubber with the sealskin, so that the wounded man would not feel the hard ice.

"Careful now," Toko cautioned, "Don't tear the skin."

John had never had to butcher a kill before. He was soon covered in blood. Finally he pried the lakhtak hide from the body, and rolled the skinned carcass to one side. Carefully he lifted Toko onto the spread-out sealskin, wrapped the ends around him and stitched it closed, using a piece of leather thong from his akyn.

Putting on his snowshoes, so that the torbasses' soles wouldn't skid on the ice, John secured the harness around himself and set off for the shore.

He was hurrying but, for the wounded man's sake, went around the knots of ice and jutting cracks, trying to step only over smooth, even ice. At first glance, you might have thought that nothing extraordinary had happened: just a returning hunter, dragging a downed lakhtak behind him. From time to time John halted and went back to Toko.

"How are you feeling?"

"Not bad," Toko tried to smile. "Put some more snow in my mouth. Even better, chip off a bit of ice with your knife. I am cold . . . and thirsty . . ."

"Just hold on," John told him, hacking at the ice, "only a little left to go until we get to the shore."

The sun was low overhead. Ice hummocks, shoreline crags, and men threw long blue shadows.

At moments it seemed to John that his heart was about to burst from his chest. It was thumping somewhere close to his gullet, there wasn't enough air – but John couldn't stop to rest. There was not a single coherent thought in his head, only a strange and senseless phrase that beat at him without cease:

"I killed a whale! . . . I killed a whale! . . . I killed a whale!"

Slowly, the shoreline neared. There they were – the Sacred Whale Jaws . . .

"I killed a whale! I killed a whale!"

It suddenly seemed to John that Toko was dead. Franticly, he threw off the harness and bent over the wounded man. John's own breathing was loud and labored, his eyes swimming with tears and salty perspiration. Then he pressed his lips close to Toko's lips. They were warm, and even trembled.

With renewed strength, John pulled the makeshift sled. He didn't feel the harness strap cut through his kukhlianka. The yarangas came into view. From this distance they did not look like human dwellings, more like a configuration of enormous boulders. But already John could tell which yaranga belonged to whom, and even see its inhabitants with his mind's eye.

He could see Pyl'mau's eyes, Orvo's face, rough as though hewn from dark stone, Armol's narrow piercing eyes . . . He could even imagine the hunters, gathering by Toko's yaranga, passing the binoculars from hand to hand . . .

But it was his gun that fired, and his bullet that is lodged in Toko's breast! If Toko died, it was far from certain what vengeance the people of Enmyn would wreak on the foreigner. A life for a life – that law is not restricted to savages. In a civilized society it is dressed in the form of law. True, a court of law would consider the extenuating circumstances that lessened the accused man's crime. It does happen that the defendant is cleared of wrongdoing. But John didn't know what kind of court the Chukchi had, or whether they had one at all. And if Toko died, there would be no one to corroborate John's story.

MacLennan halted once more.

Toko was breathing, he even opened his eyes halfway and again asked for some ice.

"We're almost there," John crooned to him, gently placing slivers of ice into his mouth. "We're almost there. You'll tell them it was an accident, right? You'll tell them?"

Toko closed his eyes, exhausted.

"Why don't you answer?" John shook the man by his shoulders, unconscious that he was causing him pain.

Toko moaned and opened his eyes.

"It was an accident? Right?"

Toko's eyes were looking straight into the sky. They were still alive, but already they were seeing another world, a world amazing in that it was just the same familiar one, with all his friends and near ones. Everything was the same here – people's faces, and their conversations, and the food, of which there was plenty. But the main thing was that there was no sadness on the people's faces in this other world; they knew nothing of hunger, backbreaking labor, suffering, cold and pain. There was only one drawback – there was not much water here, and it was the only thing that people treasured. But since it was mainly sea hunters who lived here, they were used to thirst and did not suffer much, making do with whatever water fell to their share . . .

Sensing that something terrible and irreparable was taking place behind his back, John was not watching his path now, heading straight for the yarangas. He climbed the mounds of ice and even attempted to run over the flat stretches of ice. He was sobbing aloud, howling and groaning, swallowing sweat mixed with tears, and still the words hammered in his head:

"I killed a whale! I killed a whale!"

The crowd by the side of the yaranga was very close now, but he couldn't make out the faces, only the wall of mouths that shouted at him:

"You have killed your brother only because he is not like you! . . ."

12

When the small figure of the hunter and his kill appeared among the ice-hummocks, everyone who was standing by Toko's yaranga was surprised at seeing only one person and wondered where the other had gone.

Orvo put the binoculars to his face and took a long time studying the hunter's walk.

"That's Sson coming," he said with certainty, handing the binoculars to Armol', who stood beside him.

"Looks like he's dragging a lakhtak," Armol' concluded, passing the binoculars to Tiarat.

"But why is he alone?"

"Looking at him from here, you wouldn't know it was a white man coming," Armol' remarked, and it was impossible to tell whether he meant it as compliment or as a jibe.

"A man, whatever he is, white or dark, gets used to anything," Orvo replied, and, with a graceful, almost offhand gesture that he'd picked up from the captains of whaling schooners, raised the ancient heavy binocular eyepieces to his face.

There are times when the vigil for a returning hunter lasts for hours, but it is for his wife that the waiting is longest. She begins to wait from the moment the outer door of the yaranga shuts behind her husband. It's only at midday that, busy with household chores, she is distracted from the thought of the hunter out on the fickle sea ice; but by evening, when the early winter twilight falls to earth, her waiting becomes tinged with worry, a worry that only waxes to its full strength by the time her eyes alight on a small figure winding its way among the ice hummocks. And regardless of weather – cruel frost, blizzard – the woman stands by the threshold of her home and awaits her husband. In the summer days, when the men take the hide boats out to sea, all the women congregate by the shore, silent and motionless, as though carved of stone, casting their eyes over the ocean's vast expanse.

The best part of waiting is when your eyes find the hunter coming home with a kill. Filled with a joyful trepidation, the woman wonders what prize her husband is bringing home, her heart swells with pride, and she catches the admiring glances of her cohorts, admiration laced with envy.

As soon as Pyl'mau was certain that the man among the ice hummocks was Sson, and that he was coming with booty, she returned to the chottagin and filled a ladle with water – to wet the dead animal's face, and to assuage the hunter's thirst.

Now John was recognizable with the naked eye. Only there was something unusual in his gait. Orvo was scrutinizing him intently, but couldn't make out what the matter was.

"Sson is walking strangely," the old man finally couldn't keep from saying out loud.

"Maybe he got sick, and Toko sent him home," Armol' replied.

"Sick people don't walk that fast," Orvo countered and, peering at him again, added:

"Too fast, if anything."

"Gone crazy with joy for bagging a lakhtak," Armol' conjectured. "When I got my first nerpa, I danced all the way from open water to the settlement."

"Sson isn't such a fool as you," came the voice of the usually taciturn Tiarat.

John had already crossed from the ice onto the snow-covered shore and was making for the yarangas. He was without his kamleika, his head bare. At first it was the expression on his face and his disarrayed clothing that caught everyone's attention, and then their eyes were drawn toward the strange lakhtak . . . In place of the animal's muzzle was something resembling a human head, and the human head wore Toko's hood. Pyl'mau noticed it first, and then the others did too. They all froze.

Maybe John had killed a tery'ky . . .

And only the moment when John was face to face with the people, only then did everyone see that it was Toko, wrapped in lakhtak hide.

John dragged him over to where Pyl'mau stood and fell to his knees before her, muttering in a jumble of Chukchi and English:

"It's not my fault! As God is my witness, I was trying to save him! . . . The gun went off by accident . . ."

Pyl'mau listened to this unintelligible speech, and a thin stream of cold clean water poured from the ladle and onto her dead husband's face.

"He'll tell you himself that it wasn't my fault!" John was screaming, as he crawled at Pyl'mau's feet. "He promised me he would tell you!"

Orvo unsheathed a sharp knife, cut the lashings, pried open the sealskin and there was Toko's dead body, smeared with lakhtak blubber and blood, his chest bound with John's torn kamleika.

"He won't be saying anything anymore," said Orvo in a strange, alien voice and instructed: "Carry the body inside the yaranga."

John was pushed aside, as though he were no longer a person. He sat in the snow, surrounded by the curious dogs, and watched them gently lift Toko from the sealskin, Orvo giving quiet and efficient instructions, Pyl'mau, her face stony with grief, silently throwing wide the door and holding it open until her husband's body was swallowed up in the murk of the chottagin. And over it all – a deep blue stillness and the boundless space all around, and in the vaulting sky a flock of birds, making for distant islands.

John dragged his feet back toward the shore. He made a few steps with difficulty: His legs were like cotton wool, and he felt so weary that he was ready to stretch out right in the snow. He sat down on a rock. The cold reached down to his heart. Though there was barely a touch of frost, John was shivering. Each time someone came out of the yaranga, he would hunch his head between his shoulders. He did not doubt that he hadn't much longer to live. The fear turned to cold, his heart became a piece of ice, his reason wanted to put an end this torturous waiting.

He could hear muffled voices through the yaranga's thin walls. There was no crying or wailing, as though nothing unusual had happened. People passed John and avoided looking at him: He had already ceased to exist for them . . . How cruelly life had dealt with him! First the misfortune with his hands, then Hugh Grover's betrayal, and now this . . . But why him? There are thousands, millions of happy people in the world – wouldn't it have been more just to apportion the burdens equally to everyone? There would be no one who was unfortunate or portionless, and a little bitterness would not do anyone harm. Overwhelmed by fatigue and self-pity, John wept. He sniffled loudly, smearing the tears all over his face – and the dogs watched him curiously and yawned.

The sun had gone down. The unmelted snow and the rocks, frozen through during the long winter, radiated cold. Far from abating, his trembling got worse. Some fellow came out of Toko's yaranga, carrying a walrus-hide basin. He headed for the meat pit, where he moved aside the walrus shoulder that served as a lid and hooked a kymgyt. As the man rammed his axe into the kopal'khen, John's stomach twisted in hunger. Unable to bear it any longer, he stumbled to the pit and begged a piece. The man silently held out a kopal'khen and, greedily, John sank his teeth into the frozen, slightly bitter fat. He gobbled the kopal'khen and looked at the man hopefully. A look that dogs give their masters.

"Sson!"

It was Orvo's voice. The old man motioned John closer.

"Now is the time of judgement," John thought, and wearily followed him inside the yaranga. He halted by the threshold. Orvo took him by the shoulder and led him into the chottagin. His eyes were still adjusting to the semi-darkness. He could hear a muffled conversation and the logs crackling over the fire; his nostrils detected the smell of boiled nerpa meat.

Once his vision had adjusted, John beheld almost the entire population of Enmyn inside the chottagin. People were sitting on whale spines, on the wooden headrests. Some had simply ranged themselves on the earthen floor, with deer hides spread underneath. The polog's front wall had been raised, and Toko's body was visible, laid out inside the sleeping chamber. They had already dressed the deceased in funerary garments: a white kukhlianka, white kamuss torbasses. The kukhlianka was belted, and a hunting knife hung from the belt.

"Now we'll be asking questions of the deceased," Orvo said, addressing John. "White people are unfamiliar with this rite, so I will tell you a little about it . . . Listen now. We believe that there is a world where the living cannot enter. In order to be admitted to that world you have to stop living. And this world is so far away, that those who go there will never return. A regular person can't go back and forth between the two. Only the great shamans. We have none among us. But Toko is still with us, even though he doesn't speak or breathe. And he hears us, and is ready to tell us his wishes. Look here."

Orvo showed John a smoothly polished stick, not very long and resembling the handle of an old spade.

"I'll place the end of this stick under Toko's head, and will question him. If he says 'yes,' the head is easily raised up. If he doesn't agree, the head becomes heavier, and is almost impossible to lift," Orvo explained. "There was nobody else with you. The only witness is going to tell us about it himself . . ."

John and Orvo walked into the polog and sat on each side of the deceased. Toko lay there as though asleep. His face was clear and serene, eyes lightly shut, as if he were about to open them. And from the thought that never again would he open them and look at John in his own inimitable way, nor open his lips to quietly call out: "Sson!," silent tears began rolling down John's cheeks, and his heart ached.

With a grave and serious air, Orvo slid the end of the stick under the dead man's head, and left the middle of it over his own knee, making a kind of lever.

"Bear you any ill will toward those you leave behind?" Orvo quietly inquired, and waited. Then he touched the stick, and the head rose easily. "Do you want to take anyone with you? Relatives, friends?" The old man strained to lift, but the head remained rooted to the floor. "Taking the Winchester with you?"

Toko made clear his assent. He also wished to take along all his hunting gear.

"Makes sense," Orvo remarked out loud, "he's still quite young, and he doesn't want to sit idle even there. Bear you any ill will toward the man called Sson?" Orvo asked loudly enough for all those gathered inside the chottagin to hear.

John's heart stood still. The strange thing was, he believed; believed in everything that Orvo was doing and did not doubt for a moment that Toko was really answering the questions put to him.

John peered into Toko's face. What do you say? Will Orvo understand you correctly, will he make no mistake interpreting your answer?

The stick jerked, and Toko's head stayed motionless. For a moment John thought that the dead man half-opened his eyes and gave him an encouraging nod.

John sighed heavily.

"It wasn't my fault," he said to Orvo. "Toko fell into the water, and I was trying to help him. The Winchester was what was nearest, I held the barrel out to him. But these" – he motioned to the attachments sewn into his stump – "caught the trigger . . ."

"I already know everything," Orvo answered him impatiently. "You can leave the polog. You're free to go."

John returned to the chottagin and looked around. Pyl'mau was tending the fire. Her face seemed to be carved of stone, and noiseless tears rolled down her cheeks like streams over mountainsides. Little Yako, frightened by all that was happening and unable to comprehend any of it, stood by her side. He sniffled from time to time, his whole body quivering, and then his mother would pass her hand over his head, calming and consoling the small boy.

"Lower the curtain," Orvo instructed.

The deerskins, skillfully sewn together by Pyl'mau's hand, concealed Orvo and the deceased. The old man stayed inside the polog with Toko for a long while. When he came out, his face was serene and his eyes shone with joy – wholly inappropriate, to John's mind, in such a time of sorrow.

"Toko lived honorably, and it's with honor that he leaves us," Orvo solemnly declared, and his voice was drowned in the women's wails, as though everyone had been waiting to hear the words. Pyl'mau, too, began to sob. She was saying something, but John couldn't bear to listen; he went outside.

Although Orvo's words had brought relief, the sense of guilt did not leave him.

The sun was beginning a new circuit around the sky when Orvo found him, and gently told him:

"Go sleep a bit. We'll be burying Toko early, as soon as the sun rises over the cape."

John made his way through the crowded chottagin to his own little room and collapsed on his bed fully dressed. He was afraid he wouldn't be able to fall asleep, but as soon as he closed his eyes, he fell into a deep, dreamless slumber.

Orvo awoke him at the appointed time.

A sled, loaded for a long journey, was already waiting by the threshold. It held the Winchester without its case, an akyn, leather strips for towing the dead seals, a pipe, a light walking staff and a boat hook. Only the snowshoes were missing.

Orvo, Armol', Tiarat, and Gatleh carried the dead man out and laid him on the sled. Then Orvo gestured for John to come, and harnessed him to the sled next to himself. The other men also put on the harness, and the dolorous procession set out across the snow-covered lagoon.

The snow was blinding, the sun broiled them, the runners quietly rustled over the grainy snow, and no one said a word. Only the loud, heavy breathing of the people bringing the dead man melted into the thick tense silence.

John tried to fall into step with Orvo. For him, this journey was an echo of yesterday's, when he was hauling the dying Toko on the lakhtak skin, preparing to die himself. He was looking back on that day, on himself, and a strange emotion seeped into him. John was frightened of the feeling, tried to push it away, but to no avail. The thought even crossed his mind that he might have gone mad with all that had happened. He had the sense that yesterday's John was a completely different person, so much a stranger to the one of today, that he could regard that person and judge him as he would a stranger. Today John looked at his former self with contempt and pity: the shameful weakness, the cowardice, the animal fear of death – all that belonged to another now. Even yesterday's fatigue had gone without a trace: He breathed easily, his head was clear, and only his heart bore the sadness of losing a loved one, a sadness that was filled with light, like the inchoate morning.

The Chukchi burial grounds were on the opposite shore of the lagoon. On a level hilltop, orderly rows of stones marked the dwelling places of those who had departed this world. Of many, only the bleached skulls and bones remained. The graves were strewn with spears, harpoon tips, shards of porcelain teacups . . . The snow had already melted from the cemetery site, and it was difficult to haul the sled over the bare rocky soil. Finally, using markers known only to himself, Orvo chose a place and came to a stop. Quickly, they gathered some stones and built a symbolic barrier around the dead man, whom they had taken off the sled and laid out on the ground, facing east.

Then something incomprehensible to John took place. Tiarat started to break apart the sled with his hand-ax, while Orvo used a sharp knife to cut the clothes off Toko's body, leaving him naked, and then gathered the strips in a pile and buried them under some large stones. The fragments of the sled were also neatly gathered together. On the outside of the barrier, Orvo placed the Winchester – having first bent its barrel, the spear with a broken tip, and the boat hook and walking stick that he'd broken in half. Catching John's mystified glance, Orvo explained:

"That's the custom . . . We broke the sled so that he doesn't decide to use it to come back. But the gun and the sticks we break so that bad people don't get at them. We didn't break them before . . . It was when the white men started coming to our shores, they took to robbing even the dead. They'd take the hide boat shells, the spears, the bows and arrows . . . See, there aren't any arrows left around, or bows – your kind have taken them all . . ."

Having performed the funeral rites, the men lined up next to Orvo. The old man muttered some incantations and then shook his clothing over the dead man, saying:

"Toko, take away all my future misfortunes, sickness and hardship . . ."

The others followed his example.

"Go on, Sson, you do the same," Orvo called.

John had no choice but to obey.

They took a different way back. Orvo was carrying a small plank from the dead man's wrecked sled in his hands.

Tiarat, Armol', and the other men paced ahead. Orvo told John to walk with him, and fell behind a little.

"I need to say something to you, Sson," the old man began, looking straight into his eyes. "When I was alone in the polog with Toko, he told me something important, and asked that I tell you . . . Listen, we have this custom: When a woman loses the man who provides for her children, it's up to his brothers and friends to take care of her. Usually one of her brothers-in-law will marry her. Toko had no one – he was an orphan. You were his closest friend. I'm not pushing you, I'm only telling you the dead man's wishes. He wanted you to take care of Pyl'mau and little Yako. I've said my piece, and you think about it."

Orvo quickened his step and caught up with those at the front.

John walked behind them, and his thoughts were lucid and full of joy. Stay here forever? Forget, and never again recall the past? And why not? These people had been so good to him, and had shown the kind of magnanimity he would not have expected in the world he came from. Certainly, the John of the day before could never have reached such a decision, but today's . . .

John caught up with Orvo, touched his shoulder and quietly said:

"I understand everything. I agree."

13

Right by the shoreline, the ice had broken off. Only a narrow band across the lagoon remained. A stormy south wind had pushed the ice floes far beyond the horizon. In the mornings, Orvo would go off to the high promontory and scan the sea through his binoculars, hoping to spot the first walrus herds. Two hide boats stood by, equipped with stacked oars and folded sails, with sharp harpoons.

Armol' was the commander of one hide boat, and Orvo of the other. The old man put John on his team, telling him that he was to stand at the prow as the gunner.

"After what happened, I couldn't touch a weapon," John made to refuse.

"That's nonsense you're speaking," Orvo calmly told him. "How are you going to feed Pyl'mau and little Yako? Or do you intend to beg from others, and live off someone else? Sure, you can manage like that, but for a man it's a shameful thing."

In answer, John only sighed: There really was no other way. At first, after Toko's death, the yaranga's inhabitants had lived off the reserves. Neither Pyl'mau nor John had yet recovered from the trauma they'd experienced, and they barely spoke to one another.

John spent most of the time in his tiny room. When he couldn't lie still anymore, he would go off into the springtime tundra and wander aimlessly over springy tussocks, spooking flocks of sandpipers and molting partridges. Before, from aboard the ship, the tundra had seemed to him a wasteland. In reality it was filled with life, and some of the small valleys were so picturesque that they touched even John's frozen heart. During these walks, he was surprised to note the beginnings of new ideas in his mind. He would get to thinking that the yaranga should be rebuilt, made more spacious, so that it was more comfortable for both Pyl'mau and himself, John, who had kept many of the habits of his former life. There were moments when he recalled the past. With time John became used to treating those memories with a firm hand, and willed his melancholy back to his subconscious . . . He knew now that his only concern was to build himself a life here, a life among people he'd not too long ago held in contempt, hated and feared.

The day came when Orvo announced the appearance of the first walruses on the ice. Now they could go to the hunt.

Early in the morning, Orvo knocked on the door of John's room. John rose, dressed himself and came out into the chottagin. A fire was already blazing inside, hung with a cauldron. A sooty black kettle leaned sideways on the hot coals, snorting steam clouds over the flame. Pyl'mau was busy over a wooden dish, neatly slicing up a cold snack with her pekul'.* A washbasin had been prepared for John. Old Orvo sat on the headrest log, and observed them silently.

John washed his face, dried it with a clean rag, and looked at Pyl'mau. Something was different about her face today, but it wasn't the look in her eyes, and it wasn't a new hairdo. When it came to John in a flash, he had to suppress a smile – Pyl'mau had washed her face today!

"We'll be hunting around Irvytgyr," Orvo was businesslike. "Walruses go there in waves. We'll set up on the slope in a tent. Aivanalin† live down in Irvytgyr, a cheerful people. Good singers. If we're lucky, we'll hear them and see their dancing."

* *Pekul'* – a woman's knife.
† *Aivanalin* – Eskimos.

Pyl'mau had made new kemyget* for John, with the skin of that same lakhtak that John had used to bring home her dead husband. She put all the necessaries into a capacious leather satchel – an extra set of nerpa-skin mittens, chizhi, a rattling cape of walrus intestines that had dried out over the winter . . . Many of the items had belonged to Toko.

John took the Winchester off the wall, and inspected the barrel – the metal shone . . . Pyl'mau turned her back, and pointedly busied herself with packing dry-grass torbass insoles into the leather satchel.

"It's time," Orvo said, touching John's shoulder.

John shouldered the bag, put the Winchester in its case, and stopped uncertainly by the threshold. He should say good-bye to Pyl'mau: After all, he'd be gone for many days, possibly even a month. But how is it done among Chukchi? And anyway, do they make farewells at all, and what would be the correct procedure? When the late Toko used to go hunting, he didn't even look back at his wife. But Toko would have been leaving the yaranga for a few hours, and now . . . He should say something to her.

"I'll be right there," John told Orvo, and went inside his room. For some strange reason, he picked up a pocket watch, long stopped, his notepad, and a pencil.

Orvo was still hanging around the chottagin. John quickly walked up to Pyl'mau, took her right hand between his stumps, pressed it, and quietly said: "Wait for me."

"Come on, let's go," Orvo said, and walked out of the yaranga.

The hunters were already assembled by the hide boats. Joining them, John's appearance matched theirs exactly. The same kamleika, the same nerpa-skin trousers, tucked into kemyget.

On Orvo's signal, the hunters picked up the hide boats by their sides and started to drag them over the icy band that separated them from sea-water. Carefully they lowered the vessels onto the green water and got

* *Kemyget* – high waterproof torbasses.

inside, each by his own oar. John didn't know where to put himself, until Orvo pointed to a seat next to him, by the stern oar.

The helmsman pushed off from the ice-bound shore, the long oars in their leathern rowlocks leapt up over the hide boat and then disappeared underwater. A crowd of people were standing by the shore to see them off: women, old people, children. John hadn't noticed any particular leave-taking ceremony, as though the hunters were only going to the other shore of the lagoon for firewood, back in half an hour. John picked out Pyl'mau, standing in the crowd. Little Yako was beside her, holding on to his mother's skirts.

As they came out into the open sea, they raised sails and the hide boat sailed forth with speed, noisily parting the waves.

On their portside ranged the craggy shore of Chukotka, patched here and there with the remnants of winter snow. The sea had moved right up to the shoreline, utterly swallowing up the fast-ice shelf that had seemed indestructible.

The hunters talked quietly among themselves.

Orvo was telling John about walruses:

"Walrus is everything to our people. He gives us food and grease for lamps, feeds the dogs all winter. We use walrus hides to cover our yarangas, stretch them over the hide boats. Here, these thick leather lashings are walrus skin too. We make capes from their intestines, and in the old days, when the Chukchi didn't know metal, we made arrow and spear points from walrus tusk. Used to stretch dried walrus stomach over a drum, the skin, stretched nice and tight, rattles enough to move the air – and a person's voice that beats against the drum gets stronger and carries far . . .

"This is how we hunt. When the walruses are sleeping on the ice, you have to be very quiet, so as not to startle them. It's best when there's a small wind, then you can use the sail to get near them. They're light sleepers, walruses, they can hear a single oar splashing from afar. We get in close, close enough to kill the beast for certain. Otherwise he'll get away, dive underwater. You've got to shoot under the left shoulderblade, right in the heart. Because a walrus's head is hard, a bullet doesn't always crack it . . . This is how we go at one that's in the water. The helmsman is the lookout, or I am. As soon as we see a herd, or a lone one, we go after him with full sail and oars. Walrus is a fleet sort of beast, sometimes he's very hard to catch. The marksmen stand up and try to get him in their sights. Then you can't really choose, it's only his head above the water. A wounded one can't slip away as quick. Then the hide boat comes closer, and a hunter throws his harpoon. And that's how it's done."

"I won't be able to harpoon – that means I'll have to be a shot," John concluded.

"That's right," Orvo gave him a smile.

At the close of the first day, they made camp on a sandy beach. They boiled a nerpa picked up on the way and, having eaten their fill, went to sleep in a cramped tent.

John awoke early, and while his companion slept, walked up and down the beach. He was astonished at the amount of flotsam. There were shards of wooden planks, enormous logs, pieces of ships' panels with traces of metal rivets.

Returning to the tent, John cheerfully announced to Orvo: "There's enough wood here to build a real house, a big one!"

"When we're done with the walrus hunt, we'll bring down as many logs as you need," Orvo replied. "Make yourself the kind of house you like."

"Great idea!" John enthused.

A favorable wind drove the hide boat east. Time and again, round black nerpa heads popped out of the water, but no one was shooting: They were saving the bullets for their real prey, the walrus. Orvo asked John for a piece of paper and a pencil, then made a fairly precise outline of the coast from Enmyn to the Bering Strait.

"We've come past these promontories here," Orvo was explaining with the air of a geography teacher. "By evening we'll be in Inchovin, and then it's a stone's throw to Irvytgyr . . ."

"A ship!" the helmsman was shouting.

A large ship was slowly appearing from behind a craggy cape. It had no sails. The smokestack spewed black fumes. Orvo grabbed the binoculars and scanned the ship for a long while. John, too, was anxious to have a look but unwilling to show his impatience.

"It doesn't look like an American ship to me," Orvo said, handing John the binoculars.

It was a steamship with a special icebreaking frame around the water-line. Its name was discernable on the prow, but John couldn't make it out until it occurred to him that the letters were Russian, Cyrillic. Immediately below was the Latinate inscription: *Vaigach.**

"She's a Russian ship," said John, returning the binoculars.

Now he felt very calm, and even wondered at his own indifference. He thought coolly that had this happened a while ago, his joy would have known no bounds, as the ship's appearance would have heralded his return to the familiar, so-called civilized world.

They could discern small figures on the bridge, people pressing binoculars and spy glasses to their eyes. They were looking over at the hide boat with no less curiosity than the Chukchi did the vessel. The *Vaigach* lay adrift. The Russians were waving their hands, motioning the hide boat to come closer. Orvo turned the wheel. A rope ladder was lowered from the steamship. Orvo caught the end deftly, and started to climb, with a nod to John: "Follow me."

Struggling up the slippery, iced-over rope ladder, John stepped on deck and made greeting.

* The *Vaigach* was a Russian icebreaker steamship that was constructed in 1909 and served, together with the *Taimyr*, as the operations base for a 1910–1915 hydrographic expedition to the north Arctic Ocean. (TN)

"Yettyk!"*

"Yetti," smiled a Chukcha on board; evidently he was employed as interpreter and guide.

The ship's senior officer peered intently at John, and then remarked to the warrant officer who stood beside him:

"Seems a bit pale for a Chukcha."

"That's what I think," the officer agreed. He added:

"The shore Chukchi and the Eskimos, they've got pale faces. What with all the ships that put in at Chukotka's coastal settlements! A blond one isn't so amazing. They say there's a place by the Gulf of St. Lawrence where all the villagers are the descendants of Negroes!"

"The commander of the Russian geographical expedition wants to know the ice conditions from here to Cape Billings," the interpreter turned to Orvo.

"I can show it to you on a map," was Orvo's courteous reply.

A large hydrographical map of the northeast coast of Asia hung in the captain's wheelhouse. Orvo, handed a pointer, not only marked out ice fields but gave a forecast of their movements.

The captain, well pleased, ordered some vodka to be brought for him.

"Why is your comrade so light-skinned?" the interpreter asked.

"He's white," Orvo replied curtly, gingerly clasping a small glass filled to the brim with the fiery liquid.

"You don't say!" the interpreter was stunned, and translated Orvo's words for the captain.

The latter then addressed John in good English, asking him who he was and where he came from.

"My name is John MacLennan. I live in the Enmyn settlement. That's also where my family is. Myself, I'm from Port Hope, in Ontario, Canada."

* *Yettyk* – a greeting (literally: *You've arrived*.)

"I am sorry that we didn't receive you properly. We'll remedy that right away," the captain said, with some embarrassment, and immediately gave a string of orders in Russian.

"I thank you," John inclined his head. "We were not expecting a different welcome. When I sailed on board a Canadian ship, our treatment of the indigenous people was in no way better. A cupful of vodka in exchange for invaluable information – fit reward for a native, isn't that so?"

John bowed once more and, head held high, went back out on deck.

Orvo hung back, but John didn't wait for him; with the help of his comrades in the hide boat, he descended the rope ladder.

The old man reappeared, laden with gifts. A bottle of the bad joy-water stuck out from the roomy outer pocket of his kamleika. He tossed a share of the parcels overboard into the hide boat, so as not to drop them on his way down, and only then climbed down himself.

The Russians gathered at starboard. They were shouting something, waving their hands.

The captain appeared on the bridge, megaphone in hand. Pointing the funnel's black maw into the hide boat, he shouted in English:

"Mister MacLennan, I wish you a safe journey and good hunting! If we stop by Enmyn, we'll look in on your family. Until we meet again, when we sail back from Wrangel Island!"

In answer, John waved his right stump.

The hunters pushed off and raised their sail.

In addition to the bottle of vodka, the Russians had given Orvo three packets of tobacco leaves, five bricks of tea, a splendid Sheffield-steel knife and a set of beveled sewing needles. Orvo rifled through his kukhlianka pocket and dug out a bottle of aged Scottish whisky.

"The captain told me to give this to you," said Orvo, passing the bottle to John.

"Thanks," John replied, "but this prize belongs to all of us. Isn't that right?"

"You speak as a luoravetlan!"* Orvo smiled, adding the Scotch to the pile of gifts.

The Inchovins greeted their Enmyn visitors heartily. They were about to lead the hunters to their yarangas, but Orvo declared that his troop would be bedding down inside their own tent that night.

"It's just that all your men are already there – the place we're traveling to," he mirthfully explained. "Wouldn't want anything to happen to your women."

True enough, only the women and old people had stayed behind in Inchovin. Late that evening, a blaze lit up the shore while guests and hosts alike clustered around the fire. They drank tea, strong and black, the Scotch whisky and vodka. Unused to it, everyone was quickly inebriated. The tobacco pipes, generously filled by the Russians, did not go cold. Some were trying to sing, others conducted endless conversations, muddled in both word and thought.

John felt light-headed, everyone around him seemed delightful. He was clasping Orvo, and prodding him:

"Now tell me honestly, when you talked to Toko, when he was dead, you made up the answers yourself? Right?"

Orvo gave him a somber look and said, crossly:

"You shouldn't doubt what happened!"

John had not expected such an answer. He'd been sure that Orvo would confess, in a friendly manner: "Well, yes, I did make it all up. Sorry about that, but that's what happened." Yet the old man's solemn face knocked John back. He couldn't say anything, except propose a toast to good fortune in the coming hunt.

"Still, I just have to know," John dived in again, after a sizeable gulp of alcohol burned the wind out of him. "You were unsure of me, right? You thought like this: A white man can never really appreciate the worth of our kindness and magnanimity. He ought to be punished. And so you still

* *Luoravetlan* – a true human being.

138

think that you've punished me, by making me responsible for feeding Pyl'mau and Yako . . . But I don't want you to think that! You should know that I'd resolved to do it even before you asked me. That decision eased my suffering, made me feel like a human being again. And I'll tell you frankly, I was afraid of meeting up with the whites on that ship. But see, I've passed that test, I've even surprised myself . . ."

"People who live in cold climes must keep warm by kindness," Orvo spoke softly in reply. "I think that is how every person should be. Kindness – it's the same as having a head, a nose, a pair of feet . . . There are many nations living on the earth. Each of their people carries a seed of suspicion toward those not of their own tribe. Oftentimes, they won't even see the people of another tribe as real human beings. You think that the Chukchi people don't do this? It happens. I don't know whether its good or bad, but each Chukcha is sure, deep down, that it's he who is living the right way, that there is no language better than the Chukchi, and that nowhere in the world is there such a person as him. We call ourselves luoravetlan; our speech is luoravetlan – the true language; even our shoes are lygiplekyt – true footwear . . . Some people, back at Enmyn, they had only contempt for you – until you proved that even without hands, you could feed yourself. We believed in you . . . But your own tribesmen are still very far from deserving to be called luoravetlan. I lived a long time among white people, and I know that even between themselves they can't come to agreement; as for us, they don't see us as people at all. Your folk are well-known for being like that. True, true, it's easier for the whites not to consider us as people. You have power: guns, big ships, the many strange devices you're so canny at making. But your arrogance – that's the evil that can destroy you in the end."

"Why tell me all this, Orvo? Or have you forgotten that I'm a white man, too? It would be far too simple, if everything hinged merely on the color of a person's skin," John said, and walked away from the fire.

14

The sun-bright nights in the Bering Strait left the hunters utterly exhausted. John had lost all count of days spent afloat. He became accustomed to bedding down for the night atop a drifting ice floe, he butchered walrus, knocked the tusks out of walrus heads, ate raw liver, drank bitter brew and fought to stay awake. His eyes grew inflamed from staring at the glinting seawater, his skin became as hard and brown as that of his hide boat-mates. Only his hair remained as fair as ever, and the strands of gray he'd earned that winter were barely visible. The Enmyn hunters had made a store of walrus meat on a large ice sheet that sloped into the sea. They buried the walrus hides, with their layers of blubber, the nerpa carcasses, and the leather bladders with rendered fat in the snow.

Once in a while, they would camp on the shore among a multitude of tents belonging to all the hunters that had gathered from every part of the Chukotka peninsula.

Those that didn't have tents slept underneath their hide boats. There was a single wooden motorboat belonging to some wealthy Eskimo, and it looked strange among the hide-covered vessels.

On misty and inclement days, dozens of fires puffed smoke into the sky. The hunters paid one another visits, sharing news and tobacco, partaking of tea. The Russians' gifts quickly disappeared, and now Orvo had to mix tobacco with wood shavings and carefully collect the nicotine remains in his pipe.

The Aivanalin settlement was laid out on the steep slope of a mountain that veered sharply down to the strait. The dwellings themselves were cut into the cliff face, their doors facing toward the sea and the sunrise. The settlement's streets were terraced, one underneath the other, and steps hacked out of the mountain served as pedestrian lanes.

At the edge of the little town, in a little plaza strewn with enormous, table-like flat rocks, the Aivanalin would hold evenings of song. They sang into the wind with slightly hoarse voices, would sound the drums, and the noise of their merrymaking traveled far, mixing with the cry of the birds at their rookeries, the crashing of the waves and the roars of walruses, passing by in the mists.

John toured the Aivanalin dwellings, learning about their daily lives. Though their hunting devices and hide boats were almost identical to those of the Chukchi, the inner design of Aivanalin homes and the way they were set out, was somewhat different; their pologs were smaller, and some of them contained many items of foreign provenance. John even came across a big alarm clock, ticking loudly, inside one of the dwellings. Excited and pleased, he tried to set his watch by it, but soon realized that the clock hands were indicating a strange sort of time. The alarm clock was an exotic ornament, like one of those Indian totems that were so favored by Toronto intellectuals for decorating their homes.

The owner of the dwelling turned out to be a man with a certain degree of education. He spoke good English and, to John's surprise, offered his hand in greeting.

"How do you find our village?" the Aivanalin asked courteously, introducing himself as Tatmirak.

"Frankly, I wouldn't like to find myself on these steep paths in the middle of a snowstorm," John answered.

"It's all right, you get used to it," Tatmirak smiled condescendingly. "When our children first visit a plains village, they're uncomfortable and complain that it's hard to walk . . . Can I offer you some coffee?" Tatmirak asked suddenly. John thought he'd misheard the man.

"I wouldn't say no . . . Really . . . I've even forgotten the taste of it . . ."

Tatmirak gave an order in Aivanalin and turned back to his guest with a polite smile.

"Excuse me."

"You're well versed in the white people's habits," John remarked.

"I attended the missionary school on Crusenstern's Island," Tatmirak declared, with a shade of pride. "I can count to twenty and speak English . . . Regrettably, I didn't learn to read and write."

"Why is that?"

"There was no time. Father Patrick had me living in his house. I was to tidy the rooms, cook, and bring hot water to the metal trough where Father Patrick splashed around like a walrus each evening. There was very little time left for literacy."

A woman served them two cups of steaming aromatic coffee.

John couldn't restrain himself; he grabbed the cup and took a burning swig.

"To be honest, I became bored with it, and I came back home," Tatmirak continued his story, "got married. But I learned a lot on the American island. I realized that first of all you must have dollars. Now I have a little. I have a whaleboat with a motor . . ."

"So that's your whaleboat on the beach?" John interrupted.

"Mine," Tatmirak confirmed grandly and went on: "If you've got a head on your shoulders, an Eskimo can live as well as a white man. You've got to make friends! So now we're friends with Mr. Carpenter. He gives me merchandise, and I trade it to the Eskimos for white fox. I take my dogsled around the deer camps. Mr. Carpenter gives me a share and lets me trade with the whites myself. I can get to Nome in half a day in my whaleboat, and the price for white fox there is twenty times what Carpenter offers."

"Mr. Carpenter lives in Nome?" John asked, finishing his coffee.

"No, in Keniskun," replied Tatmirak. "Would you like me to take you there in the boat?"

"Is it far?"

"Quite close. Two hours' ride."

John told Orvo that he was going to Keniskun, to meet Mr. Carpenter.

"Get him to give you some Winchester cartridges," Orvo asked. "You can pay him with these . . ."

The old man handed him a few beautifully tanned baby reindeer skins.

Tatmirak's motorboat sped south with a roar.

The Aivanalin sat at the stern, hands firmly on the tiller.

"They told me your story," he shouted, bending closer to John. "You're a trooper, a real good lad!"

Sighting the motorboat's approach, the Keniskun Chukchi assembled on the shore. John counted fifteen or so yarangas, identical to the ones at Enmyn. A bit further on, a building quite unusual in these parts – a long-house of galvanized corrugated sheet metal – caught his eye.

A tall and sturdy man stood out from the Chukchi crowd. He wore a deerskin kukhlianka and the kind of tarpaulin hat worn by Newfoundland fishermen.

No sooner had John stepped ashore, than the man ran to him, exclaiming in English:

"Hello! I'm so pleased to see you! I've heard a lot about you, and it's delightful to find you exactly as I'd imagined you to be. Please, come with me!"

Carpenter drew John along.

"I heard rumors of you last winter. I wanted to load a dogsled and come see how you were, but business . . . I set the idea aside, 'til spring. And in the spring – well, you've seen for yourself: The natives are all at the walrus hunt, and no treasure on earth could tear them away. Even Tatmirak himself, he loses all traces of respectability once he hears that walrus bellow. It's in their blood. I've known them for fifteen years. A good people, kind, caring. It's not that they haven't got their superstitions, perhaps even some vices, but compared with what we've got in our "civilized" society, it's all child's play . . . Overall, the wisest thing is to treat them like children. Take Tatmirak. A fine fellow! He's grasped the basics of trade and commerce, with time he'll make a fine businessman, in the Bering Strait region. Speaks English, went to a school, reasons well, although at times he'll act so irrationally as to make you wring your hands. I remember once, five or so years ago, I came to see him, went into his yaranga. His polog is hung with chintz, big kerosene lamps instead of oil braziers. But on the wall, just imagine, a greasy ancient amulet, some gorgon made from walrus tusk. Next to that, an engraved portrait of Major-General Dix, torn out from *Harper's Weekly*. On top of that, there's a candle burning before the American major-general, and the general's mug is completely covered in soot. Turned out that Tatmirak set up all this japery for my benefit: he'd seen candles burning before an icon, and some praying Cossacks, in an Anadyr' church . . . Ah, and here is my humble abode!"

From the outside it looked like a regular yaranga, only twice as large. Bending his head, John entered a spacious chottagin not unlike a well-furnished living room. A south-facing window was cut into the side of the yaranga, and daylight flooded in. Close to the entrance stood a cast-iron stove, its chimney climbing up to the walrus-hide covered roof. A round table with a set of chairs stood in the middle of the chottagin, and over it hung a kerosene lamp with a glass sleeve. On the right John could see the standard Chukcha polog, and on the left a door with a carved walrus tusk handle.

"That's my wife's bedroom," said Carpenter, pointing to the polog, "and this one" he motioned with his head, "is mine."

Carpenter dragged a rather weathered armchair out of a dark corner and moved it toward John.

"Please, do sit down . . ." He clapped his hands. "Mary, Catherine, Elizabeth!"

Two winsome girls between twelve and fourteen years old poked their faces out of the polog, and then Carpenter's wife – a pretty, round-faced Aivanalin – appeared.

"My wife, Elizabeth," Carpenter said casually, and spoke to her in her language, giving instructions.

Energy seemed to radiate from Mr. Carpenter. He was a good deal past forty, but had kept a slim and boyish figure. His height, sonorous voice, the remains of fiery red hair on his head, a dense beard and thick mustache gave him the look of a man with enough stature to command respect from the local dwellers.

"Mr. Carpenter, as I understand it, you've lived here for fifteen years?" asked John.

"Fourteen and a half. I settled here in the last century," Carpenter answered and suggested in friendly tone: "Let's not stand on ceremony. In Chukcha transcription your name sounds like Sson, but what is it really?"

"John MacLennan."

"Excellent!" Bob exclaimed. "I'll call you John, and I'd be glad if you would call me Bob. Okay?"

"Okay!" John agreed.

Meanwhile, without a sound the woman was setting the table. On top of a flowered tablecloth, she laid canned sturgeon, caviar, cold seal flippers, condensed milk, marmalade, and ham in containers bearing the logo of the Chicago company Swift. She served some toast on a large plate.

"The bread, surely that's not from a can?" John couldn't refrain from asking.

"Oh, Elizabeth bakes it," said Carpenter, nonchalant. "I taught her how. We've got plenty of flour, I've had the yeast brought from Nome. We can even bake sweet rolls in our oven. If you stay for the night, Elizabeth will do her best to treat you to some."

Carpenter rose from his seat, walked over to a wall cabinet that was sealed with a small lock, and took out a bottle of Jamaican rum.

"I keep the spirits under lock and key," Bob said, pouring them glass-fuls of the aromatic liquor. "The folks around here have a fondness for strong brew. Of course, it's us, the white traders, who are to blame, but still," Bob gave him a friendly smile, "now we've got to keep the bottles locked away."

Carpenter watched John take hold of the glass with his holders, not without interest.

"Incredible!" he exclaimed. "To look at you, one would never say that you have almost no hands at all! What brilliant surgery! Like the best Melbourne clinics!"

John didn't want to talk about his hands.

"You've been to Australia?"

"I've not only been there, I was born there," Bob declared. "Where haven't I been! You could say, I've crisscrossed the world! For some time I studied in the city, but it grew tedious, and I signed up with a ship going to South America. From there I went to the States and after the States to Hawaii. Hunted fur-seal off the Commodores for a few years. Came back to the States almost a rich man but the traveler's wind drove me on. When money ran out, I tried panning for gold in Alaska. And here I met Svensson, the United States's Arctic genius. Now I'm a representative and partner of a trading company that operates on Russia's Asian coast. Married an Eskimo, got children growing up. In other words, became one of the locals."

"And in all these fifteen years, you've never gone back to the States, or back home?" John asked.

"From time to time I go to Alaska," Bob answered. "But not for long. I've grown unused to all that noise. And then – there's just so much hypocrisy and insincerity down there. I've grown unaccustomed to that too. Svensson's ships bring me all the goods I need. Believe me John, your decision to stay in Chukotka makes me very glad. We'll exchange letters! Ha-ha! The first postal communications in Russia's Arctic wilderness! . . ."

Bob Carpenter was drunk. He ordered his wife around, boasted about his daughters' good looks, and pontificated at length.

"Do the Eskimos and the Chukchi actually need Christianity?" he wondered out loud, draining his glass. "To my mind, Christianity is a religion that's exclusively for whites. And converting the savages is a waste of effort and money. Let them missionize the other whites. It's them that need the word of God, and being led to the right path . . . Listen, John, how can you drink so slowly? Don't drink much, do you? Well, give it some time living here – you'll learn so well that you'll be going through a year's supply in three months . . ."

Discovering that John did not make a good drinking partner, Carpenter called for the soup. For the first time in many long months John was using a spoon and fork. It took him some time to relearn to wield them. Suddenly John heard a clock strike. The clear ringing came from Carpenter's room. The clock struck seven times, the gongs echoing in their ears for long afterwards.

Over dessert, which consisted of canned pineapple, Bob moved his chair over to John's armchair and asked, without preamble:

"How do you mean to be employed here?"

"In what sense?" John didn't quite understand him.

"Do you intend to do some sort of business? To buy pelts? Sell American goods to the locals?"

"To be honest I hadn't thought about it," John admitted.

Carpenter gave him an incredulous look.

"When I started here," he said, "the Chukchi and the Eskimo produced almost nothing of any interest to a businessman. I spent much time and effort training them to hunt for white and red fox . . . Before, they considered white-fox fur to be good for nothing: not very sturdy or waterproof. Since they got metal, they've lost interest in walrus tusk. I managed to reignite that interest, and now the hunters don't just throw the walrus heads overboard . . ."

There was a knock at the door, and Tatmirak came into the chottagin. Now he didn't look half as smug as he had aboard his motorboat. He slunk toward the table and, in an apologetic tone, as though he were guilty of something, said:

"Weather's getting worse. We'll have to spend the night here."

"Excellent!" Carpenter exclaimed and poured him a glassful of rum.

Tatmirak licked his lips, squeezed his eyes shut and knocked back the contents. Wiping his mouth with his sleeve, he uttered in English:

"Sank you very mach!"

"All right," Carpenter waved his hand. "Go on with you! . . . Dear John," turning back to his guest, he resumed the conversation, "sooner or later you'll wish to participate in trade. There's nothing else for you to do here. There's no gold. Well, there is some, according to those in the know, but it's mighty hard to get at. Farming and cattle don't bear thinking about out here. And you can't possibly be thinking of going after walrus and seal, alongside the Chukchi and the Eskimos! Therefore, all that's open to you is commerce. I'm a man of business, and I'm offering you a place in our trade concern. The place where you're living now has potential, it's virgin territory. Once in a while it's visited by ships and their merchants, people that have nothing in common with an honest trading enterprise. They make drunkards out of the natives, then rob them blind. You'd be doing the aborigines a favor by becoming our representative. Think about it. But I warn you: There's no striking out on your own, don't forget that you're treading on Russian Imperial territory. Trading without a license has harsh penalties out here. If you're caught, you'll be sent to the bowels of Siberia, to the zinc mines. And you won't leave there in one piece . . . forgive my being so frank, but I do feel an affinity for you and just want to give you a friendly warning . . . You have until the morning to think it over. There's no hurry. But I must add that, working with us, you would make a tidy fortune . . . And now I invite you to take a bath . . ."

"A bath?"

"That's right, a bath," Bob replied with a mysterious smile. "It happens to be about two kilometers from here, but a jaunt along the shore is nothing if not pleasant."

John and Carpenter walked down the shore. Clouds covered the dour gray sky. A strong steady wind had raised some waves, and the salty spray reached as far as the two amblers. Carpenter, sucking on a cigar that had gone out, was daydreaming aloud:

"Another year or two, and I'll leave here for good. I've got a solid sum tucked away in a San Francisco bank, more than enough to live out the rest of my life in comfort. I'll buy a house in Florida, open a hotel, and live to my heart's content."

"But what about your family?" asked John. "They would find it hard to get used to a foreign land, a foreign way of life."

"Certainly," Carpenter assented, and then sighed: "A pity, but they'll have to remain here. It would be cruel, inhumane, to bring them to Florida with me, from the Arctic to the tropics. Needless to say, I'll make sure that they lack for nothing."

Two streams ran into a modest pool that had been dug out of the clean sandy soil. One of them gave off a sulphuric odor.

Undressing, John and Bob climbed into the warm and bubbling water. Carpenter was moaning with pleasure. John splashed about, washing himself, scraping off many months' worth of grime, and realizing that the hardest thing to get used to would be the lack of hot water.

A bed was waiting for him in Carpenter's sleeping chamber.

He stripped naked and rapturously stretched himself across the clean cool sheets. Falling asleep, he heard the clock strike twelve, and its last bright peal lasted into his velvety dreams.

The next day, Tatmirak's motorboat took John back to the Bering Strait. In exchange for the fawn skins, Carpenter had given him the cartridges, plus a wealth of other goods.

By midsummer, when the walrus migration had slacked, the hunters began to make their way back to their home camping grounds. The hide boats from Enmyn, too, turned homewards.

When they gained the final promontory that hid Enmyn from the eye, and they could make out the yarangas, a joyful agitation seized the hunters.

Now the hide boats were spotted from the settlement. Little figures rushed about the yarangas. People and dogs were drawn to the shore. The boys raced around as though possessed, their screams carrying as far as the hide boats that were quietly approaching at full sail.

"There's my son! How he's grown!" shouted Tiarat, the harpooner, pointing to the shore. How it was that he managed to pick out a three-year-old at such a distance remained a mystery to all but himself.

"Take a look at Enmyn," Orvo said, offering John the binoculars. "What is it, if not pure joy, coming home?"

John nodded silently, took up the binoculars and leveled them at the crowd. He didn't recognize Pyl'mau right away. She was clad in a new kamleika, her thick black hair was neatly gathered into two heavy braids that fell over her shoulders. Yako stood beside her, and chattered to her about something, pointing at the hide boat.

The boats touched shore, and dozens of hands clapped down on the prows. The hunters jumped out onto the shore. To John's surprise, there were no kisses or embraces. The most that they allowed themselves to do was pat the little ones' shoulders and exchange a few words with their wives and the old people.

John stepped off the hide boat and, feeling awkward under Pyl'mau's gaze, walked over to her, stroked little Yako's cheek and asked:

"Are you in good health?"

"I am," answered Pyl'mau, and giggled.

John became flustered and hurried to join the hunters, who were busy dragging the walrus hides and meat out onto the shore. And before that, they gave it a good rinse in the seawater.

The main part of their kill had been left on the shore of the Bering Strait, in a natural icebox. In the summer, they'd gradually bring it all back to Enmyn. But for now, the hunters had brought only the choicest parts, plus the walrus hides; those needed to be dried out, while the sun was strong and there was no rain.

Orvo stood by the boats and gave orders, deciding on where the meat should be laid. The growing mounds numbered the same as the hunters in the hide boat. All the shares were equal, except that two walrus hides and ten or so tusks lay by the side of one of the piles. John decided that this was Orvo's share, as it had been his hide boat they had sailed in.

Orvo took John by the elbow and walked him right up to that very pile. Then he nodded to the others, and each hunter stood beside the mound that looked best to him.

"But I hardly need so much," John objected. "And I worked least of all."

"Take it and don't argue," Orvo cut him off. "That's the custom. Today you were given a large share because you are only starting out in life. It's a sort of helping hand from us all, and we wish you to be a good friend to us. Instead of getting angry, you could say thank you."

John reddened and mumbled indistinctly:

"Velynkykun!"

Pyl'mau was already busy with John's share. She was cutting the meat into slabs and loading an enormous leather satchel that resembled a gigantic backpack.

Orvo called out to the men:

"Help Sson with the repal'gyt!"*

The hunters rolled up the gray walrus skins like rugs, and shouldered them. After laying them down by the yaranga's outer walls, they covered them with moss and stones to keep the dogs from getting at them.

* *Repal'gyt* – walrus hides.

Pyl'mau was lugging the meat from the shore to the meat pit in the leather sack. When John made to help her, Pyl'mau emphatically shook her head.

"People will laugh," she explained. "Look – only women carry the meat."

"Let them laugh," John waved his hand carelessly. "It's not right for a man to make a woman haul such heavy bags."

"It's not right for a man to carry the leather bags," Pyl'mau was patiently reiterating. There were tears in her voice. "It's a woman's bag."

"Just help me hoist it onto my back," John said.

The bag weighed no less than two hundred pounds. It was heavy going over the blood and blubber-slick shingle. His feet kept sliding apart, and the bag lurched from one side to the other. Only the thick leather straps prevented it from falling off completely.

John managed to haul it to the pit, dumped out the meat and sank to the ground for a bit of rest. Catching his breath, he returned to shore. Pyl'mau was sitting by the pile of meat and weeping.

"What is it, Mau?" John asked, worried. "Why are you crying? Has someone hurt you?"

"Yes, someone did," Pyl'mau responded, with a sniffle.

"Who?"

"You," Pyl'mau raised her tear-streaked face. "You're humiliating me . . ."

"But it's too heavy for you! I barely managed it myself!" said John.

"Shame is heavier to bear," Pyl'mau said, and then asked plaintively: "Go on home. I'll be there soon. Please, I'm asking you."

"All right," John agreed, and called out to the boy: "Yako, let's go home!"

Once inside the chottagin, even before he had a chance to look around, John could feel that something had changed.

The earthen floor was cleanly swept, the fire pit laid with even, close-fitting stones. Yako ran on ahead, and John heard a coppery ringing. Not far from where the hunting gear usually hung, he saw a copper washstand and basin! This was so unexpected and so wondrous that he couldn't refrain from exclaiming in Chukchi:

"Kakomei!" *

"Mam brought it from the white people's big ship," Yako explained in an important voice, as he kept on ringing the washstand's little pull-handle.

John investigated this furnishing, so unusual for a yaranga, further, and discovered a convex set of letters: *Vaigach*.

He went down to the stream, brought some water and filled the basin. When she acquired the washstand, it did not occur to Pyl'mau to ask the Russian sailors for some soap. But even without it, washing his face gave John real pleasure. Afterwards, he washed Yako's face with a little cloth; the boy was not unduly thrilled by the procedure, but nevertheless boasted to his mother as soon as she returned:

"Sson and I were washing our faces!"

Inside her own home, Pyl'mau behaved differently than on the shore. Back there, she'd barely glanced at John, but now she bustled around him, going out of her way to make him comfortable. The polog's front wall was raised, there was a little table beside the headrest log, and a white deerskin spread out in the back.

"You sit yourself there," Pyl'mau motioned to the deerskin. "Rest. We'll eat, and have real Russian tea in a minute."

Pyl'mau flew about the chottagin like a whirlwind. She hung the cauldron over the fire, prepared the wooden dish, took a packet out of a large box that served as a cabinet, and laid two black tea bricks, a pack of smoking tobacco, a few large lumps of sugar, and a bottle of vodka in front of John.

---

* *Kakomei* – an exclamation of surprise.

"I traded for all these with the Russian ship. I gave four fawn skins for it, and for that thing," Pyl'mau pointed at the washstand. "The Russians only wanted two walrus tusks. What do you think, did I pay too much?"

"You're great, Mau!" John smiled, pulled the woman close and kissed her on the lips. "You couldn't have thought up a better present for me!"

Pyl'mau, stunned by the kiss, looked at John in astonishment. She pressed her fingers to her lips and said, uncertainly:

"So that's the white man's kiss?"

"Yes," said John. "You don't like it?"

"Strange . . ." Pyl'mau said softly, "like a child who got lost searching for the breast."

Pyl'mau was refusing to have a drink, but John insisted. A glassful of vodka gave her brown face a rosy glow, but all of a sudden she became silent and sad.

"Why don't you say something, Mau?" John asked her.

"What is there to say?" She shrugged, looking somewhere off to the side.

"Well, you could tell me about the ship . . ."

"They came, walked about the yarangas, traded the goods . . . Asked the old folks about the ice. They couldn't understand what I wanted with the washstand. They weren't here for long, they were in a hurry to get north, to the Invisible Island . . . And that's it," Pyl'mau's voice faded as she ended her story.

"Did the vodka make you sick?" John asked sympathetically.

"No," Pyl'mau was almost whispering. "It's just that I really wanted you to kiss me one more time, like a child lost in search of the breast . . ."

John smiled and kissed her firm warm lips.

Melting from the plentiful food and vodka, John fell asleep inside the polog. In the night, he felt Pyl'mau undressing him, and then how, after damping the brazier, trembling, she lay beside him. John embraced her. Pyl'mau was saying something, but each time she spoke he silenced her mouth with a kiss. Afterwards, he lay with his eyes wide open in the darkness, and his heart was was filling with balmy peace. "I've found myself, and my place on this earth," he thought, alive to the warm female body beside him.

When John awoke, neither Pyl'mau nor Yako were inside the polog. He heard Pyl'mau singing outside.

John stuck his head inside the chottagin:

"Mau!"

"Hi!" She bounded into the chottagin.

"Where is my . . ." John didn't know what to call a watch in the Chukchi tongue. The day before, he'd forgotten to wind it, and was now worried that it might stop. "It was in my pocket. A round thing . . ."

"A thumper-thing, that looks like an eye? With glass on it?" guessed Pyl'mau. She found the watch and handed it to him.

"Will you have some tea, or are you going to wash your face first?" Pyl'mau asked.

"First I'll wash," John answered, and then added mischievously: "I know what you were singing about."

Pyl'mau blushed and covered her eyes with a sleeve.

"I was very worried . . . I was worried that everything about you was as strange as your kiss . . . But it turns out, you're a man like any other man! So that's why I was happy."

This unexpected candor made John blush in turn, and he hurried toward the washbasin.

From that night onwards, John stayed in the polog and assumed the place where Toko had lain before him.

A few days passed, and the hunters began to ferry their kill from the Bering Strait to their own storage pits. Once in a while John would accompany them, but most of the time he stayed behind, busy with the improvements he was making to the yaranga. He had resolved to make the ancient dwelling more comfortable. He'd go to the opposite end of the lagoon in a small hide boat and tug back the water-logged timber. But when an impressive stack of logs and planks accrued by the side of his yaranga, John discovered that he wouldn't actually be able to build a thing, since he hadn't a single nail. Orvo confirmed that nails would be essential.

At the end of summer, the *Vaigach* returned to Enmyn. It had dropped anchor by the time the Enmyn people awoke one morning.

John and Orvo were welcomed on board as old friends. The captain was courteous in thanking Orvo for his ice forecast.

"Your prognosis was absolutely correct, right until Cape Billings," he said. "I must say that such fortunate conditions as this year's are few and far between, and so we managed to get to Wrangel Island without any misadventure."

Inside the captain's stateroom, paneled with blond woods, a table had been laid for them. Watching John with interest and winking knowingly at one another when Orvo was seen to be familiar with the various implements, the expedition leaders competed to show the most hospitality. Filling their glasses, the captain spoke:

"Sailing along these doleful and lonely shores of the Russian Empire, we learned that God had not withheld his bounty from this far-off land, but peopled it with a tribe that was sturdy and intelligent, capable of surviving in the harshest of climates. Enlightened visitors to this place wonder at the native people, whom only an uneducated fool would call savages. So allow me to also raise a toast to Orvo, a representative of the Chukchi tribe, who is present at this table."

The interpreter translated the captain's speech, and Orvo listened attentively. Not a single muscle moved in his impassive face, as though he were accustomed to both the surroundings and hearing high-flown speeches made in his honor. As a token of thanks he inclined his head almost imperceptibly and clinked glasses with the captain.

John MacLennan was toasted, too. The captain, who had proposed the toast, compared him to Miklukho-Maklai, but John didn't have the foggiest idea who that was. When they enlightened him, John decided to make himself quite clear and declared that he had certainly not settled among the Chukchi in order to study them. He simply wanted to live as they did, having grown convinced that the society of "civilized" people was far from ideal, and did not afford a person the chance to develop his true human virtues. John's speech puzzled the guests, but the captain lightened the mood by proposing a toast to the Canadian seafarers, who had made a large contribution to Arctic exploration.

"Gentlemen," John addressed the party, "I am very glad to have become acquainted with you, representatives of the mighty Russian people and Russian government. I must impress upon you that the best show of concern for your northern subjects would be to protect them from the robbery perpetrated upon them by merchants and the various white-fox traders. The less contact the Chukchi and the Eskimos have with white men, the better for them . . . I know that Alaska has been sold to the United States by your government. I lived there for a time, and saw Eskimos digging for garbage scraps, with the dogs, on the outskirts of towns. I shudder to think what would become of the people here, if Chukotka were to share Alaska's fate."

"Mr. MacLennan," said the captain, "we understand your concerns. But they are too pessimistic. It will be no less than a century, before civilization of any kind can reach Chukotka. As for defending the national borders, a battle cruiser patrolling the waters is planned for next year. Some time ago, there was talk of laying a trans-Siberian telegraph line across the Bering Strait and onto the North American continent, but since the success of the transatlantic cable it became needless, and so this part of Asia no longer excites any schemes but the scientific. So set your mind at rest, and live the life you have chosen for yourself . . ."

There was irony in the captain's last words, one that was completely effaced in the translation made for Orvo's sake.

The captain asked John whether there was anything he needed.

"Thank you. I have got everything that I require . . . But if you would be so kind, I'd be grateful for some nails . . ."

"We'll send a launchboat with some," the captain promised, and made his farewells with John and Orvo.

In the evening, the promised boat touched shore. The sailors carried over three crates of nails, a supply of coffee beans, four twenty-pound bags of flour, a sack of sugar and a variety of other items, the sight of which made John wonder how he'd ever gotten along without them. There was a hammer, a saw, some soap, sailors' shirts, cuts of bright chintz clearly intended for Pyl'mau, and even a few woolen blankets.

The gifts came with a letter.

Dear Mr. MacLennan!
Please accept these gifs from the Russian hydrographic expedition, and also from me personally. We would have liked to do more for you, but our resources are limited. So we share with you what we have, and hope that the modest items we send you will be of use to you. I thank you for your pleasant company and remain in the hope of meeting you again,
   Captain of the steamship Vaigach.

John read the letter, and wrote out a reply in which he praised the captain's generosity and expressed his readiness to always be of service to Russian seamen if ever they should happen upon the shores of Enmyn.

Pyl'mau was gladdest of all. She skipped from the sack of sugar to the brightly colored chintz, trying it on, sniffed the tea bricks, and chattered to John:

"What riches! We've never had so many strange new things in our yaranga! Hard to believe that it's all ours! If we use it little by little, it will last a long time. A whole year, maybe even more!"

John listened to her, smiling. When the first flush of excitement had died down, he said:

"All this isn't just yours and mine. It belongs to everyone, to all the people of Enmyn."

Pyl'mau was flabbergasted.

"What, all of that?" Her arm swept a wide arc across the piles of gifts.

"Yes," John told her firmly. "We will divide all this up, just like we do with a walrus."

"But tea, sugar, and flour, they're nothing like a walrus!" Pyl'mau countered. "Our people live well even without those. Only the real necessities of life are shared out."

"But why should I have all this, and not any of the others?" John asked.

Pyl'mau gave him a tender and pitying look and quietly said:

"All right, then. You can give a little to Orvo, Tiarat, and Armol'... But giving everything away is foolish. You're a white man, and you need these things more."

John felt a convulsion run through him on hearing those words. He gave Pyl'mau a cross look:

"If you don't want me to be angry, don't call me a white man."

15

Such days happen closer to autumn, when the nights have grown dark, and only the waves shine during the moonless hours.

The sun is sole master of the cloudless sky. It arises from the watery depths, big, clean, and red. By midday, it's sweltering on the Arctic coast, making even a light summer kukhlianka overheat.

Garlands of translucent walrus intestine (good for making waterproof capes) rustle in the breeze. The women sit in the sun, splitting the walrus skins with wide pekuls. The raw hide adheres to the wooden plank; you need to have a trained sense of the work to get equal thicknesses of hide to lie on either side of the plank.

The sun fell on Orvo and Armol', who were slicing strips of lakhtak skin. Before cutting, the skin was steeped in concentrated urine for a few days, to make it soft and to get rid of the last of the fat. Armol' held up a smelly, slippery piece of sealskin in his outstretched hands, while Orvo sliced off an even strip of leather that loops by his feet. The men might exchange a few words, but rarely, and only while they break, as the cutter's breath needs to be even to keep to a straight line and to make a leather strip of uniform thickness.

Armol' is the one who began the conversation. He hadn't known how to approach the subject at first, but now he barely paused for breath, and Orvo had to keep halting his work so he wouldn't ruin the leather.

"Why don't we drive him out?" Armol' was asking. "Let him go back to where he came from, or settle in some other village, where people are used to whites."

"But what about Pyl'mau?" Orvo said, setting to sharpening his sun-bright knife.

"We can always find some man for her," Armol' said, casually. "Someone can take her for a second wife."

Orvo stopped sharpening the knife and raised a penetrating look at Armol'. The other, unable to meet it, hung his head.

"Our people may come to grief from having a stranger here," Armol' continued stubbornly.

"What danger is there in a cripple? You're not afraid of him, are you?" Orvo's voice rang with disdain.

Armol' colored, and threw the piece of hide back into the wooden barrel.

"I wouldn't be afraid of him even if he had four arms!" he shouted. "But I don't want to hide myself when I need to speak with the gods, I don't want some stranger's eyes, that don't understand our life, to laugh at us when we perform our rites. Think, Orvo, how he was looking at us when we made the great sacrifice on the ice, by the Bering Strait."

"Every nation has its own customs and habits. Maybe Sson doesn't approve of our rites, but I haven't noticed it. Everybody did hear, though, how you laughed loudest of all when you saw Sson clean his teeth with a brush for the first time, and then at how he rinsed his mouth with water, like a hide boat being cleaned after ferrying fresh meat. Did that happen, or no?" Orvo regarded Armol' with a smile.

Armol', paying no heed, ploughed ahead:

"Maybe so it was, but it's our people's welfare that I worry about. I don't care a whit for Sson and his countrymen. If they exist – fine, if not – we'll manage very well without them! Done it for ages!"

"True enough, we've managed before," Orvo agreed. "But today we live differently than we did yesterday, and tomorrow we'll live differently from today. And it seems to me that, even in the last few years, the days only get shorter . . . Even we, people who live far from big nations and their paths, we too, have to keep up with the times . . . And I'll tell you something else, Armol': a man is always a man, however strange his customs and habits seem to another, however unusual his appearance. Don't look at a man's outside; look deep into his eyes, feel his heart – that's where his true self will be found."

"You defend him because you also lived among the whites and picked up all sorts of evil from them," Armol' said. "I don't mean to insult you, Orvo. But when a dog runs with a wolf pack for a time and then comes back to people, it will happen once in a while that he can't help but howl like a wolf . . . I know, you're hoping that John will become a luoravetlan just like us. But listen to this! The day before yesterday, he got a treasure-trove of gifts from his white countrymen, wealth you and I wouldn't even dream about, though our yarangas were hung with white fox. Did he share with you even a pinch of his tobacco? Did he treat your grandson to a piece of sugar? Or give your old lady a bit of red cloth? If he doesn't observe our greatest rule – share all that you have – then he's not one of ours!"

"Even a dog needs time to learn how to howl, and Sson is a man, after all," Orvo countered with conviction. "He came from a world where they don't like to share with one another. Everything is upside-down there: Men try to take things away from each other, though it be the other's last. How can you expect him to learn our customs right away? . . . So you say that you don't like the way he looks at us when we perform our rites. But have you thought about how hard it is for him to break free of his way of thinking, start his whole life over again, and give up what is dear to him? We don't know yet what it was that Sson sacrificed in order to help Pyl'mau and little Yako."

"As if we needed his help," Armol' grumbled. "We would do just fine without him."

The sharpened blade close to his face, Orvo lovingly appraised his handiwork and signed to Armol' to get the sealskin out of the barrel. But Armol' didn't seem to notice. Open-mouthed, he was looking somewhere behind the old man's back, watching someone. Orvo turned around and saw John approach.

"Look at him waddle," Armol' gritted through his teeth. "What a fat shiny face; he's been smoking and drinking plenty of strong sweet tea."

"Stop it!" Orvo knitted his brow.

"Yetti!" John greeted them cheerfully.

"Yetti," Armol' replied, looking away.

"Yetti, Yetti," Orvo said kindly, and corrected him:

"Sson, how many times have I told you this: It's not the person that just came that says 'yetti,' but the one who is greeting him. That is our custom. You can always tell someone is a stranger, by the way he hurries to say 'yetti.'"

"Well, he is a stranger," said Armol' with a crooked smile.

John sat down on a boulder and took out some tobacco.

"Smoke?"

Orvo readily unpacked his pipe, carved from walrus tusk. Armol' made a tobacco chew and carefully placed it in one cheek. He watched John strike a match with close interest.

"These fire-making sticks are a clever thing that the white people thought up," he said, with some respect, and gingerly took the matchbox in his hands.

"As you know," John told them, "I was given many different things. But I live with you, and all that the Russian ship's captain sent to me belongs to the people of Enmyn."

John took out a sheet of paper, both sides densely covered in writing.

"There are four times twenty, plus seven more people living in the twelve yarangas of Enmyn." John read out the names of the heads of families. He mispronounced a few of these, and Orvo corrected him. "I've divided all the flour, sugar, tea, and tobacco into four twenties and seven portions, and made twelve piles. Now I'm asking you: Does this seem fair?"

Armol' couldn't take his eyes off the paper. He pointed to the sheet and asked, his voice quivering with anxiety:

"My name is written there too?"

"Yes," John replied, scanning it with his eyes and marking the place with a fingernail: "Here's Armol'. Married, two children, old mother, altogether five shares."

"But how did you know all that?"

"Pyl'mau helped me."

"There was no need to take a woman as helper. You might have asked me," Armol' said, and spit some thick brown saliva on the ground.

"Next time, I'll certainly call you," John smiled, continuing: "But we didn't want to cut up the cloth and a few other things – you'd only get little strips. Maybe it would be better if we just decide who needs a new kamleika the most? Then we'll give him the whole thing, so we don't have to cut it."

"You are right," Orvo remarked.

"In that case, let's go back to my yaranga, we can see what should go to whom," suggested John.

"All right," Orvo agreed, asking: "Would you let us wash our hands in your washbasin? It's just that they are filthy."

"Of course," said John, "I've even got soap now!"

Pyl'mau had tea ready, and there were cups and mugs all set on the low table next to the headrest-log. A pile of pancakes, freshly baked in nerpa fat, lay on a wooden platter.

John poured some water into the basin and handed Armol' a bar of soap. The white, never-before-seen substance was slippery, and Armol' giggled like someone being tickled:

"Like he's alive! He wants to run away! Isn't used to Chukchi hands. Wild, he is . . ."

Under Orvo's tutelage he lathered his hands and rubbed them vigorously.

The old man advised him to wash his face, while he was at it.

"The little white animal, he won't bite?" Armol' asked, motioning toward the soap.

"First make a foam in your hands, then put it on your face, rub it in, and wash off," Orvo told him.

Armol' scrupulously followed the old man's instructions. Carefully smearing the soapsuds over his face, he suddenly let out a yelp:

"Eeeek! He bites! He's got my eyes!"

Armol' ran back and forth across the chottagin, knocking down whale vertebrae scattered about, and bumping into the pillars holding up the yaranga's ceiling.

"Eeeeee!" he screamed. "He's eating my eyes!"

Orvo caught Armol' and walked him back to the washstand by force.

"Rinse off the foam, rinse it well – and you'll be better!" he said. "Wash your eyes out."

While Armol' was stumbling about the yaranga, Pyl'mau was laughing merrily. John and Orvo, too, were unable to hold back their laughter.

When Armol' rinsed off the soap, and the stinging in his eyes lessened, he regained his usual self-confidence and looked around him crossly.

"What are you laughing at?" he grumbled at Pyl'mau. "See how you'd like it."

"It was the same for me, until Sson taught me how," smiled Pyl'mau, in a friendly way.

The men sat themselves around the short-legged table.

"Maybe we'll have some of that bad joy-making water first?" John offered.

"We could, a little," Armol' agreed, nonplussed.

"Mau, you can have a drink with us," John handed her a cup.

"No, I won't. You drink, and I won't get in the way of men's conversation."

At the table, John played the host, pouring the tea, asking the guests to try some pancake. The guests, stretching their lips, drank their tea noisily.

"My friends, I'd like to ask you for some advice . . ."

"We're listening, Sson."

"I want to marry Pyl'mau . . ."

Taken aback by this declaration, Orvo and Armol' simultaneously set down their cups.

"Yes, I want to marry Pyl'mau and adopt Yako but I don't know how to go about it . . ."

Armol' and Orvo exchanged puzzled glances. Armol', stuttering with embarrassment, clarified:

"So, you're saying you want us to teach you how to do it?"

"That's it exactly!" John exclaimed, happy to have made himself understood so quickly and easily.

"I respect you, Sson," Orvo said, in dismay, "but I'm no good for these things anymore, maybe Armol' can teach you how."

Armol' stared at John in total confusion:

"So whose fault is it, yours or hers?"

"There's no fault," answered John. "Pyl'mau is willing . . . To be honest, we've been living as man and wife from the day we all came back from the Bering Strait. We sleep together in the polog, in the same bed . . ."

"Well!" Armol' interrupted impatiently. "And then what?"

"And then this: She tells me that we're going to have a baby. I'm very glad, of course, but a child needs a father, and Pyl'mau a real husband."

"I don't understand anything," Armol' looked to the old man.

"Neither do I," Orvo shrugged.

"The baby that's coming, it's yours?"

"Who else's? Of course it's mine. There's no doubt on that score," John answered.

"So what marriage are you talking about, if you're already married?" Orvo was aghast.

"It seems you've misunderstood me," John said, blushing. "It's only that among white people, a man and a woman are only considered married when they go before a priest, and . . ."

"A priest, that's the white people's shaman, the one who can talk to God," Orvo explained for Armol's benefit.

"Or if they sign their names in a special book that the most important man in the village keeps," John said, "that's considered the main thing."

"I don't know what you're talking about, I don't get it," Armol' was shaking his head. "To me, the most important thing in marriage is completely different. It's the thing that makes babies. Sson, if I've understood you rightly, to my mind you've been married ever since we all came back from the Bering Strait. And if we have no man here that can talk to the white people's God, well, there's nothing that can be done about that."

"Sson, if you've decided to live according to our ways, then you're married already," Orvo concluded. "You don't need to do anything else."

"Really?"

"Well, how else?"

"So I can call Pyl'mau my wife?"

"You could have done that long ago," said Armol', and poured more vodka into the cups himself.

John showed them the Russian captain's gifts. Orvo and Armol' approved of John's method of sharing them out. Considering it at length, they decided to give the cloth to the family of Guvat, who'd been ailing for a long time.

Orvo advised John to keep three flannel sailors' shirts for himself, but John was unwilling, and offered them to Tiarat, Orvo, and Armol' instead.

"All useful things," Orvo ruefully pronounced, looking over the gifts.

"We need all these things, the outboard motor, the new Winchesters, the cartridges. It would be good to get a wooden motorboat. It's very good for sailing among the ice floes. But it's pricey. You'd probably have to give three twenties of walrus tusk for it, or a whole whale's worth of whale-bone . . ." He addressed Armol': "And here you are saying that we can manage without and live according to the ancient ways and with the ancient weapons. Would you agree to go out on the sea with only a spear, or a bow and arrows?"

"Let's hope that we can buy a wooden boat, and an outboard motor for it," John said, and asked Orvo: "Do the Chukchi pay any tribute to the Russian tsar?"

"Whoever wants to, pays," Orvo said matter-of-factly.

"What do you mean?"

"The ones who are willing, they pay," Orvo explained. "It's like a sort of offering to the Sun God – the Russian tsar."

"How interesting!"

"Nonsense," Orvo said. "They send off all kinds of garbage, things that no one wants to look at."

When they made the rounds, laden with presents, each yaranga met Orvo, Armol', and John with joy, and tried to treat them to whatever was available. People lived differently. There were some who were very poor, with torn walrus hides over their yarangas, and pologs made of half-rotted deerskin rags.

There were two old people living inside one of the yarangas. Unkempt, half-blind, they crawled about the dirty and stinking chottagin. A wooden trough stood in the middle, and both of the old people and the dogs ate from it.

"Isn't there anyone who can help these unfortunates?" asked John.

"They have no kin. Our people bring them food, clean up the yaranga once in a while."

When they were outside and on their way to the next yaranga, Orvo said:

"They should have departed for the clouds a long time ago. We have this custom: If a person can no longer feed himself, or brings in less than it takes to keep him alive, he goes beyond the clouds of his own free will. But it so happened with Mutchin and Eleneut that their sons, who could have helped them to go to the next world, are dead. So now there's no one to perform the rite, and the old ones have to suffer like this until their flames are extinguished."

"How cruel life is!" John exclaimed.

"Yes," Orvo agreed. "They were unlucky, these old ones. If their sons were alive, they would not be suffering now, but living in the next world."

The snow fell without warning. A ceaseless drizzle lasted for three days in a row and then, one morning, turned into snowfall. At first the snowflakes melted on the black earth, but there were so many that by noon the ground was covered by a fluffy carpet, and Enmyn – with its snow-capped yarangas and meat mounds – took on a bright holiday aspect.

One early morning, Yako broke the ice in the water bucket with his ladle, and commented with surprise:

"The water's gone hard!"

And Pyl'mau, heavy with child, said:

"Winter is here."

16

With the first snows came time for John to learn to drive the sled. Over the summer, the dogs had grown fat and lazy. Some of them had forgotten the way home completely, and had to be corralled from around the entire village. It helped matters little that John didn't know one from another, and so Pyl'mau ran around the village alongside him, looking.

Finally, when the pack was assembled and harnessed, John sat himself down on the sled and bravely shouted:

"Gu!"

The sled didn't budge an inch. The dogs continued to sniff at one another, evincing no desire whatsoever to obey the command. Having repeated "gu" a number of times, John came out with a string of curses. The lead dog turned his head and gave the strange new driver a look of reproach. John had to call for Pyl'mau. She said something to the dogs, and then uttered, calm and businesslike:

"Gu!"

John barely had time to leap aboard. Making a round of the lagoon and mastering the commands "kh-kh" and "pot'-pot'" – right and left – he guided the sled in the direction of the yaranga. Braking with a drawn out "G'eeeeh!" John firmly drove the hitching post into the ground and asked Pyl'mau:

"So what was it you said to the dogs to make them go?"

"Nothing special," Pyl'mau answered. "I just told them to obey you, because you're their master now."

"And that's it?"

"What else is there to tell them? Now they know what to do."

But nothing turned out to be quite that simple. The harnessed pack was stubbornly motionless, and the lead dog expressed a complete indifference to John's commands. This was a large shaggy dog with an intelligent, thoughtful look about him. There was so much disdain for John in his eyes, that the latter finally couldn't control himself; he grabbed the whip and struck the dog twice. He climbed aboard the sled and shouted angrily: "Gu!"

The leader looked back at him, but set off.

By evening, more worn out than the dogs themselves, John fell into the yaranga and triumphantly informed his wife:

"Mau! I got them to obey me in the end. They recognized me as their master."

"It couldn't have been any different," Pyl'mau smiled, "didn't I talk to them about that very thing?"

During the inclement autumn months John rebuilt the yaranga. Sometimes he had help from Orvo, Armol', and Tiarat. It became a strange, but comfortable dwelling. John didn't just blindly copy Carpenter's Keniskun yaranga. Carpenter didn't own a dog team, but John required one, and so he widened the chottagin and divided it into two halves: one for the people and one for the dogs. The halves were split by a low screen. In the people's half, there stood a roughly made table with a similarly rough stool, a large crate against a wall, wardrobelike, shelves tied to the wall with bits of lakhtak strips. John also enlarged his old closet room. Now it was transformed into a decent little room, with a big bed that was laid with fine white deerskins. The heating aspect proved more complicated. He had to place the usual stone oil lamps in the room. This way, two goals were achieved at once – heat and light.

John cut a square opening in one side of the chottagin and stretched a translucent bubble over it – a walrus stomach that had been dried and cured by a special method for making yarar drums. The chottagin was immediately lighter, and Enmyn people took to visiting John's yaranga to take a look out the window.

The polog did not suffer much alteration. Only the washstand gleamed from one corner. It hung on the wall instead of the god of good fortune, whose greasy mouth and ironic expression on his wooden face – covered with dried sacrificial blood and blubber – made John uneasy, whereas the god had taken the washstand's old place in the chottagin. At first Pyl'mau objected to the relocation, but John told her decisively that the god was much better off hanging in the fresh air of the chottagin. As for the wash-basin, it could rupture if the water froze.

Having tamed the dog pack, John could now go to the tundra along-side the other hunters. Orvo showed him the places where Toko used to hunt, and said:

"Now these are your places. You can put the bait out, for now, and when the fox fur becomes as white as snow, then you can set the traps. I'll show you how to do it."

For bait, they would bring over slightly rotted meat and beached car-casses, unsuitable for human consumption.

The sea had not frozen over yet. The changeful wind would push the icy slush far from shore, then press it close again, and during stormy win-ter nights the yarangas were battered by ice bombs, spat out from the waves.

Early each morning, the men would go out collecting the sea's bounty. Although John was more interested in good timber, he collected sea-weed, too. The taste was reminiscent of half-brined pickles.

John left the yaranga long before dawn. The waves shone in the dark-ness, and broke over the shingles with a muffled roar. It was slippery; lumps of ice constantly got underfoot. John was heading west. He made a mark on each plank and log he found by placing a stone over it. Whoever followed would know that he was too late, that the wood was already claimed by another. A pale dawn caught up with him not far from a narrow strait that led into the lagoon. It was a good time to turn back: There was no point in going on, as beyond the strait there were only steep crags that looked down on the water.

John sat down to rest. He breathed deeply, his nostrils tickled by a frosty, sea-salty air. The dawn was hard at work, trying to penetrate the clouds, dense as wet curtains. Everything that had seemed ethereal in the twilight now became familiar and real.

Only one dark object trembled at the edges of John's consciousness. There was something unusual about it: Something enormous and black was rolling in the waves not far from the strait. At first, John thought it was just a large wave. But it differed from the rest by its incredible stability.

John headed that way. The lighter the air grew, the more mysterious seemed the object. Only walking right up to it, did John realize that it was in fact a gigantic whale. The carcass was half-beached. The whale's shiny black skin was covered with shells, pitted with cracks. It appeared that the whale was dead. Maybe it had been whalers who had mortally wounded him, or perhaps he had died a natural death. The sea giant was not breathing, buffeted by the waves.

Guessing dimly that his find represented a treasure for the people of Enmyn, John hurried back to the yarangas. He went up on the grassy path to make the journey easier. A man's shape appeared in the distance. Walking up to it, John recognized Tiarat. The other was savoring some long seaweed stems.

"You're up early!" he shouted to John, mouth nice and full, and then showed him some pieces of black walrus bone. This bone is much valued by American collectors, and sometimes one fragment of it can fetch a whole brick of chewing tobacco. "What have you got to brag about then, early riser?"

"I found a whale," John answered.

"What did you find?" Tiarat asked.

"A whale."

"You probably mistook a belukha* for a whale," said Tiarat in disbelief.

"A real, enormous whale!" John shouted at him. "I'm not fooling you. Go take a look for yourself."

"I will," Tiarat said doubtfully, and quickly walked off to the west.

Then John came across Armol'. On hearing John's news, he didn't express disbelief, as Tiarat had – but still wanted to ascertain the truth of John's words for himself.

It seemed that this was the day when every man of Enmyn had decided to try his fortune in finding gifts from the sea. And although John informed each one of his find, not one of them took his words seriously. Many asked him to repeat the story again, and guessed that it was not really a whale he'd found, but a walrus or lakhtak, and most likely a belukha.

As he approached the settlement, though, John heard loud shouts raised behind him. He turned around and saw Tiarat and Armol' speeding toward him as though they were competing in a footrace.

"Hey, Sson!" shouted Armol'. "You're right! It really is a whale!"

"A huge one! We've never had one like it in Enmyn before," Tiarat confirmed.

They overtook John and ran on, heading into the settlement.

By the time John walked up to the yarangas, everyone was up and about. Excitement winged its way from one yaranga to the next: Sson had found a ritliu!† A whale! An enormous one, bigger than they had ever seen in Enmyn.

The people were hitching up the dogsleds, readying the long-handled knives.

"You've brought joy to our village! Finding such a ritliu is a great fortune!" Orvo told him.

* *Belukha* – Russian for white whale, a much smaller species. (TN)
† *Ritliu* – gift of the sea.

Pyl'mau was already at work hitching up the dogs and loading the sled with a large leather sack.

The sleds ran in an orderly line, one after another. Pyl'mau sat back to back with her husband, respectfully silent. The dogsled caravan, racing to the whale, stretched down the coastline. Yes, Sson had had unheard-of good fortune! Orvo was right when he said that he brought luck to the settlement. There were people walking behind the last of the sleds. Pyl'mau could see the crowd bringing up the rear, and it seemed to her that all of Enmyn had left the yarangas and set off for the shore. According to custom, whatever is found on the shore belongs to the one who sighted it first. So then, today her husband is the wealthiest man in Enmyn. Today even those whose hands are strong can't compete with the one who so recently was considered worthy only of pity and disdain. Pyl'mau herself had seen him in that light, at first. When Sson came to live in her yaranga, she considered him an amusing creature, good entertainment. Well, how could she have looked on him as a person, a man, when he couldn't even dress and undress himself? Sson was more helpless than a little child, and she had had no feelings for him other than pity, the other feelings all came later. His stubbornness, force of will, his rage when he saw that he was being helped out of pity, all this was surprising, and like Toko. That was how she had come to know Toko, as an orphan who had earned the respect of Enmyn by his willingness to work hard. At times, with an inner tremor, Pyl'mau could see the dead man's features in Sson. At times, the similarity grew so strong that Pyl'mau would call out to Sson for no reason except to hear the sound of his voice and be reassured that he was not Toko. Even now, it's Sson's back she feels behind her, but turning her head, it's Toko's kamleika she sees.

"Sson!"

"What is it, Mau?"

"No, it's nothing."

"We'll be there soon." John said. "Look, you can see the whale already."

Pyl'mau made a quick about-face. Even from afar you could see a commotion of people around the whale. It was like a hunk of meat covered with flies.

The hunters were already busy hacking up the whale carcass, cutting out rectangular chunks of skin together with the whitish-yellow layer of blubber. Their soiled faces were shiny with grease, jaws in constant motion.

"Itgil'gyn!"* Pyl'mau greedily reached for a piece of blubbery whale skin, sliced off a generous portion and held it out to John. It resembled the worn sole on a pair of rubber galoshes, and John made a polite refusal:

"A bit later . . ."

Orvo assumed control of the situation directly. He told everyone, including the dogs, to back a good deal away from the whale.

"The stomach can blow up so bad that you'll be covered in muck from head to toe," he explained to John.

The whale lay on his back. His belly rose sharply into the air. Armol' clambered to the very top and made a deep incision. Then he got down, and tied together two spear-knives. Taking aim, he punctured the belly from afar. With a loud hiss, a putrid fountain burst from the hole. The belly subsided, and people immediately fell to butchering the carcass.

They worked into the night. John grew hungry. Among this incredible wealth, he was the only person who felt hunger. The others had not stopped chewing for a moment. The dogs were long gone into a sated slumber, still slurping and whining in their sleep. The kids were worn out too. They had been tucked in for the night by the side of the enormous fire. Tortured by hunger pangs, John finally worked up the nerve to pick up a piece of the blubbery whale skin. The skin itself didn't taste like any-

* *Itgil'gyn* – whale skin with blubber. Considered a delicacy.

thing, or more specifically, had a faint aftertaste. The blubber was the same as usual, except that the longer John chewed it, the sweeter it became. Without realizing it, John had consumed one piece, then another, and soon his face had also acquired a layer of whale fat and the soot from the smoky blaze, where gigantic whale ribs and blubber burned together.

Armol' had burrowed through to the whale jaws, and suddenly the darkness was rent with his triumphant shout:

"The whalebone! It's all here!"

He dragged some long, taut plates to the fireside. There was enough whalebone to make a considerable pile.

"Napo!"* Pyl'mau exclaimed, and the other women echoed her as they set to scraping a white substance off the whalebone. John too was offered a taste of napo. The white substance tasted of oysters.

John lugged the meat and blubber alongside everyone else, making piles, ripping the ribs – sturdy as ceiling beams – from the flesh, and, as morning came, was so exhausted that he simply collapsed by the fire. Orvo made himself comfortable next to John.

"This is a real fortune," he said, stroking the whale whisker, cleaned of napo. "I didn't have high hopes that there would still be the whiskers inside. I reckoned this whale had been killed by a hunting schooner. That's how they always work – they kill the whale, cut out the whalebone then throw the carcass away. Same with walrus; knock off the tusks, then throw the animal overboard . . . But the whalebone is all there! Good fortune walks together with you as you start your life with us. This is a good omen, Sson. I'm glad for you."

"Thanks, Orvo." John tilted his head as a sign of gratitude.

"It is our people's custom that whatever is found on the seashore belongs to the one who spotted it first," Orvo went on. "Well, even if you wanted to keep the entire whale for yourself, you couldn't carry the meat

* *Napo* – a white coating on the whalebone.

and blubber to Enmyn in a year. But as for the whalebone, that's all yours. That is the ancient rule. I'd like to ask you, though: What are you thinking to do with such a treasure?"

Wavering a bit, John confessed:

"To be honest, I don't know myself. The whalebone, for what it is and as I understand it, doesn't really have such great value here. What do you do with it?"

"It's useful for various small items: fishing lines, sled runners, all kinds of bits and pieces, cookware," enumerated Orvo. "But only a fool would make dishes and runners from whalebone nowadays, when you can trade it for metal dishes and steel runners."

Orvo was silent for a while, staring into the dancing flame.

"So what are you planning to do with it, then?" he repeated his question.

"We'll share it, the same way we shared the gifts from the Russian ship, the same way we're dividing up the whale," John said.

"If you do that," Orvo said slowly, "your new countrymen will not approve."

"But Orvo, you must agree that I was just lucky to have seen the whale first. If I'd gotten up a bit later, it would have been Tiarat who found it, rather than being second behind me."

"But you got up earliest of all, didn't lie in bed with your young wife. You went outside, into the face of the cold morning, though you might have stayed home. Good fortune comes to the man who goes out to meet it . . . This isn't about who owns the whalebone. It belongs to you, and that's as certain as the morning about to come and the sun about to rise."

"Fine," John agreed. "I'll take the stuff. And in the summer we'll sell it to the merchants and buy whatever our people need."

"It's not so simple, this buying and selling," Orvo said. "That whalebone would fetch snowdrifts of flour and mountains of tobacco leaf. You could dress every person in Enmyn in a colorful cloth kamleika . . . But I'll give you a piece of advice. True enough, I don't know whether you will take it. I can't remember a time when a Chukcha gave advice to a white man."

"So who was it then, advising the captain of the *Vaigach?* John reminded him.

"That wasn't advice. I just told him what I knew was true . . . But now, I really do want to give you advice. The captain couldn't have done any differently, but you're free not to follow what I say."

"Why should I not follow sensible advice?" John shrugged.

"Why don't you trade this whalebone for a wooden whale boat? . . ." Orvo's voice was as though he were expressing a deep longing. Perhaps Orvo did dream of a sturdy wooden whaleboat, good for sailing among the ice floes.

"All right," John agreed. "We'll get a whaleboat and an outboard motor, too."

"It might not be enough for a motor," Orvo looked doubtful.

"It will be," John said firmly. "I know what these things cost."

"But Carpenter sets his own prices," Orvo reminded.

"Well, we won't be asking Carpenter," John countered sharply. "We'll go up to Nome ourselves and buy the whaleboat there."

"What a good idea!" With that, Orvo got up. "To work, my friends! Let's get the meat and blubber back to Enmyn."

Over the next few days, the dogsleds were busily employed. The old meat pits turned out to be too small, so new ones had to be constructed in a hurry, hacked out of the frozen earth. A part of the meat and blubber they buried in a dense and growing snowdrift on the northern face of Enmyn's mountain.

All that remained of the whale was a gargantuan skeleton with shreds of fat and flesh.

"It will attract white fox," Orvo said, and told everyone who owned fox-traps to get them ready.

Pyl'mau brought some metal traps, touched with rust, out of a closet. John cleaned them, boiled them in rendered whale blubber, and set them outside for a few days to get rid of the metallic smell.

In the darkest days of winter, when the sun did not peek above the horizon, over the innumerable paths made by fox paws, the hunters of Enmyn set their traps.

17

This year's winter was far more brutal than the last. The blizzards swept in early, as soon as the frost locked the sea in ice. Enormous mounds formed by the shore, and the men of Enmyn had to walk to their first sea hunt, since no dogsled could have passed through the monstrous conglomerations of ice.

As soon as one wind died down, another came to take its place. All of Enmyn was blanketed in snow. They barely had time to dig out the yarangas' entryways before the next burst. At first, John would dig out his yaranga's sole window, the one with the walrus-stomach windowpane, each time. But after a while, he let it go, and the only natural light inside the chottagin came through the smoke-hole.

In the rare days of calm, the hunters went out to check on the traps, returning with a rich haul each time. Orvo was despondent:

"If only we had more traps!"

It seemed that all the fur-bearing animals in Chukotka came to feed off the whale carcass. Oftentimes the traps held red foxes, rabbits, and wolverines. Once John brought home a wolverine. Pyl'mau was delighted, since wolverine fur is much better than white fox.

"But the merchants think differently," she said. "Wolverine fur isn't afraid of damp, doesn't go stiff in the cold, and is very durable. Fox doesn't even compare: As soon it's wet it goes all limp, that one."

Pyl'mau was deft at skinning the foxes, and John scraped the remaining fat off the inner side of the hides and stretched the skins over a wooden frame. They ran out of frames and he had to make some new ones. For a few days, the dried pelts would flap and flutter in the frosty air, taking on an unblemished whiteness.

This was the life of Enmyn in the winter of 1912–13. They lived calmly, without worry, knowing that the larders were filled with walrus meat and whale blubber. In the middle of a snowstorm, inside the pologs it was warm and light.

One day, John came across his notepad in the little room, which he barely used anymore. Smiling, he read his old entries, took up a pencil and wrote:

My dear diary! I haven't seen you in a long while, and if I hadn't accidentally found you, I would have forgotten you completely. What can I tell you? Not much. Life goes on, man breathes, loves, feeds, savors warmth in this realm of freezing cold and burning winds. A simple warm flame, the warm air inside a dwelling, they take on a value here that is unmatched in any other place on earth. A person is drawn toward heat as toward a celebration. And so, long live good warmth and good spirit!

John put down the pencil and was lost in thought. Lately, he'd been worried about little Yako's health. The boy looked drawn and thin, didn't eat well. John ascribed it to the lack of fresh air; because of the blizzard, Yako was spending almost all of his time indoors. And today, the child had not left his bed, just lay there, moaning quietly from time to time.

Pyl'mau, anxious, tempted the little boy with the choicest morsels, even took out some of the sugar she'd saved away, but Yako shook his head and kept his yellow-tinged eyes on the blue iris of the smoke-hole.

Two days passed like this. On the third, Pyl'mau timidly asked her husband:

"Let's call Orvo, ask his advice."

"Yes, of course," John immediately agreed, himself at a loss for what to do. He went to fetch the old man and told him about the boy's illness.

As though mindful of the humans' misfortune, the wind died down toward evening and the sky cleared. When John came out to feed the dogs, the entire northern half of the sky was awash in the Northern Lights, and large stars trembled in the polar sky.

Orvo came with some strange implements. The old man was taciturn and grave. He barely spoke to either John or Pyl'mau, addressing only the sick boy, encouraging him and asking after his health.

Finished with the preparations, Orvo asked John and Pyl'mau to go outside to the chottagin.

"What does he intend to do?" John whispered, straining to hear the sounds inside the polog.

"Heal him," Pyl'mau said hopefully. "Orvo is an enenyl'yn, you know. Only he doesn't like it if people come to him over small things, like when they have a bellyache or something like that. He only tries healing if the person is in danger of dying."

So Orvo was also a shaman, on top everything else . . . John could only marvel at the man's many facets. He was the head of the hunting club, the skilled carver of walrus tusk, the high judge, the one who remembered all the laws, the leader of the settlement, and now it turned out that he was also a healer . . .

But it so happened that nobody elected or appointed Orvo to be these things, and he was not really Enmyn's leader at all. It's just that people respected him and valued his advice. And this too – almost all the inhabitants of Enmyn were some sort of relation of his, and in the scrambled genealogies that they had tried fruitlessly to elucidate for John, the old man held a place of honor, as the eldest and most experienced among them.

A quiet singing was coming from inside the polog, accompanied by a rhythmic tapping on a drum. Orvo's slightly hoarse voice was interspersed with an indistinct chanting, and no matter how hard John tried, he couldn't make out the words.

"What's he saying?" he asked his wife.

"I can't understand any of it, either," Pyl'mau answered. "He is speaking with the gods. It's not for plain people to understand their speech . . ."

The singing and drumming grew louder and louder. The words of the incantation rumbled across the chottagin, echoing off the walls. The voice of the enenyl'yn moved inside the polog, came into the chottagin through a ventilation hole, and rang out behind John, making him turn around. The human voice was suddenly being drowned out by shrill bird cries, the growl of strange beasts. A keen mimic was at work inside the polog, and were it not for the frightened and pious expression on Pyl'mau's face, John would certainly have drawn back the curtain to get a glimpse of the old man's exertions.

"Pyl'mau!" The voice came from the yaranga's smoke-hole, descending from the starry sky.

"Toko!" Pyl'mau exclaimed, covering her face with a sleeve.

John looked up, but there were only stars looking down at them through the hole. Strange! But Toko's voice continued:

"My longing for my son has taken root inside Yako. I know that I am causing you sorrow, but will you not have pity on my sufferings? Pyl'mau, my wife, where are you?"

Pyl'mau was overcome with spiny terror. Her voice shook as she shouted up into the smoke-hole:

"Toko! If it is you, then come to us!"

"How can I join you, when you have buried me? No more breath and body have I got in this world . . . O, Yako, my only son, my beloved son! Only in you am I still living, but my longing consumes me, and I want to see you!"

Pyl'mau thrashed about, hysterical. Inside the chottagin, the dogs started howling. The ghostly shimmer of the Northern Lights radiated over the yaranga's smoke-hole.

"O Yako, come to me!" howled Toko's voice.

John knew that all this was the product of Orvo's uncanny skill, but even so, he too was covered in cold sweat. He remembered a book about primitive religions that he'd read in his student days, which described a shamanic trance. Some of the shamans had such hypnotic abilities that they were able to make crowds obey them; researchers fell sway under the illusions the shaman created. Orvo was being coy when he wouldn't agree that he was a great shaman, and John now realized that Orvo's shamanic talents were not least in the sway he held over the people of Enmyn. John had to concentrate all of his willpower not to fall under Orvo's spell, and it cost him great effort to make himself approach the polog.

With a lunge, John launched himself at the polog's curtain-door and snatched it open. By the light of the dying oil lamp, Orvo lay prone on the leather-strewn floor, staring upwards with unmoving eyes. John bent over him.

"Orvo? What's with you?" He grabbed the old man's wrist, feeling for a pulse. There was almost none.

"Orvo! Orvo! What have you done here!" John cried, and rushed to the sick boy. He was stunned: Breathing steadily and easily, Yako was fast asleep.

Orvo stirred and let out a pained sigh. John filled a ladle with cold water and pried open the old man's tightly clenched teeth.

"Is that you, Sson?" Orvo asked weakly.

"It's me. What a show you've put on! Lie still and rest now. I'm going to go see to Mau."

Weak from tears and shock, Pyl'mau made it over to the polog with John's help. Her hands shook as she righted the lamp's flame.

Orvo sat up and gathered together his shaman's tools.

"The boy will get well," he said in a practiced physician's tone. "Don't give him anything fatty, let him stick his head out into the chottagin and breathe the fresh air as much as possible . . . As for Toko, I've convinced him that the boy is happy here, and that Sson is like a real father to him. And I also told him not to bother you two anymore because you're expecting a child. I'm tired now, and I must go home."

And it was true, the boy was quickly on the mend and John would not soon forget Orvo's shamanic seance.

At winter's peak, when the red sliver of the sun was beginning to appear over the horizon, the little boy started venturing out of the yaranga again. One day he ran into the chottagin and shouted:

"A sled coming in from the west!"

At that time they were not expecting any guests from that direction. It was midwinter. Hard days, when they had to go far from the shore for nerpa. And the day itself so short, not a lot of daylight to be had – no sooner does it dawn than the sky darkens again and the shadows thrown by the shoreline crags creep up over the ice hummocks and the tundra.

John went outside and joined the other men, gathered by the outermost yaranga. Orvo's binoculars passed from hand to hand. Each man was trying to guess who the visitors might be.

"Not just one, but two sleds!" Armol' informed them, lowering the binoculars.

"Who could it be?" Orvo mused. He brought the binoculars to his eyes and studied the sleds for a long while. "Going slow . . . From afar. They've got a heavy load. A white man sitting on one of the sleds, that's for sure. Wearing far too many clothes. Look!" and he thrust the binoculars at John.

There were two sleds. They were indeed traveling slowly, but even trying hard John could not distinguish the white man, and returned the binoculars to Orvo.

"A white man on the way, right?" Orvo asked.

"Maybe," John said evasively. "I couldn't make him out."

"If it's a white man, then it's definitely a visitor for you, Sson," said Armol'. "Could be tidings from your homeland."

Meanwhile the sleds had come so near that their passengers could be distinguished by the naked eye.

"An important guest coming," Orvo concluded, and told John:

"Tell your wife to put on a big kettle."

The sleds wended their way toward the outermost yaranga. A thoroughly fur-swaddled man sprang lightly from the second dogsled and headed for John.

"Hello, John!" he shouted as he approached. "Don't you recognize me?"

The guest threw back his wolverine fur-lined hood and John immediately recognised Carpenter's balding head.

"Mr. Carpenter! Where could you be going to in such a season?"

"To pay you a visit, dear John! To see you!" said Carpenter, shaking hands first with John, and then with the rest.

"Kakomei, Poppi!" the hunters were saying to him. "Yetti!"

"Ee-ee!"* Carpenter answered with a smile, patting the men he knew on the shoulder and looking into their faces, greeting each by name. It seemed that a long-awaited guest had arrived at Enmyn, a guest everyone was pleased to see.

Truth be told, that's how it was: Carpenter hadn't come with empty sleds, and the people of Enmyn had enough to trade with the American.

"Sson," Orvo said, "go and welcome your guest, and we'll take care of all the others."

Carpenter gave orders for the goods to be unpacked and brought to John's yaranga.

"You must excuse me," John was mortified. "It's just that I really wasn't expecting anyone. Prepare yourself for an ordinary Chukcha yaranga. I haven't got any of the comforts of your own cozy home in Keniskun, least of all a bath . . ."

"No need to stand on ceremony!" Carpenter broke in. "I'm delighted to find you in good health and spirits. I see that your Arctic residency and simple life among the natives is doing you good."

* *Ee-ee!* – response to a greeting (literally: *Yes, we've arrived.*)

On entering the chottagin, Carpenter shot John a reproachful look:

"You really are a modest one! You've turned this yaranga into a dream, and in such a short while, too. Forgive me, but for a man without hands this is rather a feat!"

"Oh but I had the help of many here, Mr. Carpenter! The captain of the hydrographic vessel, the Enmyn people, and, above all, my wife . . ."

Pyl'mau walked out from the polog and into the chottagin. She had had time to comb her hair and slip on a new bright kamleika, an American silver dollar hanging around her neck from a thin deer-tendon lace.

"Allow me to introduce my wife, Pyl'mau," John said.

"A pleasure!" Carpenter exclaimed. "Robert Carpenter, Bobby to my friends, or even more plainly, Poppi, as the Chukchi and Eskimo call me!"

The visitor wanted to have a closer look at the yaranga's interior, and finding himself in John's little nook, he couldn't conceal his admiration:

"You've set yourself up in style, it's like the Prince Albert Hotel in here!"

While Pyl'mau was busy preparing the feast, Carpenter suggested they have a drink together. Digging in his voluminous luggage, he extracted something resembling a traveling bar, which anticipated every need – from an elegant corkscrew to a set of silver shotglasses.

"To your health!"

Making sure that John emptied his glass, Carpenter moved closer to his companion and began a somewhat flowery speech:

"My visit here, dear John, was motivated by my feelings of friendship for you and also by my business concerns. Don't think that you live apart from the rest of the world. Even in these parts, where human settlements are divided by enormous distances and where there is neither post nor telegraph, still there exist invisible and at times incomprehensible channels that direct information to the right address. In this case I mean your unprecedented fortune – the whale, and the excellent fox trapping. I even know certain details," Carpenter giggled and gave John a conspiratorial wink. "It was you who found the whale, and I cannot deny myself the pleasure of congratulating you on such an unheard of piece of luck! I say we drink to that and leave our chat about the whale until tomorrow. As for today, I'd like to distribute a few gifts to the people of your Enmyn. Will you allow me to use your chottagin for that purpose?"

"Of course," John answered affably.

Pyl'mau served them boiled deer tongues, jellied seal flippers, and a thick nerpa meat soup.

Carpenter ate heartily and praised the dishes.

"You manage without salt?" he asked John.

"It happened somehow that I quickly got used to unsalted food," John replied. "At this point, I don't feel a yen for it at all. When I had lunch with the captain of the *Vaigach,* everything I ate there seemed to me to be terribly oversalted."

"Oh, I feel for you," Carpenter nodded his head, "I also suffer when circumstances demand I switch to European cuisine."

Pyl'mau cleared the table and sent Yako to spread the news that the visitor wanted to hand out gifts.

Carpenter set to unpacking his bags.

Upon a tarpaulin, he laid pieces of brick tea, sugar, two-pound bags of flour, bricks of chewing tobacco, tobacco for smoking, brightly painted hard candy, lengths of cloth, beads, colored paper thread . . .

Pyl'mau's eyes watered from such an abundance of goods, and she stared open-mouthed at the wares on display. John had to remind her to go about her business, quietly, so that their guest wouldn't hear.

The closest neighbors were the first to arrive. Carpenter greeted them kindly. He handed a bag of flour, some tea and tobacco to the head of the family. The wife received a handful of beads and colored thread. Carpenter had exactly enough gift packets for every family in Enmyn. Not a single person was left out. Carpenter remembered not only who preferred what tobacco, but also who needeed beads and what kind.

To Orvo, Armol', and Tiarat he announced:

"For you, I've brought something special. If you'll be as kind as to wait until I've finished with the other gifts."

The men sat down by a low table and began the tea drinking.

Orvo was wondering anxiously whether John would help them to trade with Carpenter, or stand aside. John's face was difficult to read. He remained silent, sipping his strong tea, also watching Carpenter's movements.

Finally the last fortunate, overjoyed with his free gifts, departed. Only John, Carpenter, Orvo, Armol', and Tiarat remained inside the chottagin. Pyl'mau brewed some fresh tea and filled their cups.

"Before the tea, we'll have some of the bad joy-making water," the trader announced solemnly, and he took out the bottle. "I know Orvo is fond of this beverage."

After a drink, Carpenter handed out the personal gifts. Orvo got a pipe with pipe tobacco, plus a length of cloth for a kamleika. The others also received some cloth, and there was a bag of flour and of sugar for each. These were generous gifts.

"Now, let's get to the business talk," said Carpenter. He moved the cups aside and laid a thick and greasy leather-covered notebook on the table. "I know that your settlement has got ten twenties and fourteen white-fox tails. Beside this, eight twenties of red fox, not counting the rabbits and wolverines. I'm prepared to take all that fur immediately and give a partial payment with the goods I've brought. The rest you can order from me, and I'll note everything down here," Carpenter slapped the notebook, "then I'll drive it over in midsummer, when the American ship arrives. Right now I've got flour with me, tea, sugar, tobacco, sugar, cartridges and two 60x60 Winchesters. This way, you won't have to wait for summer. The goods have traveled to you," Carpenter shut the notebook and grinned broadly.

Armol', Orvo, and Tiarat looked at John.

"What do you say?" Orvo addressed him.

"It's hard for me to advise anything," John mumbled. "It's the first time I've been at such a trade, I'm not familiar with the prices . . ."

"Prices are the usual ones," Carpenter put in, "allowing, of course, for transport costs."

"We need many things," Orvo said, thinking. "So we will need to talk amongst ourselves, first."

"Fine," Carpenter assented. "Have a talk. But I must warn you, I haven't much time, and the day after tomorrow I intend to set out for Keniskun."

"We'll think about it for tomorrow," Orvo promised.

"And take this with you, so your noggins work better," Carpenter held the unfinished vodka bottle out to Orvo.

"Velynkykun!" the old man thanked him courteously and tucked the bottle in his waistband. All three rose and walked out together. Carpenter shook his head and gave John a suspicious look.

"They've gotten finicky all of a sudden . . . Could that be your doing?"

"I have no influence here," John answered him. "Although it is my great hope that they will come to a sensible decision."

"What do you mean?" Carpenter pricked up.

"I'd like the pelts to go toward the purchase of truly needed things."

"Maybe you know what it is they want?" Carpenter asked carefully.

"They need a wooden whaleboat. And obviously, a whaleboat needs to have an outboard motor to go with it."

"They've gone mad!" Carpenter exclaimed. "I can even understand them wanting to have a wooden whaleboat, but one with a motor! Savages that have no understanding of even the simplest mechanisms, and they wish to own an internal combustion device! It's too funny!"

"I don't see anything funny about it," John objected. "A motor would make their lives significantly easier. They would be able to bag more animals, and that means more food."

"You've definitely influenced them. And you deny it!" Carpenter said with irritation. "In that case, why don't you want to become a partner?" After a pause, he added in an insinuating tone: "Once again, I give you a friendly warning: If you strike out on your own, it won't go well for you. You have no idea what independent trade would be like here, without solid support."

"I don't intend to set myself in competition with anybody!" John said wearily. "And if we've come to friendly warnings, I must tell you frankly that I will not allow trading robbery in Enmyn. I ask you, Mr. Carpenter, not to take advantage of my countrymen."

"What are you saying, dearest John?" Carpenter smiled. "I've been dealing with them for fifteen years. Ask them if there's a single person who could complain of unfair dealing from me. More than that, a good half of the hunters from Keniskun to Cape Billings have acquired their guns from me. And not for cash, on credit! And many of them are still far from having paid in full."

"Forgive me, Mr. Carpenter, but I do understand something of commerce, and you will never convince me that you trade to your detriment, purely out of charity."

Flummoxed, Carpenter muttered:

"Commerce is commerce . . ."

"Let's save business discussions for tomorrow," John suggested. "You are fatigued from your journey, you must have a good rest."

He walked the guest to his little room, where Pyl'mau had laid out a bed and heated the chamber with a grease lamp.

John climbed into the polog, but no sooner had he undressed then Carpenter's red face appeared from underneath the upraised door flap.

"Forgive me, John," he said, in some embarrassment, "but I won't be able to sleep a wink until I'm convinced that there's no one behind you in this . . . Let me be perfectly frank: If there is someone behind you, someone who can offer you a bigger share, I am prepared to work together with you. I have experience, and as you have seen, influence over the natives."

"I give you my word, there is no one behind me!" John, annoyed and tired, waved him away. "Now, good night!"

But as soon as he shut his eyes, there was Pyl'mau, gently shaking him awake. She whispered:

"Orvo has come for you."

John stuck his head out into the chottagin.

"What now?"

"We can't do without you," Orvo told him quietly. "Come and join us. You know how important this is to us."

John got dressed and followed Orvo outside.

A fire blazed inside Orvo's chottagin, and above it was a puffing kettle. Fire-smoke and pipe-smoke billowed up around the smoke-hole. Armol' and Tiarat sat behind a wide plank set with teacups.

Orvo slid a whale vertebra toward John, and the other sat down. Granny Cheivuneh was quick in handing him a strong cup of tea.

"This is what we're arguing about," Orvo began. "My advice is to gather up everyone's pelts and buy the thing that will be useful to every-one – a whaleboat and outboard motor. Only we don't know whether our furs will be enough for such a purchase."

"You're forgetting about the whalebone," John reminded.

"If we add the whalebone, then we probably will be able to buy a whaleboat," Orvo was cheered.

"And whose whaleboat will it be?" Armol' inquired. "I've got five twen-ties of white fox, and Tiarat has only got two twenties."

"The whaleboat will belong to everybody. All of Enmyn will own it."

"I don't agree," Armol' said. "Maybe I don't need this whaleboat at all, maybe I need totally different things."

"So what do you need?" asked Orvo.

"That's my own business," Armol' muttered.

"Listen friends, I am telling you again: the whalebone and all my pelts – I haven't got as many as Armol', of course – I'm handing them over to you. Dispose of them as you see fit. But to my mind, Orvo is right. A whaleboat would open up a path to the distant places, where the walrus gather. We'd be able to hunt them wherever we wanted to . . .

"And who is going to drive the motor?" Armol' asked. "None of us have ever dealt with one before."

"I can do it," John declared.

Armol' sniggered: "But will he obey one without hands?"

"He will," said Orvo. "So we are agreed?"

"Agreed," answered Tiarat.

"There's still time to think it over before morning," Armol' said evasively.

Rising with the dawn, Carpenter appeared at breakfast having made the rounds of the entire settlement. Cheerful and contented, he plopped noisily onto the roughly built stool.

"In commerce, just like in hunting, the early riser is the one who has the luck!" he loudly declared, sinking his teeth into nerpa meat.

Over tea, he spoke to John.

"So what do you intend to do with that?" He nodded toward the whalebone, piled by one of the yaranga's walls.

"The whalebone belongs to everyone," said John.

"What a big happy family you are around here!" said Carpenter, exasperated.

"And that's why," John calmly continued, "I can't make the decision myself. I do know that my countrymen would like to trade it for a whaleboat."

"What is it with you people and whaleboats around here?" Carpenter exclaimed. "I can understand that the uneducated Chukchi might have a fascination with this new contraption. But you, haven't you seen for yourself that for these parts nothing is better than the hide boat? It's a familiar, time-tested vessel. But a whaleboat needs looking after, and it's not as though it's as quick as a hide boat under oars."

"We mean a whaleboat with an outboard motor," John clarified.

"And who is going to wind the motor?" asked Carpenter. "Do you realize, these Chukchi will take it to bits and pieces as soon as they clamp eyes on it? That's how curious a people they are. Did you see an alarm clock in Tatmirak's yaranga? No sooner had he gotten it home than the Eskimo decided to find out what's knocking around in there. He took it apart, but couldn't manage to put it back together again. The mechanic from Nome barely managed to fix it."

"It's not such a bad thing that they're curious," John smiled. "That means it'll be easy to teach them to handle the motor."

"You are an incorrigible Utopian!"

"I wish these people well."

"You have a strange way of thinking," Carpenter began in a different tone. "If we are to speak frankly, what difference can it make to you how these savages live? You'll stay here a while and then leave. There have been many here who wanted to live the primitive life, but sooner or later they all went. And it will go the same for you. That's why I am advising you to look out for yourself first. If you like – take your whalebone to Nome yourself, I won't stand in your way – but don't interfere with my trade in Enmyn."

"I am not interfering," John answered calmly. "I only ask that you consider the Chukchi's wishes and sell them a whaleboat."

"All right, they'll get a whaleboat," Carpenter promised on reflection. "But I won't be responsible for the consequences."

Carpenter devoted the rest of the day to selling the wares he'd brought along. Buyers – bestrewn with pelts, fox and wolverine pelts – crowded inside the chottagin. The women brought slippers, decorated with beads and white deer hair, and embroidered chamois gloves.

Carpenter would pick up a hide, shake it out, then blow on it, puffing his thick lips out along the grain, and toss it into the pile. The buyer would ask for the desired goods, and Carpenter handed them over immediately. If the asked-for item wasn't available, he would note it down in his notebook. Almost every inhabitant of Enmyn had gone in and out of the chottagin. It was mainly the men who traded, but a few women had come as well. Orvo and Armol' had not been among the buyers, though their wives had been there.

Tiarat bought a new Winchester and, with a guilty look in John's direction, paid twenty white-fox furs for it.

The trade finished late. Carpenter had sat over his notes for a good few hours after that. Shutting his notebook with a bang, seemingly pleased with the results, he gave a cheerful shout:

"And now we can have a drink! Business is done!"

Pyl'mau noiselessly set the table and disappeared inside the polog.

The men were alone inside the chottagin, by the light of the dying fire.

"So what did you decide about the whalebone?" Carpenter asked again.

"I'm going to follow your advice: drive to Nome and try to buy a whaleboat there."

"I'll give you letters of introduction."

"Thank you."

"That way, there will be two whaleboats in your settlement," Carpenter said with a smile.

"Do you think I can get two boats for the whalebone?" John asked doubtfully.

"I don't know about that," Carpenter chuckled. "As for one of those boats, it's Armol' who's buying. He's already made a deposit – one hundred and fourteen white-fox pelts, plus twenty of red fox . . ."

"So the joint purchase of a whaleboat isn't to be," John thought sadly.

"I think that will be even better," Carpenter said brightly. "You'll all have two whaleboats instead of just one."

"Yes, perhaps that will be better," John was thoughtful as he answered.

"You've given me a splendid welcome, and have done everything possible for me. Please accept a few modest gifts from me."

The trader rose, went to his luggage and split off a sealed, twenty-pound sack of flour, a bag of sugar and a brand new 60x60 Winchester with three crates of cartridges.

"This is for you, dearest John."

"That doesn't look like a gift," John said. "So much at once. No, I couldn't take it."

"You will offend me. You will offend me mortally and for life." Sincere disappointment was written on Carpenter's face, and his voice shook.

"Wait a moment," John dove inside the polog and returned within a few minutes, accompanied by Pyl'mau.

"In that case," he said, "accept a gift from me, too." John lay a spectacular polar bear skin at Carpenter's feet. "I bagged this animal in late autumn. He came to our settlement and knocked on my door."

"Oh, thank you! Many, many thanks!" Carpenter was moved. "Allow me to make a special offering to your charming wife."

Pyl'mau was presented with a set of needles, colored thread and a length of cloth for a kamleika.

Early the next morning, Carpenter departed.

18

Winter days resemble one another like twins. When the weather was quiet John would go out onto the ice, and when it was inclement he would work in the house. If stormy weather stretched into days, he'd spend the long winter evenings in Orvo's yaranga, listening to his tales of the ancient ways of the Chukchi people or his own sojourn in America.

From time to time there was a distinct whiff of alcohol about the old man, and John was at a loss as to where Orvo could have gotten the drink. One day he actually asked the old man about it point-blank.

"I make it myself," Orvo declared with some pride.

In the cellar beside the polog John discovered a primitive moonshine apparatus – an amazing contraption. A fairly large vessel woven out of tree-bark strips served as the reservoir. The funneling pipe was the barrel of a 60x60 Winchester. The wooden reservoir had a metal bottom, under which an everyday grease lamp gave off a low flame. Out of the muzzle, instead of a bullet exited a slow drip of murky water with an undeniable odor of fermentation.

"Did you think of it yourself?" John asked.

"Seen things like this over in America. True, those were made differently . . . But I'd got a good idea of how they work. The main thing is to have flour and sugar. And I've got plenty of those. Traded all my sables for the supply. It didn't work out with the whaleboat, and so at least I'll have my fill of the joy-making water . . ."

Orvo had been saddened by the failure of the joint whaleboat purchase. Often, brimming with the "Winchester brew," the old man launched into long complaint of man's imperfections to John.

"Maybe it's all for nothing, a person being given reason," he would ponder. "I know that boozing is no good, that's what my reason tells me, but still I drink. Reason was telling Armol': You should live together with everyone else, and the whaleboat should be bought by all of us together, but he did the opposite – bought it for himself alone. So many things we do against our reason, and mostly we don't live our lives the way reason tells us . . . So then, it looks like it's useless, this human reasoning? Eh? What do you say, Sson MacLennan?"

When Orvo began talking this way, it meant that despite maintaining his usual composure on the outside, the old man was actually very drunk indeed.

Came a true bright day to Enmyn. A sliver of the sun rose over the horizon, washing the snows and ice hummocks on the sea with pink light.

"The sun has awakened," they were saying in the yarangas, smearing the idols with grease and sacrificial blood in gratitude.

"The sun has awakened, the day has begun," whispered Pyl'mau over the wooden face of the idol that had changed places with the washstand. "Let the new day bring happiness to our whole settlement, to all people. Let good fortune stay with our hunters, and especially with my husband, Sson. He has no hands, and so he needs your protection and help more than the others . . ."

Pyl'mau swirled the blood and fat together in a wooden cup and rubbed some on the idol's mouth. The god's greasy face was smiling, and it often disconcerted John to intercept his contented, placated look.

And when the Long Days came, and they had to perform the rite of Lowering the Hide Boats, John was unexpectedly called to the men's morning gathering.

Pyl'mau awoke her husband herself and, still inside the chottagin, before he opened the outer door, hurriedly gave his face a smear of cold nerpa blood. With a bloody mug and accompanied by little Yako, John set off for the tall whalebone supports on which the hide boats rested.

Young men untied the straps that belted the hide boats to the supports and carefully lowered the hide vessels to the snow, setting them facing the sea, stern to the tundra.

As he did the year before, Orvo walked around the boats, wooden dish in his hands and incantations on his lips, scattering the sacrificial food to the Dusk, Dawn, North, and South. And just the same, the dogs collected the gods' offerings, but quietly, as though they grasped the solemnity of the occasion.

The high-vaulting sun glowed bright over Enmyn and the ritual-makers. The sky was so bright, so blue, that even the snow seemed a light blue, and in shadow the blue seemed spilled from the sky straight onto the snow.

Going on a hunt became a pleasure: a long day with warmth flowing down from the sky. Many took young boys along, training them in the hunter's craft. Yako was keen to go with John, but was still too young.

"When the ducks take flight, then I'll take you along to the sandbank. You'll throw your eplykytet right into the flock," John promised him.

"You'll definitely take me, Ateh?" * the boy would ask.

"I will, Son," John answered back.

Duck season arrived. Three-year-old Yako didn't hit anything, of course, but was still proud of being taken along by his father. Pyl'mau was glowing as much as her son. In conversation with her friends, she never missed an opportunity to mention that "Yako went duck hunting with his father."

* *Ateh* – father.

John got used to the new Winchester, Carpenter's gift, and Orvo trimmed the stock and butt, taking off some wood that he reckoned was extraneous. The Winchester took on a strange appearance, but did become much lighter.

The hunting season was a good one. Almost every day John brought home one or two nerpa, and Pyl'mau, heavily pregnant now, brought him a ladle of water with an ice chip floating inside. Every so often, before going to sleep, John would retire to his small cubbyhole and write in his notepad.

My second winter living in Chukotka is coming to an end. Memories of the past no longer trouble me. I have the feeling that I am dead to the past, and if another world, the next world really exists, then the people who end up there might remember life on earth with the same sort of feeling. Pyl'mau is soon to have a child, and so I will become deeply rooted among these people that fate has given the farthest corner of the planet to inhabit. Thank God, these people haven't many of the habits that have come to complicate the lives of modern men. Their life is simple and plain, they are honest and sincere. When they meet, there are no complicated ceremonies of greeting. One simply says to the other: "You've come?" And the other replies: "Yes." And yet sometimes the evil wind from the outside world manages to seep in. Otherwise, where would Armol's miserliness come from? Why did he decide to go against these people's ancient commandment – owning everything jointly and considering any earned wealth to be the wealth of all? Undoubtedly, the evil spirit at work here is Mr. Carpenter. But the Chukchi themselves can no longer manage without many of the things invented in the white men's world. The less my new countrymen interact with white people, the longer they will resist passing laws that create only the illusion of order, but in reality just complicate life – the longer they will preserve their spiritual and physical health . . .

One day, instead of Pyl'mau it was Grandma Cheivuneh who came out to greet him. Handing him the ladle, she announced:

"An important guest has come to your yaranga."

"Carpenter?" John asked in surprise.

"This guest isn't a man, it's a woman. And she's more important and prettier than a dozen Poppies!"

John wanted to get inside the yaranga, but the old lady barred the entrance.

"First you must be purified. Wait . . ."

Cheivuneh whispered a few words of an incantation and only then allowed him to enter the chottagin. John was already beginning to guess what had happened.

"So it's a woman who's come visiting?" he confirmed with Cheivuneh.

"Yes. A beauty with hair like the dawn," Cheivuneh answered.

"Red-haired, like grandfather Martin," John decided, and carefully raised the polog's fur-lined curtain.

"What are you doing?!" the midwife screamed. "Watch it! This guest is afraid of the cold." Paying no attention to the old woman's wailing, John crawled inside the polog. And when his eyes grew used to the murk, after a day of bright sunlight, he made out his wife by the back wall. She lay on her side, her large swollen breasts bare. Next to her, on a pile of fawn skins, wriggled something small and pink.

"Sson!" Pyl'mau's voice was a little hoarse. "Look how pretty she is!"

At first John was hard-pressed to find anything beautiful in this tiny lump of life. The child's sparse hair really was reddish. But as he looked into the tiny crumpled face, the greedily suckling little being, there was an unfamiliar and enormous tenderness alighting in his breast. Tears came to his eyes, and John whispered to the newborn:

"Hello, Mary!"

"Do you like her?" asked Pyl'mau.

"She's beautiful!" John answered. "I named her Mary. That's my mother's name."

"And I've given her a Chukchi name – Tynevirineu," Pyl'mau said.

"So let the girl have two names, then: Mary and Tynevirineu."

"Yes, yes!" Pyl'mau said happily. "Like a white person. You've got two names, haven't you? John MacLennan."

"In that case, Mary will have a total of three names: Mary-Tynevirineu MacLennan," smiled John.

"And three is even better!" Pyl'mau agreed.

Cheivuneh crawled into the polog and started shooing John away:

"Enough, enough already! You've had a look, now off you go. A husband is not supposed to see his wife for ten days after she's given birth, but we did let you in, as you're a white man. But now, go and get the gifts ready: Your guest hasn't arrived empty-handed, has she?"

"Go, Sson," said Pyl'mau. "The gifts are all in the wooden crate, in a nerpa-skin bag."

The chottagin was already crowded with people. Orvo stepped forward to greet John and showed him his little finger. John looked at the crooked, blue-nailed pinkie with bewilderment. Beside it, a second pinkie appeared – Tiarat's, then Armol's. John soon found himself surrounded by an assortment of pinkies, whose owners congratulated him on the arrival of a long-awaited and wanted guest.

"I don't understand anything," John muttered.

"It means," Orvo explained, pinkie still held high, "that now you have to present us all with gifts in the name of your guest – the newborn."

John took out the sack that Pyl'mau had been talking about. Yes, his wife had taken care of everything. Small packets held pinches of tobacco, lumps of sugar, tea, lengths of colored cloth, needles, thread and even a pair of soles for torbasses.

John wanted to go back inside the polog and spend some time with

Pyl'mau, but the guests kept on arriving, little fingers in the air, while those who had already received their gifts seemed in no hurry to leave . . . settling down for a cup of tea around the short-legged table.

"It's not a bad thing, of course, that the girl was named right away," Orvo mused aloud, "but the gods ought to have been consulted, really."

"If it's so important," John said, "it's not too late to do that."

"Yes, let's ask them anyway," Orvo advised, and sent a boy for his divining stick. While they were waiting, Orvo ordered all the men who had done what they came to do to clear out of the yaranga. Only John and Orvo, plus little Yako, were left.

"Now you have to really look after yourself," Orvo sternly enjoined his friend. "Couldn't you have had enough patience to postpone looking at the newborn girl? And this too: You shouldn't have touched your wife for ten days, and what did you do? You crawled right inside the polog, not even taking off your hunting kamleika. You've angered the gods, and only one thing might save you: They will forgive you, as someone only starting a new life. Remember, the gods are not the only ones who dislike your making these blunders . . ."

The boy brought over the divining stick, and Orvo sat down directly underneath the smoke-hole. Setting one end of the stick against the sunspot, he began lifting and lowering the other end of the stick slightly, all the while whispering sacred words. He did this for a few minutes, then laid the divining stick aside and cheerfully informed John:

"Everything's fine! I've convinced them!"

It was late in the night by the time the last guest departed. Two women who were to take care of the new mother stayed behind in the yaranga. John was about to reenter the polog, but Cheivuneh firmly forbade it and only allowed him to chat through the fur curtain.

Little Yako had been led off somewhere, and John had to lie down for the night in his little room.

For a long while he couldn't fall asleep, listening to the noises coming from inside the polog. At first, he could hear the women's muffled conversation, and then the infant's cry pierced the silence of the night. This was so unexpected that John vaulted off his bed and rushed to the door. But the cry was immediately hushed. John listened for a moment then stretched out on the bed again. That was my child crying, he thought, lying there with his eyes wide open. My first child. The person who will continue my life and carry the features of my face, my blood flowing through her veins even after I've gone beyond the clouds. What will she be like? What future lies ahead of her? Can it be that she will spend her entire life – her youth, her adulthood and her old age – here, on these deserted shores? And the old, but lately forgotten, ache for his old life gripped John's heart, and his breath caught. Suddenly he became aware that he was weeping. And he wanted so badly to have one more look at his daughter, at Pyl'mau, that he got up and, paying no heed to Cheivuneh's scolding, crept inside the polog.

The old women held something over the fire, something that resembled a piece of worn-out shoesole. The sole smelled of burnt wood. Cheivuneh was carefully scraping off the ash that formed on it, and collecting it on a piece of clean chamois.

Pyl'mau lay on the bed, and little Mary – eyes shut – slept, snoring sweetly through her tiny nose and making sucking motions with her lips. John noticed a leather pouch, similar to a tobacco pouch, at the head of the bed.

"How do you feel?" John asked, whispering so as not to wake the baby.

"Fine," Pyl'mau answered him, with a guilty look at Cheivuneh.

"I can't sleep," John said, and turned to Cheivuneh:

"Can't you burn that thing in the chottagin? All this smoke makes it hard for Pyl'mau and the newborn to breathe."

"How can you say that, Sson!" Pyl'mau said reproachfully. "Grandmother is doing everything as it should be done. We'll sprinkle these ashes on Tynevirineu-Mary's belly button, so that it heals faster."

"I'm sorry, I didn't know," John was mortified.

"And this is where we keep our girl's most precious treasures," Pyl'mau gestured to the leather pouch.

"What is it?" asked John.

"The umbilical cord and the stone blade that was used to cut it. All this has to be kept very carefully."

"All right, we'll keep it safe," and, heedless of Grandma Cheivuneh's stern glances, John touched his lips to Pyl'mau's ruddy cheek.

For ten days, John suffered under a kind of house arrest. He was not to do anything: Whether going out to hunt or doing work at home, it could all have brought trouble from the unseen but omniscient gods.

It was without him that the hide boats sailed to the spring hunt.

And when his "quarantine," as John termed his sacred idleness, was over, John discovered that he was the only man left in Enmyn. People came to him with various requests for help, settling a dispute or simply asking his advice.

Pyl'mau was back to doing all the housework, and John sat happily in the sun, watching the sleeping Tynevirineu-Mary, who more and more at once resembled the older Mary and Pyl'mau and the red-headed Martin. This unexpected combination was the source of much amusement for John, and helped pass the days of enforced leisure.

Any day now, they expected the hunters' return. The long-awaited tidings came to the yaranga via Yako, who saw himself as a grown-up now that he had a little sister.

"Two hide boats coming in, and one whaleboat!" he shouted and ran off.

Together with the women and old people, John descended to the shore.

Yes, these were Enmyn hide boats, and a white whaleboat with a black stripe on its side: So Armol' really did become the owner of a wooden boat.

The absence of wind forced the hunters to row themselves in, and the vessels were slow on the approach to the settlement. The new whaleboat was tugging a heavily laden hide boat.

Finally the hide boats and the whaleboat landed on the beach.

"Yettyk!" John shouted, rushing to meet the hunters that clambered out onto the shore.

"Ee-ee! Myt'yenmyk!" the hunters answered him. Only Orvo, breaking with tradition, walked up to John and shook his hand according to the white people's custom.

"How is your daughter?"

"Very well! She's expecting you to visit today."

"I'll come, I'll come," Orvo replied.

They unloaded the fresh walrus meat onto the beach, and Orvo began the reckoning up of shares. Despite the fact that John had not participated in the hunt, he was doled out the same share of meat and blubber as if he had gone hunting alongside everyone else.

"That's how it should be," Orvo explained. "If I fell ill, or another man did, my companions would do just the same for him."

Everyone was grateful for the fresh walrus. They pulled it up onto the beach, with bone rollers under the keel to keep the bottom from harm.

Armol' was walking about the boat with a great show of importance, gave orders, and helped insert the struts underneath it, so it would not fall on its side.

John circled the vessel from every angle, took a look at the inside and even ran his stumps over the metal-sheeted keel.

"It's a good whaleboat," he said to Armol', who'd been jealously watching his every move.

"It is a good one," Armol' agreed, barely keeping rein on his self-importance. "Now all it needs is a motor. But Carpenter didn't have one. He promised it for next year. So if you were my motor driver on the whaleboat, we'd be the most well favored hunters."

"I intend to buy a whaleboat myself," John answered.

In the evening, Orvo came for a visit. The old man picked up the new-born girl and told her:

"Grow big and beautiful!"

"Orvo," John addressed the old man, "now we should go and get our whaleboat. Straight to Nome. Besides the whalebone, I've got pelts, too."

"We'll rest up a bit, and then we'll go," Orvo concurred.

19

It was almost a month since Orvo, John, Tiarat, and a few more Enmyn hunters had gone to Nome. There had been no word of them, and Pyl'mau tried to quell her fears by throwing herself into housework and tending to little Tynevirineu-Mary.

Tying the baby to her back, accompanied by Yako, she would go into the tundra to gather edible leaves and roots. They would take some provisions along and, in good weather, spend the entire day in the tundra. Sometimes they came as far as the reindeer herders' camps that had moved closer to the sea in order to protect the deer from midges and mosquitos.

Il'motch, the head of the camp, would invite them into his yaranga and treat them to delicacies: boiled tongue, deer's-leg bone marrow, singed lips, and even plain boiled reindeer meat.

"You tell your husband," he instructed Pyl'mau, "that I wish to be his friend."

To be a deer herder's friend meant having a sure means of replenishing your store of deerskins for bedding, clothing, and the polog; and in the case of a dearth of animals on the sea, a deer herder's friend could always come to your aid.

Whenever she returned home, Pyl'mau tried to take the mountain path, so that she could see Enmyn's shore from a distance. But each day, Armol's whaleboat and hide boat were all that her eyes could see.

Once, cleaning up John's little room, she found a thick leather-bound notepad whose pages were covered in scrawly symbols, as though thousands of flies had gone over the white page and left their mark. Pyl'mau even sniffed the pages; they had a barely perceptible and strange scent. Pyl'mau knew that the pages were the record of a conversation, words, sounds that had meaning. She peered at each line, at the interwoven curlicues of each letter, and even listened to the pages with bated breath, as though it were possible to catch the set-down speech with your ear. What did John talk about on these thin, white as though snow-covered, sheets of paper, she wondered? What thoughts and musings had left their mark here? Maybe it was with this drooping letter at the end of a line that he expressed his sorrow for his past life, for the loved ones left behind in the far-off and unknown Port Hope? . . . Some long evenings, John would get to telling her about the land where he was born and where he'd lived his life. There would be yearning and emotion in his voice, and Pyl'mau would then hurry to change the topic to something else. And now John wasn't far from his home at all. There were no ships sailing straight to Port Hope from Nome but, as John said, you could first go to Vancouver and from there it was no trouble to go over metal runners on a sled hitched to a fire-breathing cart . . . When John was leaving, Pyl'mau, as befitted the wife of a hunter, didn't say a word to him. But how badly she had wanted to shout after him: Come back without fail, remember that I wait for you, and so does golden-haired Tynevirineu-Mary and your son, Yako! But she only gazed at her husband, never taking her eyes off him and saying the words in her mind. Almost as though John had heard them, he walked back to the three of them standing on the shore before getting into the hide boat. He looked carefully at Tynevirineu-Mary and Yako, and quietly told his wife:

"Don't worry, take care of the children. We'll be back soon . . ."

But a month has gone, and still they had not returned.

It seemed to Pyl'mau that her fellow-wives were starting to give her sideways glances. And one time, Cheivuneh had told her the story of how there had been a white man living in Uelen, who'd married a Chukchi girl, made four children with her and then disappeared forever, went back to America, or maybe Russia.

"Why are you telling me this?" Pyl'mau pleaded.

The old lady pursed her lips, embarrassed.

Taking advantage of Orvo's absence, Armol' had moved the device for making bad joy-making water over to his own yaranga, and fitted it with the barrel of his own Winchester.

In a drunken haze he'd descend to shore and sing songs, dancing around the snow-white whaleboat with its black stripe.

One day, in a very inebriated state, he came by Pyl'mau's yaranga. She was feeding the little girl, while Yako was polishing off some cured walrus meat that he cut off the rib with an enormous hunting knife.

"Yetti, Armol'," Pyl'mau affably greeted him.

"Ee-ee," Armol' lowered himself heavily to a whale vertebra and fixed his eyes on the little girl.

Tynevirineu-Mary left the breast, suddenly gave a wide smile and laughed noisily.

"Kakomei! She's real."

"Did you doubt that I could give birth to a real baby girl?" Pyl'mau said, offended.

"It wasn't you I doubted, but Sson . . ."

"But why?"

"It's hard to explain it to you, a woman . . . But this is what I think: Can a white willow-grouse and a black raven have a child together? And will this child be able to fly, even if it is born?"

"As you see, this baby is real enough, and I'm sure that Tynevirineu-Mary will fly."

"Won't such a long and heavy name drag her down to the ground?" Armol' deliberately and slowly stretched out the syllables: "Ty-ne-vir-i-neu-ma-ree . . ."

"You might like to know that a third name can be added to those. That's the custom with white people. And then the girl will be called Tynevirineu-Mary MacLennan," challenged Pyl'mau.

"One who tries to live according to another people's custom is like a duck that caws like a raven," Armol' told her in a pedantic tone.

"What's to be done, then?" Pyl'mau shrugged. "Tynevirineu-Mary is the daughter of two nations. What's wrong with her being able to caw like a raven and quack like a duck?"

"You can't be argued with!" Armol' said angrily. "You're the same as you were before you were married . . . Just the same . . ."

Suddenly Armol' went silent, as though he were seeing something in the distance. He stared into a fixed point in space for a long time, and all the while deep furrows gathered and relaxed on his brow.

"He was my best friend . . . And when they entrusted us with wearing the sharp hunting knives, we swore to always be side by side, to help not just one another, but also those near to us . . . Well you know that when a friend dies, it's up to the surviving one to take care of his wife. I should have taken you into my yaranga and made you my second wife. But you chose another. The one who had killed your husband . . ."

Together with fear, outrage was kindling in Pyl'mau's heart.

"Now I'll have to think, before I reach out my hand to help you," Armol' went on. "Sson should have come back a long time ago but he hasn't, and I don't think he ever will. I know white people very well, and I see through them. They never see us as their equals. They despise us and laugh at our customs. Having touched us, they wash their hands, and after speaking to us they rinse their mouths with water and rub their tongues with brushes on sticks. You might say – but what about Sson? Yes, he's different. But if he'd been a real white man – with hands – he'd quickly change his tune and wouldn't live among us. So when he was left without his hands, he lost some of his pride because he couldn't live with his own people as an equal, but here he still felt himself to be a little above us . . . And now he's learned to shoot, get food for himself and even make speeches on paper with little marks . . . Now he's become like his folk again, and so . . ."

"Armol'!" Pyl'mau shrieked, so frightening Yako that the boy burst into tears. "Get out and never show yourself in our yaranga again! Never come back, bringer of black thoughts! Poison drips from your tongue, and it's a wonder it hasn't eaten your mouth away!"

"Pyl'mau! Come back to your senses! Think what you're saying!" Armol' lurched from the whale vertebra and backed toward the door. "If you crawl by the entrance to my yaranga, I won't open the door to you . . . Think, you'll be left all alone!"

"It's not true! It's not true!" Pyl'mau was screaming, as she pushed Armol' back.

Retreating, Armol' tripped over the yaranga's doorstep and fell flat on his back and out of the yaranga. Pyl'mau stopped to catch her breath, and it was then that she heard an unfamiliar sound: mosquito singing or else the twang of a thin metallic string. She stepped over Armol', lying prone, and shouted to Yako:

"Run along with me, son!"

The unfamiliar sound was coming from the shore. With an effort, Pyl'mau made out two black dots on the horizon. Could it be John returning? She ran down the gravelly slope and stopped right at the waterline, mindless of the waves that lapped at her torbasses.

Pyl'mau was straining to see but the sudden flow of tears impeded her vision.

"One whaleboat and one hide boat!" someone called out.

"Look how quickly they're going!"

"They've got a motor! A motor!"

"And they're tugging the hide boat!"

Pyl'mau saw nothing. She took a step and someone grabbed her from behind:

"Crazy woman! You could drown this way!"

Pyl'mau turned back sheepishly, wiped her eyes with the sleeve of her kamleika and only now could make out the approaching boats.

The whaleboat flew over the water like a bird. Its speed was such that the tugged hide boat flopped from side to side. The roar of the motor grew louder and louder, and the people of Enmyn listened to the unusual sound with curiosity and surprise.

"Like singing," said old Cheivuneh, stopping next to Pyl'mau.

"I can see Orvo!" someone shouted. "He's sitting at the helm."

"And there's Sson!"

"Sitting by the motor!"

The whaleboat was very close now. The motor's noise lessened, and then stopped altogether. The boat glided toward the shore. Tiarat jumped off the bow and onto the shingles.

"Yettyk! Pykirtyk!"* came voices from every side, and the men on the whaleboat answered:

"Myt'yenmyk!"

Pyl'mau couldn't take her eyes off John and, turning the little girl's face his way, pointed to him, saying:

"There's your father! Your father's come back! He's coming ashore to meet us."

John took the motor out of its well and put it in the whaleboat.

They dragged the whaleboat and the hide boat from the water. The men who'd just returned loaded their family members with gifts and went off to their own yarangas.

John set down a large cloth sack and two crates – one bigger than the other – in the middle of the chottagin.

* *Pykirtyk!* – You've come.

"How big and lovely you've grown!" he said, on looking his wife and children over.

"We really missed you," Pyl'mau smiled. "Every day we looked to the sea."

"We did," Yako confirmed.

Pyl'mau looked at John, and it seemed to her that he had come back different from the man who had left, and her heart was a bit uneasy at this.

"Why do you look at me so strangely?" asked John.

"It's just that I'm very glad," Pyl'mau sighed. "Don't you be angry with me, but at times I did think: What if you he doesn't come back . . . His home isn't far from there . . ."

"Darling Mau!" John embraced her and kissed her. "Wherever I am, wherever the winds may blow me, the home nearest and dearest to me is this yaranga, and the nearest and dearest people are you Mau, Yako, and little Mary."

"Tynevirineu-Mary," corrected Pyl'mau.

While his wife was preparing the food and lighting a fire inside the chottagin, John was unpacking the presents from his bag. He dressed Yako in a brightly colored jacket, erected a cloth bonnet upon Mary's head, laid out bricks of tea, sugar, tobacco, and then picked up a smallish box of redwood. Yako was following his father's every move.

"What is it that you're making, Ateh?" he asked.

"Wait a minute, you'll find out," John replied.

And when he attached an enormous ear-shaped pipe and started to wind the handle, Yako hazarded a guess:

"I know – it's a motor!"

"You're almost right," John carefully lowered a shiny head with a bird's neck on top of a spinning disc that looked like a charred tree-trunk ring.

The chottagin was filled with unusual sounds, and Pyl'mau, startled, almost dropped the hot kettle.

Then a woman's voice began to sing. The dogs that were lounging inside the chottagin pricked up their ears and stared at the pipe's wide maw in bewilderment. The woman sang of something very dear, very heartfelt, and listening to her, Pyl'mau felt an aching yearning in her own breast.

"What is it?" she whispered, as though afraid of frightening the voice away.

"A gramophone," John answered.

When the song was over, Yako tiptoed up to the pipe and peered inside. Finding nothing, he turned to his father:

"So where is she?"

"Who?"

"The singer."

"She stayed behind, far away from here, and it's only her voice that is here," John attempted to explain.

"She stayed behind, and her voice traveled here?" Pyl'mau's voice contained both fear and astonishment.

"Well, yes," John replied.

"Poor thing!" Pyl'mau wrung her hands. "Why did you do that? How can a person live without a voice? How is she going to talk now?"

John took a long time explaining the mechanics of sound recording, but neither Pyl'mau nor Yako could understand a thing.

When he wound up another record, Pyl'mau asked, as she listened to the man's voice:

"So that one's mute too, now?"

Then John did his best to explain that the people singing out of the wide wooden pipe haven't lost their voices at all. It was more like they'd shared their voice with the record, the thing that looked like a sliver from a charred tree stump.

"And those people's voices didn't even get weaker?" asked Pyl'mau.

"No," was John's firm answer.

Pyl'mau calmed down and listened to the music with obvious pleasure, no longer pitying and commiserating with the singers who'd lost their voices. Still, it was Orvo who explained the principle of sound recording best of all, when almost all of Enmyn gathered in John's yaranga to hear the gramophone.

"It's a kind of frozen echo," said Orvo. "This black record is like a steep crag – it reflects voice and sound. Only the crag gives the sound back right away, but the record holds it and can repeat it many times."

Only Yako was not completely convinced by the grown-ups' explanation. To him, it seemed that the most convincing explanation was that there were little people with musical instruments inside the box.

So when he and Tynevirineu-Mary were the only people left inside the yaranga, Yako – left behind as a babysitter – dragged the music box into the center of the chottagin, under the light coming from the smoke-hole. The pipe was easily taken off: Yako had seen his father attach it. Carefully inspecting the box he discovered nail studs. These little nails were just the same as on the Winchester, and to pry them out of the wood, you needed a screwdriver. But when you haven't got a screwdriver, the end of a hunting knife will do just as well.

Holding his breath, Yako lifted the lid . . . but instead of the expected little people he found only metal parts. Yako unscrewed them one by one, but the little people were nowhere to be seen. Bitterly disappointed, Yako shoved the unhinged mechanism wrathfully back into the gramophone, put back the lid and carried the music box to its place.

"There's nothing there," he mournfully announced to his baby sister, who was staring at him with her round little eyes. "No little folk."

When the Enmyn people came that evening to hear the music, John discovered that the music box was silent. The winding handle turned easily in its nest, and inside the wooden box itself, the mechanism parts rattled around from side to side.

Yako sat in the corner, half-dead with fright. He realized that he'd ruined the music box, despite having tried to make sure all the innards fit back inside.

"What could have happened to it?" John was puzzled as he turned the handle and gave the box a shake.

Pyl'mau's eyes met her son's. His mother walked over to him and Yako said, guiltily:

"I was looking for the little people."

"You've been told already, haven't you – there are no little people in there!" Pyl'mau shouted and grabbed the boy by the ear.

Yako's pained and frightened wail filled the entire chottagin.

"What are you doing?" John took the boy away from his furious mother. "Calm down, Yako. It's a good thing that you took a look. Good boy. There's nothing wrong with trying to find out new things. Only next time, ask me to help you. All right, Yako?"

The little boy stopped crying and nodded his assent.

They fixed the gramophone and during the wet autumn evenings, a wind orchestra sounded over the quietened village. Negro singers' voices rent the damp cool air.

The motor whaleboat brought excitement and a new way of life to Enmyn. Now the distances were made shorter, and it was no great challenge to take a trip to Uelen or Keniskun. The only thing they did have to worry about was the fuel.

"If only the motor could eat nerpa or walrus fat!" Orvo daydreamed. "Then we'd go far out on the sea, where nobody's hunted yet, where the animals aren't wary."

The hunters had been to the Inchovin breeding ground, but there was not much walrus this year, and their main hopes remained in hunting along their own shores. But it so happened that the ice came early this winter.

20

A churning icy porridge had moved up to Enmyn's shoreline that morning. High waves launched themselves at the frosty shingled beach, spitting enormous chunks of ice onto the shore. A number of them reached so far they punched a hole in the roof of Tiarat's yaranga.

There were some days of sleet. Enmyn's paths froze over, and it was a struggle to get from one yaranga to another. The dogs didn't stir from the chottagins, and the people themselves were loath to leave their warm dwellings.

Each time John ventured out to pick up some supplies of meat, the sky seemed to him to be gathering lower and lower, and the waves creeping ever nearer the shore, as though nature, alien and hostile, were trying to swallow up the small and lonely human outpost.

One night, a strong frost descended, a veil of dry snow covered the ground and leveled the ice-churned surface of the sea.

Buckling "crow's feet" onto their shoes, the hunters walked out onto the new ice. A path to the sea stretched from each of the yarangas, and by nightfall, these paths were ruddy with fresh nerpa blood.

John sat inside the polog, attending to some broken straps on his snowshoes. A stamping of feet soon filled the chottagin.

"Yetti!" John shouted through the fur-lined curtain. "Menin?"*

* *Menin* – Who.

"Ghym,"* Orvo's head poked inside the polog, and then another head popped up beside his.

"Remember him?" Orvo nodded toward his companion. "This is Il'motch, the one you lived with when Kelena healed your hands."

"Of course!" John exclaimed. "I remember him very well!"

Having put away two large mugs of tea, Il'motch looked to Orvo with anticipation.

"John," Orvo turned to their host, "Il'motch has heard a lot about your music box, and he'd like to hear it play."

"Sure thing," said John. "Yako, go on and wind us up some music!" A naked Yako reached into the corner and asked his father:

"Do you want me to put on the woman's voice or the man's?"

"Which would you like?" John consulted with Il'motch.

"We can listen to the man's voice for now," Il'motch said, shooting Orvo an oblique glance.

The nomad listened attentively. Indeed, the expression on his face suggested that he understood every word of the jaunty cowboy song by Dean Morgan.

When the record was finished, Il'motch gave a word of praise:

"Good singing. Loud."

After the man, they listened to a woman's singing and then to a Negro church choir. The visitor was well pleased with the concert.

"I came to give you a present, Sson," he declared.

"That's right," Orvo corroborated. "Il'motch is going to be your tundra friend. For now, he's brought you two deer carcasses, a few hides, kamusses, fawn skins, and deer tendons to use as thread. All this he gives to you as his friend."

"Oh! Thank you!" John was overwhelmed by such generosity.

So Pyl'mau had guessed correctly when she told him about Il'motch's intention to become John's tundra friend. Well then, it would be both

* *Ghym* – I, me.

flattering and useful to have such a friend. Only what could he offer him in return? And should this be done immediately?

"John and I will come to visit you soon, before you move camp too far from us," Orvo told the nomadic reindeer herder.

As soon as the guests finished their tea and departed, John asked his wife:

"Maybe I should have given return gifts to Il'motch right away?"

"No, it isn't done, to give gifts back right away," Pyl'mau answered. "Otherwise it would look more like a trade than an exchange of gifts. When you go visit him in his camp, that's when you'll take him your gifts."

A few days later, Orvo and John loaded their sleds with presents for the reindeer herders and set off into the tundra. John's sled held a variety of small items purchased in Nome – lengths of printed cloth, coarse white calico for kamleikas, thread, needles, bits of lakhtak skin for shoe soles, leather strips, and two nerpa-skin containers of clarified seal fat.

They spent the first night in the tundra. Orvo dug some twigs out from under the snow and made a blazing fire, heating up some tea over it. They dined on cold kopal'khen and boiled nerpa meat; then, surrounded by their dogs, they bedded down in a snow-lined hollow.

The weather was calm. Flares of the Northern Lights promenaded across the starry night, and the moon's narrow crescent was etched sharply into the sky. Lying there for a while, eyes wide open, John called to Orvo:

"Are you asleep?"

"I'm not," the old man replied. "I'm lying here and thinking: Could I ever have imagined that two winters and two summers later we'd be going to visit Il'motch again, you and I. And not as a white man and a luoravetlan, but simply as two people who live the same life . . . And it wasn't so long ago, now was it? So does that mean that our ways are not so strange to you now?"

"The first time I made this journey, I too never imagined that it would be my path to you. You wouldn't believe how frightened I was. To be honest, I didn't even think of you as people."

"This is not new to me," Orvo replied. "When I found myself on a white people's ship for the first time, it was like diving headlong into another world. I didn't know the language or any of the customs. They laughed at me, teased me, beat me when the mood took them. For some reason, they loved offering me soap to eat. How much soap I had to gobble, before they showed me a little respect!"

Orvo sighed heavily, and the sleeping dog-pack leader sighed in his sleep, too, as if in concord.

"The thing that divides us from one another is stereotypes about others and wrong ideas about ourselves," John said. "I think that the biggest mistake might be this: Each nation thinks that it's the only one that lives in the right way, and all the others have turned their backs on this right way, for one reason or another. In itself, the idea is harmless. It even helps keep order in a society. But when a nation tries to change another's way of life forcibly, that's when things go wrong. Dear Orvo, if only you knew the whole bloody history of the civilized world!"

"No one has tried to change our life here," Orvo answered.

"Didn't they try to change your gods?" asked John. "I know all about the Ananalin and the North American Indians. Our main shamans, the servants of the white gods, dream about converting the savages – as they call them – to their own faith."

"They wanted to change our gods here, too," Orvo replied. "The bearded white shamans drove around from camp to camp, passing out metal crosses and white shirts. You had to be dipped in water and accept the whites' god, to get one . . . Many people accepted him."

"What do you mean?" John was surprised. "So you're Christians?"

"What harm did it do us to believe in another god, too?" In the darkness, Orvo went on, "In those times, such a thing as a metal cross that you could make a fishhook out of was hard enough to come by. On top of that, adults were given a whole packet of tobacco leaf. And why should we have refused the white god? My countrymen took him up and said, Why shouldn't there be such a god as this one? They would set him next to their other gods and pray to him just the same way. This is how they reckoned: If the god that the whites brought really is all-powerful and all-knowing, he won't evict the host gods that took him in under their roof. So for a while, these new gods lived together with our old ones, and were eventually forgotten. Truth be told, they were not much use, since they didn't know what our lives are like, didn't know about the sea and the reindeer. And then, they didn't take to our food . . ."

"What?" John was amazed. "You fed them, too?"

"Of course!" came Orvo's reply. "Gods need to eat. But the blood and blubber rotted the paper, and soon enough all that was left of the sacred image was dirty rags. Those who got wooden gods held on to them for longer, but in the end threw them out, too, or gave them to the children to play with."

John was not a religious man, but such a casual approach to religion made him uneasy. Not without a secret design to trap Orvo, John asked him:

"So what would you say if a white person treated your gods the same way?"

"He'd probably be right to do it. It's no good forcing your own gods on someone else."

John was amazed at the simple and true answer.

"Yes, you're right . . . I've thought about your way of life a great deal. To my mind, the less we come into contact with the white people's world, the better. Do you agree, Orvo?"

Orvo took some time to answer. "I've thought about it myself," he said. "We can't withdraw from it completely. But I agree with you about everything else, Sson."

They arrived at Il'motch's nomad camp by midafternoon of the following day. John struggled to recollect a familiar place, but although the yarangas were the same, the surrounding landscape was different. It seemed that the nomads had set up camp in a different location from last year's.

The dogs were straining to make straight for the reindeer herd, but the pack leaders drove them on, then veered off to the side, where a welcoming crowd was waiting for them. Il'motch stood out from the others by virtue of his height and his festive chamois-leather outfit. He greeted the visitors and, after giving his deer herders instructions to feed and chain the dogs, led Orvo and John into his yaranga.

John inspected the inside decor of the nomad dwelling with curiosity. The design in general was the same as the seashore Chukchi's, but every part of the deer herder's yaranga was notable for its lightness. There were no walls, as such, in the yaranga: A tent of sueded or simply shorn deerskins stretched over poles formed the yaranga's outer shell. Inside it hung a polog, looking a bit cramped to a seashore dweller's eye. There was a fire lit inside the roomy chottagin.

"I'm very glad that you've come to visit me," Il'motch said with some ceremony, "make yourselves at home."

John presented his gifts to his tundra friend. Il'motch accepted them with restrained dignity, giving them a cursory glance.

"Velynkekun!" he said, and ordered for the gifts to be cleared away.

Finding a quiet moment, John consulted with Orvo:

"Didn't Il'motch like my gifts?"

"He did," Orvo said with certainty. "It's just that giving presents is the usual thing between friends, and it doesn't do to look them over."

"Il'motch," John turned to their host, "could I see Kelena?"

"You can," Il'motch nodded, "she'll be glad to see a person whom she's saved from death."

The old lady didn't keep them waiting. On seeing John, she gave out a loud wail:

"Kyke vyne vai!* He's come, the healed one! Kyke! How hale and hearty he is!"

John presented her with a length of cloth for a kamleika, tobacco, and beveled sewing needles.

"Velynkykun!" Kelena thanked him, and asked permission to take a look at his hands.

Deftly, the old lady's lean sinewy fingers went over every stitch, every fold, with surgeon's skill. Having looked her fill of her handiwork, Kelena couldn't help saying delightedly:

"Well made!"

Orvo and John were put up in the camp leader, Il'motch's, yaranga. A second polog had been made for them. In the night, John was awakened by the sound of the wind. He lay inside the darkened polog and the specters of the past crowded around him. It seemed to him that time had turned back, and once again he was in the same situation as two years ago. He even felt the ghost of pain in his wrists.

The storm was clearly audible inside the nomad's dwelling – the walls here were thinner, and the whole of the yaranga smaller. John didn't manage to fall asleep until morning, not properly. He kept nodding off, then waking, reality mingling with dreams. Hearing a slight noise inside the chottagin, he stuck his head out of the polog and saw Il'motch.

"You awake?" Il'motch greeted him and shook his head regretfully: "Blizzard. No good."

A light snow fell through the opening that crowned the yaranga's central cone. What an amazing construction is a yaranga. John had noticed that if there is the tiniest hole in the wall – from a nail, or something else – even the smallest blizzard blows in a snowdrift. But the smoke-hole, which could accommodate a person climbing in, admits only a snow flurry!

---

* *Kyke vyne vai* – a woman's exclamation of surprise.

Il'motch drew back the deerskin that served as a door and disappeared into the glowing twilight of the blizzard.

All that day, Orvo and John were the only men in the camp – all the herders had gone to see to the reindeer. Il'motch returned late in the evening. He took a long time patting himself down in the chottagin, beating the snow from his kukhlianka and torbasses with a piece of deer antler.

"This blizzard is staying for a while," he informed them. "It's warm. The snow is wet, sticky."

"A southern wind?" asked Orvo.

"That's the one," Il'motch replied.

"A bad wind," Orvo gave John a worried look. "It could knock off the ice on shore. And when the frost comes after the blizzard, the snow will harden and make it difficult for the deer to feed."

"As soon as the wind dies down," said Il'motch, "we'll move to a different pasture, on the southern slope. The wind blows off the snow, there."

For three days and three nights the yaranga shuddered in the wind bursts. At the third night's waning, the wind became weaker and the frost stronger. At noon, they began to roll up the yarangas. Barely an hour later, all that was left of them were black circles and the fire pits. The reindeer people packed all the equipment and household items into the sleds. The herders drove up the reindeer herd, caught the draught animals – enormous big-horned bulls with large sad eyes.

By midday the caravan slowly set off for the blue mountains ahead. Il'motch, having said his farewells to Orvo and John, raced to catch up with his moving camp in a light dogsled that looked as if it were made of lace.

21

The wind was at their back. It blew up their kamleikas like sails, made curlicues out of the huskies' tails. The heavy snow didn't rise up, and so the whirlwind only polished it, pressing it to the ground. John had never moved in a sled at such a speed. They only allowed the dogs one rest stop, feeding them and having a snack of slightly melted deer meat. There was no way to light a fire in such windy conditions, and the travelers had to make do without tea.

By the next afternoon, they sighted the familiar shoreline crags. It was twilight by the time the sleds drove up on the lagoon ice, where the blizzard had left long furrows of hardened snow. On the icy smooth surface, the wind was so strong that it drove the sleds faster than the dogs could run, and the shaft dogs had to turn away from the front.

The settlement seemed to be crouching to earth, afraid of being carried of into the sea by the wind. John and Orvo were scanning the yarangas.

Orvo's sharp eye immediately registered that the repal'gyts had been blown off some of the yarangas. The hide boat supports had been knocked down.

A chill worry was creeping into their hearts. This kind of wind could do much damage.

John found his yaranga with his eyes and noted with satisfaction that it was still intact. Only the outbuildings' chimney pipe had been completely sheared off by the wind.

Where the snowpath led from the lagoon to the yarangas, a welcoming party was assembling. There were only three. They stood there, bent in the face of the wind, barely managing to keep their foothold on the rock-hard snow.

They were Tiarat, Guvat, and Armol'.

"Trouble!" Armol' shouted from afar. "The storm has taken the whaleboats and the hide boats!"

Orvo braked his sled.

"How could it have happened?"

"We did everything to save the boats," Tiarat launched into an explanation. "We froze the anchors into the ice, packed the whaleboats in snow, but it didn't help. The wind knocked the snow away and tore the thick straps as though they were cloth threads."

"The whaleboats flew in the air like they'd grown wings," Armol' butted in. "They all took off at the same time, like they'd decided to fly away home, and then they smashed on the ice hummocks and splintered to pieces . . . Oh, the misfortune!"

John directed his pack to his yaranga. The dwelling was filled with sadness, as though someone dear and precious had died. Even the children behaved quietly and in a restrained manner, and little Tynevirineu-Mary silently pressed up against her father's soft curly beard, as though able to comprehend the immeasurable loss.

Orvo, who'd come to see him that evening, said:

"Nobody could have prevented this disaster. A storm like this only happens twice in a hundred years . . ."

The wind continued to rage. The yaranga shuddered and creaked like a ship caught in a stormy ocean. Stray air currents managed to get inside the polog some mysterious way and shook the lamp's flame.

Pyl'mau was quietly crooning a lullaby to Tynevirineu-Mary, and her singing merged with the blizzard's song.

John listened to her with a sense of wonder, that his wife's voice weaved so naturally into the wind's humming. The melodies of her song and the storm were the same.

For a long time Orvo sat deep in thought, listening with John to the singing of the woman and the storm.

"We've gotten too proud," Orvo said quietly, "stopped honoring Narginen.* The Outer Forces, they've shown us what's what . . ."

John was about to teach the old man otherwise, explain to him that this was a natural disaster, against which there is no insurance, but some strange feeling of helplessness held him back. In Orvo's words there was promise of explanation and consolation.

"We wanted to live other than the way nature decreed," Orvo continued. "And it was as though a rainbow fog rose before my eyes. I couldn't see rightly anymore. And everything was going so well – there seemed to be more animals by the shore, the sea often offered us ritliu, the weather as good as could be expected, we were fortunate in the hunting and in the meetings with white people . . . Even sickness passed us by for a few years . . . And here's the punishment for our sins . . . It's not the first time that I can remember. At first everything goes well, and such a life starts up that even ancient old ones, who are long awaited in the world beyond the clouds, are in no hurry to leave the earth. The yarangas are full of cheer, and the larders are full of meat and blubber. People come together for feasts and merrymaking more often than for sacred sacrificial rites, and man starts to believe that he is the strongest and the smartest, and that he is the only master of the earth. And this is how it goes, for a time. But then, nature, Narginen, the Outer Forces, take away all the extraneous

* *Narginen* – the external forces that guide all life.

229

things – people who were born not out of need, but out of lust. They send down diseases, famine, they destroy the food stores that breed laziness in people. This is the kind of storm the Outer Forces use to clear away all that can lift man above them . . . It's as though Narginen is reminding us: I'm master here, and it's only on my sufferance that man lives here at all . . ."

Orvo's harsh, grim words dropped into John's consciousness, and his soul grew with unease.

"How are we to live now?" It was a cry from the heart that John couldn't stifle.

"Narginen will tell us, himself, how to keep going," Orvo called back. "Let the gods go back to their places, and man return to where he's always been."

The storm raged for a few more days. The wind had blown the ice floes far beyond the horizon. The open water in a winter sea seemed strange and unreal. It was just as wildly impossible as a man promenading naked in the middle of a blizzard.

The blue sky and sparse clouds, racing in the wind, were reflected in the water. The people were impatiently awaiting the day the wind died down and they could venture out to hunt.

Before then, John had never noticed just how much the dogs consumed. And although it was enough to feed them just once a day, the twelve toothy maws demolished as much kopal'khen as three people could eat in two or three days.

When John fed the dogs himself, he tried to cut down on the regular amount.

"It wouldn't do any harm if the dogs ate a little less these days," he once told his wife.

Pyl'mau looked at her husband with surprise:

"But they're half-starved as it is . . ."

"Well, they're not really doing anything right now, or bringing any food . . ."

"There isn't a single person in Enmyn right now that is hunting for food, but still everyone wants to eat, and everyone eats to stay alive," Pyl'mau countered.

"That's people, and this is dogs."

"What's the difference?" Pyl'mau shrugged. "They eat the worst scraps anyway."

Despite the catastrophically dwindling food supplies, in each yaranga they continued to feed the dogs, and such extravagance was a source of astonishment to John. Once, he even suggested to Orvo that the number of dogs in the settlement should be reduced to the bare necessity.

"Maybe you want to start yourself?" Orvo chuckled.

After the blizzard, there came such a frost as to make the sea freeze over immediately. Always covered in ice hummocks and haphazardly strewn with ice-floe splinters, now its surface was unusually even and smooth.

The hunters wasted no time in going out to hunt. They raced on their sleighs, on runners made of walrus tusk. Pushing off with the sharp metal-plated end of their sticks, they slid to the polynyas* over the slippery ice, and came home with a kill by eveningfall. Fires blazed again inside the chottagins, the delicious smell of fresh meat drove out the stench of rancid whale blubber. The hunters were in a hurry: The first light wind would crumple and destroy the mirror smoothness and raise up ice hummocks once more.

And soon this came to pass, the sea taking on its usual winter appearance, riven with ice hummocks and hoary rocks. The moving ice porridge drove the old ice floats back to the shore. The sleighs were relegated

---

* *Polynya* – an air hole in the ice cover, usually formed in places with rapid current. (TN)

to the children, and the hunters hitched up the skinny dogs for the long journey to the polynyas.

The fierce frosts cracked and split the ice nightly, but the open water receded farther and farther from shore and you had to get up near the middle of the night to catch the short interval of daylight out by the open water.

One evening, an agitated Pyl'mau ran into the yaranga and told them that Mutchin and Eleneut were lying dead inside their dwelling.

The old people had breathed their last some days ago, and the hungry dogs had had time to gnaw on their bodies. John couldn't look at them without shuddering and evaded participating in the funeral by pleading ill health.

After the funeral, Orvo himself set the empty yaranga alight, and the noisy smoky flame rose high toward the heavens.

"Each of these fires brings closer the hour when all our nation will go beyond the clouds," Orvo said meditatively, watching the dancing blaze. "Have you seen how many empty camps and abandoned yarangas are rotting all along the shore? Some settlements have disappeared completely. Our people are waning quickly, and it scares me. Our women give birth rarely, and barely any children survive. So many of them die here, with not enough time even to get used to their names! And yet, once our people were great and mighty!"

"There's no need to look at life in such a grim light," John answered. "It's not for nothing that man exists on earth. It can't be that the Chukchi will simply disappear from the face of the earth . . ."

Snowfall powdered over the charred remains of the yaranga, and the names of the deceased were quickly erased from the memories of the living. John felt that the unfortunates were so soon forgotten because in their heart of hearts Enmyn's inhabitants secretly felt responsible for those deaths.

Once he mentioned this to Orvo, but the old man said, irritably:

"Here on earth, the only people with the right to live are those who can provide food not only for themselves but for their progeny."

"And what if misfortune befalls you?" John knew that the question was a cruel one.

With a smile of unexpected serenity, the old man looked back at John and gave a firm answer:

"When I see this happen, I will go beyond the clouds myself."

Hunting turned into a grueling labor. Having to climb out into the cold from underneath a warm coverlet was torture.

Pyl'mau would be the first to rise and prepare breakfast. The hunter had to be fed for the entire long cold day ahead. Only one grease lamp would be lit inside the polog. Its light and heat had been plenty, until the heavy frost hit. Now, silvery patches of frost appeared inside the polog's corners.

The children slept under a deerskin blanket, tightly huddling together.

John would eat his breakfast in silence and, with a chilly revulsion for the cold and for the stars' blue flickering, step over the threshold.

The snow crunched loudly underfoot, and this single sound within the frosty silence spread far around, filling the white space with a nasty creaking. It followed the hunter the entire way. And the way was long, through tall ice hummocks, through conglomerations of broken ice. It had been a long time since they used harness teams in Enmyn: The half-starved dogs had gone wild, having to fend for themselves, and wouldn't allow themselves to be caught.

Frost bound the polynyas. No sooner did a melthole appear, than it was drawn over with new, translucent ice.

John moved from one frozen water hole to another. Gradually, the ends of his toes would freeze, and so, from time to time he had to knock one foot against the other, to restore feeling. It was a good thing that he had no fingers – there was no need to worry about mittens, and he could load and unload his Winchester with his holders in any weather.

It was hard to distinguish the boundary between the fast ice and the moving ice, which had so few breakages that the nerpa themselves had to blow out vents in order to get a breath of air.

John hurried on.

Slowly the stars faded and the brief winter day began. It would last for two or three hours, and only in that window of time would you be able to distinguish a nerpa's dark head on the surface of an ice-free patch. Quickly, it grew dark, and John returned to Enmyn by starlight and the glow of the shooting Northern Lights.

He would walk past the yarangas with his head low, ashamed of his failure. Then he grew used to it. The worst was meeting little Yako's hungry eyes. But Pyl'mau, unshakeably calm, acted as though everything was as it should have been. It was a wonder how she managed to produce food at all and, eating his fill, John would collapse onto the cool deer-skins, to venture out once again in search of animals the next day.

Once, he frightened off a polar bear. The beast rushed away over the ice hummocks and disappeared into the snowy whiteness. His kill was left behind on the ice – an almost whole nerpa carcass, with an opened belly and a skinned head.

The bear had lain in watch for the nerpa, waiting for it to surface through the blowhole. You need incredible quickness to catch and extract such a cautious and dextrous animal through a narrow hole. John was jealous of the polar bear's luck.

He inspected the carcass and saw that it was only a little damaged, and hadn't even had a chance to freeze. The pink liver was covered with a thin layer of ice. John took out his hunting knife and cut off a few slices. After having a snack, he threaded a leather strip through the animal's muzzle and and started dragging the nerpa back to shore.

Ascending from the shore to the yarangas, he had a moment of doubt: Can it be a good thing, taking the marine animals' food away from them?

But remembering Yako's hungry eyes and Pyl'mau's visibly thinner body, he strode decisively toward his dwelling, trying to pass the other yarangas as quickly as possible.

Pyl'mau was already standing by the door with a ladle. Silently, she poured some water over the nerpa's head and gave the rest of the water to John. The small ladle shook slightly in her hand, and a lonely piece of ice rang out against the tin.

When they had dragged the nerpa inside the polog, John made a perturbed confession:

"I took the nerpa away from a bear. Not sure whether it was a good or bad thing to do . . ."

"I remember, sometimes Toko did that," Pyl'mau answered calmly. "You took what was yours according to the right of the strongest. The gods will be pleased."

Taking off his hunting gear, John crawled inside the polog. Yako sat by the nerpa's head and stared greedily at the animal's half-closed eye. John gouged the eye out with his hunting knife, pierced it and handed it to the boy.

For little Tynevirineu-Mary he sliced off a piece of liver.

Pyl'mau lit a second oil lamp, and the polog brightened. Today she was lively, joyful at the provider's success. She spoke animatedly, frequently throwing her husband tender, slightly worried glances.

By the light of the second oil lamp, John scanned the polog. He had a vague sense that some change had taken place inside the dwelling, something taken away, or else something added. John slowly moved his eyes across the interior, until they stopped at the corner post, where instead of the copper washbasin, hung a wooden idol!

"You see, he sent us luck," Pyl'mau said with a sheepish smile. "As soon as you left for the sea, I took him in from the cold, warmed him up and pleaded with him for a long time to be kind to you."

"And where's the washbasin?"

"I've hung it up in the chottagin, where it was before." Pyl'mau was nervously crumpling the edge of a deer hide. "I was thinking, you almost don't wash at all anymore . . . And the god ought to hang in his own place . . ."

And in truth, John had lately ceased to practice personal hygiene. One morning, approaching the washstand, he remembered the bitter frost outside the yaranga's walls, he could feel how instantly the cold would pull on his washed face, stripped of a protective layer of grease, and he didn't wash it . . . Afterwards he didn't touch the washstand at all, and it hadn't done his health any harm.

"And here's another reason the god should be right here," Pyl'mau continued, in an ingratiating tone. "I want a son. Yako needs a companion, with whom life will be less hard . . . Why don't we just let the god stay with us."

"All right," John waved his hand tiredly, "butcher the nerpa, I want to eat."

No sooner had Pyl'mau hung a little cauldron over the fire, than guests began to arrive at the yaranga. No one asked for anything. They came by for no reason, or for some trivial reason, but not a single person left empty-handed.

John saw there was less and less of the nerpa, and a few times he almost shouted to his wife: "Enough!"

Late that night, Orvo's dry coughing came from the chottagin and then his gray head popped inside the polog.

The old man had a look at the recently returned god and hummed with satisfaction.

"We should set nerpa nets," he said. "We're running out of cartridges, and there's less and less open water. Got to drill holes and set up the nets."

This was the first time John had heard of nerpa being caught in nets.

"We'll spread the nets, and you can go see your friend Il'motch," Orvo

single human figure could be seen between the yarangas, and not a single column of smoke flew over the tents.

John fell inside his yaranga's chottagin and, groping for the fur-lined curtain, climbed into the polog.

Attracted by the yellow-flame tongue, he heard his wife's weak voice:

"Is that you, Sson?"

"It's me, Mau."

"Did you bring anything?"

"I didn't find the deer camp. Only spoor . . .Where are the children?"

"Here," Pyl'mau answered. "They're very thin . . . Asking for food all the time . . . I'm already down to boiling old torbasses. I've scraped out the meat pit. That's what we manage on."

"Anyone going out to sea?"

"They go, but there's little good. It's been rare for someone to come back with a kill, from the day you left. No cartridges."

Pyl'mau stoked the fire in the grease lamp with a stick, and hung a little pot over it.

Yako crawled out from underneath a heap of skins and stared at John. The boy's ribs stuck out sharply, while between his shoulderblades and his neck there were clearly visible hollows, like pits in the swarthy, hunger-roughened skin.

Tynevirineu-Mary lay quietly. For a minute she opened her blue eyes and then shut them again, as though the brazier's glow were unbearably bright for her.

"What's wrong with Mary?" John said, alarmed.

"She's hungry," came Pyl'mau's despondent reply. "I give her the breast to suck, but there's nothing there."

A foul-smelling soup had boiled in the pot. Fighting revulsion, John swallowed it.

"Have you been eating the dogs?"

"What are you saying! How could we eat dogs?"

"It's better than boiling lakhtak strips that were cured in human urine," countered John.

Regaining a little strength, he decided to pay Orvo a visit.

Beside the yaranga, the dogs were rumbling as they chewed on the remains of the sled's leather holding straps. Seeing the human, they ran off. It was only now that John noticed that the walrus-hide covers of each yaranga were chewed up to the height within reach of the dogs.

Orvo lay inside a darkened polog, with his two wives.

"The thing I was most afraid of has happened: Il'motch has moved his camp to the Forest Boundary . . . He could feel it, the old man, that we'd come to him for help . . ."

Orvo's breathing was short and broken, something whistled and gurgled in his chest.

"We have to do something," John said, after a pause. "We can't just meekly wait for the end."

"So what do you suggest?" Orvo asked apathetically. "There isn't any strength to hunt. It gets dark by the time you find a melthole, and there's barely any open water anymore as it is."

"We can eat some of the dogs. I don't understand it: People are starving to death, while there are animals who can save our lives, just running about. It's not as though they don't eat horseflesh in some parts, and in some Eastern countries, they even consider dog meat to be a delicacy . . ."

"Maybe we will come to that, eating dogs," Orvo answered tiredly, "but that's the last resort. After the dogs, it's usually the turn of the dead. Then they kill and eat the weak ones . . . Until a person has eaten dog, he can still consider himself a human being . . ."

"Well, I did eat dog meat!" John declared, with a challenge. "So then, I've stopped being human?"

"Don't speak that way, Sson," Orvo pleaded. "Check my nets. Maybe something has been caught."

In the morning, forcing himself to swallow the stinky leather-strap brew, John went out looking for Orvo's nets. There had been no snow for a month, and on a hardened early-snow cover there was no need for snowshoes. The even white surface blinded his eyes. And really, the Long Days, the pre-springtime season had arrived long ago, but the people in their famished stupor hadn't noticed it come.

The old man had spread his nets far afield, and only by the late dusky twilight did John reach them. It took another hour to hack them from the ice. The first net had some worm-eaten seal bones, but in the other was a nerpa, nearly whole. John, cheered by this, cleaned out the nets and spread them again, with the intention of returning the next day.

With a load of seal bones and the nerpa carcass, John returned to Enmyn.

Despite her weakness, Pyl'mau came out to greet him with the usual ladle and its floating chip of ice.

It was hard to divide the spoils into twelve equal shares.

"We should put more into Orvo's pile," John said.

"No, let each family get the same amount," Pyl'mau disagreed.

"Why should I feed Armol', who is stronger than me and could have gone to check the nets a long time ago?" John said, annoyed.

"Don't be angry," Pyl'mau lowered her voice, "there's no room for anger when food is being doled out. Let everyone get his share. The sun doesn't decide which person to give the most light and heat, it's the same for everybody."

"I'm not competing in generosity with the sun! First of all, I want to feed my children, and only then all the rest!"

Almost forcibly, he took a hunk of meat from each share and threw them in the pot that hung over the grease lamp.

Afraid that John wouldn't give the other inhabitants of Enmyn anything at all, Pyl'mau gathered together some pitiful bits of meat and bone, and went to make the rounds of the yarangas.

Alone with the children inside the polog, John tried to stoke up the flame in the grease lamp. He took the little black baton, made out of some unknown material, and started to scrape the fat-soaked moss to the edge of the stone vessel. The flame did grow bigger, but so did the soot. Trying to manage it, John only put the flame out altogether. Darkness came over the polog. In the quiet, he suddenly heard Tynevirineu-Mary's wail. Feeling for the child's thin, trembling body, John drew her out from underneath the pile of deerskins and held her close. The little body burned him, as though on fire. The baby girl was semi-conscious, crying quietly. Incredible, that there can be so much heat in such a tiny creature!

John rocked the crying girl and pleaded with her:

"Mary, dear, don't cry, just wait a little longer. Mother will come soon, she'll light the lamp, and we'll all eat fresh hot meat. Don't cry, my baby girl."

John crooned to the little girl, and it seemed to him that she was beginning to breathe more evenly, her fever leaving. His eyes slowly got accustomed to the dark: A little light seeped into the polog through numerous bald spots in the hide covers.

"My little bird, little trouble . . ." John whispered in English. "Why was it you who drew the lot of being born here? . . . Somewhere else, thousands of lucky children smile at the warm sun, smelling of milk, but you, my blood, are burning up in this accursed ice-bound land! My darling! My little polar flower! . . . Why are you so quiet? You've stopped crying? Yes, sleep for a bit . . ."

John talked to the little girl, and his heart grew more and more heavy, as though a black cloud were moving over his soul. Dread of something terrifying and inevitable filled the cramped polog to the brim, rising up like dark shadows in the corners. Trying to push away his worry, John would raise his voice:

"My darling! Winter won't be forever, spring will come after, and we'll see the green grass again, and eat our fill! . . ."

A weak ray of light stretched from the smoke-hole to the corner pole that supported the polog. The god was hanging there. This time, his face did not seem emotionless to John. Some sort of vengeful and malicious expression had appeared on the god's face.

John broke off his talk with his daughter. The god's look pierced his heart like an icy needle, and cold viscous sweat ran down between his shoulderblades, raising fear and fever.

"Hey, you, idol!" John shouted, beside himself with terror. "Stop it! I still don't believe in you, and I don't accept you!"

He lay the child on the bed and rushed to the god. Ripping it off the post so savagely that the entire polog shook, John threw it out into the chottagin.

"Vyne vai!" he heard Pyl'mau's voice. "What have you done? Oh, it will be nothing but trouble for us! Oh, the misfortune!"

John peered into the chottagin and saw his wife kneeling before the cast-down god.

"Get up!" he screamed in a terrible voice. "Don't you dare abase yourself before him! No god – not yours, not ours – is worth that. They are liars, all of them! Get up, Mau!"

"A terrible misfortune is waiting for us, Sson," Pyl'mau said in a voice that was quieted by the depth of her emotion. "How could you do that?"

Pyl'mau stretched her arms out to the god, who lay on the frost-covered earthen floor, and in that instant, a dreadful wave shook the yaranga, knocking the frost from the wooden struts. A steady blue light filled the room.

John ran to the outer door. A large round lightning bolt was rolling toward the sea, giving off little flickering balls of flame. When it collided with the first ice hummock, it fell apart into a multitude of sparks and expired. Where the sea joined the shore, there was a black crack – the source of the thundering noise. John went back inside the chottagin and found Pyl'mau unconscious, clutching the wooden idol to her breast.

John barely managed to drag his wife inside the polog.

Having come to, Pyl'mau made some fire, lit the grease lamp, put the god back in his place.

"Sson was fighting with the god!" Yako informed them weakly from underneath the deerskins.

"Oh, the trouble! The punishment! Look Sson, she's fading, our Tynevirineu-Mary!" Pyl'mau picked up the baby and clutched her to her frail chest. "Descended from the Dawn is dying!"

The blazing lamp shone onto the pale almost lifeless little face. Tynevirineu-Mary silently pulled open her eyelashes and sweetly, plaintively, looked at her father. A long, drawn-out sigh escaped her tiny chest together with a barely audible moan.

"Sson! Go to the god and beg for forgiveness!" Pyl'mau screamed hoarsely. "Oh, Sson! Beg him to intercede for the girl, beg him . . . Sson, don't you want our little Dawn to live? Or do you want her to fade, never having risen to a bright day?"

John was frozen with terror. In the shaky lamplight, the idol made faces at him. It seemed that the merciless wooden eyes were staring right at Tynevirineu-Mary's cooling body. In two bounds, John leaped to the corner post where the god was hanging, and unexpectedly for himself, began whispering:

"Don't! Have mercy on the girl! I promise not to touch you again. I'll feed you well and your face will always be shiny with fat. Just don't, don't, don't . . ."

His whispering turned to loud sobs.

The hungry Yako started to cry underneath the deerskins, and soon the yaranga was filled with weeping and groaning.

Suddenly, Pyl'mau's heart-rending lament broke off, and she said, in a somehow surprised voice:

"She's gone beyond the clouds!"

Tynevirineu-Mary's little head lolled. The fog had already drifted over her widened and frozen blue eyes.

John accepted the cooling body from his wife's hands in silence, and carefully laid it on a deerskin. He stretched the eyelids, already rigid in death, over the large blue eyes, and pressed them closed.

He heard nothing that went on around him. He thought of nothing, remembered nothing, crushed by the measureless weight of grief that filled all of his being.

He didn't hear Pyl'mau feeding little Yako, chastened by his encounter with death; he didn't hear the arrival of old Orvo, who, listening to Pyl'mau's story, took a long while whispering with the god.

Orvo tried to talk to John, but to no avail.

After twenty-four hours had passed, Orvo pulled a child's sleigh with walrus-tusk runners up to the yaranga. Pyl'mau wiped clean her daughter's body, and dressed it in white funerary garments.

Orvo was about to carry the deceased child out, but John barred his way. "I'll do it myself."

Ascending the funerary hill and seeing the bodies of old Mutchin and Eleneut, half-eaten by animals and starving dogs, John shuddered and told Orvo, bewildering him into silence:

"I'll bury my daughter according to our custom."

Not in Enmyn, not in the whole of Chukotka, had a person who had gone beyond the clouds ever returned: Yet John brought Tynevirineu-Mary's body back to the settlement.

Pyl'mau, speechless with fear, could say nothing to her husband, and Orvo said bitterly:

"He's gone mad with grief, your husband."

John upended the contents of his sailor's trunk, placed a square of bearskin over the bottom, and laid his daughter inside. The rigid body had stretched out, and barely fit inside the copper-cornered trunk.

John cut a plate from an old tin can and engraved it with a nail. He nailed it to a wooden cross, and only then, accompanied by the steadfast Orvo, again ascended Funerary Hill.

A metal crowbar and a shovel lay on top of the box together with the cross.

John chose a spot and, strapping the crowbar to his stumps, set to breaking the ground that had been frozen through to rock-hardness.

Orvo crouched further off. From time to time, bits of frozen earth reached him, melting over his wrinkle-furrowed face and running down in muddy little streams. John hacked tirelessly. Orvo was watching him and remembering the rosy-cheeked young man who'd been terrified by his misfortune, meek one moment and wild the next, puppylike. Not much was left of the old Sson. Here was a person who had gone through ordeals and grief, and who was no longer afraid of anything.

The perma-frost was slow to give way. After a few hours of backbreaking labor John was only knee-deep in the little grave.

When the late sun disappeared, John and Orvo lowered the small trunk containing Tynevirineu-Mary's body into the little grave, erected the cross with its metal plate, and covered the grave with a mound of earth.

Orvo stepped aside, and John sank to his knees before the cross and its plate bearing the words: *Tynevirineu-Mary MacLennan. 1912–1914.*

Orvo took apart the sleigh runners and leaned them against the mound.

It was a long descent from the funerary hill; John and Orvo were silent.

Reaching the foot, Orvo glanced at the icy seascape, gave John a shove and said, alarmed:

"Someone coming through the ice . . ."

John and Orvo halted. Two figures appeared from the ice hummocks, figures vaguely resembling humans. They were heading for the shore.

"Tery'ky!" Orvo whispered, terrified and with the full intention of running for it.

"Wait a minute!" John caught his sleeve. "Even if they are tery'ky, now is just the time to meet them up close."

"Sometimes they eat people," Orvo said, his voice shaky.

"I doubt we'd tempt them," John said with a nervy smirk, and shouted across to the strange creatures, who had meanwhile come in range of human voice.

"Who are you? Where are you coming from?"

The figures stopped, and Orvo and John heard the reply:

"I'm Captain Bartlett, a member of Stefansson's* expedition. With me is the Eskimo Kataktovik.

* Vilhjalmur Stefansson (1879–1962) – Canadian explorer and ethnologist. In 1913 he headed the Canadian Arctic Expedition, which ran into difficulties when the ship *Karluk* was crushed by ice floes as it lay adrift, waiting for Stefansson and his small team to return from a coastal foray. The *Karluk*'s sailors were later rescued, but despite the wealth of geographical and ethnographic data collected, the expedition was not considered a success by the Canadian government. *The Adventure of Wrangel Island* is Stefansson's account of the expedition. (TN)

23

The travelers had two lakhtak carcasses on their sled. Pyl'mau speedily dragged them inside the chottagin, thawed them out and butchered them. Having fed the guests, she laid out some bedding for them next to the grease lamp, where it was warmest. The conversation between the visitors and her husband was conducted entirely in English. Pyl'mau couldn't make out a single word, but she was guessing that the travelers were neither hunters nor traders. The footwear they had taken off, and their clothes, bore witness to a long and arduous journey through the ice hummocks. There was barely anything left from their lakhtak shoesoles, and Pyl'mau had to take out the last of her stores in order to fix up the unexpected guests' shoes and clothes.

The one John addressed as "keptein," was white, and the other man, who had almost no part in the conversation, resembled a Chukcha but was more likely an inhabitant of the other side of the bay.

Bustling about, Pyl'mau would forget herself, moving without thinking, yet once in a while she would halt as though struck against an invisible obstacle, and tears streamed from her eyes of their own volition. At those moments, John would give his wife a look of reproach, and his voice would grow louder.

The guests had brought a small reserve of tea and coffee. Pyl'mau warmed the aromatic brew over the grease lamp and poured it into age-blackened cups.

Captain Bartlett, nearly melting from warmth and food, was acquainting John with the work and the aims of Vilhjalmur Stefansson's ambitiously scoped expedition.

In brief, the driving idea of Stefansson's expedition was to prove to the civilized world the possibility of living and existing in the Arctic vastnesses independenly of outside aid. To break the deeply rooted belief that the Arctic was a pitiless wasteland, incapable of providing subsistence . . .

John listened quietly as he drew a mental picture of the colossal resources that had been required to equip the expedition, the number of people uprooted, to prove that the icy Arctic expanse harbored life.

"Sir," John interrupted the captain, "I don't quite understand why all this is necessary. All right, you've proved that this relatively inaccessible pole is home to living creatures, but what for? Surely the very fact of the existence of the different peoples of these Arctic regions prove the possibility of man's existence here?"

"But it's one thing for an Eskimo or a Chukcha, inured to the weather, and quite another for a white man," the captain objected.

"Frost is equally damaging to the one as to the other," John said sharply. "Look at the Arctic inhabitant's dwelling, at his clothes – everything is geared toward protection against the cold. I don't deny that a certain hardiness has developed in him over the ages, but to speak about the evolution of a particular type of human being is nonsense."

"Mr. MacLennan," Bartlett began, after giving John a polite hearing, "I repeat, the goal of our expedition is to take information back to civilized society, and not to resolve the question of how close the Arctic dweller is to the rest of humanity. I don't deny the importance of this problem, and more than that, I have the highest opinion of the physical and spiritual attributes of the Northerner. The work of our expedition is to open up the Arctic to the whole of humanity, to prove that man can exist in this region without help from the outside world."

"What for?" John had waited for the captain to finish speaking with impatience.

"In order to explain it to you, I would be obliged to repeat once again everything I've just told you," was Captain Bartlett's courteous reply.

"As I understand it, the whole idea of this expensive expedition is undertaken to prove to the people inhabiting more southerly latitudes the possibility of their living in the Arctic?"

"That's exactly right," Captain Bartlett concurred.

"So that they could head for the Arctic without fear?" John went on.

"Yes," the captain replied.

"Well, who asked them to come here? Why would they be so inconsiderate as to encroach upon the very place that, by supreme right, belongs to these people who have forsaken lands more suitable for human habitation? Why would you appropriate discoveries made by these people for yourselves, with hardly a mention of those who have made these discoveries long before the polar expeditions? More than that, you even change the place-names of these parts and introduce them to humanity as newly discovered lands . . . You've got Kataktovik with you. He's not only your eyes and ears; he's also your nursemaid, sled driver and provider of meals. But I am certain – when you report your expedition's findings, let's say in Toronto University's School of Geography – you'll credit Kataktovik with merely an assistant's role . . ."

"Mr. MacLennan," answered Captain Bartlett, holding himself in check, "I gave you no grounds to be voicing such suppositions about me."

"Forgive me." John hung his head. "I buried my daughter today. She died of starvation and a nameless disease. She is buried on top of the hill from which we sighted you . . . Forgive me."

"We are deeply and sincerely sorry for your loss . . ." There was a note of real compassion in Captain Bartlett's voice. "Our appearance, when you are in a grieving state, can only be mitigated by the extraordinary circumstances in which we find ourselves . . ."

"Once again, I ask your pardon," John lifted his head and looked the captain in the eye. "I must have offended you, but again, I ask that you pay no mind to that. The problem at hand is much more important. We are talking about preserving peoples, and the way of life that they have chosen for themselves . . . I remember when I first arrived here, I asked old Orvo how to explain his love for this land, which from a so-called civilized person's point of view, neither offers any comforts nor shines with particular natural beauty. His answer, back then, was that no one else besides his people wanted this land . . . But now, it's become wanted by others, and I fear for the future of the people who live here."

Captain Bartlett weathered John's stare.

"I understand, and more than that, I share your concerns. But I am hoping that there are enough reasonable people in the world to stand against the forces that could destroy the Arctic peoples. Our expedition's mandate includes a comprehensive study of local languages, ethnography of the peoples inhabiting the relatively inaccessible pole's environs."

"In the name of what, this study?"

"Primarily in the name of science," Captain Bartlett answered after momentary reflection. "It's possible that the summation of our research will be a recomendation to our government."

"But have you asked these people whether they need intervention by a government of which they have the haziest conception, and which they did not elect? Maybe the best thing is to just leave these peoples alone, and to sail a hundreds-of-miles-wide berth around the regions they've tamed and called home?"

"Mr. MacLennan," Captain Bartlett's voice was stern and stately, "the peoples inhabiting Canada's northern territories are a part of the Canadian people, and they cannot remain outside of progress, which will inevitably reach even those parts. The issue now is how to make sure that the journey these tribes are faced with will not be tortuous and tragic . . ."

"Wait a moment," John interrupted yet again, "is this progress necessarily a desirable thing for them?"

"To be honest, Mr. MacLennan, politics are of little interest to me. Perhaps it is you who are right in this, and perhaps it is the Canadian government. As for myself – I'm an American, hired as staff by Vilhjalmur Stefansson, the captain of the lost ship *Karluk*. Let's end this debate, so aimless and futile for us both . . . I am very glad that we met, and if it's no secret, would love to know how you got to this place and what it is that holds you here."

Without going into too many details, John told his story. Even in his dry and spare recounting, it made an impact on Captain Bartlett.

"I understand now," he said thoughtfully. "But your loved ones left behind in Port Hope, haven't they a right to know that you're alive? Your mother, your family?"

"I don't know," John said quietly. "Perhaps they have gotten used to the thought that I'm no longer among the living. I'm dead to them, and it really is so. Because I will never be able to go back to the past . . ."

"Mothers never believe that their children are dead, if they should happen to disappear far from home," Bartlett remarked. "Give me your parents' address. I will only tell them that you're alive, that you have found your happiness here and have no wish to return. I think it will be easier for them that way."

John raised his head, looking over his dwelling – the deer-hide walls, Pyl'mau and Yako lying in the corner hardly daring to breathe – and uttered:

"There's no need. Let everything stay as it is."

He moved away from Captain Bartlett, wished him goodnight and went to lie beside Pyl'mau.

"He wanted you to go with him?" Pyl'mau asked.

"Go to sleep."

"I understand everything. He was calling you, reminding you about your mother . . . I've noticed, when you're talking with a white person, you become like a stranger, as though a different Sson has taken your place . . . What did you answer him?"

John let out a heavy sigh:

"You know very well the only answer I could give him . . ."

Pyl'mau caught his sigh:

"Maybe it's true, you should go back to your homeland? What's left for you here? Tynevirineu-Mary's cold grave and nothing else . . ."

"What about you, what about little Yako?"

"What are we?" Pyl'mau sniffled. "We're from here, this is our land, strewn with the bones of our ancestors. Go back home, Sson, where it's warm, where there's always plenty of food, where your family is. When you leave, you will still be in my heart; I will never forget you. In the dark evenings, when it's too dark to see who you're talking with, I'll talk to you and I'll be glad that you are happy. Go back, Sson!"

"Hush." John laid a hand on his wife's shoulder. "I couldn't leave this place. It's as impossible as if I were to decide to become a different person. Sleep untroubled."

Waking in the middle of the night, John could feel Pyl'mau's body shaking stiffly under his palm; she was crying.

The yaranga's occupants were awakened by heavy footsteps in the chottagin.

It was Orvo and Armol'.

"Sson!" Armol' informed him excitedly, "The ducks have flown. We were so hungry that we didn't even notice spring arriving! If your guests have shotguns, we're saved! The sky is black with duck swarms."

Tuning his ear, John could hear the rustling of thousands of wings. He dressed in a hurry. Captain Bartlett and Kataktovik followed suit. They took out their shotguns, and Enmyn's starved silence shattered with the thunder of volleys.

The ducks were flying in such dense flocks that you could shoot blind-folded. With dull thumps, the birds fell and fell onto the snow. The lifeless settlement rang with the loud barking of the dogs, who had appeared out of nowhere, and the shouting of the people, who were diving into the midst of the squabbling dog packs to wrest the birds away from them.

The dogs tore at their clothes and bit them, but the people paid no attention to that, returning the blows, prying the still-warm ducks from canine jaws and taking them back to the yarangas.

John ran around with everyone else, screamed at the dogs, growled. His hands became covered with teethmarks and scratches, and his clothes hung in tatters.

When the shooting came to an end and the late twilight descended over the earth, fires were set to blazing inside the chottagins, and the scent of boiled meat, the smell of food and of life, long forgotten by the starving people, floated from yaranga to yaranga.

So great was their impatience that the women didn't pluck the ducks, but skinned them. Cauldrons bubbled over great fires.

"Your arrival has turned out to be our salvation," John told Captain Bartlett. "Duck meat will give strength to those who were on the brink of starving, and the men will be able to go out hunting again. A great thanks to you."

"Not at all," the captain replied, wiping the gun down with a cleaning rod and inspecting the barrel in the firelight. "I am glad to have been of help to you, and that our guns finally had some use. During the sinking of the *Karluk* in the Arctic Ocean, our supply of rifle cartridges was lost. All we had left were the shotguns. That's what we hunted polar bear with, and seal."

With a nonchalant air, Kataktovik was scalping the duck heads of their multicolor feathers. Back home, they made fancy clothes and headdresses out of the feathers, ones that fetched a good price from the white people.

Spending two more days in Enmyn, Captain Bartlett and Kataktovik provided the village inhabitants with a few days' worth of duck meat. Then the hunters went out to ply their craft. Armol' bagged two nerpa, and brought the news that the ice was checkered with large meltholes and crevices, where fat spring nerpa frolicked.

The visitors needed to get going toward the Bering Strait, from where they intended to cross over to their own side.

John caught a few dozen of the stringy dogs, and wrangled together two workable packs.

Early on a spring morning, when a dazzling sun rose over the distant hills, the dogsleds set off down the coast toward the ancient Chukchi settlement of Uelen. The second dogsled was driven by the imperturbable Tiarat, even more withdrawn after the long hungry winter. He didn't even call out to the dogs, just looked at them with a kind of intensity and, meeting his eyes, the leader of the pack drew himself in as though from a blow, and dragged the rest of the dogs along.

Captain Bartlett sat on John's sled. His stern face, weathered by the northern winds, was anxious. He told John that there were people waiting for help, left behind on Wrangel Island.

On the way to Uelen they stopped in a few small settlements where people were only beginning to recover from the long hungry winter. Disaster had touched the entire region from Enmyn to Cape Dezhnev.

Between the Neshkan and Inchoun settlements, set on one of the sandbanks that stretched far into the Arctic Ocean, the travelers came across a lonely snow-covered yaranga. No one came out at the dogs' barking. After digging out the entrance, they looked inside, a terrible scene lay before their eyes: From underneath the collapsed polog protruded half-eaten human bones. John carefully raised the hides and saw the bodies of a man and a woman. Their eyes had been pecked out, and there was only the thinnest layer of skin left on their faces.

"Here is the true face of the North," John quietly told Captain Bartlett. "Look and remember. And when you make your reports to the geographical societies, don't forget to mention the dispossessed, the people of the North, who can be not only loyal and obedient guides, but also true heroes. For ages they have been battling a merciless enemy – the Arctic climate. Instead of monuments, it is their bones that remain in this ground, and yet these people do not retreat, they stubbornly cling to these frozen limbs of Mother Nature."

The sleds were slowly moving away from the desolate yaranga. In the calm of the spring evening, the crows cawed loudly as they circled over the yaranga's smoke-hole.

"This is terrible," Bartlett said with a shudder. "Such a small folk, to lose so many!"

"If the resources that you've spent on proving man's ability to exist in the Arctic and in looking for new lands had been used to plumb the soul of the Northern man, all the world and humanity would be graced with a wealth much greater than a scrap of icy wasteland lost in the Arctic Ocean," John said quietly, but with certainty.

The famine had also come to Uelen's people, but not in the same degree. Here, there were none of the shadows that remotely resembled human beings that the travelers had met in the other settlements.

Spending the night and feeding the dogs, the travelers made for Keniskun and Robert Carpenter.

The trader met his visitors with boisterous exclamations and, without letting them collect themselves, immediately ushered them to his natural bath, the hot springs.

"I read about Stefansson's expedition in last year's papers!" Carpenter declared over dinner. "This is a grand undertaking! Truth be told, it interested me more than the beginning of the war in Europe!"

Carpenter felt free and easy with his guests. He talked loudly and kept on giving orders to his wife and daughters, so that they had barely any time to bring more and more victuals.

Somewhat to the side, Kataktovik and Tiarat made themselves comfortable at a separate little table. They ate in silence, paying no attention to the white people's talk.

Captain Bartlett, mellowed by his reviving bath among virgin snows, raised one toast after another.

"I propose we drink to the steadfast people of the North!" he announced, nodding toward Kataktovik and Tiarat.

"In that case," Carpenter remarked, "they should have some, too."

They agreed amongst themselves that John and Tiarat would not be going further. Robert Carpenter would be responsible for the captain of the *Karluk* from here on.

"Go back to yours," the merchant told John in a paternal tone. "I heard that you've weathered a hard winter. Lost your whaleboat . . . Harsh, the North is, harsh!" he repeated it, making a concerned face. "It's hard around here, when you're not used to it."

John and Tiarat took some cartridges, gunpowder, a little tea, sugar and tobacco on credit, and then set off on their journey back.

Captain Bartlett and Kataktovik headed south, down the craggy coastline of the Bering Sea. After a while they met with Baron Kleist, an official of the Russian government, who assisted them in getting to Providence Bay. From there, Bartlett sailed to St. Michael in Alaska on the whaling ship *Herman* and sent the Canadian Naval Department a report of what had happened.

The Russian government and the United States of America, whose shores were closest to where the catastrophe had occurred, agreed to save the remains of the *Karluk*'s crew, marooned on Wrangel Island. The Americans sent the ship *The Bear* to the subpolar island, the Russians, the icebreaker steamships *Taimyr* and *Vaigach*. But the Russian vessels, already within sight of the island, suddenly turned back, having received the order to return – Russia was at war.

Beyond the Far Cape, on a narrow shingled beach, the walruses came to breed. Winter survival depended on how many animals they could bag here. According to Orvo, this breeding ground had lain empty for many years. The walruses had abandoned the spot for a long time after some American schooner had organized a hunt there. The sailors went down to the water in half a dozen whaleboats, approached the peacefully sleeping beasts and opened fire. Shots thundered in the crisp, silent autumn air, blood spurted like fountains over the shingles, touched with the first frost. The gigantic animals were dropping their toothy heads onto one another and turning still. The surf was blood-red.

Having decimated the breeding ground, screaming, the sailors rushed to shore. Each of them held an enormous axe, and used it to hack the tusks from the half-dead walruses.

When the schooner, loaded with walrus tusk, sailed away, the people of Enmyn – who had been observing this savage hunt – came down onto the beach. Tears stung their eyes. Their hands that held the spears, useless now, trembled. "I somehow managed to hold my people back, or they would have attacked the sailors," Orvo confessed. It was from Orvo that John learned that after their breeding ground has been fouled, walruses might leave the place for a long while, even forever, and move to a different spot.

"It's a good sign, the walruses coming back to their old breeding ground," Orvo said, as he and John walked up to the Far Cape to get a look at the hundreds of fat bodies that had waddled up onto the shingled beach. "The gods have not left us without their mercies and have rewarded us for the sufferings that fell to our lot last winter."

Orvo had uttered these words solemnly, and from the shingled beach, the old walruses called back to him as they frolicked and luxuriated in the icy tide.

With each passing day, the number of animals on the beach increased, and soon nothing except a grunting mass of bodies could be discerned from the high promontory.

The men gathered in John's yaranga to discuss the impending hunt and divide forces so as to get as many walruses as possible and ensure a serene and well-fed winter for themselves.

The past winter had left a visible mark on each of them. Even the proud Armol' had something new in his step, as though something in his joints had gone awry. Over the summer, the people had regained strength, got back their confidence, yet as the cold days grew nearer, their recent privations preyed more and more often upon their minds.

Pyl'mau brought every single cup that could be found in the yaranga into the chottagin, and set to feeding her guests. There was some flour left from the Uelen supply, and everyone got half of a large pancake fried in nerpa fat. They drank the tea noisily, slurping it from the cups.

Orvo stared at the bottom of his old faience cup and inspected the hieroglyphics carefully, as though he might divine something from them.

Unexpectedly for everyone, the first to make himself heard was Guvat, Enmyn's poorest and quietest denizen.

"I've had plenty to eat and drink. If there's nothing else to do, may I go back home?"

Everyone turned toward him.

Burly and awkward, Guvat stood in the middle of the chottagin, grinning like a fool.

"If that's how you see it, you're free to go!" Orvo said harshly. "And everyone who agrees with Guvat, you can all shove off to your yarangas."

The old man fixed the hunters with a dark, angry look.

"When, when are we going to stop behaving like children, never thinking about our future? When I look at Guvat, I see in him all of our carefree foolishness. We have one desire – to be well fed. Today's fat grows over our eyes, and we can't see tomorrow's famine . . . Yes! Today we have eaten well. But remember last winter, and you'll taste boiled straps on your tongue! Your ears will ring with the dying moans of your family! You have no memory!"

Orvo paused, cleared his throat and continued:

"We'll go after the walrus together, and position our people so that not a single large animal escapes to the sea. We have to kill the grown ones, no touching the pups. They are our living stores."

Guvat, who'd been standing to the side, now quietly sat back down in his place.

The hunters agreed with Orvo.

When everything had been decided, and silence crept over the chotta-gin, Armol', who'd so far been quiet, suddenly spoke. He straightened up sharply, and flexed his shoulders, becoming, for a moment, that old jaunty and lucky ankalin* who feared neither sea nor tundra.

"Orvo! The trouble isn't our not looking forward. The trouble is the white people's ships. We'll wait and wait until it's time to go after the wal-rus. And then the whites will come in their ships, shoot their cannons – and there'll be only gun smoke left of our breeding ground, and of our hopes."

"So what do you advise?" asked Orvo.

"Get our own cannons to fire against the white people," Armol' joked with a crooked grin, and a glance at John.

"Why don't we hear what the white man himself has to say!" Guvat suddenly offered, as though trying to brush off Orvo's accusation that all the laziness and recklessness of their people was epitomized in him.

"What can I say?" John shrugged.

They would never forget, would they, the people of Enmyn, that he was not one of them. And they'll remember it every time some trouble comes from those they call the white people . . .

"What can I say?" John repeated. "If the wolves are circling the herd, what does the reindeer herder do? He goes to protect the herd and takes weapons with him. I think that this is exactly what we need to do."

"You are right," Armol' echoed. "But how will you catch up with a fast motorized ship in a hide boat with oars? They'll run away, or else open fire."

* *Ankalin* – coastal dweller.

"I don't think they're all criminals aboard the ships," John objected. "Are all white people the same? Many of those who reach our parts are decent enough. They study our seas, currents, ice floes, discover new lands . . ."

As he was speaking, John began to feel uncomfortable – what did the scientific interests of Stefansson's expedition matter to the Chukchi? They had to protect their lands and sea dominions, and of course, the most sensible thing white people could do was to leave the inhabitants of the North alone.

"If there are no objections, I'll be responsible for protecting the breeding ground," John said. "If anything happens, I'll answer for it with my life."

No one dared look John in the eye. Heads lowered in agreement, the men were breathing heavily.

"It was a good thing you said, that you'll guard our sea herd," Orvo said, and turning to the others, concluded: "But everyone will help."

First of all, they had to set a watch over the paths to the breeding ground. There was only one pair of binoculars for the whole village – Orvo's, and the old man treasured them. They finally agreed on Orvo's keeping a watch himself, but sometimes giving the binoculars to some-one else, to those he trusted especially.

It was harder to resolve the challenge of a quick approach to a ship, if it should try to get near the walrus nursery.

"We'd never catch it on oars," Tiarat frowned. "And if the ship's got a motor, then it's all over."

"But I've still got a motor and a supply of gas," John remembered. "From the whaleboat. Maybe it can be fixed to the hide boat? I'll give it a try."

Armol's ears pricked up, thinking of his own whaleboat that had been carried off by the hurricane.

"How can you fix a metal motor to a hide boat? It's the same as giving a rabbit wolf's teeth," he said gloomily.

"It's the teeth that everything depends on anyway," Guvat remarked with a deeply thoughtful air. "As soon as the hare shows his wolf's teeth – all the animals will flee from him."

"I'll have to try it first," John thought, "and only then show them. Maybe Armol' is right: the hide boat won't be able to take the motor's power and will break apart as it goes."

Tiarat was considered the settlement's best woodworker. The frames of each of Enmyn's hide boats had been made either by him or under his supervision. Looking at the elegant construction devoid of a single nail, held together with sparse wooden spikes, but primarily with lakhtak strips, it was hard to believe that this miracle had been envisioned complete in his head. There was not a single scrap of paper, not a line drawn in the making of this astounding creation.

So it was Tiarat that John came to, resolving to talk it over with him – whether it would be possible to shore up the hide boat so that it could hold the weight of the gasoline motor.

Tiarat lived on the outskirts of the settlement, almost on the bank of a noisy stream that sparkled in the cold sun's rays. It was a well-chosen spot for a yaranga. There was water near at hand, and the mound over the stream served as a natural buffer against the winter snowdrifts.

The yaranga was not especially prosperous, but everything was sturdy and well set in its place; even its inhabitants stood out by their cleanliness, somehow unusual among the Chukchi. Tiarat had eight children. His eldest, married son lived here, too, as well as an impoverished nomad – the suitor of Tiarat's middle daughter, the beauty Umkanau.

Tiarat was working on something as usual, but he immediately put aside his gatteh – a small crosscut axe – and hailed his guest with reserve and dignity:

"Yetti!"

"Ee-ee," John replied, and sat down on the polished whale vertebra that had been offered him. John noted at once that in this many-peopled yaranga, they took care of their clothes, polishing the seats so as not to tear the pants.

He'd brought along a page from his notepad and the stump of a pencil. As he outlined his idea, John drew it on the page.

Tiarat bent low over the drawing, and John could feel the other man's hot breath on his own face.

"The metal paws won't be able to grab the thin planks on the stern," John was saying, marking it with the pencil.

"Even if they did grab, the planks still couldn't take it," Tiarat observed. "But this can be fixed, we can make an additional, special plank for the motor. It's simple. Like this."

He plucked the pencil stub from John's loop holder and confidently drew a new stern, rigged up and strengthened with the motor in mind.

"This is how it could be done," he concluded and added: "But the first thing is the hide boat itself. When the hide vessel goes over water, it's always under sail or with oars. The mast stands in the keel, on the sturdiest part of the hide boat, as though right on the backbone. The oarlocks on the sides, they're also pulling the boat through the water evenly . . . Need to think about that. Think very hard. It could happen that the motor will make the hide boat wrinkle and shrink like an empty leather sack. We'll think about that, and you also think about the motor. It's all in working order, right?"

The motor was all right, but it couldn't do any harm to dismantle it once more, oil some of the parts and check the magnet.

John extracted the motor from the cellar where it had lain all winter, carefully tucked in among burlap and hides, and set it down onto a walrus skin spread out in the middle of the chottagin. The news that John was about to "butcher" the motor sped like lighting through the village, and the curious flocked to his yaranga.

So as not to get in the way, the guests sat down a little to the side, leaving John and his motor the lighter part of the room, under the round smoke-hole in the roof.

In the universal silence, when the only sound was the metallic clanging, John took out the flywheel with some difficulty. With bated breath, the people followed his every move. When the heavy, shining flywheel bearing the convex legend *General Motors* was set down on the walrus skin, an old woman whispered, with unfeigned terror:

"He's taken off the head."

"Picking at the brains . . ." the others echoed.

"Getting to the feet, now," said Yako, when John separated the three-bladed propeller.

Yako was helping his father.

Pyl'mau had a rag ready, and thoroughly wiped down each component of the engine.

"Likes cleanliness, the motor," said one of the spectators.

"All white people like cleanliness," another concurred.

"But a motor isn't a person," countered a third.

"Much alike, though . . . Head, shoulders, feet . . . You almost expect it to speak . . ." said the old woman with a shiver.

"Yes, when the motor starts working, it makes a buzz, like giving a long speech . . ."

On the whole, all the component parts seemed to be in order. Under John's supervision, Pyl'mau and Yako oiled them and John, to everyone's surprise and delight, reassembled the motor.

"Kakomei! Kyke vyne vai!" came from every side.

Still, the most crucial part still lay ahead: They needed to test it out, but had nothing on which to mount it. Again, it was Tiarat who came to the rescue. Immediately comprehending what John required, that same day, after a few hours, he brought special wooden trestles, tightly held together by lakhtak strips instead of nails.

"And this, for the water," Tiarat suggested, "we'll put the motor's feet into the barrel."

John could only marvel delightedly at the design talent that he so suddenly discovered in the quiet and modest Tiarat.

First of all, they had to test the magnet. Asking Tiarat to hold the wire to the cylinder, John wound the flywheel. Tiarat was knocked to the side with a loud scream.

"He hit me!" he shouted, pointing his finger at the motor from afar.

John burst out laughing.

Tiarat looked at him, confused: A person's been hit and he's laughing. John explained the origin of the knock to Tiarat, but the latter, listening politely, flat-out refused to touch the wire again. They agreed that it would be Tiarat who pulled the flywheel's string. Approaching the motor with some trepidation, Tiarat hesitantly picked up the string, pulled it, and quickly ran off, fearful of receiving another blow from the perfidious motor.

There had been a spark. They poured the gas into the canister. The motor should now start. John made five, ten, twenty pulls, but the motor was silent. His shoulder hurt, his neck ached from the repeated pulling, already many of the spectators had gone back to their yarangas, and still the motor wouldn't start. John tried unscrewing the spark plugs, fixing the gaps between contact points, adding gasoline into the carburetor, but the motor maintained its stubborn silence, with only a dumb and unwilling infrequent shudder. It was dead.

"Seems that with a person, too, if you take him apart and then put him back together, you couldn't wake him, either," was the weighty conclusion of Guvat, the most patient of the observers, as he headed back to his yaranga.

While John was fiddling with the motor, Tiarat had been rigging up the hide boat, drawing up additional ribs, and making the stern extra sturdy – so sturdy that you could hang two motors off it! But the hide boat had no use for a dead engine.

John wouldn't leave it for the next few days. When it began to get dark, he would cover the taciturn motor with furs and head home a broken man.

Pyl'mau tried not to ask about anything. Silently, she'd serve the food and help him undress, and when her husband crawled inside the polog, she'd helpfully bring him the brightly printed instruction manual about the use of the smooth-running, gasoline outboard motor from General Motors.

John didn't want to look at the advertising brochure, sick to death of it, but a little while would pass and he – yet again – would pick it up. Line by line, he scanned the instructions, trying to figure out just where the problem lay. In his mind's eye he took apart and reassembled the motor, following the gasoline flow from tank to cylinders – and he just couldn't understand a thing.

He had despaired of getting anything out of the stubborn device. Done with refitting the hide boat, Tiarat began coming by to help John more and more often. Together they picked over the motor yet again, but to no avail.

Once, when John had returned home and was finishing his tea, a victorious droning burst into the chottagin. It was the working motor! Except that the sound of it was somewhat strange, unusual. John was outside in a heartbeat.

Shaking on its fragile shelf, held together with lakhtak strips, the motor roared, spraying water from the barrel underneath the propeller in every direction. Tiarat was standing nearby, watching the quickened and unleashed engine fearfully.

"Who got it to start?" John asked.

"Himself." Tiarat made a clumsy attempt at a fib, and sheepishly added: "I only wanted to touch him a little."

John cut off the motor and then pulled the flywheel cord again. After two or three tries, the motor started working. It was alive again!

"So what did you do to it?" John asked.

"Honestly, nothing," Tiarat pleaded. "I was just touching him a little, just like you do it."

There was a pitiful, guilty look in his eyes. John considered it best to drop the question altogether, so as not to upset his comrade, especially now that the people of Enmyn had started to follow the motor's noise to its source.

"You're a real magician," John had time to whisper to the bewildered Tiarat.

The next day they tested the hide boat. Just in case, they decided to do it in the lagoon.

The flimsy little craft was brought ashore and lowered into the water. John lugged over the motor and, with Tiarat's help, carefully fixed it to the stern of the light hide boat. The boat sat low instantly. Tiarat and Armol' climbed aboard. The others wished to observe the hide vessel's behavior from the shore.

"Get in, get in," Tiarat beckoned. "The lower the hide boat sits, the better."

"What if sits too deep?" Guvat said, looking innocent from his place in the crowd, hands deeply hidden in the pockets of his deerskin kukhlianka.

Tiarat threw him a reproachful glance, and gave John a questioning look.

"Let's go," John shouted.

They rowed the hide boat a length from the beach and turned toward the opposite side.

John pulled the flywheel cord. The motor roared, yanking the hide boat with such force that Tiarat, standing beside it, almost fell overboard.

A wave of foam rose up behind the stern and rushed along with the hide boat as it sped across the lagoon, nose held high, scaring off the cormorants. The birds were all but knocking into the boat's hide-bound sides. The people left behind on the beach were shouting something, waving their arms, but it wasn't possible to hear them, as the motor's triumphant song drowned out all other sound.

With a specially made leather ring, John held on to the motor's steering handle. The hide boat was pliant, responding to the lightest touch. It vibrated from keel to sides, the leather stretched over the hide boat's frame vibrated too, creating ripples that streamed by and lingered behind the stern.

The motorized hide boat was at least twice as fast as a wooden whaleboat. The yarangas, the Whale Jaws, the funerary hill sped by. John wheeled the hide boat around and made a flying pass of the beach, splashing the onlookers with water and the smell of gasoline.

Breaking out once more into the lagoon's open space, John took course for the Pil'khyn strait that connected the lagoon with the ocean.

"What do you think, can we get past Pil'khyn?" he screamed into Tiarat's ear.

"We can!" was the other's confident reply. "Only we should keep to the right shore. The left has a large rock, the motor can break its legs on it," and Tiarat nodded toward the motor, as though it was a living creature.

Navigating through the strait, they came out onto the ocean's level surface. The water was thick, heavy, but even so the nose of the hide boat sliced through it easily. It seemed to John that this time, it had risen even higher and was flying through the air, barely skimming the water with its keel.

"Do you want to drive the boat?" he asked Tiarat, standing near, with a look. "I want to," the other answered happily, and reached out his hand.

Feeling the engine's live force, Tiarat shivered at first, but then his face took on such a contented and peaceful aspect that John had to turn away to hide an unbidden smile.

Smoothly winding the handle, Tiarat would curve around the sparse icebergs in their way and then revised the hide boat's flight path, trying to keep to a straight line of course.

Not a half an hour later, the outermost of Enmyn's yarangas came into view, and then the lonely figure of a fisherman, guarding the nets. John was surprised by the empty shoreline, but then he realized that all the people were waiting for them on the other side of the shingled sandbank, by the lagoon.

They had had time to come ashore and drag the hide boat out onto the beach, before they saw the people of Enmyn running in the distance. Guvat was in the lead, windmilling his long arms.

"How did you get here?" he shouted from afar, with sincere disbelief.

"We flew in the air," Tiarat answered calmly as he was carefully unscrewing the bolts that had fixed the motor to the hide boat.

"Really?" Guvat's eyes went wide. "True, true! I'd heard that the whites can do even that! Right?" he turned to John.

"We came into the lagoon through Pil'khyn."

It was plain on Guvat's face that he didn't believe his fellows.

While they were walking up to the yarangas, Armol' suddenly held John back by his sleeve.

"This is very important!" he whispered heatedly. "Now I know what I need to do! You don't need to buy whaleboats – you need to buy motors! The main thing today is speed! Look, we went around the lagoon five times faster than on oars. That means it was more like five hide boats going, not just one. If I had a motor . . ."

In his excitement, Armol' was even lost for words. He was seeing himself at the wheel of a motorized canoe, speeding across the sea.

"It's dangerous out among the icebergs," said John. "You hit one at that speed, and it's straight to the bottom."

24

And yet John was unable to make the first patrolling trip any time soon: Pyl'mau had given birth to his son. It was Yako that met John as he came in from a day of hunting. The boy was loitering beside the yaranga, at loose ends.

"A brother has come to visit us," he said in the tone of a grown man imparting a very significant piece of news.

"You don't say!" Joyfully, John rushed for the chottagin, only to be met with old Cheivuneh's implacable stony face. She barred the way with her arm, dry and wizened like a gnarled branch, and sternly told him:

"Think about your son's future!"

John spent a few days out of action, retreating to his long unused cubbyhole. He slept on the hard cot, surprised at how his own perception of comfort had changed over time. An he even wondered whether, if this were his native house in Port Hope, he would feel as peaceful and contented in the spacious living room in front of the fireplace on a long winter evening as inside the snug warm polog. Picking over his personal items that had become useless, John discovered his notepad and read the last entry with a smile. And then he had an epiphany: How unbelievable all this was! Here he is, reading the last entry, and a completely different person arises before him, a person left far behind. In turn, that person's thoughts are read and even spoken out loud by a whole other person . . .

Well, now, let's see! John picked up a pencil, stuck it through a special holder loop and began writing on a clean page:

My son was born. My own son, born on this barren ground. Last winter, I buried my daughter . . . How did it happen, that I cannot even conceive of leaving this shore? It isn't that my daughter is buried here or that the people near and dear to me live here. Then what is the root of the matter? It's as though each passing day takes me further away from that ideal of manhood instilled in me from childhood and reinforced in my studies. I've even started to believe in these idols, in my own way, or more precisely, in the forces behind them . . . Maybe it's because here you need to keenly feel your humanity every day, every hour, in order to survive. Or, to be more precise, I am trying to feel my way toward the true ideal of humanity. Besides, what is a person, and what does he live for? What's brought him into this orderly, clearly outlined world, and made him invade it?. . . Around here, they don't ask such questions – of themselves or of others – they just live. A son was born. He will live and fight for the right to be called a human being in this cold land, hunt animals, learn to love the MacLennan line and continue it . . . Somewhere in the distant future, there will live the legend of the white man who stayed among them, and who sired strange Chukchi – in whose line of descent sometimes unusual features surface. And maybe, some day, one of them will feel emotion rise up in his soul, but he won't know that it was Shelley's poem or Chopin's Ballade No. 1 he was remembering. He will hear them in the inaudible breath of the flowering spring tundra, in the freezing wave that runs over a shingled beach . . . Be happy, my son, Bill-Toko MacLennan!

Snowflakes came down from a clear sky, and the sea was clear, too. The water had become heavier, it no longer had its summer weightlessness and elasticity. Lazily, the waves would roll over the frozen shingle and slowly draw back, leaving a salty layer of ice on the rocks.

They brought the hide boat down to the beach with great care. The light little boat was resting on the shoulders of four men, who walked over the slippery, hoarfrosted stones. Tiarat walked behind the hide boat carrying the motor on his shoulder, and Yako trotted in the rear, with an important look about him, dragging a long oar with leather-loop rowlocks.

The patrolmen who were stationed up on the high promontory had reported seeing a vessel in among the ice floes. It had passed a long way from shore, heading for the Invisible Island. The piece of news was alarming to Enmyn's inhabitants, especially those who'd been given the task of guarding the breeding ground.

The news forced John to hasten the time of his going out to sea, despite the fact that the traditional quarantine for a new father had not yet passed. He talked to Cheivuneh about it himself.

"If you are concerned about my new son's future," John said respectfully, "would it not be better to think about what he's going to eat? Remember last winter. How many lives were taken by the famine, how many newborns went beyond the clouds, though all the rites had been observed at their births and their fathers had stayed the full length of the required hermitage?"

"It was not I who decreed these customs, and not even my ancestors. They were born together with our people," Cheivuneh answered him. "If you start thinking about whether it's reasonable or unreasonable, then life itself will turn out to be unreasonable."

"But still, we have to try and make it so that the custom works for the people's well-being first of all. The ones who thought it up or created it, they were thinking of the people's good, weren't they?" John mildly objected.

Cheivuneh's stony expression remained unchanged, but something twitched in the folds of her wrinkles, the spark of a new idea glimmered in her eyes.

"If we don't go out to meet the white people's ship, they could frighten off the walruses, as they've done before. If the Outer Forces punish me for breaking the tradition, then it's better that I alone suffer than all of us together. Does this seem sensible?"

Cheivuneh bowed her head and said in a whisper:

"Just don't forget to make an offering to all the directions – Dawn, North, South, and Dusk – before you go out to sea. And don't forget your household god."

"All right, Epekei." *

"And go see your wife and son."

"All right, Epekei . . ."

With Tiarat's help, the Outer Forces were endowed with bits of tobacco, deer meat, and drops of blood. John managed the household god himself, giving his face a generous smear of nerpa fat and drawing a tough stalk of chewing tobacco over his lips.

And now, calm, confident, they were walking to the shore to enter the sea and meet the unknown ship. John was propping up the hide boat's stern with one shoulder, and his eyes took in the back of Guvat, walking in front of him, and beyond him – the sea's expanse, which seemed so serene and peaceful at this distance. There was barely any ice on its surface, and it was hard to believe that within a short while, this boundless expanse would be covered over with thick ice, piled with sharp-nosed ice hummocks, and they would have to seek open water far from shore, sometimes traveling tens of miles. John was trying to match Guvat's step; even the sway of his torso was identical to that of the man who walked

* *Epekei* – grandmother.

ahead. It was only right by the shore, when there was a single last step to be made, that John looked at himself as if from afar, at the way he'd sacrificed to the gods and even whispered incantations along with Tiarat, how he was walking with his countrymen . . . Something moved within his breast, a thought glimmered in his brain, but then Guvat's voice interrupted his musings.

"Let's set it down!"

There was hardly any surf. The water, heavy with frost, splashed lazily close to shore, and rainbow parachutes of jellyfish hung almost motionlessly over the clean bottom, rocking gently in time with the ocean's breathing.

Yako spotted a tangle of seaweed in the frosty shingle, pried it free with the tip of one of his torbasses, bit off half and offered the rest to his father.

The seaweed, something John had grown very fond of, was pleasantly refreshing on the tongue, and its taste held something faraway, familiar, as though it were not a marine plant but a fresh cucumber, just plucked from the vegetable patch and lightly salted.

Businesslike, Tiarat checked on the stern rigging and carefully attached the motor's little claw-hooks to a specially built system of thick wooden planks and lakhtak-skin lashings.

The motor's propeller was raised high in the air, so as not to dent it when they pushed the hide boat off from the shore.

"You know, we're doing everything wrong!" Guvat, who had also got lucky with some seaweed and whose loud satisfied munching filled the beach with noise, piped up all of a sudden. "It should all be the other way around."

They had to suffer him a good while, until they could manage to fish a genuinely useful idea from his muddled speech: It would be safer for the propeller to push the hide boat into the water stern first. Then the propeller would immediately be in deep water, and the hunters could climb in more comfortably.

"You, too, have common sense, once in a while," Tiarat said with surprise.

When the hide boat was rocking in the water, Yako jumped in first, and John after him. Last to climb aboard was Guvat, who pushed off the light craft and neatly folded the docking rope.

They decided to row from shore, so that the motor's roar did not reach the breeding ground and frighten off the animals. Steadily, the oars dipped into the heavy, viscous water, and thickly the drops plunked down, rolling down the long oar blades. Only the creaking of the oarlocks broke the silence. The people did not speak amongst themselves, and not just because each one was busy with a task of his own, but such was the old custom – hunters don't open their mouths when there is no need. Noiselessly, with a light splash, the nerpa came up to the surface, but the hunters had no weapons with them – the crash of gunshots was also unwanted in the virgin silence that protected the great walrus gathering.

The low, pebbled sandbank was now in view. Truth be told, there was no sandbank anymore – it was completely blanketed with gray-brown bodies. If you let your eye slide up the steep rocky side, on the very top you would see the observers. Today it was Armol'and Orvo who stood there.

John thought about the old man. Lately, Orvo had become reclusive and only rarely looked in on John. And when he did, more and more often he'd speak about his ailments, about some kind of small creature that had taken residence in his chest and whose hungry squeaking woke Orvo up some nights. "He's gnawing at my innards," Orvo would say and start to cough. The coughing racked his whole body, now grown thin and old, that had once seemed to John to be carved from an incredibly durable species of wood. According to Orvo it would seem that he was not much more than fifty, and yet he looked closer to seventy. Yes, life here was not easy, and one year spent on the shore of the Arctic Ocean was worth two, even three, years lived, say, on the shores of Lake Ontario.

"Ateh, look, lakhktak," Yako diverted John away from his somber thoughts.

A shiny round head was swimming silently in front of the hide boat. From afar it seemed human, especially the eyes – large, black, expressive, filled with such deep wisdom that you couldn't look into them for long. Time heals everything, even wounds that seem to be inscribed upon the heart and soul for life. It was a long while since the mention of lakhtak stirred the terrible memories of the horrors John had lived through, dragging the dying Toko, wrapped in lakhtak skin, down the fast ice.

Now Toko had come again. He came in the guise of a new person whom Pyl'mau had carried under her kind heart in the harshest and gloomiest days of the hard winter. And the winter itself no longer seemed so dark from the vantage point of today, a day that promised well-fed winter evenings, the Northern Lights frolicking in the skies. And even the raging blizzard that shook the walrus-hide covers of the yarangas seemed a pleasant music, a music that acquits the man who is sitting inside a warm polog surrounded by his loved ones or lost in listening to distant and misty legends. Satiety, the certainty of tomorrow, and long slumber when the penetrating winter fog begins to steal in. You go off into that dream at the edge of fog, and when you wake, a new day has dawned, and you can even see a sliver of sun creeping behind the horizon in its long chase of the escaping winter.

John's musings were interrupted only by short commands from Tiarat, who was directing John where to point the steering oar. But the commands were few and far between, and there was only the ringing of water drops rolling from the oars' blades stretching out over the vast expanse and the creaking of the leather oarlocks on the ancient vessel that carried on its stern the latest invention built by man to replace the labor of his hands – the gas-driven outboard motor from General Motors.

"I see a sail!"

The oars hung motionless over the water, the creaking of the lashings stilled. "A ship coming to our shore," added Tiarat, clapping a big flat nerpa-skin mitten above his eyes as a visor.

"Have we come far out enough to start the motor?" John inquired, as he pulled the steering oar out of the water and prepared to replace it with the propeller and wheel of the outboard motor.

Tiarat glanced at the shore, at the far-off breeding ground that seemed, from here, merely an unremarkable narrow strip, much the same as all the other shingled sandbanks on the Arctic coast. The hide boat had come far out to sea (evidently there was a seaward current here helping the oarsmen); the walrus were no longer distinguishable.

"Now, the loudest sound for them is the noise of the surf, and they're not silent themselves," said Tiarat, lowering the mitten from his eyes. "They won't hear us."

He moved from the bow to the stern, to help John with starting up the engine.

The cooled-down motor took a long time to start. It just spluttered in a disgusted manner.

And meanwhile, inexorably, the ship continued to come closer. Already you could see the water-stained rigging, and the ship's body, marred by the ice. The people on the hide boat threw themselves desperately into awakening the motor. The pull cord went from John back to Tiarat, from Tiarat to Guvat, who pulled with such zeal that the whole hide boat shuddered. But, to everyone's surprise and delight, the motor roared, and Guvat, miraculously leaping over Tiarat and John in the packed boat, found himself back in his place.

The hide boat raced toward the ship like a bird on the wing. The keel shook a little, as clinging water rolled smoothly underneath. Under the translucent walrus hide, green water rushed by.

The ship grew larger with each passing moment. Only a few minutes passed before Tiarat began to brake. The ship heaved to, and lay adrift.

This was the schooner *Bear* of the Canadian Naval Department, coming back from Wrangel Island with the surviving crew members of the *Karluk,* that had been crushed by the ice in January of 1914.

On the bridge, John sighted Captain Bartlett, who recognized him:

"Hello, Mr. MacLennan! I'm very glad to see you in good health! Please, come aboard."

The schooner sat low in the water, and the men from the hide boat climbed aboard the wooden vessel without difficulty, eschewing the aid of the gangway. Setting foot on deck and greeting the captain once more, John looked around and, not seeing Yako next to him, turned back.

The boy was standing in the hide boat looking at the whites, at their immense wooden ship that could probably hold all the people of Enmyn and their dogs, too, eyes wide with both curiosity and fear. And another, surprising, discovery immediately set him apart from his stepfather: Standing next to the captain, ateh, Sson, suddenly became just as distant and unreachable as all of those white people crowding on deck and curiously peering at the natives that had arrived by motor hide boat, Sson in his Chukchi clothing, and the little boy who was clinging fearfully to the side of the hide-bound vessel.

"Come here, Yako!" John called.

"I'm scared, Sson," Yako confessed in a quavering voice.

"Come here, son, I'll help you up," John said calmly and firmly, and stretched his leather-wrapped wrists out to the boy.

Fighting his fear, trying to control the revolting tickling somewhere behind his knees, Yako obeyed, and having climbed up on deck, stood beside his stepfather.

"My son," John said. "His name is Yako."

"I'm pleased to see you again," Bartlett smiled, offering his hand.

Yako had never before had to make greeting according to the white people's custom, not outside gameplay, when he was pretending to be a white man, but now he had to do it for real. The captain's palm was hard as a spear handle.

Captain Bartlett invited everyone to the cramped wardroom.

The steward set the table with tea and rum, and sweets for Yako. The captain entertained them cordially, telling them all about the hazardous journey to Wrangel Island.

"We'd lost hope and had resigned ourselves to our unfortunate comrades' having to spend another winter ashore. But one day, the ice that had amassed by the coast broke, and we were able to come ashore in a launch and bring back our friends. The *Karluk*'s epic adventure ended relatively well, but our boss, Vilhjalmur Stefansson, is already considering a plan for a new expedition, with the intent of colonizing the island, setting up a permanent settlement there . . ."

"Wrangel Island belongs to Canada, then?" John inquired, taking a sip of his rum-laced coffee.

"It's hard for me to say anything conclusive about the matter," Captain Bartlett replied. "Ancient custom tells us that land belongs to those who live on it. And as far as we could discern, at present Wrangel Island is uninhabited, and will be owned by the country that colonizes it."

"I doubt that the Russian government will take this lightly," John objected.

"Right now, the Russian government is busy with the war in Europe. These northern territories are nothing but a burden. Recall the sale of Alaska."

The Chukchi respectfully listened to the white people's strange conversation, and it was strange for the men of Enmyn to see their own fellow-countryman Sson as someone in a position to discuss this unknown but evidently important business. Perhaps they were talking about how the current ice conditions were favorable to seafaring: The tops of far-off mountains had long been covered by snow and yet there was still no sign of sea ice near the shore, and only when the wind blew from the north did a white stripe appear on the horizon and quickly disappear again.

At the end of the discussion, Captain Bartlett expressed a wish to come closer to shore and replenish their water supply from a waterfall that dropped into the sea two miles or so east of the Enmyn Cape.

"Take as much water as you need," John answered, "but my friends and I would ask you not to use your engines and not to make too much noise. I'd like to especially ask you not to shoot: We're protecting a walrus breeding ground. It's our only hope for an untroubled winter. If someone frightens off the animals, we'll be left without food or fuel."

"We will respect your wishes," was Captain Bartlett's courteous reply, as he ordered the raising of the sails.

Tugging the hide boat, the *Bear* moved slowly, catching barely perceptible air currents within the enormous cloths of its sails, currents that couldn't even raise a speckle over the smooth surface of the sea, heavy from the cold.

In sight of the village, John and his people went back to the hide boat and returned home. The *Bear* went a little farther east, and the sailors set to ferrying the fresh water, using the freshly scrubbed launch boats to collect it.

The schooner required a great deal of water, and the vessel was there all night. In the morning, sparse ice clumps floated closer to Enmyn's shore. It was time to hunt the walrus.

Before the ship departed, Captain Bartlett paid John MacLennan a farewell visit. A heavily laden launch bumped up against the shore, where almost all of Enmyn's inhabitants were already assembled. Not far from the men, the women stood in a separate group, among them Pyl'mau with a fur-swaddled infant.

With a firm handshake, Captain Bartlett told John:

"I thank you most sincerely for your help, and please believe me, I stand in awe of your character. Allow me to present your son Yako with this sailing atlas of the northern seas, published by the Canadian Naval Department," and he handed a heavy, lavishly printed tome to Yako, who was standing beside his father.

Then he gave gifts to the people of Enmyn in the name of the Canadian Naval Department. Noticing the baby in Pyl'mau's arms, he said to John:

"Oh, I see you've an addition to the family?"

"Yes," John answered.

"And what is this new citizen of the Arctic called?"

"Bill-Toko MacLennan," John replied.

"I wish you all prosperity and happiness," and with that, Captain Bartlett climbed aboard the launch. The sailors picked up their oars and moved off toward the schooner.

John set off in the direction of the Far Cape, to have another look at the breeding ground. Despite the late autumn, the sky was clear and high. The sun had long gone, but it was still light from the glowing sparse new ice, thinly covering the earth and the seashore crags.

And John MacLennan's soul was just as clear and light.

Tomorrow all the men and boys of Enmyn would be going after the walrus.

25

They'd sharpened their spears well in advance. The spearheads were so sharp that you could have used them to shave. This was demonstrated by Tiarat, who scraped a little growth that resembled the head of a calligraphy brush, off his chin.

Long before dawn, the settlement had come alive. At John's urging, they made the Great Sacrifice a little to the side of the Far Cape, rather than directly underneath it to avoid making unnecessary noise. All the dogs were locked up inside the chottagins, or else chained up at the eastern end of the village, where enormous snow and water-bleached whale skulls had been dug into the pebbled beach.

The thin fiery stripe of the approaching dawn was growing with remarkable speed. But it only seemed that way – time was moving at its usual pace, and it was the impatient hearts of the hunters that pulled forward the moments too quickly.

Orvo stood with his face to the dawn, whispering the sacred words. It struck him that if the prayers of all nations and religions were translated – the big ones and the small ones, ancient and new – their import could be reduced to three words only: peace, bread, health. Peace, understood to be not merely the friendly relations between governments and peoples, but also the wish to respect the inner life of another and not befuddle him with useless and unusual temptations, to cherish the peace and life of another human being without trying to measure him with one's own stick. And as for bread and health, well, that was self-explanatory. Except that here, bread is the enormous assembly of blubbery beings wiggling to and fro on the pebbled sandbar under the Far Cape.

In his hands, Orvo held the now-familiar sacrificial vessel. A plain wooden dish, shiny with long use and the grease of foods allotted to the gods.

Half-closing his eyes to narrow slits so as not to miss the first ray of sunlight, Orvo waited for the great heavenly body to appear. The Enmyn hunters hung back behind him, silent shadows. Somewhere in the distance, the chained dogs were whining softly. Frozen moisture poured from a cloudless sky in the shape of snowflakes.

Finally! The first ray sparkled through. It burst from the icy, whitewashed horizon and hit Orvo, standing motionless, in the eyes. The old man's voice rang out, and, uttering the last of the incantations, he began to scatter the sacrificial offering, each wave of his hand accompanied by new words.

John's spear had been adapted so that the handle would not slip off the leather clamps on his wrists even when they became slick with blood. Although, by rights, the ceremonial sacrifice should have had a calming effect on the hunters, it was difficult to fight the agitation that was part and parcel of the approaching hunt.

They walked past the yarangas via the beach. Like stone carvings, the women and children stood by the dwellings. They were seeing off their breadwinners.

The shingle was hardened with frost. The usual creaking of torbasses went unheard. And, despite thick and springy tundra-grass insoles, every so often a toe would be painfully stubbed against an upright piece of rock.

They were twelve going to the walrus hunt. Only ten of these could have been considered real hunters, and as for the other two – Tiarat's sons Chupliu and Ergynto – this would be their first hunt of this kind.

The seascape stretched out before them from the top of the Far Cape. They could clearly distinguish the white stripe of ice on the horizon, the ice floes appearing as so many pieces of white cloth scattered over the smooth plane of the sea.

The packed gray mass of walruses lay in the usual spot, on a narrow sandbar. From here, from the top of the Far Cape, you could already hear their deep, heavy grunting and intermittent exhalations, as though sighing with terrible foreknowledge.

With great care, the hunters descended the rocky slope, cautious not to let a single pebble roll down to disturb the animals. Before the descent, Orvo warned the hunters: They must start killing the walruses from the beach, to cut off a means of escape for the wounded ones.

"You've got to hit him quickly and to the death," these were Orvo's parting words, his voice trembling with agitation. "A wounded walrus will run away and tell the others what a terrible place this is – the sandbank under the Far Cape. And he'll show them his wounds. Don't let any that are not whole and untouched leave. Go mostly for the old ones, don't touch the cows. That's all. Let's get moving."

Carefully leaning on the handle of his spear, John was third in the descending column of hunters. The shingled sandbar was looming closer, and he could distinguish individual animals. His nostrils took in the pungent smell of excrement, malodorous breath, mixing with the fresh scent of encroaching ice.

Already, some of the walruses were anxious, raising their heads and swinging their blunt pointy-whiskered and tusked muzzles from side to side. A displeased snorting issued from the pink jaws with their rows of strong white teeth.

Orvo made a sign with his eyes, and the young hunters leaped from the hillside straight into the gentle incoming surf.

John rushed to follow the others. Remembering Orvo's instructions, he speared the animals under the left shoulder blade, as he'd been shown.

Despite its thick layer of blubber, walrus skin turned out not to be especially thick, and the well-sharpened blade entered the animal's body with comparative ease. Moaning hoarsely, the walruses would raise their heads and collapse onto the shingle, slippery with blood and urine, meekly, with resignation, as though each had come to this sandbank precisely to end his life's journey in just such a manner. John speared one walrus after another, in bitter, hardened silence, trying not to think about the fact of his killing a living creature, a body that might even be feeling the heartache of its impending doom.

The young men stationed by the surf-line had not let even a single wounded walrus escape. The ones to leave were the cows, the strong young bulls, and the very young pups who still had only small white growths instead of tusks, reminiscent of unkempt snot-nosed children.

The surf was streaked with red. The rising sun dappled its rays across the rock, greasy with blubber and blood, across the sweat-shiny faces of the hunters. Their arms were tired, their heads throbbing from the nauseating smell of blood and the walrus bodies, and there came a moment when John realized that he could not make another single blow. But no sooner had he thought this than Orvo's voice rang out:

"Enough! Let the rest go back to the sea!"

The young men parted ranks and freed up a passageway to the open water. But the walruses were not especially keen to get in, sensing that this was not the native element that was for them both the cradle and the medium of adult life. Still, it was worse to be on this blood-stained ground, among their suddenly silenced and motionless brethren. The walruses swam out to sea, looking back in bewilderment, and emitting loud anxious bellows, as though calling to those who had for some strange reason decided to stay behind among the two-legged ones with their deadly rays fixed onto long sticks.

Tiarat took out a big knife and slit the belly of a young walrus that was lying nearby. He extracted the steaming, still-quivering liver, and sliced off a large portion for each of the hunters. The liver was warm, with a sweetish tang. It was excellent for slaking both hunger and thirst.

When they had their fill, the hunters fell to butchering the carcasses. Great skill and dexterity was essential for wielding the long hunter's knife, and so John was employed instead in dragging the hides and chunks of meat off to the side, and helping to sew up the enormous kymgyts. By evening, two hide boats of women had arrived to help. They had brought with them cauldrons and fresh water. Fires came ablaze on the spot that had only recently been teeming with walrus life, and thick smoke streamed up to a sky swathed in a thickening frosty mist.

Together with the women, the children had come. They wandered around the dead animals and poked them with sticks, miming the hunters. Yako played with them, and soon his festive kamleika, sewn from a ten-pound flour sack, was soaked through with blubber and blood. But the boy was delighted! Screaming, he dashed between the half-butchered carcasses, leapt over them, sank his sharp teeth into the juicy pulp of raw walrus liver and, every few minutes or so, ran to his ateh, to help thread the thick uncured hide-lashing that stitched together the gigantic kymgyt. Each of the hunters carved his personal mark on his own kymgyt, and so each kymgyt was prepared according to the owners' individual tastes. Pyl'mau had been placing chopped hearts and kidneys, layering the meat with strips of lard, in some of hers. Tiarat's brand, for example, was the picture of a deer, as his ancestors had been born of tundra dwellers. Orvo was cutting out the inypchick – the killer whale – character. John stamped each kymgyt with the letter J, until his wife perplexedly inquired:

"What animal does that sign represent?"

"That's the letter *J,* the start of my name."

"But your name is Sson, not Jay."

"That's what you all call me, but really, my name is John."

Pylmau set down her pekul' and stared at her husband, puzzled:

"What do you mean – really? So then, all this time we've been living with you, we've been calling you by a wrong name?"

"Oh, it's no big deal," John waved his hand, "Sson, John, what's the difference?"

"How can you say that?" Pyl'mau was aghast. "A man's whole life is in his name. A man who loses his name, loses his life!"

"Mau, this isn't the time to be talking about it," John tiredly replied, "let's wait until we're back home, and then we can discuss the matter at leisure."

"I wouldn't think of talking about something important right this minute," Pyl'mau shot back, insulted. "But why did you keep silent and put up with it for so long, when we kept calling you by the wrong name? . . ."

"So what sign did you use when Toko was alive?"

"A hare's head. Toko was a very fast runner, and so the name Miliut – hare – became his nickname. But his real name was still Toko."

"Let's do this, then," John suggested, "I can't draw a hare, and anyway it would be hard for me to do without hands. You put a hare on the kymgyts, and I'll do my J."

"Let's do that," Pyl'mau agreed, and busied herself with the next walrus.

Night had come and gone unnoticed. Only by morning, when dawn blushed over the east, did they see that almost all the work was done: Under the stony incline, on a shingled sandbank, there lay a neat row of kymgyts – each family having done exactly what was required. The remaining carcasses they hacked to parts and piled inside an enormous stone larder, cut into the crag itself untold centuries ago.

They brought some of the kymgyts back to the settlement, and stacked them in uverans, earthen pits whose bottoms glinted with permafrost even in the hottest height of summer. The rest was left beside the Far Cape, painstakingly covered over with stones so that the white foxes and wolves, and especially polar bears, could not steal the cache.

It took a few days to cart the fat, hides, meat, bundles of half-cleaned intestines – material for future waterproof cloaks – enormous and heavy yellowish tusks, flippers – everything that walrus could give to man, even the whiskery heads. Everything was either brought over to Enmyn or carefully stashed in the stone depositories of the Far Cape.

The people of Enmyn looked forward and into the face of the coming winter with confidence. Steadily, but without undue haste, winter equipment was being prepared, snowshoes were being patched up, winter clothing sewn, new torbasses, kamleikas from the cloth presented by the Canadian Naval Department. All that was lacking were some deer hides. But at this junction, as though apprised of the Enmyn people's needs, Il'motch had moved his herds closer to the seashore and presented himself in John's yaranga like an old friend. He arrived with a gift of a few skinned deer carcasses and lots of kamusses for torbasses. Among the array of the deer herder's gifts were a multicolored fawn skin and some specially cured skins for a warm winter kukhlianka.

"All this for me?" John was at a loss for words.

"Yes," Il'motch said solemnly. "For you are my coastal friend, and I offer you a part of my wealth, and the things you need."

It was hard to think of an appropriate return gift for Il'motch.

26

The reindeer herd settled in on the opposite side of the lagoon. And there, in a cozy narrow valley, whose stream was glazed with a thin layer of ice, stood the tentlike tundra yarangas, haloed in blue smoke – as each day there were visitors from the coastal settlement, a feast always had to be ready.

John drove up his dogsled from the seaward side. The pack sensed a deer herd was grazing just beyond the hill, and pulled in that direction. But the pack leader, obeying John's quiet commands, held a course for the first yaranga belonging to the camp elder and chief, Il'motch.

His host had sighted John from afar and came out to meet him together with his sons – tall young men with slightly bowed legs. Eventually, John learned that the curvature of the reindeer herders legs owed not to their riding the deer, but to a peculiarity of the children's garments. Little boys wore special pants, with a little codpiece, just like a sailor's. The codpiece was packed with moss that was replaced as and when necessary. Sometimes the mothers were too busy, or the boys themselves prefered to ignore the small discomfort caused by the dampness, so they carried on running up and down the tundra tussocks, merely trying to keep their legs wide apart. The springy tussocks gave a deer herder's walk elasticity, and when he walked over even ground, his walk was a sight for sore eyes – it was as though he were dancing rather than walking.

Il'motch's sons rushed to the dogsled, grabbed the ostol from the visitor's hands and brought the dog pack to a halt.

"Amyn yetti!" Il'motch stepped forward with a wide smile.

"Ee-ee," John replied, and followed his host inside.

Il'motch's traveling yaranga was different from the one John had seen on the two previous occasions. There was nothing extraneous here, and the polog had been sewn from sheared rather than long-haired hides, to make it easier to transport . . .

"I'm always very glad when such a guest comes to visit me," Il'motch continued with a warm smile, motioning broadly for John to sit down on a snow-white deerskin.

"Before I sit down, I'd like to unload the dogsled."

"Don't you worry!" Il'motch raised a hand. "My sons will unpack everything and bring it right inside the chottagin. They'll feed and tie up the dogs."

And true enough, no sooner had the words left his lips than the young men appeared in the cramped doorway, carrying the bundles of gifts. John had decided to deviate a little from what Pyl'mau had advised and presented his tundra friend with walrus hides, fat that had been poured inside whole sealskins, pulled off stocking-style, lakhtak for shoesoles, dried walrus meat on the bone, and a few bits from Captain Bartlett's parting gifts.

Il'motch wasted no time in opening the pipe tobacco tin and, taking in a delighted draught, became engrossed in the picture of Prince Albert, with cane and top hat, pictured on the canister.

"If he showed up here in the tundra with such a bucket on his head, the wolves would run from him, much less the deer," he said thoughtfully.

Wordlessly, John nodded to indicate his agreement. But it seemed that Il'motch did not wish to be taken for a person of limited perspective, and so went on:

"Your beasts would be frightened of me, too, if they saw me in the stuff I'm wearing right now. Right?"

"I doubt it," John replied. "In winter, our shepherds don't look much different from the Chukchi tundra dwellers."

"Shepherds don't, maybe," Il'motch agreed, "but this person," he tapped a blue fingernail against the tin, "he's an unusual sort. He needs to put such a long head somewhere, right? So he has to wear that kind of strange hat."

John couldn't suppress a smile:

"He's got a perfectly normal head. As for the tall hat, it's only worn on holidays. Like the chamois overall that you wear on big visiting trips."

"You don't say," Il'motch was sincerely surprised. "And here I thought his head was that long, too."

Falling silent for a while and watching the women preparing a treat for John, Il'motch resumed the genteel conversation:

"Yes, many wonders on the earth! And we don't even know everything about it. Listen to one storyteller, and it seems that the earth is something like a bowl that's floating on the sea. Another says it's made up of layers. And we're on the top layer, and the ones who died recently are in the next one down, and so on. They say there are shamans who can talk to such distant ancestors that the ancestors don't even recognize them. That's what our storytellers and wise men say, and what about yours?" Il'motch inquired.

"Our wise men have proven that the earth is like a ball," John informed him.

The scientific determination of the earth's shape did not produce an effect upon Il'motch.

"Well then!" he exclaimed, with almost a kind of joy. "Yours are saying strange things, too!" And he continued, but in a serious tone:

"No way to find out everything, though. You should know yourself.

What you want, how good your life is on the earth? . . . And it's enough to know where the grazing lands are, what rivers and mountains there are around, and where . . . The head, for our guest!" He curtly instructed a woman who was setting up a large wooden trough on a short-legged little table. "Clear enough, there are wonders in all the lands. Now I've heard, is it true, that in the lands of the white people there are springs of the bad joy-making water?"

Now the purpose of this conversational thread became clear to John, and with a smile, but firmly, he said:

"Nonsense! There are no such things!"

"But the fat for the rumbling engines," Il'motch objected, displaying an unexpected and astonishing possession of the facts, "so then, that doesn't flow from the ground, either?"

"The fat does flow," John answered, "but there aren't any springs of bad joy-making water."

"It's not right, what nature does! Not right!" Il'motch's disappointment was palpable, and, in the near certainty that his guest had not picked up on the hint, suggested they begin the meal.

But here John finally extracted the whiskey bottle from his pocket and set it on the small table, next to the trough full of boiled deer meat.

With a passing glance at the bottle, and noting that it had not even been opened, Il'motch, reining in his impatience with all his might, ordered:

"Women, bring cups."

Now it was John's turn to marvel at Il'motch's willpower. The deer herder comported himself as though a bottle of whiskey was a commonplace thing at his table. He drank, trying not to show any greediness, or desire to take a large swig.

Under his guidance, John ate the deer's head, and had to admit that he'd never had anything as delectable before. Even before they sat down to eat, Il'motch had issued an order for a few large rock-salt crystals to be placed on the table.

"When I heard that you came looking for my camp last winter, I was much grieved," said Il'motch. "My heart bled, when tidings came that your daughter was dead. Oh, if only I'd been near you then with my herd!"

Having eaten his fill, John attempted to find out from his friend how many heads his herd numbered.

Eyes half-closed, Il'motch was silent for some time, noiselessly moving his lips.

"My own reindeer, the ones with my brand, will be forty or so twenties," Il'motch answered. "But in our camp there are also five other yarangas. They don't have as many reindeer. Some have only one or two twenties. I let them graze near my own herd. I don't mind it. And it's not as boring for them."

John tried to imagine the combined headcount. If you took, say, fifty reindeer per household on average, that would mean that Il'motch controlled a herd of a thousand reindeer. That he was the real owner of the herd and the decider of the fates of those living in the camp – of that there was not a doubt. "So you're a capitalist, after all," John thought with some irony, recalling his student days' discussions of the new teaching from the German philosopher Karl Marx. But aloud, he praised his tundra friend:

"They look good, your herders – well fed, neatly dressed."

"And that's all because I don't let them get lazy," Il'motch, on whom the alcohol was beginning to take effect, said smugly.

After the meal, John let his friend understand that John was giving him the remainder of the liquid inside the bottle.

"Velynkykun," Il'motch thanked him politely, speedily snatched up the bottle and secreted it somewhere in the bowels of his traveling home.

Over the course of the evening, Il'motch had repeatedly sampled the bottle's contents, and the darker it grew, the more talkative he became. And when they lay down to sleep, he suddenly told John:

"I met your countrymen in the tundra."

"Probably Captain Bartlett and the Eskimo Kataktovik?" John conjectured. "They'd been to see me too."

"No, not them, very different people. The kind I've never seen before in my life!"

"What kind, then?" John was intrigued. "Maybe they were Russians?"

"I can tell a Russian from an American as easily as I can tell a dog from a wolf, even at a distance," Il'motch boasted. "Those people were Americans. They're easy to recognize by their talk. They were rummaging in the mouth of the springs, by Lake Eeonee, as happy as if they'd found the source of the bad joy-making water. They came to our camp, asked for some deer meat, but they had nothing to trade for it except yellow sand that looked like dried baby shit, like an infant's that's still at the breast . . . One of them did give a knife, though. They offered weapons. But when I had a look at the kind of weapons they had, I lost all interest in them. They were measly little guns, in leather holsters, like the children of big guns . . . I still gave them two carrion deer. We don't eat that kind here – dead of hoof rot! But the whites were glad of it, all the same. Starved-looking, they were, hairy up to the eyes . . ."

Il'motch fell silent, and a trickling sound was heard in the darkness.

"You've become a real luoravetlan, and I can tell you all of it," Il'motch went on. "We moved camp from Lake Eeonee, and two moons later, on our way to the coast we went the same way back. We found only human remains by the side of our sacrificial hill. They'd long been eaten by the birds, but you could tell from the clothing that it was a white man. There were no other things with him. There was a round hole in his skull. From a bullet. I was surprised – so then, the little guns can kill a person after all . . ."

John's sleepiness had evaporated. Hardly breathing, he listened to Il'motch's tale, not daring to break the flow with a careless or inappropriate question. There was no doubt in his mind that the two had been gold prospectors. So these wolves had managed to reach even here, and the story told by the old reindeer person was only the usual kind of tragedy to accompany such ventures.

"The second one turned up in the mouth of the Big Stream. He hadn't been killed. Either he died on his own, or the wolves got him. Lying next to him were two of the little guns, a shovel, and two little bags of that yellow sand they offered to trade us for the deer."

This time, Il'motch's silence was a long one. He turned to and fro on his deerskin, evidently battling the temptation of one more sip from the bottle. Finally unable to restrain himself, he glugged and gurgled in the dark.

"And then what?" John couldn't wait any longer.

"And that was the end of it," Il'motch answered calmly, with a wide yawn.

"What about his things? The bags and the little guns?"

"You know we never touch dead ones' things," Il'motch replied. "It's all still there."

Agitated by what he'd just heard, John sat up in his bed.

"Listen, Il'motch," he said. "You can't even imagine the kind of trouble that has passed your people by! If even one of them had reached home and told them that you could pan for the yellow crap in your streams, that would be the end of you and your homeland. Crowds of white people, for whom the yellow sand is more precious than anything in the world, would flock here. They would have trampled and set fire to your pastures, annihilated the deer, taken your women and dug up the ground until they couldn't find even a tiny piece, a single yellow grain of sand, anymore. Then they would have shot each other, fought, and maybe even started a big fight – a war . . ."

"I've heard that right now the Russian land is running with rivers of blood," Il'motch answered him. "But what you're saying now, how horrible! Can it really be true?"

"It's true," John said. "And I beg you not to tell anyone about what happened. And if another searcher of gold sand wanders into your lands, drive him out, and make him run faster than a hare."

The pleasant, wine-induced mellowness that had taken hold of Il'motch turned into alarm.

"If that's how it is, I'll cut out the tongues of everybody in this camp!" he said with fright. "No one will dare even think about it."

Early in the morning, John was departing Il'motch's camp. His dogsled was overflowing with the gifts of his tundra friend.

Still not completely recovered from last night's shock, Il'motch made a mysterious face, took John to the side and whispered:

"I remember well our nighttime talk."

It was not a long way back, and about two hours later John was at home, where his whole family greeted him outside his yaranga.

Yako was overjoyed at the presents, but although Pyl'mau was smiling too, there was something unusual and unfamiliar in her smile. She was uncharacteristically inhibited in her manner toward him. Over the evening tea, John finally determined to ask her what had happened.

"When a husband goes to hunt, or sets off on a journey," Pyl'mau's voice was solemn, "his wife always fears for him, and holds his image in her heart, and silently remembers his name . . ." All of a sudden, she sniffled: "But this time, it was hard for me to do . . ."

"Why?" John was perplexed.

"Remember what you said about your name at the walrus breeding-ground?"

John recalled it and was about to say that it was all nonsense and nothing to worry about, but managed to bite his tongue just in time. Evidently, the matter was not as simple as it had seemed to him – here, a person's name was synonomous with their very existence, and altogether this was both logical and fair.

"You have to teach us how to say your name right," Pyl'mau

demanded, "even if it's hard for us. But we can't do without it. And then, when you go out hunting or on a long journey, it will be your name that rings in my soul, your real name, and not some nickname."

"Very well," John replied, looking serious. "I'll teach you to say my name right."

It took a few evenings for not just Pyl'mau, but Yako too, to be able to pronounce it clearly and correctly, ringingly: John!

And, at first, it was strange for John to hear the clear and sonorous John instead of the now-familiar Sson from Pyl'mau's and Yako's lips.

Winter had descended all at once. The ice had come near the shore one dawn and pressed its weight over the flimsy pebbled beach, threatening to push it into the lagoon. John was awakened by the crashing sounds of the fast ice. He was about to go outside, when a strong wind and big snowflakes, akin to buckshot in consistency, hit him in the face; a real winter blizzard with a frosty edge that burned.

John let out the dogs that had been allowed to roam free inside the chottagin, shut the front door tightly, stopped the cracks in the walrus-hide coverings with some thin wood planks and returned to the warm polog, where three grease lamps gave off a bright blaze, where he could hear the cooing of baby Bill-Toko as he played with Yako, where Pyl'mau – Polar Fog – moved about noiselessly and gracefully, wearing only a thin loincloth, her large breasts swollen and both their dark tips capped by snow-white droplets of milk.

27

The sun vanished. For one last time, it had glinted a sharp red edge over the ragged line of the mountain range, and these days all they had of it was a steadily brightening dawn that every day melted into an evening twilight and slowly died away, relinquishing the sky to the stars, the moon, and the tireless swathes of the Northern Lights.

There were times when John came back from the shore late in the day. On quiet days, they would light a bit of moss that floated in seal fat inside the chottagin, close to the entrance, and its flickering reflection danced on the hardened snow. A multitude of these little lanterns drew the hunters homeward from the sea, and each of them knew their own beckoning light without fail.

Every so often, John and his cohorts went out to the sea. Sometimes they drove into the tundra to check on the traps they'd set, and then, instead of nerpa carcasses, their dogsleds brought back snow-white and fiery-red foxes or smoky wolverines.

On stormy evenings, Orvo, Tiarat, and the other inhabitants of Enmyn would gather in John's yaranga.

Sometimes the tea drinking carried on long into the night: They related ancient legends or prodded John to talk about the white people's customs and lifestyle in exhaustive detail.

John often marveled at how easily the Chukchi navigated in the tundra and on the open sea. Most of the hunters could sketch the shoreline between Enmyn and the Bering Strait with a good degree of accuracy. Orvo, who's been farther south, could recreate the promontories and lagoons from Uelen to Anadyr from memory, but had only the haziest conception of the outside world beyond.

During one of these long evenings, John was telling them about the exploration and colonization of Canada, about the endless wars between the English and the French over possession of this part of the New World. That happened to be the day that his tundra friend, Il'motch, was in for a visit. This time, he was in no hurry to move camp to the forest borders, and even tried to convince John to go to Carpenter in Keniskun, to "buy-some-sell-some."

"And this, too," John told his quietened listeners. "Those people warred among themselves and never once asked the native people for permission to run riot in their hunting grounds, burn their forests and sail enormous paddle-steamer ships down their rivers – ships that caused all the fish to die and rise belly-up to the surface."

When everyone had gone home, and only Il'motch remained in the polog, he said to John:

"I know who that story was meant for. I'm keeping quiet, and I've ordered everyone else to forget everything about those two whites."

Il'motch did finally manage to get John to go to Keniskun: They were running low on supplies of cartridges, tobacco, and tea. Genuine merchants had passed Enmyn by that year – perhaps they were wary of John's presence there, or possibly they felt that the gifts supplied by the Canadian Naval Board were plenty for such a tiny settlement. Meanwhile, the people of Enmyn had stored up considerable quantities of white fox and wolverine. There was walrus tusk, the women had crafted fur-lined house slippers that were always happily bought up by the Keniskun trader. John asked Orvo to come along, but the other had refused, for some reason, bidding Armol' to take care of his business.

In mid-February, when the sun had appeared once again, a four-dogsled caravan moved off toward the Bering Strait.

They made stops in small settlements, sometimes pitching camp right under the blue crags where they would steep tea and shave off bits of frozen deer meat. It was a pleasant journey – there was not a single blizzard for the duration of it, except that somewhere around the Koliushin-skaya promontory they had some flurries. But Tiarat said that it was never quiet inside this particular pass.

As befitted a tundra friend, Il'motch considered it his duty always to be beside John and share his tiny canvas tent. Over the course of an evening, he'd take a long while wheezing and groaning, turn from side to side and hold forth on how it would be best to buy the bad joy-making water from Carpenter first, and only then all the rest of the supplies.

"We've done without all that before," Il'motch reasoned. "And we can live without it now. But the bad joy-making water! Your heart dries up and your stomach shrinks out of longing for it."

"Why is it that you love the joy-making water so much?" John asked him once. "Isn't just living enough?"

"A mouse in his hole is just living," Il'motch observed sensibly. "I don't want to just live, I want to feel something, too. And that's what the bad joy-making water gives me."

"A typical alcoholic," John thought to himself. If Il'motch had had a limitless supply of the bad joy-making water, he'd have drowned his thousand-strong herd in it long ago.

"So, do you know why Orvo didn't want to come with us?" Il'motch asked, and there was a sly edge to his voice.

"Why?"

"He's taken offense, and he's upset with you."

"But what for?" John was surprised. Lately, Orvo had seemed somehow different, but John had ascribed this to his ill health.

"Because before, I was his tundra friend, and a close one, too, but now

I'm yours . . . we were good friends, friends for real," Il'motch was off down memory lane. "I used to come to see him, young and vigorous then, and he'd go and ask me before bed: Which one do you want to sleep with tonight, Cheivuneh or Ve'emneut? And I'd do the same, of course, when he came to visit me in my camp. One of my sons that you saw, that was Orvo's doing!" Il'motch informed him with a tinge of pride.

"But that's not a nice thing, changing coastal friends like that," John said reproachfully.

"Well, even a friend isn't just for no reason, but to be useful for something," was Il'motch's artless reply. "When you decided to stay in Enmyn, I knew right away that I'd be your tundra friend. Who are the people coming to for advice these days? You. Before, it was Orvo. And anyway, it's cheerier in your yaranga – children, music, always tea on hand, and sometimes even a drop of the bad joy-making water . . . Yes, sir," Il'motch drawled with conviction, "it's a good thing to be friends with you."

"You know what, friend of mine," John said decisively, "go and move yourself to Armol's tent! I've suspected for a while that your friendship for me is far from being disinterested, but I didn't think that you'd confess it so openly. Some friend!"

Il'motch realized that he'd spoiled everything with his foolish chatter, but it was too late.

"You're throwing me out?"

"No, I just want you to vacate the space," John dryly replied.

"What is going on here?" asked Tiarat as he crawled inside the tent. "Il'motch shows up in our tent, shouting at me: Go sleep with Sson! Can't stay in the same tent with him any more! He smells bad!"

"Well, if that's all he said, so much the better," John said mysteriously, and shut his eyes, intending to fall asleep. Il'motch's behavior, his words, they had lifted the curtain on something that John had not noticed before. The relationships between people around here are far from simple . . . Turning to and fro for a while, he called to Tiarat.

"You asleep?"

"How can I sleep, with you creaking on the snow like that?" Tiarat answered him testily.

"Tell me, what's going on with Orvo? I'd thought that it was ill health that changed him, but I get the feeling now there's something else amiss."

"He's getting weaker, the old man," Tiarat replied, "getting sick. Bad luck for him, of course, not having any sons of his own, but there's nothing for it now. He's already standing on the threshold of old age, he's looked ahead and has not seen anything good there, so it makes him a little worried. And so now he's become solitary, irritable. The old friends are walking away from him, no new friends in sight. It's bitter cold for a lonely man, in the face of one of our winds," Tiarat concluded and, after a moment's silence, added: "And he's a very good man, too, he's done a lot of good for people, held them back from much foolishness."

They spent the night in Uelen, in the large lively settlement. They had intended to set off for Keniskun on the following morning, but it turned out that Carpenter himself had just arrived.

"Keniskun can wait!" Carpenter declared to John. "We'll spend a couple of days here. The best singers and dancers on the coast from Enurmin to the Cross Bay have gathered here. Big celebration! A real Christmas! You'll be glad you stayed to see it!"

Despite John's protestations, Carpenter moved him into his own place. The trader was occupying a separate polog inside the yaranga of the well-to-do Uelen Chukcha, Gemal'kot, to whom Carpenter was both a friend and a distant relation by marriage.

The yaranga was a substantial one, and built if not for centuries of use, then at least for many decades. It boasted a spacious chottagin, divided into three sections: the actual chottagin, where the dogs came to warm up and where barrels of blubber and pickled greens lined the walls, with a hearth paved in large flat stones. The second chottagin was next to the pologs. There, the inhabitants ate, worked animal hides and skins and ground frozen seal blubber in stone mortars. And the third chottagin bore the clear marks of the owner's association with Carpenter. The walls were hung with firearms, equipment for winter hunting, and even a copper whaling harpoon that looked more like a tiny cannon. Carpenter's polog was set up right in the middle of this "living room," and the yaranga's owner would give the small "gate" a polite tap, before entering it.

Gemal'kot turned out to be a tall man, his hair streaked with bright gray. He was closely shaven, with the exception of a mustache. His entire form, body and face, exuded self-assurance and strength. He spoke English adequately and, according to Carpenter, had been to the United States more than once, going as far as San Francisco.

Gemal'kot was unfailingly courteous – not once had he allowed himself to enter Carpenter's dwelling without warning, or break into a conversation. But behind all this lurked power of a kind to make John note, and not without a certain malice, that Carpenter's glances at their host were far from haughty.

On the very first evening Carpenter launched into the conversation that John had feared most.

"I haven't got certain intelligence, not yet," said he in a lowered tone, "but there are rumors that finally, gold has been found on Chukotka. Some experienced Alaskan prospectors were here. Their prognoses are rather encouraging. And if it's true, can you imagine what's going to happen here! And us, John, we'll be the first! Right now, the Russian government is too busy to give thought to the north. There's war, and if I'm not mistaken, they are losing it. The Russian csar's wife is a relation of the German Emperor – so what victory of Russian arms could there possibly be? Most likely, these northern regions will go to America or Canada. In the end, there's not a big difference between the two. What do you say to that, my dear friend John?"

Carpenter's voice had a wheedling ring to it that smacked of Il'motch.

"Why don't you, Mr. Carpenter, ask Gemal'kot, or even Il'motch? It's their decision, their land, after all."

"Oh, do stop it, John, we're not children, and neither are we delegates of a charity convention!"

"Mr. Carpenter, I tell you again that I've decided to stay among these people, willingly and forever. I will not only live among them, but will use all my power to protect their land with all its riches above and below ground from the encroachment of strangers."

"No one intends to encroach upon either their land or their way of life," Carpenter said patiently. "For God's sake, let them herd their deer, hunt walruses, trap white fox. But we'd have to be utter fools to let the gold, d'you hear me, John MacLennan, gold, go to some third party. To be completely straight, it's us, the pioneers of the north, those who have weathered its harsh climate and managed to make friends with its people, gain their trust, it's us who have a certain right to being rewarded."

"Mr. Carpenter, we are speaking two different languages," John attempted to forestall him, but the trader waved his hand dismissively and went on:

"I know of your intentions, and I've met a good many unusual people in my life. But all these unusual people became quite common, at the sight of gold. Would you like me to show it to you?"

Carpenter reached into his belt and brought out a small bag, resembling a tobacco pouch. With a cautious look from side to side, he poured a small pile of yellow sand, the one Il'motch had dismissively described as dried infant's excrement, into the palm of his hand. The trader moved his hand closer to the fire and asked John, triumphantly:

"How do you like that?"

John found it curious. The contemplation of the gold sand had not aroused any extraordinary sensation within him. It only reminded him of how, a long time ago, getting ready for his travels he'd secretly dreamed of returning to Port Hope a wealthy man, and how chief among the many ways of achieving this was the very method proposed by Carpenter now – to find gold and pan for it in a tundra stream.

"I know where you got this gold from," John surprised himself by saying. "This is gold from the streams that empty into Lake Eeonee."

Carpenter recoiled as if he'd beed burned.

"How do you know that? The man swore that no one except himself, no one, knew about the treasures of Lake Eeonee," he said, with alarm.

"Every secret comes to light, in the end," John said tiredly. "I'll keep silent for now, but if it comes into your head to organize a big gold mine or something in that vein, you'll have only yourself to blame. The Chukchi will throw you off their lands."

"Well now, well now," Carpenter muttered with real surprise, as he put away the little bag of gold.

Uelen was lively and animated in these clear frosty days, and there was a multitude of passers-by crowded in every street. The local dogs were at a loss for whom to bark at first. The visitors had assembled a dog depot at the seaside by the large icebergs that had not managed to float down to the Pacific Ocean that summer, tying up their sled-dog packs to some wooden pikes, frozen into the ice.

There was a fire blazing in each of the yarangas, food being prepared and an astonishing amount of tea being drunk. Carpenter could not allow such an opportunity to pass by and opened a small shop in the dog section of Gemal'kot's yaranga. He did a brisk trade in brick tea, sugar, treacle. The hunters were buying cartridges, gunpowder, buckshot. Twice, the dogsleds had to be sent back to Keniskun to pick up more goods.

The trader made no more mention of the gold sand to John; he grew pointedly considerate and attentive.

On the appointed day, the hosts and the guests gathered together inside a large newly made wooden building. The Russians had intended to open a school, or possibly some government office, but because of the war, the building lay empty, and today, with the volost'* chief's permission, it was being used for the entertainment.

Inside the building it smelled of fresh paint. Winter sunlight beat at the windowpanes, the wooden tread boards creaked underfoot – all around him were the sounds that John MacLennan had grown long unused to. And it was not even so much a matter of familiarity, but that the noise was unusual in these circumstances and did not sit easily with the crowd of Chukchi and Eskimos in their fur-lined kukhliankas, their brightly colored cloth kamleikas, and festive beaded torbasses.

They were coming into the wooden yaranga, peering from side to side, touching their fingers to the painted walls and looking down at the wooden floor with wonder, as though it were the deck of a ship.

The Chukchi and Eskimos found their places right on the floor, as it was clean and shone with new paint, while the singers and dancers arranged themselves on a small dais made by the slightly raised floor of the next room and fenced in by removable screen walls.

The Uelen masters were the first to sing and present women's group dances. The large ochre drums obscured the faces of the singers, who were singing directly at the tightly stretched walrus stomach. The sound reverberated and, as it grew stronger, created the illusion of a mountain echo.

The women danced with abandon, eyes half-closed. John watched them, and emotion stirred in his breast. He was thinking that, even a few years ago, had he seen these dances, heard these songs, at best he would have condescended to allow that they had a certain interest for specialists. But now he was genuinely moved, moved to the depths of his soul, by this dancing and these songs that were almost without words – only a melody that conveyed the wind's howl, the rustling of tundra grass under a caressing summer breeze, the waterfall's thunder, the shadows of wind-

---

* *Volost'* – Smallest administrative division of csarist Russia. (TN)

blown clouds on the surface of the sea, the ringing peal of blueing ice, and much more, all the things that are called life, in its great variety and, at the same time, its great simplicity. The women's movements were expressions of unspoken tenderness; they never appeared undressed before a stranger's eyes. And they were glad that now with their supple bodies they could speak of a loving heart, of a concealed desire. They were a little shy, and so the maidens' eyes were half-hidden under their long eyelashes.

John watched the dancing women and his thoughts went to Pyl'mau, to her tender, loving look. He remembered her penetrating, gentle voice, her devotion to him, and once again it seemed that no one could take him from this land now, or tear him away from these people who had become his family.

Now came forward a slender youth, almost a boy still, the famous Aivanalin dancer, maker of songs and melodies, Nutetein. He was performing a song-dance about a seagull caught in a storm on the sea. But the story was not about the bird, but about those whose turbulent lives are filled with storms, about the ones who never lose their hope of reaching the dreamed-of shore. There were only a few words in the song, but they were all that was needed, and therein lay the song's true poetry. Poetry, thought John, chooses the most vital, the most genuine words.

Nutetein was succeeded by the Uelen vocalist, dancer, poet, and musician – a young man named Atyk. John peered into his face and marveled at its beauty. This was true masculine beauty – the beauty of an intelligent, strong-willed and inspired face, illuminated by the flame of poetry and the joy of living.

Applause was not the customary thing among the natives, but Carpenter, never bound by conventions, clapped loudly, expressing his delight and approbation.

"Honest to God, there's something in it!" he commented loudly to John, seated beside him. "Know what I mean? There's something there!

You sit there listening to these plain simplistic songs, like a wolf's howling, and suddenly you realize that they stir up some emotion, touch some chord in your heart."

"Because this is genuine artistry! A genuine art!" MacLennan repeated.

"Now really, there's no need to go that far!" Carpenter drawled. "Although I do agree with you, there is an embryonic art in some of the dances. Of course, in the right hands, if this were polished up, transposed to real musical interests, some of it could be good entertainment even in the States . . ."

"They've got no business going anywhere near the States!" John cut him off abruptly. "Let everything of theirs stay here, because only they understand it and feel it as it should be understood and felt."

"Well," Carpenter conceded, "maybe you are right."

Carpenter was clearly trying to win John's goodwill. The old trader was annoyed at himself for feeling guilty around the handless cripple, as though he'd done something wrong in his eyes.

By evening, the celebrations moved to the snowy expanse of Uelen's lagoon. Runners armed with staffs set off on their long journey right from the beach. They had to run roughly fifteen miles. The reindeer herders got a few fawn skins ready for the victor, and Carpenter, the main source of prizes, stuck a flat bottle of whiskey into the snow, to await the best runner.

In a marked-out circle, wrestlers were also competing. Divesting themselves of their kukhliankas, bare to the waist, they gave off steam in the frosty air, trying to grab a hold of one another's slippery bodies.

"Do you have these sort of gatherings often here?" John asked Gemal'kot, who was standing beside him.

"Every year that we manage to have a mild winter," Gemal'kot answered readily. "But you must come in the summer. That's when the most interesting stuff happens. They come all the way from Nome for the celebrations, not to mention the islands of the Bering Strait. Then we get a second Uelen growing right here, on the seashore . . . Come and see," Gemal'kot repeated his invitation. "When the spring hunt is over and the walruses start to bunch at the breeding grounds, that's when we get together."

"I'll come for sure," John promised.

The festivities continued by the light of the moon. The runners were murky shadows. They slid noiselessly across the moonlit snow and seemed to be merely drawn onto the landscape.

The winner, and this turned out to be a deer herder from the Katryn tundra, deftly plucked the bottle from the snowdrift by its neck, and with the same light step walked off toward the yaranga where he was staying. The yaranga's owners followed suit, accompanied by the envious glances of the spectators.

They walked back to Gemal'kot's yaranga together. Their host walked slightly ahead, while John and Carpenter were walking together behind him.

"These people have a healthy temperament, and the right life path," John spoke heatedly, still under the influence of all he'd seen and heard. "They don't need any other intoxicants."

"Perhaps you're right," Carpenter was cautiously assenting. "But so often they don't know the difference between what's valuable and what's not worth a cent. One way or another, they need people like you. Just to keep up rational interaction between the world of the white men, as they call us, and them. I'll tell you frankly, that it was only when I opened my shop that the raiding of these shores by merchant ships has come to a stop. Now the trading company of the Russian merchant Karaev is about to set up shop here. I've thought long and hard about how to deal with him, and came to the conclusion that we have to cooperate with the Russian government. There's nothing else to do. Especially as the Russians have no intention of interfering with our company's commercial operations."

"I'm not quite sure why you're telling me all this," John shrugged.

"Forgive me, but I see a cultured and educated person," Carpenter said courteously. "You say that you intend to devote your life to the flourishing of the Chukchi people, and I can make you an offer to join forces."

"I'm afraid I won't be of any use to you. I live just the same way as all the Chukchi or the Eskimo. I have no other means of survival than my two hands. The sea and the tundra feed and clothe me. As far as I'm aware, you don't go hunting, don't set nets or traps – you only trade. And so the only thing that distinguishes me from the native people is the color of my skin."

Carpenter fell silent. And in his silence there was anger and helplessness.

"Well then," he gritted through his teeth, "it is true, you and I are speaking different languages."

On the next day, Enmyn's dogsled caravan set out for Keniskun. Making the necessary purchases and having taken a final dip in the mineral baths, the travelers made their way back, cutting a significant length off their journey by setting course from Keniskun through the tundra and toward the Koliushinskaya promontory.

Two weeks later, the heavily laden dogsleds entered Enmyn from the east, and next to each of the yarangas, people stood waiting to greet them.

28

And now it is the year 1917, wrote John MacLennan in his diary. *The year was ushered in during this bright and vivid night, amid the blaze of the Northern Lights, in the flickering of the stars, unusually large for the north. They don't celebrate a new year around these parts. Here, there is a wholly different cycle of life, a different rhythm. A new being is chirping in my yaranga – my daughter, Sophie-Ankanau MacLennan. She was born in the autumn blizzards, and that is how Pyl'mau explains the unusual whiteness of her skin . . .*

From the chottagin came the sound of footsteps, and John called out to the newcomer from the polog.

"It's me!" Tiarat informed him, and stuck his round, neatly barbered head through the fur curtain.

Tiarat watched John write with curiosity:

"You're very nimble with those loops!"

"Did you know that the new year arrived today?" John inquired with a certain exultation.

"Really!" Tiarat was surprised to hear it, and looked around the polog carefully, as if the new year could have simply walked in and concealed himself in some corner.

But there was nothing noteworthy inside the polog. In one corner, Pyl'mau was breast-feeding the baby girl and simultaneously stoking the flame beneath a low-hanging kettle. In the other corner, Yako and Bill-Toko played with small seal teeth, making intricate designs on the walrus-hide floor. The protector of the hearth with his countenance shiny from sacrificial fat, and the sparkling copper washstand hung from the corner posts.

"The year nineteen hundred and seventeen has come," John continued, mentally reckoning up how many twenties there were in nineteen hundred.

"That many?" Tiarat marveled. "I've heard white men counting years, but I can't figure out how it is that they can see the arrival of the new year in the polar night. It must be a hard thing to do?"

John had wanted to explain about chronicles and calendars, but after some thought, decided to change the topic to something else, since the explanation was likely to take some hours, and he doubted that Tiarat would appreciate the necessity of such precise timekeeping, especially on these glacial winter evenings that made it seem as though the flow of life itself had stopped.

"Can I have a look?" Tiarat reached for John's notepad.

He was poring over the filled pages, and again John had the same feeling he'd had when Orvo had examined his words, that Tiarat comprehended something of the written text – such was the concentration on his face.

"How I'd like to learn to do that!" Tiarat said longingly, as he returned the notepad to John with a sigh of regret. "It must be wonderful to understand what you've marked and take back the spoken words, like turning back to look at your own thoughts."

"But I'm writing in my own language, not in Chukchi," John said. "Now if your language had its own signs, then it would be no big task for you to draw and understand them as easily as you do prints in the snow."

"Can it be such an impossible thing, to come up with some squiggles for our language, too?"

"Perhaps it can be done," John assented. "But some learned people would have to study your language carefully, first."

"Why should the learned people study our language?" Tiarat said in surprise. "It's enough that we know it well ourselves."

"I have no doubt that you know it well, meaning that you can speak it. But in order for a language to have the squiggly signs, we need to know what it's comprised of. For example, every person who lives along the coast has seen a deer, but what a deer is like on the inside – not everyone knows that."

"But to find out what the deer is made of, you'd have to kill him first," Tiarat objected. "And what about the language? How can you kill that? You'd probably have to kill everybody who speaks it."

"There's no need to kill a language, in order to study it," John replied. "Here I am speaking the Chukchi tongue, thinking in Chukchi, and I can even write your name using English letters."

"Try it." Tiarat gave John a pleading look.

On a clean page, John set down Tiarat's name in large letters. The Chukcha picked up the sheet and took a long time scanning it, as though trying to discern the features of his own face within the letters' curves.

Pyl'mau, unable to contain her curiosity, looked over Tiarat's shoulder and suddenly said:

"Doesn't look like him at all."

"Why not?" Tiarat asked, insulted.

"In the middle, something is bulging there. But you're a well made, handsome man."

"True, true," Tiarat agreed. "Not exactly like me, you can see it right away." With a sigh, he commented: "You can just feel how it's made with foreign letters . . . Now if they were our own. Here," Tiarat carefully poked a finger at the notepad, "it looks like I've decked myself out in a white man's clothes."

One day, Tiarat was chopping up a large kymgyt for the dogs. Before plunging his sharpened blade into the frozen walrus hide, he took some time to peruse his family's mark, a diagram of two crossed oars.

John had come up to him, pulling his own kymgyt by a short-handled boat hook. Tiarat stopped and moved his eyes to John's sigil – the letter *J*.

When he was done chopping up kopal'khen for both his and John's packs, Tiarat asked:

"Do you think you could teach me the white people's talk? Your own language?"

While making the plea, he was looking at his own feet, like a misbehaving schoolboy.

"Could be done," John answered readily, and felt a flush of pleasure: Now there would be something to pass these long winter evenings. "It's even possible to learn making the marks and recognizing them as you learn to talk."

"That would be something. But I wouldn't so much as dream of it."

"We'll start tonight, there's no sense in postponing it," John said firmly.

Tiarat ran home to change his clothes and then presented himself at John's yaranga. When he removed his kukhlianka, Pyl'mau couldn't suppress an admiring exclamation: Tiarat's mighty physique was clad in a silk top of clearly Eastern origin. Fighting valiantly to smother his own smile, John joined in his wife's expressions of delight.

The paper and pencil had been readied. Naturally, John had never before played the teacher's role. After momentary reflection, he decided that it would be best to begin with mastering the immediate surroundings.

Pointing to Tiarat, he uttered:

"Man!"

Tiarat shuddered, but collected himself and nodded to indicate his agreement.

"Woo-man!" John shouted, moving the finger to Pyl'mau, who'd returned to her lamp.

"Woo-man!" Tiarat assented with a whisper and, out of sheer nerves, bore down on his pencil so heavily that the graphite tip immediately cracked.

Dully, he followed the black bit with his eyes, as it rolled down to the end of the page, then gave himself a cuff on the head.

"What have I done! I broke it! Broke the fragile little thing with my big paws!"

"Don't worry Tiarat, we'll sharpen the pencil again," John reassured him. John was trying to speak deliberately at the top of his lungs, on the assumption that the louder he spoke the easier it would be for Tiarat to learn. Having yelled the names of some items inside the yaranga into Tiarat's ear, the man dripping with the sweat of mental work and anxiety, John decided to test him. Tiarat's memory turned out to be first-rate, and he named the items in English with barely a mistake.

"Let's keep going!"

"Wait, Sson," Tiarat pleaded. "Can I have a drink of water?"

He emptied a big ladle with greedy gulps and asked for another. The silk shirt was splotched with dark sweat stains.

At this point, John elected to make a start on introducing his pupil to a few letters of the alphabet.

Tiarat copied them onto his own sheet of paper with relative ease, even repeating the defects of his teacher's own handwriting.

"Excellent!" John exclaimed, peering at the sheet. "And now we'll learn the pronunciation of these letters."

Yako had wedged himself beside Tiarat. He listened attentively to his father and, noiselessly, moving only his lips, repeated all that the other said.

"Give the child some paper and a pen," Pyl'mau intervened on behalf of her son. "Why entertain just yourselves? Maybe it's even more interesting for the boy."

Even through his swarthiness, Tiarat's face colored with shame. He could feel it himself, that he was engaged in a task not his own, a trifle, that would never be of any use in his life. It's not as though he were going to talk to his countrymen in English. And as for trading with the merchants, Orvo's language skills were more than enough, and now they had Sson as an interpreter, besides. What could be better! As for reading and writing, there was no practical use at all. Just a game, as Pyl'mau had pointed out.

"Let him learn, too, that's the way," John said seriously. "Only, Mau, you really shouldn't say that literacy is a useless, trifling thing. In the world where I've come from, one can't even imagine life without the ability to read and write."

"But here?" Pyl'mau objected.

"What do you think?" John turned to Tiarat. "Don't you find that the woman talks too much?"

"You're right, there," Tiarat agreed.

The lesson came to its conclusion without any more interruption. Yako gripped the pencil in his hand and tried his very best. The pupils were almost equal in aptitude, as John noted to himself, but Yako's reactions were quicker, and he was, on the whole, a little sharper.

Each free evening, when John and Tiarat were not too late in returning from the day's hunting, an unlikely school opened session inside the yaranga, with two students and the pedagogue, John MacLennan.

Spring came, and was followed by a short but task-filled summer. In the autumn they once again went to hunt the walrus breeding ground; they had to ward off incoming schooners, of which there were a surprising number. The sailors talked of a revolution happening in Russia, of a new government. Alarmed, Orvo at once asked John:

"What do all these rumors mean?"

But John hardly understood any of it himself. He managed to obtain a two-month-old newspaper from a passing schooner belonging to the Hudson Bay Company. One thing was clear from the article, that the csar in Russia had been replaced by a parliament. But in the same small piece, they spoke of warring political factions within the country, some mysterious Bolsheviks led by a certain Lenin. John was nonetheless surprised to discover that, despite the events that were rocking the enormous country, the war with Germany continued.

"They've deposed the Sun Lord," John explained.

"But he was sitting so firmly on his golden seat," Orvo shook his head doubtfully. "A few years before you, a Russian shaman – a priest – came to our settlement. He said that the Russian csar is the mightiest power on the earth. And he's sitting so firmly on his golden seat that no one could move him. The Sun Lord had talked to God . . ."

"Well, he had to leave his golden seat after all," John said.

"But why did they have to take him off it?" asked Orvo.

"Evidently, other people besides him also wanted to govern the land," John ventured.

"What odd people. Didn't they have enough of their own problems to worry about?" Orvo commented with disdain. "The csar did everything well, and besides that, he had great experience. They shouldn't have taken him off."

"How can you be so sure that all the csar did was good?" John asked.

"How else," Orvo was agitated. "He didn't insist on our worshipping his gods. Besides that, unlike our neighbors the Yakuts, we were freed from the mandatory tribute and could pay only as much as we wanted to. Is that so bad?"

"Yes, that's true enough, from this standpoint the Russian csar was quite suitable for the Chukchi," John observed.

Ignoring the irony, or perhaps not seeing it, Orvo said:

"After all, who knows what the new government will bring to these parts. Maybe something that will be bad for all of us."

John had to agree with this rational conclusion but said with some hope:

"But how long will it be before the new government even reaches as far as Chukotka!"

This conversation took place on the eve of winter, while the new ice began to spread over the sea and the light grew less with each passing day, as if every afternoon some giant were slicing off a crescent from the cold winter sun. Another winter was rising before John MacLennan, but he did not fear it and calmly greeted the tidings of coming inclement weather, the frozen rivers, the steadily growing ice shelf that pushed the frontier of drifting ice further and further from the continent.

By now, Yako and Tiarat were writing English words easily enough, and could address one another and their teacher mock-seriously, using the words they'd learned. One evening, Tiarat was visibly upset as he came to the lesson.

"What's wrong?" John asked him.

"I've wanted to tell you for a long time now," Tiarat spoke with embarrassment, "but I was afraid you'd stop teaching me . . . They found out that I'm trying to make and decipher the prints of human talk on paper, and they started to laugh at me. Even my sons are laughing. Today I was talking to Orvo, and he asked if it was true that I'm learning to read and write from you. I told him the truth. He thought about it, the old man, and then declared that nothing will come of it. And when I showed him that I can do it already, he mocked me. Told me how he'd heard you say that reading and writing is totally useless to Chukchi, that it's just as alien to them as white skin and fair hair. Did you say that?"

"Yes, I did say it," John confessed. "But I meant that it's useless in general, if every Chukcha, say, suddenly became literate."

"And you still think so now?" Tiarat asked.

"I'm sure of it," John said with feeling.

"Then why do you teach me and Yako?"

"If you and Yako know how to read and write, there's no harm in it to anybody."

"The harm's started already," Tiarat declared. "I'm a laughingstock. People turn away from me and suspect something evil in my wanting to learn the white man's language."

"Are you trying to tell me that you won't be learning anymore?" asked John.

"I haven't said that yet."

Tiarat found himself in such a quandary that he pulled his overall off his head and wiped his perspiring face with the furry side, an old habit of his.

"It would be good if you taught reading and writing to anyone who wanted it," he finally managed to express.

John thought about it. He knew his settlement neighbors well enough. From a sense of competition, from a desire not to be left behind the others, every one of them would want to learn. Because Yako was being taught, the other children must follow suit. That would mean having to open a real school and devote all his time to teaching Enmyn's inhabitants. Then who would go to hunt, travel to Keniskun for goods? And besides, there was neither paper nor writing implements, not to mention textbooks. All this John explained to Tiarat in a patient and businesslike manner:

"Let's think this through together, what is it all for? A Chukcha has no need to read and write, not in hunting, not in household work. It would only take up his time and stir up thoughts and desires that would distract him from real life."

"You are right!" Tiarat exclaimed almost with joy. "Yes, maybe that's enough. We've had our fun, now it's time to stop. Ooh," he pulled on a cord and opened up the collar of his kukhlianka. "Feels better now."

John was saddened at how easily Tiarat rejected learning. He sensed that this man, born and raised inside a yaranga, in the perpetual pursuit of food and warmth, was in his own way exceptional, gifted. Everything he touched acquired strength, beauty, and some kind of distinctiveness. For all that, Tiarat was astonishingly selfless and could live only on the bare necessities. He did not have reserves, so precious to Armol', nor did he have a second dogsled and spare dogs. If he came into possession of something extra, he'd immediately and joyfully give it to his nearest neighbor, usually the feckless and needy Guvat.

John studied with Yako for another stretch longer, then the first reading and writing lessons in Enmyn quietly ceased, all by themselves. John even neglected his diary for a long time, not returning to it until the fateful day when Carpenter, in a state of panic and confusion, came to pay him a visit.

29

Carpenter collapsed into John's yaranga on one stormy morning that glowed with the falling snow. He took a long while dusting himself off, shaking out his torbasses and fur-lined trousers, prying icicles from his beard.

"The Bolsheviks have taken power!" he blurted into John MacLennan's face with a kind of despair.

John shrugged.

"Russia is ruled by Lenin and the Bolsheviks!" Carpenter repeated. "Do you understand what I'm telling you?"

"That's the problem, I don't understand a thing yet," John serenely replied. "In the meantime, come inside the polog. Pyl'mau will prepare your room."

Pyl'mau was bustling around inside the little room where John once lived, trying to light a tiny iron stove. The strong wind kept on slurping up the flame, occasionally even blowing it into the room. Pyl'mau struggled for a good while, before the fire took, and the stove's sides flushed with the heat.

"Dear John!" Carpenter went on. "I felt it my duty to come to you and warn you of the danger. The Bolsheviks have designs on the north, too. The Soviets have already come to the Kamchatka; they are operating in Anadyr'. How can you have so little trust in me, when I dropped everything and raced to warn you before anyone else. I could easily have left on my own and abandoned you to the vagaries of fate. My dear friend, I see in you not only a man of the same blood, but an exceptional human being, who might be destroyed by a Bolshevik bullet."

"I don't understand," John was supremely calm, "why is it that you're so frightened of the Bolsheviks? You've never even seen them."

"But the things they're doing!" Carpenter clapped his hands to his head. "They've executed the entire royal family, they didn't spare even the small children."

"Flip through any history textbook, you'll find far more horrific crimes," John reminded him.

"They take away everything a man has and hand it out to the poor. They don't look at whether a man's actually acquired his wealth by his own labors, and not by robbery; for them, a rich man has only one name – bloodsucker, exploiter. No, you must leave immediately! I offer you my help. If you wish, I'll send over dogsleds, give you money – anything you want. I'll tell you frankly, my heart bleeds to see the destruction of a lifestyle so hardly won. One of these days, the happiness you've achieved by the sweat of your brow, by your sufferings, could be shattered to pieces. I grieve for you, dear John!"

Carpenter had almost shouted the last words, before covering his head with his hands.

John was looking at those big hands and thinking: Why would Carpenter suddenly overflow with tender feelings for him, and even come to him at the height of winter? To offer his selfless aid in escaping from the Bolsheviks? There was something suspicious in this unexpected show of devotion on the trader's part.

Pyl'mau served the meal, filled the cups with strong tea and left them, so as not to impede the men's talk.

Carpenter ate greedily, his fingers were soon greasy and covered with fat. Even while he was chewing, he never ceased to talk, and his speech flowed uncontrollably, as if a dam had burst.

"You know that I receive the papers regularly," he was saying. "Obviously, you can't believe everything they write in our American newspapers. But if even half of what they write about the Bolsheviks is true, it would be better by far to live among cannibals. Their leader, Lenin – he's a monster! He's demanding the inception of a communist government not just in Russia, but all over the world, inciting the workers to take over their factories, throw out the owners – in a word, he's a crazed rebel! A pirate! They've proclaimed the motto: 'He who doesn't work, doesn't eat!'"

"I've already heard that motto here, in Enmyn," John interrupted his guest. "He's not worthy of living, the man who can't feed himself. Roughly the same sentiment."

With the coming of the tea, Carpenter's verbal flood had a rest, and John could ask him the question that had been burning on his lips all along.

"So when are you leaving?"

"You mean leaving Chukotka?"

"Yes."

"Our firm will have some sort of cooperation with the new government, at least in the early days. The Bolsheviks wouldn't dare leave this enormous region without any supply lines, and they haven't yet any merchandise of their own. In all likelihood, we'll be granted a concession for continuing to trade. In any event, I've been ordered to remain at my post. As soon as the Strait opens, we'll bring out all the white fox, and as for the store of goods at my trading station, it barely exceeds a thousand dollars' worth. Even if they confiscated everything, it shouldn't prove a heavy loss."

"Me, I don't even have five dollars' worth of possessions," John remarked with a smile.

And by that smile, Carpenter knew that his trickery had been exposed. John had realized that he was being pushed to leave Chukotka so that

Carpenter could remain in complete possession of not only the entire shoreline, but more importantly, of the gold discovered in the streams that flowed into Lake Eeonee.

"That's right," Carpenter said in a chastened tone. "But you have no right to be here, no official leave to live in Russian territory. You're an alien, settled on foreign soil without authorization!"

John was smiling wordlessly.

"What is it, what holds you here?" Carpenter railed, beside himself. "What is it that you've found in this deserted land? Why, if you had a yen to go live among the natives, didn't you choose a better place?. . . It's not only in the north that primitive life exists, there are tropical islands, too. You declined trading, you don't want to take part in the gold-mining project at Lake Eeonee, you don't need anything and you're happy with your life! But surely a person must need something. He can't simply exist, like some sort of vegetation. What is it that binds you to this place?"

In answer, John held out his stumps, capped with their leather bindings.

"Everyone here has forgotten that I have no hands," John said quietly. "I feel like a full-fledged, valuable person. Valuable to my family, to my friends, to the little community that peoples Enmyn. Here, I'm a human being – do you understand? – a human being! I have no fear of the Bolsheviks' coming. Naturally, I find their doctrine alarming, their denial of any kind of personal property. But, just think Mr. Carpenter, what property does a Chukcha have? What property do I have? And meanwhile, those among whom we live are, with rare exception, a trusting folk. Simply put, it is my duty to stay with them as difficult times loom ahead. I must be with them."

John fell silent and his eyes fixed to the bottom of his cup.

"Dearest John!" Carpenter's exhortation swelled with pathos. "Now, now I see that you are a truly noble spirit! I am in awe of you . . . It was not just the question of our firm's prestige and my duty to the Hudson Bay Company, my employer of nearly twenty years, that played a role in my decision to remain. It was also concern for the fate of these small arctic nations – the Chukchi and the Eskimos."

Carpenter's voice shook from an overflow of emotion.

"And regardless of our personal relationship, it's for their sake that we should cleave to one another. After all, we are the only whites on the entire stretch of coastline between Enmyn and Keniskun . . . "

"And the only sensible men among these children of nature?" John had caught Carpenter's intonation exactly, as he finished the sentence.

"That's it exactly!"

John wanted to say something sharp, but held back, thinking tiredly that Carpenter would never be changed in his own views nor brought around to another's. He is so certain of his superiority that if you told him, for example, that he was no better than, say, Tiarat – the trader would think the suggestion absurd.

Carpenter rooted around his nerpa-skin traveling sack, richly ornamented with beading and deer hair, and pulled out an opened bottle of Scotch.

"Let us drink to solidarity among men!"

John drank in silence. After a moment, he felt that he would be happy to embrace the entire world, and even Carpenter seemed to be a decent fellow, however misguided. And anyway, what had he done that was so reprehensible? He'd spent all his life far from home, his only goal to save up some money, buy a little house and live for himself, only for himself . . . *His* life had not been easy, either.

"I heard that you've acquired a gramophone," said Carpenter, "and though I do have one of my own, it's possible I haven't heard some of your records. Allow me to get it going . . ."

"Yako!" John shouted. "Bring the music box."

Carpenter selected a record and put on a yearning melody. The trader listened, eyes half-shut, and seemed to be wholly surrendered to overwhelming emotion.

"The enchantment of music, it's inexplicable. No sooner do I wind up the gramophone than I immediately recall my own childhood, despite the fact that there were no gramophones yet. There was an Italian organ-grinder walking the streets and playing tunes . . . Long-gone childhood, irrevocably lost . . . By the way, Mr. MacLennan, where were you born?"

"Port Hope, on the shores of Lake Ontario."

"Beautiful country," said Carpenter. "Haven't been there myself, but I've heard about the place. Serenity, the splash of warm waters, greenery, quiet streets that lead to the lake . . . Yes, it must be hard to give up all that. By the way, are your parents still living?"

"When I left they were living," John answered, a longing stealing into his soul, while the music and Carpenter's voice awoke memories long-hidden in the most secret and sensitive corners of his heart.

He rose to his feet and roughly knocked away the membrane, stopping the gramophone.

"Enough! Time to sleep. Whoever doesn't work, doesn't eat. And I've got to go out hunting on the sea tomorrow morning."

. . . By the time John had returned from the coast, Carpenter was already gone – he'd driven to Il'motch's camp, intending to set off for his home in Keniskun from there. That's what it said in his note of thanks, left behind in the little room where the trader had spent the night. He'd been generous with gifts for Pyl'mau, leaving a supply of flour, tea, sugar and a box of cartridges.

John read the note, and uneasy thoughts colored his mind like dark shadows: Now what does he want, that Carpenter?

Pyl'mau speedily butchered the freshly killed nerpa and set the meat to boiling. She divided up the nerpa's eyes between the younger children, Bill-Toko and Sophie-Ankanau. Yako, who saw himself as a grown man and carried a real hunter's knife on his belt, generously declined his share of the delicacy in favor of his baby sister and little brother.

As he waited for his meal, John took out his well-weathered notepad and, after a moment's reflection, wrote:

I have the distinct feeling that Carpenter will try and get rid of me the first chance he gets. My being here has complicated matters for him, although I don't really interfere in his business. Let him trade, let him even pan for gold on the sly, as long as he doesn't pick at the hearts and souls of these people, whom he's been robbing blind with a cheerful smile on his face . . . But a revolution, that is more troubling. If, on the one hand, the Russian csar didn't pay much attention to Chukotka, then at least the government has had more sense than to repeat the mistake of Alaska. And what can be expected of the Bolsheviks? A completely unknown quantity! Maybe they'll decide to sell Chukotka to Canada or the United States! Who knows whether the twentieth century will be the century that the Chukchi and the Aivanalin disappear forever from the face of the earth . . .

"John! Food is ready!" Pyl'mau called out from the polog.

"Hey-hey! I'm coming!" John stopped writing midsentence and shut the notepad. He didn't feel like writing anymore. Not in the right mood. Even the faint signs of the coming long spring had not kindled that pulsing warmth in his heart. "Is it that I'm getting old?" he thought testily, as he carefully crawled inside the polog, making sure not to let any cold air inside.

30

The spring raced swiftly by, in sleepless nights out on the sea, in the wake of walrus hunting, and the short lull came when it was possible to transport the kill back to the settlement and store it away.

The shore was clean and deserted. The hide boats had all been raised up on high supports, to guard their coverings from hungry dogs who, although well fed, had no objection to enjoying a bit of walrus hide pickled in seawater.

The *White Carolina* came to Enmyn in the early hours.

John was already on his feet when he heard the cries outside:

"A ship! A ship coming in!"

Men were already assembled on shore, and Orvo's binoculars made the rounds from hand to hand.

"A very beautiful ship!" said Tiarat, as he passed the binoculars to John.

The vessel slowly neared the shore. A sailor stood at the prow, measuring depth with a hand-held plummet. The ship was so near that the sailors' voices were discernible in the morning silence. With a thud, the anchor dropped in the water and the ship came to a full stop.

A launch boat was now hanging over the water. As soon as it touched water, the sailors jumped down into the boat. Last to get inside was a woman.

"A woman coming to pay us a visit!" Orvo said, with surprise, handing John the binoculars.

John pressed the lenses to his eyes. Yes, it was a woman, wearing a dark coat of rough cloth and a wide-brimmed felt hat, her gray hair teased out from under the brim by the wind. It was as though he'd been struck in the chest, and he almost dropped the binoculars. He was afraid of believing in his own intuition, but with each passing moment he grew more and more certain that it was she, his mother.

The launch was almost at the surfline when John knew for certain that it was Mary MacLennan, and he swayed. Tiarat asked him, concerned:

"What's with you?"

"My mother's come," John whispered back.

The launch touched shore, and the sailors helped the woman disembark. John's feet were frozen to the shingle.

Mary MacLennan intently scanned the crowd of people on the beach.

"Where is my son?" she asked.

"I'm right here," John said, and stepped forward to meet his mother.

At first, Mary MacLennan drew back, seemingly unable to recognize him, but in the next instant, an inhuman cry shattered the morning stillness of Enmyn.

"Oh, John! My boy! What have they done to you!"

John embraced her, held her close, inhaling the long-forgotten scents of home, and an uncontrollable stream of tears sprang from his eyes. A taut bitter lump in his throat kept him from uttering a single word.

"I've found you, my precious son! I've found you!" Mary MacLennan spoke through her tears. "The Lord has heard my prayers. I'd thought I would never see you again, that you were dead . . . My darling, my boy! Eight years! Eight long years I've thought you lost forever . . . Father didn't live to hear the joyous news . . . Let me look at you."

She drew aside a little, took a step back.

"What's happened to your hands?"

"Mom," John whispered, "I don't have hands. Not for a long time . . ."

"Oh, the misfortune, what a misfortune!" cried Mary, throwing herself upon her son's breast.

"Mom, I've gotten used to it, and I don't feel the lack. The people here, they've taught me to use the gun, the spear, and the knife. I can even write."

"But why have you never sent word?"

"Forgive me, Mom," John hung his head in shame. "I'll explain everything later."

The people of Enmyn stood to the side and watched the meeting of mother and son. The sailors did, too.

Thuderstruck by the astonishing news, the remaining souls of Enmyn were descending from the yarangas to the shore. Pyl'mau was at the head, carrying little Sophie-Ankanau in her arms. Yako and Bill-Toko ran up behind her. Pyl'mau did not walk over to her husband. She joined the rest of Enmyn's inhabitants and, together with the crowd, stood silently observing John and his mother.

"John, dearest," his mother said, "go and pack. You mustn't stay here a moment longer. This is the end of your sufferings, the end of your black night, the end of your nightmare. Wake up, John, you've come back to life for me and for all your loved ones . . . And Jeannie, she too is waiting for you . . . Let's go, John. I can't stand to look at the faces of these brutes. I can't even imagine what grief you've had to suffer from them. They must have taunted you, mocked you. It's nothing, John, it will all be forgotten, it will slip from your memory like a bad dream . . ."

John listened to this flood of words and his heart broke with pity for his mother, and for himself. He saw Pyl'mau, standing together with the children surrounded by the others, and the deceased Toko's words came to mind: "You'll leave, and all the days you've lived here will seem like a dream. A dream in polar fog . . ."

"Mom, dear Mom," John's voice shook with agitation, "calm down and try to hear me and understand. Only let's go to my yaranga, we can talk there . . . Alright, Mom?"

"No, Son, I can't stay here any longer. I fear losing you again."

"Don't be afraid, Mom," John smiled sadly. "I won't disappear. Come with me."

Mother and son walked up the shingled beach toward the yarangas. The crowd followed them at a distance, Pyl'mau and the children at its head.

John led his mother past the yarangas, past the tethered dogs, past the walrus entrails hung out to dry. At the threshold of his home he halted:

"Mom, this is my yaranga. This is where I live."

"Poor John," Mary MacLennan said with a sob, and bending low walked into the daylight-dim chottagin.

John followed her inside and, while his mother was looking around, took out a deerskin and spread it by the side of the polog.

"Mom, come and sit down here."

Mary MacLennan walked past the hearth – a cauldron of walrus meat cooling atop it – and lowered herself heavily onto the deerskin.

"And this is where you've been living all this time, all these eight years?" his mother asked.

"Yes, Mom," John answered. "All these eight years."

"How awful! No one could have stood it. But now it's all behind you, my son, all behind you!" Again she fell to sobbing, cradling John's head to her breast.

He listened to his mother and remembered Toko's words: "It will end, your dream in polar fog, and you will barely recall our shores."

A shadow moved at the door. John raised his head and saw Pyl'mau. She was watching her husband, her eyes filled with tears. "She's already saying her farewell to me," John thought and, untangling himself from his mother's embrace, cried out:

"Come inside, Mau!"

Pyl'mau walked inside, uncertainly. Sophie-Ankanau was in her arms. Yako and Bill-Toko sidled in behind her, tightly holding hands.

"Mom," John turned back to his mother, "I would like to introduce my wife. Her name is Pyl'mau. And these are our children, Yako, Bill-Toko and little Sophie-Ankanau. We had another child, a girl, Mary. But she died . . . Come and meet my wife, Mom . . ."

Mary MacLennan gazed at Pyl'mau with horror.

"It's impossible!" she cried. "I can't believe that my son married a savage! It's impossible, John! Impossible!"

Pyl'mau understood everything. She backed to the door, pushed the boys outside and fled into the path herself.

"Mom! How could you say such a thing!" John rose to his feet. "You've insulted my wife, my children. How could you do it? I always had faith in your intellect, and you must understand that the John of Port Hope ten years ago doesn't exist any longer. There is another John now, one that's gone through trials I wouldn't wish upon my worst enemy. You wrong my new friends, Mom. It killed me to hear you say those words . . ."

"Darling John," Mary MacLennan spoke heatedly, "be yourself once more! I do understand, it will be hard for you to go back to your old life. But that's nothing, it will pass, it will all fade away and your life will return to its natural path. Pack your things, John!"

"Wait, ma," John said. "Calm yourself and hear me out. Look inside your own heart, Mom, and ask: Is your son capable of abandoning his wife and children?"

"But is she truly your wife? Is she your wife in the eyes of God and the law?" Mary MacLennan asked harshly.

"She is not my wife under the eyes of God, and not in the eyes of the law either," John answered her. "She is my wife under a much more important and authoritative power than an imaginary god or a hypocritical law. Pyl'mau is my wife in the eyes of life itself!"

"John, dearest, let's not speak of that ghastly woman again. I suspect that you fear them. Don't worry, John, we'll buy you back, we'll give them money, anything these savages want for your release, they'll get. Let's go now, dearest John, let's go!"

Mary MacLennan stood up and tugged at John's sleeve, as though he were a small, unreasonable boy.

"No, Mom. I won't move an inch from this place. I just can't do it. I can't simply blot out my own self, my children, the life that has made me a man again! I cannot do it! You must understand me, Mom!"

"Oh John, you are breaking my heart . . . All right, darling . . . Say good-bye to your . . . your loved ones. I'll wait . . . I'll wait aboard the ship, not to get in your way. And tomorrow, I'll come back for you . . . Only tell me honestly – they won't do anything to you, will they?"

"Oh, what are you talking about, Mom!"

"All right, all right, my child," Mary MacLennan quickly said.

John escorted his mother to the beach. As he walked, Enmyn's people followed him with their eyes. He sensed them at his back, whipping him like a scourge.

"If it hadn't been for a kind soul from some village on the shore of the Bering Strait, a trader, I'd never have known where you were, or whether you were dead or alive. It was he who sent me a letter and told me of what had befallen you. Son, you must always remember his name – Robert Carpenter."

"Robert Carpenter?" John was stunned.

"Yes, it was he who sent me the letter. Do you know him?"

"Do I!" John exclaimed. "I've been to visit him more than once, and he's come to see me, too."

"What a kind heart he has," sighed Mary MacLennan.

John helped his mother get into the launch boat, kissed her good-bye, and she had a moment to whisper:

"Your last night, John, in that terrible shack, and away from your mother . . ."

John returned to his yaranga. All its inhabitants were already home.

Pyl'mau was starting the fire and the boys were playing with their baby sister.

John sat down on a headrest log and held his head in his leather-covered stumps. Thoughts drummed inside his head, though how badly he wanted to get away from them, to forget himself, to switch himself off, if only for a little while, from all that had weighed upon his heart since this morning! How far beyond his mother he'd gone! And even if the impossible were to happen, and he did return to Port Hope, he would never again be able to resume his former way of life.

"Will you have something to eat?"

Pyl'mau's voice startled him. He raised his head and saw a pair of eyes, dark with grief. John shook his head no.

Pyl'mau crouched down beside him, right on the earthen floor.

"Why did your mother leave?"

"She'll be back," John replied.

"I know how hard it is for you," Pyl'mau let out a sigh. "Only, I'll tell you this: A man can always find another woman, but there are no other mothers for him in the world. Go to the ship. Thank you for everything. It won't be so hard for me to bear losing you: After all, I'll still have something of you, Bill-Toko and Sophie-Ankanau. You can go with a clean conscience. You've done all that a real human being could have done!"

"Be quiet!" John cried.

Pyl'mau was shaken: Her husband had never shouted at her.

John ran from the yaranga.

All day he wandered the tundra, ascending to the Far Cape. He met the sunset atop Funerary Hill, by the sideways-slanting cross with its tin marker: *Tynevirineu-Mary MacLennan, 1912–1914.*

In the morning, the launch boat once again headed for the shore. Alongside her son, Mary MacLennan walked up to the settlement. She flatly refused to enter the yaranga.

And again there were pleas and tears. The mother begged the son, but

John seemed to have turned to stone. In the evening, the launch took Mary MacLennan back to the ship.

John went back to his yaranga and found Orvo, Tiarat, and Armol' inside his chottagin. They were drinking tea, served by Pyl'mau, with great concentration. John sat down beside them and Pyl'mau silently handed him a cup.

Orvo took a loud swig of tea, carefully set the cup on the edge of the little table and solemnly began:

"Sson! We've come to tell you something important, to give you our advice. We see how your mother grieves and suffers. It pains us to see this, and our hearts break for you, and for this old woman, and for Pyl'mau and the children, too. We have thought long and hard on this. We pity both you and Pyl'mau. But it would be better if you left with your mother. We have grown to love you, and have no other feelings toward you. Our affection gives us the right to offer you good advice. We'll never forget you, but always will remember that the Chukchi of Enmyn have a dear and close friend among the whites, one who became a real brother to us. Go, Sson! Remember us sometimes."

John's throat was constricted with sobs. He didn't notice the tears streaming down his face.

"No! No! I'll never leave you! I will stay here, and no power on earth could drive us apart!"

"Think of your mother, Sson," Orvo said quietly.

"And who is going to think of my children?" asked John.

"Don't you worry about them and Pyl'mau," Orvo answered. "Your children will grow, and your wife will have everything she needs. There are no poor or dispossessed among our people. If we starve, then we all starve together, but food is something that's always shared . . ."

It was now three days that the *White Carolina* had been anchored off the shore of Enmyn. Each morning, a launch boat would push off from the ship and a stooped woman in a dark rough-cloth coat and high rubber boots would come ashore. John would hurry to meet her and carefully walk her up the shingled spit to the yaranga.

In all this time, Mary MacLennan had not entered her son's dwelling again.

Mother and son slowly climbed up the slope to the yarangas, walked past the hide boats on their supports, past the earthen meat pits, shut tight with the shoulder blades of whales. John tenderly settled his mother on a flat rock, and sat down at her feet.

It took the woman a long time to catch her breath.

"John," she finally began to speak, in a voice that shook with emotion, "tell your mother one more time that you've positively decided to stay."

John nodded wordlessly.

"No, you tell me so I can hear it!" his mother was insisting, looking at her son with eyes bleary from crying.

"Yes," John quietly managed.

His mother gave a deep sigh.

"I consent to your coming together with these people that you persist in calling your family. If you find it so difficult, so impossible to break with them, then fine, bring them along . . ."

In his mind's eye, John drew the picture of Pyl'mau, Yako, Bill-Toko and little Sophie-Ankanau entering the house on the shore of Lake Ontario, promenading on the manicured little paths of the municipal park, and, grinning, said:

"Now, Mom, you're a sensible woman . . ."

"Oh, John!" the old woman sobbed.

"Don't, Mom, don't . . ."

John wrapped his arms around his mother and helped her up.

They walked down to the shore, where the *White Carolina*'s little sloop danced in the waves.

"So this is it then, John," his mother said, brushing away her tears. "Farewell."

John helped her into the boat. He did everything quite mechanically, and it even seemed to him that it was some internal mechanism that drove him. Inside him, everything had hardened, set to stone. Only when the boat was a few feet from the shore did he realize that he hadn't even kissed his mother good-bye.

"Mom!" he shouted in desperation. "Good-bye, Mom!"

The mother turned to face her son.

"Oh, John! My boy! It would have been easier for me to see you dead than like this!"

RAINMAKER TRANSLATIONS
supports a series of books meant to encourage a lively reading
experience of contemporary world literature drawn from diverse
languages and cultures. Publication is assisted by grants from the
International Institute of Modern Letters (modernletters.org),
a nonprofit organization dedicated to promoting the literary
arts and literary activism around the world.

A Dream in Polar Fog was designed by David Bullen Design
and printed at The Stinehour Press in Lunenburg, Vermont
on 60lb. Mohawk Vellum